I'd once watched two feline chaagra posture for the right to rule a choice hunting ground outside my village. It was a blustery affair of raised hackles, bared teeth, and swishing tails. Mascha and I eyed each other similarly, standing at the foot of his bed. I was fully prepared to argue about the cage again. The only way he'd get me back in there was if he dragged me over and stuffed me inside it. I ignored the surge of lust that came with the thought of such rough handling.

Mascha looked toward the cage, then sighed. "You may share my bed. I won't touch you; I swear it."

TIPORI

A TALE FROM DESSOS

CINDY L. SELL

ÆTHER AND ASH PRESS

Author's Note

Tipori is a spicy enemies-to-lovers romance set in the world of *The Last Draegion Saga (TLDS)*. It can be read apart as a standalone, or as a spin-off tale following *Embers Rising: TLDS Book Two.*

This book contains dark themes and explicit scenes unintended for audiences under 18. Reader discretion is advised.

If you are sensitive to certain topics, please review the list of content advisories on my website: www.thelastdraegion.com

See the back of this book for a pantheon guide, translations, and pronunciations.

Island States of Rillion
West Aivenosian Sea
CAPITAL CITY
CITY
TOWN
FERRY ROAD
TRADE ROAD
ISLE OF JOHSCHIIR
Johschiir
Alahiir
Sommal's Pass
Yzehn Dunes
Sommal
Yzeron
Sands of Sumiir
ISLE OF CABRION
Yzamet
Tohred
Cabrion
Alleschii Rainforest
Oulaziim
Capital Road
Alleschii Road
ISLE OF EPILLON
Epilloni Channel
Epillon
Iiqestra
Straits of Fate
Durgost
Oennian Channel
Johrfallen
allus
Smugglers' Cove
Oenna
Durgostian Channel
ISLES
Scharvillost
OF
Feschur
Gosche
Naskatam
Merchants' Road
Tradego
avet
Keschrallam
Rahbiir
ISLE OF DURGOST
Mines of Naskatam
SCHARVILLOST
Keschrallam Channel
Mt. Escha
Saphgram Trade Route
Spicers' Highway
Amahz
Tahamel
Narillinon
Casterion
Silk Road
Carimmisec
Mines of Tahamel
rinon
Hadrion
Marillinoni Savannah
ISLE OF MARILLINON
Qiiterian Jungle
Khestian Ocean
Mines of Kheskaria
Kheskaria
0   40
LEAGUES

For Tim.
Sorry you get the smutty book, love.
But hey—writing it was fun, wasn't it?

Chapter One

Mascha

Sunset over the city of Durgost was said to be the most beautiful in the world.

Light scattered across the horizon in dazzling rays of tangerine and gold. Darker violets clung to the easterly faces of clouds, and the sky was painted in rich shades of scarlet and burgundy. Many poets likened those reds to the ripe skin of Aivenosian apples or the fine mane of a prized Rillanese stallion.

To me, they were the color of blood.

From the adoration of pit fighters in the Durgostian Arena to the way crowds cheered as unruly slaves were whipped at public posts, this city was caught in a love affair with violence. In the distance, the market streets were still packed with people who had clamored to get a view of the spectacle I'd created at one such post. I could still feel the pressure of that gods-cursed weapon in my hand. Stomach churning, I turned from the balcony railing, only to catch the sky's reflection in my palace windows. I scowled and looked down at my bloodied palms.

Why did it have to be today, of all days?

Screams echoed through my mind. The same screams that had awakened me every night this week. They resurfaced now and then like an ache from a long-healed injury. To have been forced to such violence again today—the anniversary of that horrific day—it was a disgrace. My fingers curled around the blood.

Black-violet mist coalesced in my periphery, offering distraction. I turned my attention to the image of a young page walking toward me. Three heartbeats later, the Aetherial image dissolved, and my slave appeared in earnest, his waifish figure clad only in loose-fitting white trousers. Raffi traced the path my Foresight had predicted, his black curls bobbing with every step. He bowed with the same skittish imprecision as his image.

I frowned.

"Master..." Raffi paled, his gaze darting to the red stains on my shirt.

Rumors were already spreading. It wouldn't be long before the entire country knew what had happened. Today would serve as a reminder of whom I was, and no one would dare draw my ire after this.

No one, perhaps, except for Maralla.

Johtan Shasnaram, the other slaves called her. Unbreakable. And by Silonas, I was starting to believe it.

"Speak."

Raffi shifted, keeping his gaze downcast. "The Amins are here, Master. For their quarterly. Lady Anelliiq looks lovely tonight."

The Amins' quarterly. Of course. In all the excitement at the market, I'd forgotten whom I was to bed this evening. "Thank you, *raschu*. Has Scherazeme been prepared to receive Lord Amin?"

"Yes, Master. And Emmi, if he requests another."

Ludicrous. Anelliiq had informed me years ago her husband only lasted a few minutes. It was a waste of two of my prettiest slaves, but protocol demanded I honor Wali Amin's request. I had neither wife nor concubine, and a deal couldn't be sealed without a fair exchange of flesh.

"Very good. See them brought to the red dining hall and have Hasanthe distract the Amins with a tour of the palace gardens. I will be along shortly."

"Yes, Master."

Raffi began another faltering bow. I caught him by the chin. Any future master would beat him for such an improper display, and I would have no one to blame but myself.

"Ease the tension in your back and bend at the hips." The half-dried blood on my hand stuck to Raffi's jaw. "And clean your face before you attend my guests."

I released him. Raffi took several breaths before repeating the gesture. His next bow was smoother, nearly flawless. He had the makings of a great steward, if only he could get past his fear of correction. Coupled with his pleasant looks, he would fetch a fine price at auction once I finished processing him.

I left the balcony for my chambers. With no other slaves around to witness, I hesitated at my bedroom door and centered myself for another fight.

Fading sunlight splashed against the sheer drapery surrounding my bed and glinted off the bars of Maralla's cage. It seemed Silonas favored me; she lay asleep on the steel floor. Her slow, shallow breathing eased the knot between my shoulders. I'd already lost my head once today, and she would surely call attention to it when she awoke. Much as I'd tried to temper her over the past six months, I had yet to find a single subservient bone in her body.

Wet lacerations marred her lavender skin. The blood on my palms grew heavy with accusation.

Normally, I left the unsavory task of whipping the slaves to my half-brother, Tasari, who enjoyed causing pain, but Maralla had left me no choice. I, Mascha of the Rorsch Hekkai, third in line to the Chancery of Rillion, could not be viewed as weak.

I took extra care crossing the floor to the washroom so I didn't disturb her.

The cold marble soothed my feet. One fingertip grazed the saphyrum stud in my earlobe, and I summoned Aether from the arcane metal. Black-violet mist burst into flame inside the shower's overhead reservoir. By the time I had discarded my clothing and opened the tap, steam streaked every surface in the room.

I scrubbed blood from my skin and washed sand and dirt from behind my ears. Once the reservoir ran dry, I stepped out of the shower box and toweled off, avoiding the tender slash across my abdomen. I had to hand it to Maralla; her reflexes were impeccable. No one had gotten the drop on me like that since I was a slave myself.

Water dripped down my shoulders as I combed my hair back. The ends were starting to curl again; I would need to schedule a trim soon. I shook droplets from my beard and groomed it, too, then braced myself against the vanity. My attire for the evening was laid out on my bed, which meant I inevitably had to re-enter my bedroom. After applying an extra layer of mint oil and delaying as long as I could, I mustered my courage.

Maralla slept on. Thank the gods.

She was breathing steadily, but I knew how excruciating her injuries must be. I was no stranger to that end of the whip.

One night with those wounds was enough. In the morning, I would take her to Hasanthe for healing.

I dressed in black trousers and a white cotton shirt. The infernal red doublet beside them could burn for all I cared. With the Amins' quarterly contract for Rorsch Hekkai security already drawn up, there was no need for formal negotiations this evening. Lord Amin would be anxious to dip his cock in something warm, and Lady Anelliiq, gods bless her, would be grateful that something wasn't her.

With one final rallying breath, I slid my mask of decorum into place. I closed the bedroom door, passed through the small library, and out through the suite's anteroom.

I did my best to ignore the phantom screams echoing down the corridor behind me.

Scherazeme and Emmi knelt by the hearth, their bronze complexions lit by crackling flames. Tattoos adorned Scherazeme's upper arm and cascaded in floral patterns down her left side. Emmi's finer features were framed by lush waves of midnight hair and thick eyebrows, the envy of every native-born Rillanese woman to cross my doorstep.

Both wore nothing beyond thin platinum collars and four ruby piercings adorning ears, nose, and navel. The piercings denoted their high status among my slaves. Two more could make either of them concubines, but I would sell them before condemning them to that fate.

Their discipline was unrivaled. They could have been statues, but for the delicate rise and fall of their breasts, and the way Scherazeme straightened when I approached. Always so eager to please me. She was a work of art.

"Good evening, *raschan*."

"Good evening, Master."

"Saolanni smiles on you, Master."

I suppressed a snort. Emmi's favored goddess had nothing on the god of fortune. Saolanni may have graced me with life, but it was Silonas who had seen me this far. Nevertheless, I tilted her chin up. Her lips were soft and full as ripe sickleberries, and she tasted just as sweet. She closed her eyes and returned my kiss, one hand straying between her thighs.

"Master, may I?"

I smiled against her mouth. "You're an eager little thing tonight."

She blushed and lowered her gaze. After claiming Scherazeme's lips in the same manner, I retreated to the dining table. "Yes, both of you may. I suspect Lord Amin will not dally long with conversation."

And if he injured either of my women in his haste, I would have his foul head.

I surveyed the new kitchen slave's work. Three places were set appropriately at the table, and not a fingerprint marred the silver. The white tablecloth was pleated perfectly at the corners. Black-veined violets filled the room with a lovely aroma and provided a stunning complement to the scarlet rug and drapery.

I glanced toward the servants' entrance. "Vassu, attend me."

The new slave appeared, quiet and demure—a far cry from the beastly wretch my men had dragged through the foyer a few weeks ago. Half-Syljian, like myself, and edging into his youthful fifties, his pointed ears quivered as he bowed and fixed his gaze on the floor. "Yes, Master?"

"Did you obtain assistance with these preparations?"

He swallowed. "I asked Hasanthe to procure the flowers, Master. He said they were your favorite."

"They are, indeed." Satisfaction tugged at my lips. "And these corners? Did Farrah pleat them for you?"

"No, Master. I did them myself."

"Excellent." I brushed my saphyrum earring and summoned its energy. "Lower your trousers, *raschu*."

Though he didn't meet my eyes, relief flooded Vassu's face. He did as instructed, revealing his caged member already swelling in anticipation of its freedom. I murmured the incantation to banish the terrible device, and once the cage disappeared in a cloud of Aetherial mist, he fell to his knees.

"Thank you, Master," he sobbed, kissing my feet. "Thank you."

"Remember who holds the key to your pleasure." My fingers sifted into his brown locks. "Good behavior is rewarded, while belligerence and disrespect are met with suffering. I expect you will not displease me again."

"I won't, Master. I promise."

The lively shake of his head drew a chuckle from me. "Go. Take the rest of the evening to enjoy yourself."

Vassu nearly fell over himself. He rushed to tie his trousers and bowed, murmuring more platitudes, before bolting from the room. Emmi and Scherazeme paused in attending themselves to stifle giggles.

I shot them a smirk. "Behave, now. Remember your manners."

"Yes, Master."

"Apologies, *meschiir*."

My smile grew at the brightness in their eyes, the color in their cheeks. For the first time all week, the dark clouds looming over me parted.

Voices outside the dining hall grew louder, and both women sobered. Emmi's hand crept back between her thighs. I ignored the heady scent of her arousal and turned as Hasanthe swept in, white robes swirling. His mountainous frame filled the doorway, his scarlet and gold-embroidered headdress brushing the ornate wood.

"Here we are, my lord, my lady." The healer's deep voice resonated like a Dennian horn, and red tassels swung from his sash as he waved the couple inside. His enthusiasm was a sight to witness; had he been a fighting slave in the arena, he would have been a fan favorite.

"An hour past time," Wali Amin groused, his dark face and beady eyes framed by rolling neck folds. The misty black image of my Foresight predicted the path he would take to thrust a finger into my chest. "If you think—"

I stepped away from his intended route, and with the sudden shift in possible futures, the phantom image vanished.

"Please accept my apologies for the delay, Lord Amin." Placating the ill-mannered boar left a sour taste in my mouth, but my employer would expect no less. We needed his subjects calm and compliant to preserve the delicate hierarchy of the upper and ruling castes. I pulled out the nearest chair for the lord to sit. "A matter of Rillanese safety was most pressing this afternoon."

As Wali floundered, I redirected my attention to Anelliiq. Her maroon bodice hugged her sultry figure and contrasted with her sea-green Aivenosian complexion. A collar of fine rubies encircled her neck. "Lady Amin, you are a vision."

Even avoiding my gaze, as was proper, Anelliiq's emerald eyes glittered. She glided into my arms and kissed my cheek. "It has been too long, Rorsch Hekkai."

"I missed seeing you for the spring equinox." I cupped her face, letting my thumb brush the new scar along her sharply angled cheekbone. Understanding passed between us in the way it could only among decades-old friends.

A hot coal lodged in my belly. We would have words about that scar later.

She cleared her throat and stepped toward the table. I pulled out her chair and kissed her temple once she settled. "I pray you'll join us for solstice. The Chancellor promises this year will be the finest gala yet."

Wali scoffed and slapped the table. "Of course it will. It's always better when that bastard Neborov doesn't attend."

Neborov.

Visceral upheaval was the theme of the day, it seemed, but I choked down my revulsion. It wasn't like Neborov Ideghis V to miss the largest social event of the year.

My grip tightened on Anelliiq's chair. "Ideghis will not be in attendance?"

The thought of House Ideghis, the Master's house, on this day of all days, was enough to fracture my composure. Fortunately, the Master was long dead, as were Ideghis II and III, whom I'd also served before winning my freedom in the arena. Still, my animosity toward that house had never wavered. If not for my employer's favoring of it, I'd have demolished House Ideghis years ago.

Wali's eyebrows shot skyward. "You haven't heard? I thought you, of all people, would know."

"Tell me."

My quiet demand wiped the taunting look off Lord Amin's face. The man might be an imbecile, but at least when confronted with true peril, he had enough sense to appear cowed. He straightened the cutlery beside his plate.

"He's supposedly in talks with Aegren's boy. He's after the mine."

The saphyrum mine. Of course. After the last outbreak of weeping pox had taken his father, Aegren I, Asuul Aegren II had found himself on the verge of bankruptcy. He was in the middle of selling off assets, and aside from his estate grounds, his saphyrum mine was the most lucrative sale he could make. If Ideghis—the wealthiest house in Durgost—was his buyer, Aegren would want for nothing by the time the deal closed.

"Rumor is he's scheduled a tour for the first week of Faeza. There's no way he'll make it from Tahamel to the capital in time." Lord Amin wetted his lips. "And when the trade commission gets wind he's about to break anti-monopoly law, they'll slap him with a fine so big he'll not dare show his face in Epillon."

No doubt, Wali would file the report with the trade commission himself. House Amin and House Ideghis had been at war for as long as I could remember.

Unfortunately for Wali, Ideghis V had most of the commissioners in his pocket. He was even offering free use of his Syljian slaves to Commissioner Uuli to strengthen some component of his breeding program.

My gut churned again, and I turned away. I didn't care about Aegren's mine. The bastard could sell it to whomever he wanted. My own private mine supplied me with all the saphyrum I needed. But for the sake of a reprieve from Ideghis at the summer gala, I hoped Wali could actually delay the sale.

I settled into my high-backed chair and snapped my fingers. "Scherazeme, Emmi, attend us. My guests are hungry."

Chapter Two

Mascha

Dinner didn't last long.

Wali was already making use of Emmi's throat by the third course, and I led Anelliiq away with a silent gesture to Scherazeme, ordering her to load the man up with more wine. If he passed out on his plate again, the slaves could spend the rest of their evening in peace.

Silence greeted us as Anelliiq and I reached my chambers. She knew the space well and wasted no time gawking in my anteroom as the younger wives and daughters did. She made for the sitting room, her gown whispering across the polished tile. While she began setting pieces on the piccara board, I selected my finest Durgostian vintage and a pair of gold-rimmed goblets.

I paused outside the library and listened, staring past the rows of leather-bound books to my bedroom door. Ever since I'd isolated Maralla in my quarters—a precautionary measure to keep her from influencing the other slaves—she'd made a point of causing as much disruption as possible while I sealed my employer's contracts. Her particular favorite was banging her spellbinders against the bars of her cage.

But no sound came from the room beyond. Maybe for once, I wouldn't have to Silence the room to disguise the noise. Maybe at last, her rebellious nature had come to heel.

"You're missing a fool chip, Mascha."

In the privacy of my sanctuary, Anelliiq could finally abandon her formality.

"Try behind the drawer." I resumed course and entered the sitting room. "Sometimes those smaller chips slip through if the slaves aren't careful putting them away."

I tried to recall which of my chamber slaves had picked the board up last while Anelliiq searched inside the table. Odessa was usually more careful, but Catari had left here deliciously spent after Lord Belfahr's visit last week. I'd refrained from ravaging Belfahr's daughter as my heart had desired, so poor Catari had endured my appetite instead. I supposed I could forgive the poor thing for losing her head.

Anelliiq slid the drawer back in place. "Not there." She checked under the table, then sat up and wrinkled her nose.

"It's alright." I pulled the cork from the bottle and set it down in the chip's place. "This will do."

We played and drank wine. I ignored the random bursts of Foresight that would have helped me win the game in favor of moves meant to prolong it. All the while, we studied each other, awaiting which of us would address the dragon in the room first.

Finally, I could bear it no longer. I reached across the board and touched the scar on her face. "Wali?"

She met my eyes—a breach of protocol for any woman or slave. "Fausch."

I started. "Fausch?"

Her eldest son had just come of age, and even at fifteen, he had a heart blacker than his father's. Rumors claimed he'd beaten one of the house slaves within a fingerspan of her life for spilling wine on his innix-skin rug recently. Only the gods knew how such a monster could have come from Anelliiq's womb, though as Wali's firstborn, he was bound to be spoiled and cruel. One day, he would inherit House Amin and all its assets, and I would have to suffer his presence in the social hierarchy as I did so many others. It was simply the way of things.

"Tell me."

She sighed. "I stepped between him and his brother. Really, Mascha, it's not important."

"It is to me."

"And what are you going to do?" A combative edge sharpened her tongue. "It was within his right."

It shouldn't have been. No man had a right to put his hands on his mother—but I didn't say it. Better to accept what couldn't be changed. My eyes dropped to the board, and I took one of her sentry chips with my assassin. Then I listened again to the silence.

Not even the crackle of a hearth disturbed us. Odd how even now, with Maralla a room away and out of sight, guilt ate at me. But surely her silence wasn't that of shock or mute terror. She was only sleeping.

Regardless, I *needed* her to break, or she wouldn't survive long in another master's house.

"You keep doing that."

I sipped my wine. "Doing what?"

"Glancing toward your room. She's in there, isn't she?"

"She is."

Anelliiq leaned back on the low divan, goblet in hand. She leveled her perceptive stare on me, her forest-green lips pursed. "What happened in the market today?"

"You tell me." I had to know what others were saying. My employer's emissary would come knocking tomorrow, and I would not be caught off guard.

"They're saying she stumbled into a vendor's stall. That you whipped her until she slumped unconscious against the post. Some say you, the fearsome Mascha, dealer of death, rifted away with her corpse."

I scoffed. "Is that so?"

My legacy still lived, as I'd hoped. It was why I'd claimed no noble title or surname after winning my freedom. Even though I'd ascended to the highest caste of the wealthiest country in the world, I wouldn't allow them to forget what the Master made me.

A killer.

A Champion.

Mascha—death.

Anelliiq's gaze hardened. "But I know you better than that. What really happened?"

A slow sigh escaped me. If there was anyone in this world I could trust, it was Anelliiq. I fought the urge to rise and pace the room, instead opting for another sip of wine.

"There was a boy begging for scraps in the Saffron Square." I placed the glass on the table. "Maralla bolted from my side, took off her diamond earrings, and gave them to him. Then she covered his retreat by stealing a knife from a nearby vendor."

"Caelyn's wrath." Anelliiq's mouth fell open. "She attacked you?"

"Yes."

"And you spared her?"

Any slave who pulled a weapon on her master should have been executed on the spot, hung in the street, and left to rot as a warning to others. It was Rillanese law.

"Yes."

"Why?"

Kaana'ruh ke'aave tipori.

The words, in Syljian, whispered through me like the night wind, cool and soothing despite the late spring heat. They were ingrained in my earliest memories, and like the screams, they traveled with me through time.

Remember to have mercy.

I'd let them soften me today.

"I gave her twenty lashes," I said, as if that answered her question, "and I made certain they covered us both in blood. Then I cut her loose and rifted away before anyone sorted out the mess I'd made of the vendor's stall to cover things up."

She smoothed a wrinkle from her gown. "You took an enormous risk."

"I know." My chest constricted. "But Ani, I couldn't kill her for helping a child."

Anelliiq fell into contemplative silence, brows drawn inward.

The need for movement finally won me over, and I left my chair as if to outrun the memory of all that blood. Distant screams filtered into my awareness, but I shoved them aside. Those screams belonged to another—*her* blood spilled a lifetime ago. They held no power over me now.

"There's something else, isn't there?" Anelliiq's voice was quiet. "You haven't been sleeping. You never do around this time."

My body drew taut as a bowstring. "Don't," I snapped at my oldest and dearest friend.

Wisely, she lowered her eyes, and I spun away to stalk the floor. Today would soon pass, and this wretched anniversary would fade. The screams, the reminders, the blood would all fade, and things would return to normal. I just had to be patient with myself.

A distinct rustle of cloth drew my attention.

"Come and help me with these."

When I turned, Anelliiq was shaking the laces of her corset and watching me over her shoulder. The last of my anger eroded with the invitation. We still had a deal to seal this evening.

Expertly, I tugged the laces through, and the corset hit the floor. Her shift and petticoats soon pooled atop it, until every fingerspan of her beautiful sea-green skin was laid bare.

Mature beauty was too often overlooked in Rillion, slighted for younger, more pliable bodies with little experience in their own pleasure. I enjoyed teaching the young ones what their men often denied them; it made them willing, even eager, to come to my bed. But there was true magic in the confidence of an older woman.

Anelliiq knelt and took me in hand through my trousers. Aching tightness grew as her palm skimmed my length and the fingers of her opposite hand untied the laces. Cool air touched me, and then warmth, as her lips and tongue staked their claim.

I shuddered. "Silonas slay me."

With silent dedication, she went to work making my knees weak, alternating between firm strokes of her hand and practiced movements of her mouth. When my breathing grew ragged, I sank my fingers into her perfectly coiffed hair, knocking pins and jewels to the floor.

I pulled her mouth from me and bent to kiss her. "Let me have you." My demand rumbled through the space between us.

"Yes, Mascha."

After shedding my shirt and trousers to feel her softness against my skin, I sank into her on the bare tile. Always wet for me, always willing. Baosanni take me, she was still mine in every way but name. Tiny scars marked her nose and eyebrows where diamond studs had once been. She was the closest I'd ever come to taking a concubine.

Her emerald nipples, pierced through with the steel bars that marked her as a nobleman's wife, peaked in invitation. I caught one between my teeth and traced it with my tongue.

"You'll come for me twice tonight." Bracing myself on one elbow, I guided her hand between us. "Say you understand."

"I understand."

Her breath caressed my ear, her teeth nipping at the sensitive tip. Gooseflesh rippled across my back and I groaned as her silken heat clenched around me.

"Gods, I've missed you."

Her breathy chuckle hitched when I began my rhythm. Long, deliberate strokes pressed her into the floor. Her legs hugged my hips, her free arm wrapped my shoulders, and her knuckles brushed my pelvic bone with every thrust. Her cries mingled with my pleasure, and I drove her to the top of her first climax with single-minded determination.

"Mascha," Anelliiq rasped. "May I?"

I grinned. Some habits never died. "*Ciir*. Come for me, Ani."

Head tilted, eyes grown distant, Anelliiq's entire body arched into mine as she obeyed my command. A deep ache settled low in my belly, but I held back. Long ago, I'd mastered the art of controlling myself. The Master had seen to it. Forced to perform as often as I was forced to fight, I'd learned quickly the consequences if I came too soon. Those lessons had served me well as I grew into my power.

Feral need rose within me, as sharp as the knife wound Maralla had scored against me in the market. The slash had torn open during our coupling, and blood was weeping across my abdomen. My eyes closed against the pain, and the blackness in my soul fought to overtake me—the same instinct that had kept me alive in the arena, when the roar of a crowd and the smell of blood rolled over the sand.

Anelliiq tried to slip her hand from between us. I seized her nape and pressed her close to trap her fingers. "You're not finished."

A moan passed her lips. The familiar sound, equal parts desperation and apology, signaled her sinking deeper under my control. I could do anything to her past this point, but there were certain precautions we had worked out over the years so that I never went too far.

"Look at me, *rascha*."

Already fallen so far into her former role, her response was automatic. "Yes, Master?"

"How do you make it slow?"

"*Kavvur.*" Discomfort.

"And how do you make it stop?"

"*Gheschal.*" Distress.

"Good girl." Her eyes rolled back at the words. I thrust once, firmly, to reclaim her attention. "This is going to hurt."

Though her gaze didn't level with mine again, her voice rang with challenge: "Do your worst."

The chains of my resolve snapped. I took her once more on the floor with my hand at her throat, then balanced against the wall as she clung to my shoulders, and finally from behind with her face pressed into the divan. When at last I spent myself inside her, she shattered for the second time and slumped against the cushions. Victorious, my chest heaving, I gathered her to me and wiped her sweaty hair from her face.

"My good girl," I whispered again, my lips brushing her ear tip. "You make me proud."

She lifted her chin in silent offering, and I claimed her mouth in a lingering kiss.

I always enjoyed her visits. Sometimes I hated myself for selling her to Wali, but despite his rough treatment, she had more opportunities with him than she could have ever had with me. She was free—at least, as free as any woman could be in Rillion—and she could bear all the children she wished without fear that they would end up in the fighting pits. Nor would she ever be harmed in a plot against me.

For long minutes, I held her, until she drifted off in my arms. The blood from my knife wound had painted her skin in a few places, and my chamber slaves wouldn't fill the shower reservoir until morning. I could send for them early, but a warm basin and a cloth would serve just as well.

I hoisted Anelliiq up and carried her into the library, then backed through the bedroom door to place her on my bed.

"Thank you," she murmured, eyelids fluttering.

"Always a pleasure, Lady Amin."

Stillness blanketed the room as her breathing slowed to the steady cadence of sleep. I turned for the washroom, but an eerie foreboding settled over me. The silence felt off. Hollow, even.

Something was missing.

My fingertip brushed my earring, and saphyric energy flooded me. I scanned the room, searching the Aetherial eddies for signs of trouble.

But it wasn't a phantom image that turned my blood to ice. It wasn't a prediction that made my gut twist and my breath seize.

No. It was the clash of numbing disbelief and creeping certainty that pulled my feet across the rug to the steel cage in my room.

The barred door stood ajar, and the lock hung open. In the center of the cage lay a single piccara chip. The gap-toothed grin of the fool mocked me from the floor.

The cage was otherwise empty.

Maralla was gone.

Chapter Three

Maralla

I T WAS A LONGER climb off that gods-forsaken roof than I'd expected. I was shaking by the time my bare feet hit the ground. Fog obscured my thoughts and vision, and I collapsed in the bushes surrounding the courtyard.

Precious minutes wasted.

I'd timed my escape to coincide with the biggest gap between patrols. That window narrowed with every passing moment. I stared into the branches swaying overhead, cursing my body for its infirmity. Six months on a slave ship and another half-year as Mascha's captive had made me frail as a newborn kitten.

Blackness encroached. I blinked furiously and shook my head. I couldn't fall asleep here. Not when I was so close to freedom. I had to get up. Had to move.

Rolling over, teeth clenching around a groan, I squinted through the branches to the moonlit garden beyond. Coastal wind cooled the spots where fresh blood soaked my stolen shirt, but each laceration pulsed through my back like a war drum. The cacophony of pain and heat threatened to compromise my entire mission.

I set my jaw and started forward. Fallen petals clung to my elbows, and brambles clawed at the trousers I'd taken from Mascha's wardrobe. Fortunately, the bastard owned at least one pair that wasn't made of silk.

I'd nearly reached the garden path when light speared the darkness.

I froze.

A slave dressed in chiffon padded by, only spans from my hiding place. His leather sandals whispered across the stone, and gold rings flashed at his earlobes. He tended the garden with all the diligence of a loving steward, as if his back wouldn't be stripped of its flesh for over-pruning his master's roses.

The nagging ache in my back mounted as I lay cramped between two bushes. With bared teeth, I steeled myself and accepted the pain as if breathing through labor contractions.

Mascha's slave lingered so long at a nearby nightthorn hedge, trimming, trimming, trimming with those stupid shears that I considered stabbing him through his neck to make it stop. I had no time for this. A blow to the ulnar nerve to disarm him, a quick puncture of the carotid artery, and he'd be dead before I vaulted the gate.

A staggering notion. Was I so desperate to escape that I valued my freedom over an innocent man's life?

Part of me didn't dare answer.

Whether his death would be a mercy, I couldn't say. So many of Mascha's slaves viewed their master with adoring eyes, despite his control over every facet of their existence. At least this one didn't have a torturous metal contraption over his genitals. Those could turn even the staunchest man or woman into a simpering courtesan within a matter of days. Only the open wounds my own device had left after weeks of near-constant wear had spared me from that fate. Thank the gods Mascha had changed tactics just in time.

The slave finally moved on.

I dragged myself from the bushes, peered around the closest hedgerow, then dashed across the cobbled path. Through the garden, down the grassy slope, stopping only at the gate. Mascha's clothes were a poor fit, and I had to roll up the trouser legs to keep from tripping on them, but their dark color helped me adhere to the shadows. I passed the Aetherians on patrol without incident.

Aetherians on patrol. I scoffed. What an absurdity to be so rich, one could have the world's strongest arcanists delegated to guard duty. What few Aetherians I had under my command might have been warlords in their own right, had the Alliaansi not banded us together against the sorcerers who'd driven us from our lands.

I made for the cliff overlooking the Durgostian harbor. Over a dozen spans below me, surf crashed against the beach. The cliff was easily as tall as the smaller merchants' vessels in the distance. I sucked in a breath and braced myself. If I slipped and died here, it was still better than staying a slave.

I scooted over the edge, belly scraping against the ground. Hand under hand, lamenting the loss of both my sword-hardened calluses and my magic, I lowered myself down.

The wounds across my back pulled open, and my world listed. I paused in my descent to will the feeling along. Whether it was caused by blood loss or the dizzying height, I couldn't let it deter me. This was my chance—possibly my last chance—to get back home.

I'd mapped my escape weeks ago and practiced it mentally a dozen times, vowing that when Mascha at last presented me with an opening, I would seize it. He'd been distractible, inattentive, and sleep-deprived all week. Between the night terrors and the Deal-Breaker's envoy demanding an update on my progress, I could tell Mascha was feeling the pressure to deliver results.

So much the better. A desperate enemy was a reckless one, and rashness bred mistakes.

Almost there. My back screamed in protest, and my atrophied muscles quivered. I glanced down to plan my next foothold in the moonlight. Mist and sweat slicked my grip. Loose stone tumbled from beneath my toes.

Saonis miraar. Gods above.

I grabbed for a handhold and missed. My stomach stayed behind as I fell the last three spans to the beach.

Breath and agony burst from me; the night sky exploded with brilliant color. Sand and rock ground into my back, and my lungs spasmed around a breathless scream.

I fought down the tremors threatening to shake my bones apart and curled inward, wheezing and writhing as I struggled to retain consciousness. For long minutes I lay there, uncertain whether the roaring in my ears was the sound of ocean surf or the Aether burgeoning from a rift in the Wall, ready to devour me whole.

Someone could have heard all this. I couldn't linger here.

I scraped myself back together, color fading too slowly from my vision, and adjusted the silk headscarf disguising my white hair. Both scarf and sand clung to my sticky shoulder blades, and dark spots painted the beach. But no alarms sounded. No voices filtered down from the palace grounds. For as far as I could see in the moonlight, I was alone.

I kicked clean sand over the patch of blood and checked the rest of my meager provisions: a bead of saphyrum stolen from a sconce, a bundle of hard bread and candied fruit harvested from my meals over the last week, and a flint pilfered from the palace kitchen.

The nail I'd pulled from the market's whipping post pressed snugly against my thigh, wrapped in silk shreds from Mascha's fanciest shirt. It was my only weapon, and I'd gambled with my life to get it. It had made a handy pick for the lock on my cage, and if the bastard hadn't welded the spellbinders encircling my wrists in place, I could have picked those locks, too. But I didn't need my magic or my sword to best him; his own hubris was weapon enough.

Steeling my spine, I turned toward the specks of torchlight in the distance. Mascha would be balls-deep in some poor woman by now. If he stuck to his routine, I had an hour or two before he noticed my escape. Enough time to stow aboard a ship leaving port tonight. Most crews wouldn't sail after dusk, but high tide and clear skies both worked in my favor. A boat with time-sensitive cargo and an experienced crew wouldn't be that hard to find.

Waiting until morning wasn't an option. Mascha wouldn't announce that he'd lost a high-profile slave, but as the Rorsch Hekkai leader, he didn't need a reason to close the largest port in the world. As long as his employer, the Deal-Breaker—the true power in Rillion—approved the action, Mascha could grind this entire country to a halt to find me.

My legs grew heavy as I fought through the dunes. The port seemed to grow farther away with every step, like a mirage in the desert. Sand abraded my feet, and for once, I longed for those scabbing silk slippers. I'd ripped mine lunging for the knife at the merchant's stall, and they'd come off when Mascha dragged me to the post.

At least I'd guessed correctly that after six months of processing, I was worth more to him alive than dead. Many Rillanese slaves went to Baosanni's Gate unbroken every year, but my execution would have been the first blemish on Mascha's reputation.

My escape would leave a mark far more irrevocable, and when my steps faltered and I hit the sand, that knowledge alone provided the strength I needed to carry on.

Still, his behavior lately was a curiosity. Whatever dreams he'd been having must have appealed to the kernel of empathy he possessed. *Tipori, tipori*, he would mumble in his sleep. *Tipori daatahl.* Mercy for her. All while turning in his bed like a spitted boar over a fire.

Frankly, I didn't care what that meant. He could keep his demons; I already had plenty of my own.

Careful to cast no shadow, I stuck close to the bluff until I neared the docks, then heaved myself up to street level.

The view from Mascha's balcony had allowed me to map the maze of storage sheds and shipping crates. Though goods were always coming and going from Durgost, the port landscape stayed roughly the same. Slaves loaded pushcarts onto the docks, over the gangplanks, and onto the ships, while hired crews directed them and oversaw ship maintenance and repairs.

By day, I could have been spotted easily. Tonight, only a few docks remained occupied. One ship hoisted cages full of coral crabs off its bow with a system of winches and pulleys. Another was a domestic vessel just big enough to ferry goods across the channel to Epillon. A third ship bore the Eidosinian crest—the Sorcerers' Guild's open hands on a background of green and gold.

Fire seared my blood. My people's southern neighbors had murdered my mate, Nalerta, and our two adult children last year. I could still see my family's faces as they died: Nalerta, throwing me out of the path of a poisoned arrow, his teeth bared in a snarl; Elliaana, our eldest, lips blue with frost viper venom freezing her from the inside out; and Rysios, his ever-tangled hair rendered to ash as his features vanished behind a wall of flame.

We'd fought one bloody war after another with Eidosinia while they tried to wipe us from existence. And though my instincts screamed for vengeance on the mage standing watch on the forecastle of that ship, I had neither magic nor weapons to rid the world of one more black-robed carrion feeder.

I closed my stinging eyes until the surge of grief and rage passed. If I wanted to get home to my sister—the only surviving member of my family—I needed a clear head.

The fourth ship flew no banners and appeared the most promising. I could deal with pirates or independent sailors. Any danger they posed could be mitigated by sex or violence. Men were simple creatures, after all, and I had no problem using my body to exploit their baser instincts.

Peering around a stack of crates, I watched a black-and-gold-liveried guard walk past. Mundane—without magic—I wagered, and armed to the eyebrows. At my best, I could have killed him with nothing more than the nail pressed to my thigh. But even if I hadn't been injured, leaving a trail of bodies wasn't a good look for me.

Boards creaked under his feet. I made note of which ones to avoid.

He disappeared around the stern of an Aivenosian longship. I darted across the boardwalk and hunkered beside a mooring to wait out a pair of slaves wheeling empty pushcarts toward the fishing vessel.

A splinter lodged in my foot on the next dash through shadow and fog. I kept going, whisper-quiet as I dove behind a second mooring, then a salt-crusted supply shed.

Two more docks.

Nearly there, and Laangor's balls, did my back hurt. The scent of fresh blood lingered beneath the docks' miasma of pine tar, algae, and sweat. I steadied my breathing against the prospect of yet another journey in a cargo hold. At least this time, I wouldn't be chained beside a hundred others in various states of injury and sickness.

I suppressed a shiver. The stench of fleshrot and death had taken weeks to scour from my skin. I would never forget that moldy air, those slimy walls, the press of bodies and mingled fluids…

Crii'ruh. Stop.

I couldn't lose my nerve now.

Teeth bared, I slipped from behind the shed and skirted a circle of lantern light to the next dock—the sorcerers' berth.

I knelt in the shadow of a cockboat waiting to be loaded on its new vessel. My hand flexed around an imaginary hilt, as if I could will Dawnbringer, my Aetherial sword, into it. But the mage on deck was looking away from me, and the only activity beside the Eidosinian vessel came from a group of slaves hauling supplies up the gangplank.

I forced my fingers to relax. One more dock, and not a guard in sight.

A plummy voice wafted across the water. "...then get the rest of the saphyrum aboard."

Saphyrum.

My breath caught, even though it shouldn't have. Rillion was the biggest exporter of saphyrum in the world.

"Why me?" a second man whined. "Just have the slaves do it."

Squinting around the cockboat, I found the familiar barrels corralled in the light of two lanterns. Dozens of them. Enough to supply all of Aon'In—the Alliaansi's stronghold—for months. How in the Wastelands had I missed those?

"They're likely to pilfer some when we aren't looking. Now go. The Councilor's getting impatient."

A grumble answered him, followed by purposeful footsteps that reverberated through the dock beneath my palm.

I warred with the plausibility of stealing a handful of beads for myself. Even to mundane Syljians, saphyrum was as essential as food and water. It was the true reason behind the sorcerers' disdain for us, the reason they'd destroyed our cities, taken our land, and driven us north. Since it was also the source of all magic—the only way to access and manipulate the Aether—they felt compelled to hoard it like the dragons of old.

If I wanted to avoid saphyrum sickness, I would need more than one bead for the months ahead. The spellbinders' steady-but-useless trickle of saphyric energy would keep me alive, but it was akin to drinking watered-down juice to stave off hunger.

Teeth clenched, I surveyed the unmarked ship, searching for signs of magic among the crewmen. No flashes of white-violet light. No rifts simplifying the transport of cargo. No saphyrum lanterns illuminating the ship. It wasn't a damning assessment, but it wasn't a good one either.

Indecision gripped me in a vise.

Barked orders issued from beside the sorcerers' ship. The whiny mage rattled off something in Rillanese, too fast for me to catch more than the words "*raschun*" and "*porfiir*" with any confidence. Apparently, he wasn't above disobeying orders and relegating his task to the slaves after all.

The mage folded his arms and watched the collared men load one of their pushcarts. I counted the spans between the cockboat and the closest barrel. Forty paces or so, mostly in shadow, but with no cover between me and the last twenty spans.

It was risky, but I could make it.

"Hey!"

My stomach hit the boardwalk.

Sharp footsteps slapped behind me, and I bared my teeth. Damn my inattention. I was smarter than this. To let someone sneak up behind me...

I reached through the hole in Mascha's trousers for the silk-wrapped nail and turned, readying to lunge from the darkness.

The Rorsch Hekkai guard strode past me. He addressed the mage using the trade tongue. "Harbormaster says you haven't cleared those barrels through customs."

I blinked, too stunned to let the tension ease from my legs.

Whiny groaned. "Tell that rat bastard to check his manifest again. Sarikkian already filed your paperwork."

As the two men squared off, I sagged against the dock and willed my racing heart to calm. I must be losing my touch. There were too many eyes on that saphyrum haul.

The irony of my near-fatal mistake wasn't lost on me. Desperation, indeed.

Two more members of Mascha's police force shuffled over as the sorcerer and the first Rorsch Hekkai continued bickering. When a commotion on deck signaled the appearance of more mages, I took their distraction as an opportunity to slip away toward freedom.

Two slaves were hauling a cart up the unmarked ship's gangplank. With every nerve buzzing, I hurried toward the stack of crates still waiting to be loaded. One lid was nailed down, but another came away with a sharp screech.

I froze and swept the area for movement.

Raucous laughter carried from the foredeck, and a female voice cajoled the sailors in Rillanese. A male voice followed, bellowing a demand for more ale.

Drunken and aroused—the usual state for men in Rillion. For once, it was the perfect combination for me.

I shot one last look at the boardwalk before removing several bolts of silk from the crate and submerging them under the dock. I worked as fast as I dared and climbed into the crate, mindful of protruding nails as I shifted more silk bolts to one side to make room. Once I folded myself up, knees drawn to my chest, I pulled the lid shut. Soft footfalls creaked across the dock moments later.

Then the crate lurched into motion.

Chapter Four

Maralla

I AWOKE CRAMPED AND sore with metal digging into my neck and wrists. Dread doused me like a plunge into the frigid waters of Taaru'Kallii, and a strangled yelp clawed up my throat. I threw my arms into the blackness, the movement strangely absent of rattling chains, and my knuckles smashed against something hard. The pain returned me to my senses.

Cool, soft silk and dry wood—not sweaty, feverish skin—greeted my fingertips.

Heaving breaths slowly brought the pounding in my chest down to a light canter as I remembered the evening before. The market, the cage, the cliff. Sand and surf. A ship.

My fingers closed on the nearest bolt of fabric, my mind still disbelieving, until the ring of a distant bell and calls for more sail filtered through my awareness.

I touched my thighs, my arms, my throat. The nail beneath my trousers was still tucked in silk, and my stash of provisions strained at Mascha's shirt. Everything was here. *I* was here, and though his familiar scent of saffron and leather still clung to his clothes, I had to be leagues outside his reach by now.

At last.

Waves of joy and relief crashed over me, staggering and unstoppable, and manic laughter bubbled to the surface.

I was free.

Had I not been seated already, I might have fallen over in my triumph.

I clapped both hands over my mouth to quiet my sobs. Though I was on a ship bound for Tiior-knew-where, I still wore Mascha's collar and spellbinders. Until we were far outside his influence and at no risk of turning back for what would be a hefty reward, I couldn't be discovered.

Eventually, I would need bartering power and a blacksmith, preferably in a country where slavery was illegal and the locals might take pity on me. I could only pray our next destination wasn't the northern shores of Rillion.

But, gods, I was *free*.

The finer details of my passage home would come later. For now, not even the radiating ache all over my body, the sticky mess of my back, or my need to piss could dull my mood. I ran shaking fingers through my hair, and quietly laughed again as I stared into black space.

For long minutes, I savored the knowledge of my escape, until the pressure in my bladder could no longer be ignored. As I listened for voices outside my crate, I flexed each muscle group, starting at my toes, to wake them up. If I rushed to stand, I risked further injury, and I'd rather void my bladder right here than be unable to fight.

Wood creaked, doors opened and closed, and the occasional sailor called in a tongue I didn't recognize, but nothing sounded close. I shifted into a crouch and carefully pushed on the lid.

It didn't budge.

I pushed harder. The lid had come away easily last night. I couldn't have cinched it down that tightly, not from the inside...

Something must have been placed on top of my crate.

The realization reverberated through me like a death knell.

No. No, this couldn't be happening. Another push, my palms slipping against splintery wood.

No, no, no. How could I have overlooked this? Of course they would have stacked these crates for transport. Scabbing *gods*, how had I been so short-sighted?

The box's sides began to close in, and my lungs spasmed for air. I would suffocate in this pile of grossly overpriced and fragile cloth. To escape my captivity, only to find myself trapped in a box with meager food and no water—

I scowled. This was *not* how my story ended.

Shifting my legs beneath me, I lowered my head, pressed my ravaged shoulders against the lid, and pushed.

Wood groaned and nails squeaked. A slight bowing of wood near one corner spurred hope, and a sliver of gray appeared against the blackness. My muscles protested, and my wounds sewed fire across my upper half. Breathless, I dropped to the floor and the world plunged back into darkness.

Whatever was pinning the lid still allowed some movement in that one corner. If I could just leverage more force there, I could squeeze out of the gap. Fingerspan by fingerspan, I shifted bolts of fabric around. The slow shuffle spurred my annoyance, but I counseled myself to patience.

One of the bolts crackled in my grip. I paused, squeezing that spot again. A spicy musk, coupled with the sweetness of citrus, filled the crate.

Foreboding spider-walked down my spine. Very carefully, I set the bolt aside and reached for another, then another. Each time, the telltale sound came once more, and the citrus scent grew stronger.

There was no mistaking it. These bastards were smuggling keallite.

I tugged my headscarf over my face, counting myself fortunate I hadn't disturbed those bundles sooner. If I'd fallen asleep breathing that spice, I could have overdosed and died never knowing it. Gods willing, my exposure wouldn't elicit its more notorious effects. Addiction, illusory images, and euphoria were common; it was said not even conquering the world felt better. But a dirty dose could break a mind beyond the most skilled mastermind's ability to repair it. Even Mascha shied from keallite, and he was the most indulgent man I'd ever met.

To further filter out the dust, I forced saliva into the cloth around my mouth and nose. Mindful not to bang the silk about, I shuffled round until I was crouched beneath the loose corner.

A smooth board lay at the heart of each bolt of silk. I wiggled the keallite free of the nearest one and set the pouch aside. Blood trickled down my back, but the pain seemed lessened, as if I'd been touched by my sister's healing magic. I felt stronger, more alert. Sort of giddy.

I ignored the implications of that and pushed against the lid. Cooler air filtered in, providing a surge of relief that washed away all traces of my fatigue. I wedged the board into the gap, then grabbed another, and another, until four bolts jutted from the lid. Merely a handspan more and I could fit through. I eyed the gap and the boards, their straight lines turning wavy the longer I stared. I blinked the illusion away, then summoned my strength.

With a solidness to my legs that I hadn't felt since my youth, I shoved the lid upward while holding the silk wedges in place. I reached out to grab a fifth bolt, all too aware of the mounting pressure in my bladder.

Wood groaned above me, and something shifted.

I paused, listening.

The tension on the lid gave way, and the weight on my shoulders vanished. Bolts of silk thumped the top of my head, and an explosion of splintering wood sounded loud and damning in the quiet space. The lid fell back against my shoulders, and I cut my arm on a protruding nail as I flailed to remain upright.

The sharp scents of vinegar and dill hit me. I turned, wide-eyed, to the broken barrel lying next to my crate. Light filtered through the deck grates above and glistened against rough, oblong shapes.

Pickles. Gods-damned pickles.

I scrambled out of the crate and yanked the barrel upright, feet splashing in the pungent brine. Vinegar stung my wounded soles. Several hasty armfuls of pickles later, I realized the pointlessness of my attempts to put them back in the barrel. A shoddy clean-up would look more suspicious than the barrel left on the floor.

I shoved it back over and flicked pickle juice off my hands. The bread I'd stowed in Mascha's now vinegar-soaked shirt squished against my abdomen.

And I still needed to piss. I tossed the wet silk bolts back into the crate, then replaced the lid. There would be better places to hide.

I balanced against another crate to wipe the brine from my feet, before slinking away from the disaster to relieve myself in a corner.

Boots clomped across the floorboards overhead, heading for the ladder down. Swearing, I tugged up my trousers and ducked behind another stack of crates.

"Bleeding Torris can't stack a hold to save his mum."

A second man laughed. "Aye, made me ten eighi richer. I told Sombrai we wouldn't make it to Denna before the first one fell."

Scabbing Wastelands. Of course they were going to Denna. Where else would a multi-million gran shipment of illicit spice be headed than Rillion's most corrupt city? If that was our next stop, I was in trouble. The Rorsch Hekkai had been making efforts to police its docks to bring the drug cartels to heel, and once the cargo cleared out, I would be easy to find.

"That lout ain't good for it," a third said. Heavy steps on the ladder signaled the men's descent. "You're better off coaxing coins out of a courtesan's arse."

More laughter accompanied the first man's single-word incantation. "*Luminos.*"

Light flooded the cargo hold.

My eyes watered against the familiar spell, but in a way, it was a boon to know there was a mage among them. Where there was one bead of saphyrum, there would be more. Though, getting it from an arcanist while I was spellbound would require tact—*after* the unloading in Denna.

I peered around the stack, spotting a fourth man with them. A black stripe ran the length of his bald head, down to the tip of his nose, and three more stripes ran along his chin. He sniffed the air and pointed.

I'd only heard stories of the Dasch'Kalliir—mute assassins who worshipped Baosanni, god of death. Some claimed the Dasch'Kalliir were so skilled at the art of death that they could cut a man in half before he ever felt the blade.

The first speaker, a Mautori man, held his glowing bead aloft. Twisting horns jutted from his skull, and his fur-covered snout resembled that of an ox.

The sailors approached the broken barrel, and the second man—a human, as far as I could tell—kicked it. "Told you. Idiot stacked 'em wrong."

I let out a slow breath while the men scowled down at the pickles.

"Bleeding useless," the Mautori muttered. He gestured to the third man, whose green complexion and rounded ears marked him for only half-Aivenosian. "Get a broom. Captain better take it out of his coin."

My shoulders drained of tension as the third man started for the ladder. While the human folded his arms and leaned against another barrel, the Mautori swung his bead around, assessing the surrounding cargo.

The tang of citrus lingered on my lips. A need for movement gnawed at me like a hunger no meal could sate. The keallite sharpened my vision when I focused, but wavy lines and false movement distorted my larger field of view. An itch began in my limbs, and I shook off the imaginary horror of roaches crawling beneath my skin.

"Well, what have we here?"

Gods curse it. I'd only looked away for a second.

Despite my heart's attempts to escape my chest, I peered back around the crate. The half-Aivenosian was just returning with his broom, and he paused beside the grinning Mautori.

The assassin crouched beside the pool of brine and studied the silk crate. A thin, dark smear colored the side of the lid. He swiped at it and rubbed his fingers together; an unmistakable reddish tinge gleamed in the saphyrum light.

I clenched my jaw, all too aware of the blood soaking through my shirt.

"We've a stowaway, boys," the Mautori said.

Their snickers raked across my eardrums. Though my palm itched for the nail tied to my thigh, I couldn't fight them, even with keallite bolstering me. I had no idea how long this low dose would last. If I moved from box to box, I could try to stay hidden, but there were only so many places to hide aboard a ship. I needed to claim a better hand. Bargain somehow.

The half-Aivenosian bared his rotten teeth. "Cap'n ain't had a reason to keel-haul nobody for some time."

Eyes closing, the Dasch'Kalliir rose, and the scent of hot iron—of magic—seared my nostrils. He turned toward me as if he could hear my pulse thundering in my veins. Our eyes met even through the cloak of darkness.

"Spread out," the Mautori said, waving to the others. "He can't have gotten far."

The assassin lowered his chin, unmoved, and continued to stare at me.

My position was already compromised. I lifted my arms and rose. "That won't be necessary."

Heads turned. Three pairs of eyes leveled on me. The Dasch'Kalliir, however, sank into the shadows. I prepared myself for the kiss of cold steel along my spine.

The human pulled a knife from his belt, but he held it like a savage, point down and useless unless his opponent was already on the ground. "A woman," he sneered.

"I didn't mean any trouble." Daring a smirk, I recalled the name of the man accused of botching their loading procedure. "Bleeding Torris shouldn't have placed those pickles so precariously."

"Precarious pickles," the Mautori snorted. "Step into the light."

It rankled to obey orders from a man, but in this, I had no choice. I held my chin high as I approached.

"Little worse for wear, there, Pickles," the half-Aivenosian drawled. "That's a dainty collar about your neck."

"It's made of pure platinum, and yours, if you can remove it for me."

With my luck, these brutes would find removing my head from my shoulders easier. I didn't know if the metal was really platinum, but it seemed like the sort of stupid, costly thing Mascha would do. Hunger sparked in the human's eyes, and he started forward.

The Mautori held him back. "The punishment for assisting runaway slaves is steep."

"Well, you weren't supposed to assist me, much less find me. But now that you have, I suppose we can help each other." I kept my hands raised, trying to ignore the buzz of keallite and the way it made my fingers warp in my peripheral vision. "I don't want to go back, and it would be in your best interests if the Rorsch Hekkai don't find me in your possession. I'll stay quiet about you helping me if you drop me at the next port outside Rillion."

While the others guffawed, the Mautori—apparently the only one with a spark of intelligence about him—bared his flat teeth against my veiled threat. "What makes you think the Rorsch Hekkai would believe your word against ours?"

I hoped my smile was as feral as it felt. "My punishment is the same either way, whereas you would spend six months in a Rillanese prison"—I nodded toward the silk crate—"plus whatever time for sneaking all that keallite aboard."

The human tried to push past. "Not if I cut out your Chaos-sworn tongue—"

The Mautori shoved him back. He spoke curtly in that unfamiliar language, and the human scowled.

While they bickered, I appraised the smugglers more closely. All three were tattooed and shirtless, but the loose lobes of the Mautori's wide ears had once been pierced and heavily stretched. An old scar cut his right eyebrow in half, and he was easily four handspans wider through the shoulders than I.

He passed his saphyrum to the half-Aivenosian, whose grin mimicked the grisly slash of an executioner's blade.

A decision made. My luck had just run out.

I reached for the nail too late. A wall of fur barreled toward me, and the Mautori seized my face.

My laugh sounded sharp and deranged even to my own ears. Of course it had come to this. Sex and violence, after all.

The Mautori lifted my chin. I leaned in and reached up to touch his chest. It felt like I reached forever. Scabbing gods, the bastard was enormous. This was going to hurt.

"I assure you my tongue is more useful intact." I tried to stay calm, tried to retain control. This wasn't my first time at the whims of lesser men.

His chuckle rumbled beneath my palm. "Alright, Pickles, we'll give you a chance." His sneer stretched taut in a facsimile of sympathy. "Suppose you'll have to prove to the whole crew why we shouldn't throw you overboard."

They were going to do it anyway.

A snarl burst from me as my feet left the ground. The Mautori slammed me into the deck, and light exploded in my vision. I fought against the star-studded blackness, against the pressure on my arms and the shredding of cloth.

Cold and pain. Faces appeared, and their laughter drove spikes of rage into me. I screamed. I arched, freeing one arm to strike the bastard on my left. My knuckles sang, and I got one knee up before the Mautori's beastly weight crushed me against the floor.

The human pinned my wrists while more hands pried my knees apart. I clung to the image of their blood painting the deck while mountains of fury and pain drove me higher.

And as if the gods themselves had heeded my ire, wood and metal shuddered.

Alarmed cries rang out above deck. The human hesitated. I wrenched my hand from him and tried one last time for the nail.

Something struck the hull, and all three men flew sideways. I didn't care to ponder what could have thrown a ship like that. My fingers found the nail. Elation flooded me, sharper and sweeter than any keallite-addled stupor. I stabbed into the nearest man and kicked at another. I stabbed again, and my grip slickened with blood.

My blood. But keallite numbed the new gash in my palm as well as the pain in my back. Without Mascha's shirt and trousers, my exposed wounds ground into the planks. I rolled onto my stomach and pushed off the floor.

Furry hands seized my calves, dragged me back, and flipped me over. "Go see what's happening," the Mautori snapped at his companions.

"And let you have all the fun?"

"Yeah, piss off."

I swung the nail at him. Flesh parted beneath his eye, and he roared. His fist smashed into my face.

The nail clattered into oblivion, and I tasted blood.

The rustle of fabric cut through the ringing in my ears. I lay there dazed, unable to will my body into movement, but I had to keep fighting; I couldn't let them win.

Familiar, rhythmic footsteps reverberated through the planks above me. I struggled to surface, tried to make sense of them, but the pressure between my thighs brought me back. The Mautori's crushing grip anchored my waist, and black malice glinted in his eyes.

"I'm going to make you regret that," he snapped.

Pressure mounted into pain, then agony. I screamed.

Black-violet mist coalesced in a halo around his head. An explosion of light blinded me. The Mautori jerked forward once, twice, with a wet crunch and a choked gasp. He stopped fingerspans from crushing me, eyes glassy with shock. His spittle slathered my face, and my stomach heaved.

In my periphery, his companions exploded into red-black mist. The Mautori's body lifted seemingly of its own accord and fell to one side, face down on the deck.

I stared, stupefied, as Mascha stepped over him. Windswept brown hair curled over his shoulders, his violet eyes aglow with magic. His twin battle axes, rumored to have been forged by the god of suffering himself, jutted from the Mautori's body. Mascha waved his hand, and the weapons vanished into mist. My savior, my captor, moved like a shade of death as he knelt and plunged his hands through muscle and bone into the gaping holes flanking the Mautori's spine. Teeth bared, he ripped my assailant's lungs out of his back and crushed them in his bloody fingers.

I didn't realize I was trembling until he looked at me. I snapped my jaw shut.

He let the mangled organs fall. "On your feet, *rascha*," he growled. "It's time to go."

Chapter Five

Mascha

IT WAS LIKE LOOKING into the past.

Blood darkened Maralla's thighs and streaked her belly. Her braids hung in tangles, half-unraveled and caked with grime. Swelling already distorted the white warrior's runes over one eye. Her scream still reverberated in my ears, blending with the distant howls of terror and agony from my dreams. The scents of blood and male arousal nearly drove me back into my frenzy; the strain of resisting it forced my heart ever harder against my ribs.

I focused on the smell of vinegar and dill to ground myself. Drew a breath. Then another. I wasn't too late this time.

This time, I'd killed them all.

Whether Maralla would thank me later was irrelevant. I rose from the corpse of her attacker, wetness cooling up to my wrists. My command still hung in the air between us. Apparently, the mascha—my signature kill-stroke—was disturbing enough to stun even a former legion commander.

Her eyes darted toward the scarlet remains of the sailors. Trousers, belts, and boots piled in two dark rings. Even for a skilled Aetherian such as I, breaking a body into its simplest form was no small feat. Fatigue burrowed into my limbs with the deadly promise of Mage's Folly should I cast much more.

While Maralla collected her wits, I turned toward the dark figure near the hull. Jhamar slipped out of hiding and opened a nearby crate with ease. White powder dusted the crimson silk within.

My jaw clenched. I ignored my body's traitorous pining for that vile substance and suppressed a shiver.

Several bolts of the fine fabric had been removed, leaving more space inside than usual. Jhamar tilted his head and his eyes flicked toward Maralla. We seemed to draw the conclusion at the same time.

He replaced the lid, then approached me with a mask betraying no sense of accomplishment or victory. He bowed with his forearms crossed—acknowledgement of a fulfilled contract. I'd hired the Dasch'Kalliir months ago to track rumors of keallite smuggling along the Dennian Channel. No one expected an assassin to care about spice, so it was easier for him to move about than any of my Aetherians.

I returned the gesture, then nodded to Maralla. "Did anyone else see her?"

Jhamar's slate gaze never wavered from my face. He shook his head, but pinched his thumb and two fingers together to drag them up his throat.

I nodded. He was right; her scream was enough to warrant suspicion. And truthfully, I had no qualms about killing spicers.

I withdrew a platinum assassin's coin and passed it to him. Baosanni's symbol—three leafless trees—gleamed on the coin's surface. "You know what I expect."

Jhamar pocketed the coin and dragged three fingers over the marks on his chin—a vow of service. The blades at his belt glinted as he climbed the ladder. Moments after he disappeared above deck, the guttural sounds of killing and dying began. I returned my attention to Maralla.

The flicker of Foresight was my only warning.

She was on her feet, so close that the blow intended for my throat pushed air against my skin. I caught her wrist and drove my thumb into a nerve cluster. Her fingers went slack, and something clattered to the floorboards.

Her howl echoed through the cargo hold. One bare foot stomped on my boot. I turned aside to dodge a knee to the groin, seizing her chin in my other hand. Nose to nose with her, I paused.

Dilated pupils. Enhanced reflexes. Abnormal stamina, despite her injuries. The most ill-trained fighter could be dangerous on keallite. Maralla would be lethal.

The prospect excited me more than I cared to admit.

She thrashed, snarling, and another Aetherial image predicted split futures of a blow from her free hand. Maralla was a tactician—one of the best in the northern hemisphere. She'd discovered my Foresight early and, despite the magic's rarity, learned how to force uncertainty into what should have been unequivocal out-comes.

Rather than block either future, I let the blow land. Her fingers snagged in my beard.

"Peace, *rascha*." I held fast to her, one arm across her back, her blood wetting my sleeve. "You must know when you've lost."

"Ass-eared mongrel," she spat. "I'll look upon your grave."

My grin only inflamed her further. She went for a punch. I spun us both to throw the blow off-target, but pain still bloomed where her knuckles glanced off my jaw. With each attempt to break my hold, her movements grew less precise—a sign that she was coming down from the high. When at last she overbalanced, I swept her feet from under her and wrestled her to the floor.

She hit the ground with a cry. Our legs entangled, her chest heaving against mine. A slave-binding could have ended this sooner, but I had to conserve my arcane energy for the rift back to the palace.

I waited while her short, angry breaths warmed my neck. Her struggles weak-ened, her body ceding to mine with each passing moment. I pinned her wrists and blocked another hold-breaking attempt with my knee.

Gods help me, she was fierce, like a tiger that wouldn't be caged. She bared her teeth, and I couldn't help pressing my growing arousal against her thigh. Though I wouldn't take her against her will, I *would* remind her of her place.

The ship swayed, and the object she'd dropped rolled into a square of light from the grate above. I glanced toward it, and my jaw went slack.

A nail.

And not just any nail. One like those driven into a pier. Or a post. Cold prickled my fingertips, and the triumph surging through me faltered.

The feral smile that pulled the warrior's runes tight over Maralla's cheeks rankled me as much as it claimed my grudging respect.

I'd wondered what had gotten into her yesterday. She'd been in Rillion long enough to know drawing steel against me should have prompted her execution right there in the street. And yet, she'd chosen to gamble her life on my hesitation, all to acquire a nail capable of both picking locks and puncturing flesh.

"You planned this." I couldn't keep the awe out of my voice. "All of it."

A savage spark set Maralla's gaze alight. Her laugh bordered on hysterical. "Except the last bit, anyway. That was my mistake."

Her venom poisoned what little victory I'd savored in besting her. I'd grown complacent and inattentive with her better behavior, and she'd used my blunders against me. By all accounts, she should have won this battle. Only Silonas's favor had allowed me to catch her before she slipped out of reach.

This game we played had gone on too long.

"Your first mistake was believing you would succeed at all." I shifted to my knees and straddled her waist, keeping pressure on her wrists. "Now, are you going to walk out of here under your own power, or do I have to bind you?"

Her amethyst eyes narrowed to a dagger's edge. She met my gaze—a breach of protocol for which any other master would have beaten her bloody—and her expression softened. "I'll walk."

I didn't trust that softness for a moment. "If you make a fool of yourself, you'll regret it."

My fatigue aside, I considered a slave-binding anyway to insulate myself against further risk. Only hours ago, she'd elected to take a whipping to procure her means of escape. It seemed punishment, like the long list of other disciplinary techniques I'd tried, was no longer effective.

Jhamar's path across the ship quieted, and his footfalls creaked against the floorboards overhead.

I hauled Maralla up and pushed her toward the ladder. "Move, *rascha*."

She dragged herself up the rungs with the gracelessness of a cat escaping a plunge into icy water. When we emerged from the hold, she hit her knees on the sun-drenched planks, and eerie, keening laughter shook her entire body.

Alarmed, I shot up the last three rungs and cupped her face. "Maralla?"

She gripped my wrists and laughed harder, though her pupils dilated normally in the shadow of my chest.

I released her, and she folded in on herself, clutching her stomach. Tears streamed over her nose and more barking, mirthless sounds erupted from her throat.

"Have you gone mad?"

"*Cii*—" She hiccupped and wiped her nose with the heel of her hand. "*Ciir*, I think so."

I hesitated. "Can you walk?"

She shook her head, grinding her temple into the deck.

A keallite crash, then. Or perhaps her capture after such a masterful escape attempt had broken something inside her. The poor wretch still held on to the hope of ever returning home.

I looked around for bystanders. The midmorning sun glinted off Jhamar's ashen pate. He lingered nearby, wiping blood from his needle-thin blades.

"Is it finished?"

He tucked away his steel, crossed his arms, and bowed.

"Very good. You may accompany us back to Durgost or take the cockboat wherever you wish. My men can assist you if you choose to depart."

Jhamar nodded and turned toward the gangplank spanning between the smugglers' ship and mine. Hooks and ropes secured my leaner vessel to the ship's side.

Maralla quieted beside me, though silent hiccups still shook her. I tried to touch her face again, but she snarled and slapped my hand away.

It came as no surprise. She always denied my attempts at comfort. My own snarl threatened as I took in her bruised thighs, bloodied back, and swollen face.

This didn't have to happen. She shouldn't have run away, shouldn't have been on this ship, shouldn't have been within arm's reach of such wicked men.

All I asked for was obedience. I was fair to my slaves. I tried to protect them from the cruelest realities of my world. Of all the slaves who had passed through my care to the auction block every year, of the hundreds of faces and names I'd committed to memory, only Maralla refused to see.

"Why?" I asked.

She sniffled, but said nothing.

"Why do you keep doing this?"

Maralla curled tighter, a silent refusal.

I seized her hair and forced her head up. "Why do you make me hurt you?"

Her mouth twisted into a vicious slash. "I don't."

"Yes, you do." I couldn't tell guilt from fury; both lodged firmly between my lungs. "You practically beg for it. You *plan* for it."

Her gaze sharpened with scorching clarity. "Let go of me."

"If you would just submit, then all of this could end."

"Never."

The urge to strike a slave had never been so strong. My open hand drew back of its own accord and I shuddered to a halt, eyes squeezed shut against the base impulse. For a master to lose control before his charge was folly, and I'd already demonstrated too well her ability to burrow under my skin.

I lowered my arm, muscles quaking with restraint. She studied me with that too-shrewd expression, her wits having returned from wherever keallite and her capture had sent them. Part of me wished to send them back. A larger part found their familiarity comforting.

I didn't want to hurt her. Cruelty was never my method of choice. But if discipline and reward couldn't make her a proper slave, then I was running out of options.

"After all this time"—I struggled to keep my voice even—"why must you still defy me?"

"Because..." Maralla's voice broke, her body shivering with the aftereffects of the drug. "Because it's the only agency I have left."

My lips parted.

Helplessness—a concept I understood well. I'd spent a third of my life at the mercy of the Master. And I knew that if a man should try to assert his will over mine after all these years, my response would be no different from hers.

Silence reigned between us. Numbly, I reached for her, and this time, she didn't fight me. I hoisted her up and carried her across the ship, across the gangplank, and tried to ignore the look of longing she threw down to the waves. Her despair seeped into me, and I steeled myself from offering empty assurances.

I stepped onto my employer's ship. Two dark-skinned Aetherians in jade robes greeted me. Svaronei's Aethersight had traced Maralla's whereabouts off the coast, and Vhedja's manipulation of the winds had allowed us to catch up to her.

Vhedja, the slighter of the pair, spared a curious look over his hooked nose at the source of all the excitement. "Orders, Rorsch Hekkai?"

Word of Maralla's escape couldn't reach the rest of the nation. Only the most discreet of my men had attended this spectacle. But these two were the Deal-Breaker's creatures, and they would send news of this encounter to our employer within moments of our return. The Deal-Breaker would expect as few loose ends as possible.

I lifted my voice so all those gathered on deck could hear. "The cargo hold is full of keallite." I nodded toward the smugglers' ship. "This was a mission to apprehend the smugglers, and they chose violence over surrender."

Scattered assent met my words. Ropes creaked and sails snapped overhead.

I turned, holding Maralla close, and looked at Vhedja. "Burn it to the water-line."

Chapter Six

Mascha

The Rorsch Hekkai Palace drifted into view above the bluffs lining the Durgostian Channel. Wind tossed my hair over my shoulders, and I breathed in the crisp scent of the sea. I didn't sail often—the Aetherians in the Deal-Breaker's employ Walked me through the Aether most of the time—so I relished the rare opportunity to enjoy mundane travel. Now that I'd reclaimed my wayward slave, and I had a lead on our latest keallite epidemic, my most recent crisis seemed to be drawing to a close.

Maralla knelt on the bow at my feet, wrapped in spare bed linen. Steam practically billowed from her tapered ears. If she could have stood beside me without collapsing, I was certain she would have done so to spite all protocol.

Footsteps approached, and I turned from the railing.

Svaronei folded his arms inside his jade robe. His strong shoulders and square jaw lent well to his handsome figure, and though he was a handspan taller than I, he possessed the presence of mind not to loom by keeping a few paces between us. "Want me to Walk you in?"

"That won't be necessary." I could rift us from here. "Take Vhedja and check the port manifests for the source of that silk. I want the portmaster's men questioned about their lapse in cargo checks yesterday." If we could find which house had supplied the silk, we would also find our next lead on the origins of that keallite.

Svaronei bowed. "Yes, Rorsch Hekkai."

As he turned away, I summoned saphyric energy from my earring and slashed a black-violet rift into the Aetherial Wall. A brief cyclonic wind formed as the sea air poured into the man-sized void.

I offered my hand to Maralla. "Come, *rascha*."

Her growl might have passed for the roar of wind, but I knew better. She clapped her hand into mine and tried to rise, only to tumble again when her knees failed her.

I swept her into my arms. As her head came to rest on my shoulder, I stepped over the mouth of the rift and into the blackness beyond.

Myriad colors streaked by in a blur. Normally, one would not Rift Bend beyond line of sight or through unfamiliar terrain. Aetherial travel could cause permanent disfigurement or even death if a rift spat its caster into a wall or other object on the exit side. Fortunately, I knew my palace corridors as surely as I knew my name.

The rift let out into a wide corridor on the third floor, and the break in the Aetherial Wall snapped closed behind me. A sea scent clung to us as I carried Maralla toward Hasanthe's infirmary. Half-asleep in my arms, she perked up as I passed the turn for the disciplinarium.

"Where are we going?"

"You want me to whip you again?"

She glared at me through her white lashes. "You can try."

Torn between commending her bravery and condemning her ignorance, I chose to laugh instead. "If I drop you, it will hurt."

"I'd prefer if you didn't."

"Then be silent."

For once, she obeyed.

The silence was short-lived. When I turned the next corner for Hasanthe's chambers, Maralla's snowy eyebrows nearly touched her hairline. "The healer?"

"*Ciir.*"

Certain the remorse would show on my face, I kept my attention trained on the doors at the end of the hallway. I couldn't go another moment without addressing her wounds.

"*Tipori?*"

I lurched to a stop. "What?"

The word parted so softly from Maralla's lips that it could have been the caress of a ghost. *Her* ghost. She'd died so long ago, and still her words haunted me: *Kaana'ruh ke'aave tipori.*

It was merely a coincidence. We shared a language, and our Syljian dialects were not so different. The Master had preferred the purer, northern Syljian over one tainted by Rillanese. I'd since adopted a blend of the two languages partly out of necessity and partly in defiance.

Maralla held my gaze and threw her lance again, surer this time. "*Tipori.*"

Mercy.

It shouldn't have been my undoing. Silonas slay me, I couldn't afford any more mistakes. Her haughtiness dissolved, replaced by curiosity. My jaw worked as I contemplated how to respond.

"*Ciir,*" I finally managed. It was just a word, after all. One with no more power than any other. "But don't press your luck."

Maralla relaxed against me, clearly content with her new knowledge.

I suppressed a groan and called through the infirmary doors. "Hasanthe!"

The healer's assigned slaves, Emmi and Charice, opened the doors to a large room draped in soft linen. Embroidered red accents paid homage to Hasanthe's patron goddess, Shavaan. Incense wafted from a golden altar between two rows of beds.

I seated Maralla on the closest mattress and called again. "Hasanthe!"

"I'm coming, I'm—" Hasanthe ducked out of a private room and froze. "Sweet Shavaan." He hurried to my side, and his dark hands engulfed Maralla's shoulders as he bent to inspect her back. Then he regarded me in disbelief.

News from the market would have reached him by now. He wouldn't question me in front of the slaves, but he knew how I felt about harming them.

Though I didn't owe him an explanation—he was my employee first, and my friend second—I still grappled with the need to deny the worst of the rumors. Anelliiq had sworn to say nothing of my disappearance, and Wali wouldn't bother to ask her about it. He would only grumble about my 'savage behavior' in his social circles, then go about his business of slandering Ideghis V as if nothing unusual had happened.

But the way Hasanthe was looking at me now forced my guilt deeper. I glanced toward the slaves and tossed aside any thought of telling the truth. It was better they believed I could do this than send them out with gossip.

"Heal her, please. She's been bleeding a while."

"I can see that." Hasanthe's disapproval was poorly masked. "These will scar."

I folded my hands, feigning nonchalance, though the thought of such permanent evidence of my failure formed a hollow in my stomach.

He sighed and addressed the slaves. "Don't just stand there, *raschan*. Bring fresh water and towels."

The girls moved to obey, and Hasanthe wove strands of white-violet light into two palm-sized sigils. Maralla held her chin high while Emmi and Charice wiped blood from her back and belly. The water in the basin grew redder with each pass. Her only indication of pain or embarrassment was the stiffening of her shoulders when Charice reached the bloody trails along her thighs.

Maralla snatched the towel from her. "I can do that," she said, and swiped at the evidence of her assault before passing the towel back.

Understanding smoothed Hasanthe's brow. Having counseled me on certain aspects of my past, he knew I would never harm anyone that way. Too many nobles had requested forceful performances from the Master over the years, and none of his slaves had been immune to a night on the breeding bench if we displeased him. Though my body still reacted positively to the violence, I'd experienced both sides too much to glean any satisfaction from it.

Still, that left Hasanthe with questions. I maintained my stony resolve and made a subtle gesture, promising to speak in private later.

The door opened behind me, and a distinctly chemical smell rolled in with the newcomer.

Slighter of build than I, with the Master's rounded ears, soul-black eyes, and disarming smile, my half-brother Tasari was every bit our father's son. He could have easily passed for a full-blooded human, though he was over one hundred and twenty years old.

"Hasanthe," Tasari purred, placing his leather satchel on a nearby mattress. Glass clinked as he rummaged and withdrew two empty flasks. "I need more egg serum and distilled water. Be a dear and get them for me."

Hasanthe kept his attention on his task, and healing magic flowed from his sigils to Maralla's wounds in white-violet ribbons.

Tasari snapped his fingers. "Come now, my pox cure won't make itself."

"You can see I'm busy. Come back later."

"Well, if you're going to be rude about it, I'll just get it myself." Tasari paused. His low whistle echoed off the walls as he appraised Maralla. "My, my."

He tossed both flasks over his shoulder, and they shattered on the floor. Smartly, Maralla lowered her gaze, and Tasari flashed me his brightest smile. "You really did put our resident brat in her place. I couldn't believe it when I heard."

I didn't rise to the bait. He knew I took no pride in wielding a whip.

He started toward her. "Does she still bite, I wonder?"

Aetherial images flickered through my vision, too many to predict whether Maralla would react as poorly as she had during their last encounter. She'd been tied to the post on Correction Day, and he'd tried to dose her with a new potion made to heighten the sensation of pain. I'd condoned it, hoping it might bring her to heel, but she'd kicked it out of his grip and spilled the only vial across the sand.

The closer he got to her, the higher my hackles rose. "You will not disturb Hasanthe's work."

"I just want to see if my marks are still there."

Aside from the Correction Day whippings, I only utilized my brother's taste for pain when all other avenues failed me. I'd spent too much time processing Maralla already, and Tasari knew it. He'd demanded I turn her over to him months ago, but I'd denied him, arguing that the risk to my investment was too high. He killed more of the slaves assigned to his care than he broke, and he still had a few test subjects languishing in his quarters.

Not for the first time, I stepped between him and Maralla. "Be about your business."

"Oh, come now, Mascha. You never let me play with that one." He thrust out his lip like a child. "Just look at her. She turns such pretty colors."

"All the same"—I mirrored his sidestep to stay between them—"if I needed your help, I'd have sent for you."

"So possessive." Tasari rolled his eyes. "She must have one magnificent cunt for you to keep her all to yourself."

We'd never coupled, in truth. Not even caged and heavily dosed with raspaati had she submitted to me.

Tasari stepped wide, and I tracked his movement across the room. Before he disappeared into the storeroom, he turned back, all smiles once more. "Saarach was looking for you, by the way. He's been waiting in the courtyard for over an hour."

Gods damn him.

Of course Tasari wouldn't have led with that knowledge. He never had to suffer the Deal-Breaker's emissary. I looked to Hasanthe, who thrust his chin toward the entrance without breaking concentration.

"Go. I'll take care of her."

Fatigue tugged at me, but I could manage one more rift. Then I would have Raffi cancel my appointments for the afternoon and take some time to rest.

I summoned saphyrum and slashed through the Wall. Wind tugged me toward the rift as I took one last look at Maralla.

"Behave," I warned.

Though my command was as empty as a peasant's larder, I reached into the rift and pretended her quiet stare was anything but calculated.

In my haste to see the Deal-Breaker's emissary gone, I neglected to ask *which* courtyard the bastard was in, nor did I give any thought to changing my shirt. Quite the vision I must have been, showing up late, harried, and covered in blood.

Saarach turned from his study of a rare Skriian orchid and regarded me impassively. He dabbed at his wizened face with a handkerchief, his hairless cheeks and pointed ears made pink from the rising heat. He didn't allow the weather to affect his mood, however. I was always impressed—and a little unnerved—by the man's even-keeled nature.

"Rough morning, my lord?"

My eye twitched. I was no lord, nor did I wish to be, and all of Rillion knew it. "You could say that. What do you want?"

"I'm certain you know already. He is displeased, Mascha. This dip in your performance has caused him great distress."

"You can assure him both incidents have been handled." I folded my hands too tightly and made a conscious effort to relax them. "I've already sent Svaronei and Vhedja to deal with the lapse at the port. The situation is under control."

He nodded toward my bloodstained attire. "Is it?"

"Yes."

"Hm." A parchment-thin smile touched his lips. "Nevertheless, he requires assurances. He has entertained your little tryst long enough and demands you put an end to it. If you cannot break the slave, you will turn her over to Tasari for processing."

Bile rose in my throat. "That's not necessary. Her payoff will be worth the investment. I just need more time."

"You've said this before. I'm afraid our employer disagrees." Saarach's tone remained neutral. "Our country looks to you for order, and yet you don't have order in your own household."

"That's—"

He made a curt gesture for silence. "A slave causing disturbances at market, sneaking out at night, escaping from the port. It is disgraceful. Next time, you may not be so fortunate in containing this disaster, and then we may have a revolt on our hands."

Heat rose in my face, though I couldn't argue the point. Any lesser noble whose slave escaped his estate was made a laughingstock, his business deals defunct, and his reputation shattered. *My* loss of control would inspire slaves all over the country.

But I knew what became of those in Tasari's care. No one, free or enslaved, deserved that. "She *will* break. And when she does, her reputation alone will net him more profit than any slave sold this year."

Saarach fanned himself with his yellow robe, tilting his head.

"I ask for patience." I couldn't think of it as a plea. Wouldn't. "He knows the best investments take time to mature."

Finally, Saarach lifted his chin. "If you insist on this course, the Deal-Breaker is willing to offer you one more chance. But if you don't bring the slave to heel, you may find it is easier to unmake a man than it is to make him."

His clinical delivery of the threat drove my predicament home better than anger or exasperation ever could. Indeed, the Master might have made me a Champion, but the Deal-Breaker had made me a free man. In exchange for placing my Freedom Wager in the arena, I'd agreed to work for him, enact his plans, and assure national security. It wasn't just my reputation on the line, but my livelihood. A step too far, and I could lose everything I'd built over the last eighty years.

Worse, if a revolt were to occur, a loss of riches and station would be the least of my concerns. The Deal-Breaker's wrath was swift, and he could devise a punishment far worse for me than death. I could be the next victim to Tasari's grisly experiments. I could find myself returned to the pits, to the Master's house even, where I would be a slave once more, forced to produce more champion fighters and see more of my offspring die in the arena.

My pulse throbbed at my temples, and I blinked haloes from my vision. Perhaps turning Maralla over to Tasari was the wiser course.

But no, my thoughts were spiraling. I couldn't condemn her to that fate. Not while I could still do something about it. I would surrender this country to invaders before I would allow a revolt to come to pass.

"Give him my assurances. I will do what is best for Rillion."

Saarach bowed. "May Silonas favor you."

I didn't bother to repeat the false sentiment. Saarach turned, passed beneath a pergola laden with yellow jasmine, and departed through the courtyard gate.

For long minutes, I scuffed along the meandering paths between flowerbeds, pondering this new ultimatum. Break the unbreakable, or let her die a slow, torturous death.

It wasn't much of a choice, and yet I'd failed at the former repeatedly over the last six months. Corrections, caging, pauper's rations of fish and bread, even withholding her worldly pleasures and rewarding good behavior had gained me nothing. It was clear there wasn't enough raspaati in this world to soften her to her own desire. She'd resisted for so long that her genital cage had cut into her legs.

It didn't help that I admired the woman. In many respects, she reminded me of Anelliiq. Both were tenacious and intelligent, capable of strategy and subterfuge. But while Anelliiq could see reason, Maralla only entertained it if it suited her.

I stopped at the apex of a wooden bridge and frowned into the water below. Exotic blue fish darted between the rocks. A yellow-shelled turtle swam upstream and settled in a patch of sunlight. Aquatic vegetation danced in the current, steadfast in its anchorage yet willing to bend with the stream.

Maybe that was the key. I'd spent six months fighting Maralla's nature, trying to alter it, rather than bending with her. Even if there was little I could afford her in that respect, the illusion of autonomy was almost as effective as autonomy itself.

We desired the same thing, really. I wished her gone, and she wanted to be free of me. I only needed her to behave long enough to sell her. Whatever she did once she left my household was none of my concern.

But I *was* concerned. She'd outsmarted me last night, and escaping my palace was no easy feat. It meant timing the movement of every sentry on rotation perfectly. It meant mapping her escape over days, if not weeks, and waiting for the exact moment to strike. I had no doubt if I sold her to another house, she would escape her new master within a few days—a bad look for me, unless I took steps to mitigate the damage.

If I could maneuver her into a lesser house, I could blame her new owner's ineptitude and poor security. My flawless reputation for breaking slaves would insulate me from accusation. Even the most docile slave would run if given the chance.

I pushed away from the railing and started for the palace doors. Such a plan would require her cooperation. Her escape couldn't happen too soon after the sale. It meant patience. Trust.

I scoffed. It was a desperate move, but I couldn't stomach the thought of mutilating her further. I had enough slaves' blood on my hands.

Maralla had a mind for war. She would see the merit in this. If she didn't, we might both find ourselves at the whims of lesser men.

Chapter Seven

Maralla

The drop from keallite's euphoric high struck me like a cudgel on the ride back to the palace. But by the time Mascha returned to collect me from Hasanthe, I was clear-headed and already planning my next move.

I couldn't allow despair to cripple me. My foiled escape wasn't a failure so much as an opportunity to gather information. I'd proven it *was* possible to leave the palace grounds and board a ship. I just hadn't known to factor in Svaronei, who—according to talk among the crew—had tracked me to the smugglers' vessel through Aethersight. Next time, I would remember. Next time, I would get my hands on a wardstone to circumvent him.

'*Tipori*' had likewise revealed a weakness in my unshakeable captor. The slaver, who only hours ago had ripped a man's lungs from his back and misted two others in defense of his so-called property, had been struck speechless by that one word.

Tipori daatahl. Mercy for her, he begged from his dreams, for a woman—a lover, I guessed—who'd once suffered greatly in another's hands.

I could exploit this.

It seemed to pain him to look upon the new scars on my back, so I refused the blouse and skirt Hasanthe offered. I strode naked ahead of Mascha all the way to his quarters, rather than a half-step behind and to his right like a good little slave. He didn't correct me.

I reached the master suite, folded my arms, and turned to face him.

He averted his gaze and opened the door. "After you."

Strange—not even my posturing got a rise out of him. But I wouldn't be thrown off by that subdued tone.

"What a gentleman," I hissed.

Still, he didn't react. No scowl. No steely glare. Not even a twitch of his jaw. I sniffed and brushed past him. He shut the door behind us, locked it, and waved a hand to set the rift ward on the wall. The large chunk of saphyrum powering the ward emitted a soft blue glow.

He turned and opened his mouth, but I knew the drill. *"Go to your cage, rascha. Sit like a lady, not a slut, rascha. You'll not speak unless spoken to, rascha."* It was always the same.

Before he could derive any satisfaction from barking orders at me, I stalked through his chambers and shoved the bedroom door open. My cage stood ajar, and I paused only briefly before forcing my feet over the tile. This was not a battle worth fighting. I would save my energy.

I sat cross-legged—like a slut—on the metal floor and slammed the door shut. Gooseflesh exploded over my skin, but I closed my eyes and let the cold seep into me. It was so close to the feeling of northern winter that I could imagine myself back home, breathing pine-laden air, crunching through knee-deep snow, holding my sister close. Orowen would have never let my back scar so badly. Even before she'd donned the robes of a priestess, she'd made herself an accomplished healer. I wished I'd told her before I left for Sessia how much I loved her. She'd surely received word about Nalerta and our children by now.

I shoved the rising tide of grief aside. There would be time for tears later.

Mascha's footsteps drifted over the rug and stopped not far from my cage. I opened my eyes, but didn't find him looming over me like I expected. Instead, he sank down at the foot of his bed and rested his face in his palms.

Curious.

Mascha had never taken me to the healer after a whipping before. He never showed remorse for the things he did or let himself appear overwhelmed. His meeting with the Deal-Breaker's agent must have gone poorly. A smile tugged at my cheeks.

He'd forgotten to lock my cage. Now was as good a time as any to unseat him from his proverbial horse. I wetted my lips.

"What was her name?"

He stiffened, his bloody shirt pulling tight across his shoulders.

"The woman in your nightmares."

He rose from the bed and turned away. Emotion like I'd never heard throttled his voice. "She is no concern of yours."

A confirmation. I tracked him across the room to his dresser. "Was she important to you?"

His top drawer screeched open, and he stared too long into it.

"She must have been." My eyes narrowed. "Something terrible happened to her."

His white-knuckled fist slammed atop the vanity so hard that it shook the mirror. "Enough!"

I flinched.

The room trembled as he turned back. Sconces rattled, and the lines of his windows and bedposts wavered as the Aether itself responded to his anger.

I wasn't stupid; I knew when to quit. My gaze slid off his, and he returned to his dresser. As he removed his bloodied shirt, I studied the extensive network of scars across his back—the way the light dipped into the hollows. A uniform, rectangular patch of scar tissue adorned his hip where a brand had once been, and his shoulders bore jagged lashes, as if from a whip laced with glass.

I'd seen his scars many times before, but I didn't fully understand them until today. Stories abounded about the champion pit fighter who'd gone over a hundred matches without defeat. His legend had seemed exaggerated and his signature move, the mascha, made more gruesome with time. Now, having witnessed it myself, I could almost respect his restraint among the slaves.

Even so, I refused to fear him. There was nothing he could do to me that my enemies hadn't already done.

He retrieved a bell-sleeved shirt from the drawer and tugged it over his head. His reflection betrayed his attempts to calm himself as he braced against the dresser, unmoving.

Finally, he sighed. "This isn't working."

"That's no jest."

I couldn't suppress the retort any more than I could stop the wind from blowing. Mascha met my gaze in the mirror, then turned and crossed the floor to sit on his bed facing me.

"I've been going about this all wrong."

"What do you mean?"

"Processing you." Elbows balanced on his knees, dried blood staining his nail beds, Mascha curled and uncurled his fingers. "I've been doing it wrong."

His posture didn't lend well to whatever air of nonchalance he was attempting. I tilted my head. "Is that supposed to be a consolation?"

"No. Merely a statement of fact."

If this was a trap, I couldn't work out his angle. I waited, hoping he would get to the point sooner rather than later. Hasanthe might have mended my wounds, but the tender new flesh between my legs made sitting like this uncomfortable. Still, I would bear it, knowing it annoyed him.

"I'm not going to hurt you anymore. It serves no purpose." He drew in a breath. "Consider your processing finished."

Despite the steel teeth likely to snap closed on me at any moment, I couldn't help my spark of hope. "Release me, then. Let me go home."

Dry, humorless laughter rasped out of him. "I'm afraid it's not that simple. Your antics yesterday have attracted the Deal-Breaker's attention. He will never allow it now."

As swiftly as hope ignited, he snuffed it out.

"To the Wastelands with him." I leaned forward until I could feel the cold radiating from the bars. "You shouldn't let him control you."

Mascha scoffed. "He is the reason I am free. I pledged myself to his service, and I'm not in the habit of breaking promises."

"What's your plan, then? If you were going to kill me, you could have just left me on the ship. Why rescue me?"

'Rescue' was too strong a word, and it left a sour taste in my mouth. Mascha blinked, as if he were just as surprised to hear it. But I kept my chin high and stayed the course.

"I want to be rid of you just as much as you want to be free of me," he ventured. "But I cannot permit your escape under my care. It's bad for my image."

I cast my eyes skyward. "*Ciir*, because Mira forbid you look like a mortal."

By the gods, he actually smirked. Though the look was gone by the next breath, the echo of genuine humor lingered in his eyes. "I have a proposal for you. A way we can both get what we desire."

My lips pulled back. He was baiting me. He had to be. But the absence of his usual arrogance gave me pause. "I'm listening."

What else was I going to do anyway?

"Prove yourself the proper slave. I can sell you to a new master—one certainly far less equipped to deal with you than I. Then, after some time has passed, and he grows complacent with you, you will have another chance to escape."

Preposterous. He just wanted to parade me around like some obedient, doe-eyed trull. Wearing his jewels, fucking his friends, kneeling for him. Why he thought I would ever agree to debase myself like that—

My disgust faltered.

A new master. A chance to escape. Mascha continued to study me, searching, as if waiting for me to catch up.

He was serious.

"You really think that will work?"

"My palace is one of the most heavily fortified facilities in the country. Only the Chancellor's Palace and a few of the biggest estates can compare. You nearly escaped here several times, and you succeeded last night. What do you have to lose?"

Nothing, aside from maybe a familiar jailor. If I let Mascha sell me, I would trade an enemy I knew for one I didn't and an environment I hadn't mapped to the point of navigating with my eyes closed. But if my study of Mascha's patrons was any indication, few were as cunning as he, and fewer possessed magic. Escape would be simpler without Aetherian guards, towering walls, and obedient slaves who would gladly rat me out for an extra hour of free time.

Still, I hesitated. "What's in it for you?"

"I'm sure you've heard the rumors by now, *Johtan Shasnaram.*"

Unbreakable. One of the few Rillanese phrases I knew well. Indeed, other slaves whispered about my defiance of Mascha with a mixture of reverence and fear. Some of his most doting slaves thought me foolish, because how dare I not desire his pleasure as they did? Yet, the majority found me entertaining. Maybe even inspiring.

I could see how that might be a problem for the king of all slavers.

"I need you to help me correct them." His bed creaked as he rose to crouch before my cage, his eyes leveling with me through the bars. "I want your total obedience for one month. Only a month. Culminating in an appearance with me at the summer gala hosted by the Chancellor."

I quirked an eyebrow. "You want to take me dancing?"

"I suppose you could say that." This time, he let his smile linger. "The gala is the second-biggest event of the year, next to the winter solstice. There will be hundreds of nobles in attendance, and deals of many kinds will take place. I can tailor the offers better there than on the auction block, where any number of men might fight over you."

He lowered one knee to the rug and steadied himself with a forearm on top of the cage. Scents of saffron and mint underlay a stronger male musk and hints of leather. My nose twitched.

"But this requires trust between us," he said. "I have to depend on you to perform as my slave in earnest, and you must allow me to maneuver you into the right house. If you can agree to these terms, you could be on your way home by winter."

My lips parted. The prospect proved too sweet to contain my shaky sigh. On a ship home by winter. I could see my sister by next summer. "A month."

"*Ciir.* One month of obedience, and then we can be done with each other."

My father always said I would have less trouble stabbing a man than I would holding him to a promise. But Mascha seemed sincere, and it beat having to best his security again—security he would only tighten now that I'd revealed its weaknesses. This way, I might not even need a wardstone to bypass his Aetherians.

One month. Thirty-six days of obedience—feigning meekness, serving his guests, sealing his deals, bedding whomever he demanded—for another chance at freedom. Nalerta would have been appalled, and it went against everything we'd ever taught our children, but I had no sense of loyalty or modesty left to preserve. As painful as that was, I couldn't let it deter me. If it got me closer to home, I would gladly make my body a weapon.

But a simple agreement wasn't enough. Something had compelled Mascha to offer this arrangement. The Deal-Breaker probably had his balls in a vise. If that was the case, I could manipulate the odds further in my favor.

"I need assurances."

His gaze caught fire, as if the thought of negotiating thrilled him. "Name them."

"First," I said, ignoring the answering spark in my chest, "you'll not inform anyone else of this plan without my approval."

"Agreed. That goes for you as well."

"Second, you will sell me only to a weaker house that is well-positioned near a port to facilitate my escape."

"While ideal, that significantly limits my options," Mascha said. "I will agree on the condition that if such a house is outbid or unavailable, I'll get you as close as I can, and delay should the Rorsch Hekkai be contacted to assist in your retrieval."

We were mincing words now. Fine. I turned his amendment over, seeking weaknesses he might exploit later. Though, I didn't detect that he was trying to cheat me. He was known for keeping his word, even to his slaves. He'd once canceled a deal with an emerald merchant who'd insisted on bedding Emmi when she'd been promised a week off due to her particularly painful courses.

I clicked my tongue. "Third, you'll replace these spellbinders with false ones."

He laughed. "Nice try, but I'll only ensure you are delivered to your new master with basic ones. You've already demonstrated your talent for picking locks."

It had been a long shot, but he had a point. I shrugged. "Fine."

"If that is all...?" He paused, at which I nodded again. "I have a condition of my own. If we are to do this, there can be no mistakes in your etiquette. I know you understand what is expected of you because you consistently do the opposite."

Still cross-legged as I was, I didn't bother to feign confusion.

His expression hardened. "I mean it, Maralla. Your presentation must be perfect. At least in front of others."

I sucked in a breath. Let it out.

Eyes down, speak only when spoken to, use titles of respect to address all men and free women...

I clenched my teeth around a growl.

Thirty-six days. I could do this.

I extended my hand between the bars. His fingers closed around my wrist, and I gripped his in turn.

"Alright," I said. "You have yourself a deal."

Chapter Eight

Maralla

The thing with Rillanese deals, I'd learned, was that only free men could make them. Women were disallowed from participating in business, using magic, and even owning assets. Most of the pompous pricks wouldn't even treat with foreign parties who were women, unless some specific conditions were met.

It was to these conditions I turned as I roused myself that afternoon on the floor of my cage, sore and shivering, with a vow that today would be the last time I slept that way.

Despite our deal, I was under no illusion that Mascha would suddenly start treating me with the respect I deserved unless I fought for it. Fortunately, I was well-versed in matters of war.

Distant bells chimed the fifteenth hour. I paced the study while Mascha sifted through his ledgers. He called in Raffi, his messenger, and exchanged words in Rillanese. A mouthful of rocks couldn't help me emulate the sounds they made, but I caught the name Bastian Clairmont and a few other words that put Mascha's order in context. As the boy hurried away with a summons for Rillion's most esteemed jeweler, I approached Mascha's desk.

"I want my own room."

Mascha snorted. "Absolutely not."

He didn't even look up from his parchment.

I braced myself against the desk, blocking the light from the windows. His quill scraped to a stop.

"A deal requires two or more free parties entering into a binding agreement, *ciir*?"

His lips pressed into a line. "*Ciir.*"

"Then, the nature of our relationship asserts that I am not your slave, but your business partner—a *guest* in your home. And I'm certain none of your guests would find a cage to be an acceptable sleeping arrangement."

"You obviously don't know some of my guests," he quipped. "While I concede Rillanese law disallows formal agreements between free men and slaves, it also states a business partner may not be a woman."

Grateful for all the legislative texts written in the trade tongue he kept stocked in his library, I smiled and said, "A *domestic* business partner, you mean. Your country makes an exemption for foreign powers. I still hold rank in the North-lands, whether your false documentation confirms it or not."

He leaned back in his chair. The longer he studied me, the more my resolve hardened. He wouldn't broach the subject of who I was outside of Rillion, or the papers fabricated by the Iceborn slavers who'd sold me to him, but I wouldn't let him forget.

"And how would that look to the rest of my household?" He waved the idea aside. "A guest room is out of the question, and private quarters are reserved for slaves of higher station. Unless you plan to let me pierce your genitals, the answer is no."

Only in Rillion would genital piercings be a mark of station. Gods help me, but I almost took the bait. The ache in my spine from that scabbing cage was making me reckless.

Something predatory crept into Mascha's expression. He rose and mirrored my posture, his hands flanking his ledger. His gaze raked over my near-nakedness, as if he sensed my thoughts lingering. "Or perhaps you like the idea of my fingers between your thighs. I hear the *araschavka* makes one much more sensitive."

I recoiled, realizing too late it was exactly the reaction he'd hoped for. His laughter rang with triumph, and heat seethed from my skin.

I would *not* let this bastard get the better of me. "Then I'll sleep in the slaves' quarters."

He rounded his desk, still grinning. "As if I'd risk you corrupting my well-behaved women. Our current arrangement serves us well."

I caught his wrist as he brushed past me. "I won't be kept in a cage like a dog."

Darkness flickered across his face, his amusement a casualty of war. "Release me."

The demand rumbled out of him like thunder. Air left my lungs in a rush, and I inhaled just as violently. But after several grudging seconds, I obeyed. The apology I might have offered anyone else for invading their space shriveled on my tongue.

Mascha stepped in close, his nose mere fingerspans from mine. "Remember your part, Maralla. A slave doesn't put her hands on her master without his permission."

This was going to be much harder than I thought. We stared each other down while I contemplated all the ways I could crush his stupid nose.

To my surprise, Mascha looked away first.

"I truly don't want to hurt you, but I will if you leave me no choice."

That note of earnestness threw me further off balance. I fumbled for a response as he made for a nearby decanter and poured a tumbler of brandy.

I recalled how he'd crouched over my attacker this morning, blood-slicked up to his forearms, body quaking with rage. Still, I'd be a fool to mistake vengeance for a sign of altruism. I folded my arms and rolled my shoulders to ease the tightness in my scars.

"We're meeting Bastian this evening," he said. "You will attend us at dinner and allow him to take measurements for your gala attire. He's the most forgiving of my guests when it comes to mistakes in etiquette."

A test, then. Bastian was Mascha's friend, and an Eidosinian expatriate, not native Rillanese. From my observations, I'd gleaned that he followed local customs only as they pertained to his business endeavors. He also preferred men, thank Mira.

Mascha swirled his brandy. "I expect you to do your best all the same."

His hand quivered. The motion was so subtle that it could have been a trick of light. It could have been fatigue. But it didn't take a mastermind with the powers of psionics to recognize what it truly was.

Anxiety. The mighty Mascha was nervous.

I glanced toward the bedroom, an idea taking shape. He had to be in one serious predicament to make a bargain with me. That meant there was much more riding on my obedience than he let on. More than the nightmares, more than '*tipori*,' maybe more than his reputation. How far could I push him?

And what would happen if he broke?

Bastian arrived promptly at eighteenth hour.

Mascha and I emerged from his quarters, freshly bathed and slathered in costly fragrances. He smelled of mint and sandalwood, while vanilla and rose clung to my skin—a layer of decadence ill-suited for me, but Mascha had refused to see reason.

He wore a gaudily embroidered vest over a shirt the color of his eyes. I traced the lines of silver thread in an attempt to keep my gaze downcast and my gait steady, one half-step behind his right shoulder.

For once, the silk dress he'd provided for me concealed more than it revealed. Extra ruffles extended from the collar to hide my nipples. Soft lace whispered against my upper thighs, and though I still hadn't *earned* the privilege of small-clothes, at least it covered my ass.

We entered a private dining room that could have fit all the Alliaansi leadership and over half our top military officers at one table. Bastian had already helped himself to the wine; he rose from his seat with a grin and swiped a stray brown curl from his forehead. "Mascha, my boy! Silonas smiles on you."

Mascha grinned. "His fortune is a gift, indeed."

He caught the jeweler's sleeve at the elbow in an embrace reserved for more intimate meetings. Bastian followed suit, his ring-laden fingers glittering with rubies.

I hung back as they exchanged pleasantries, my mouth watering at the array of meats and cheeses on the table. All that food for two people. It took a feat of will to suppress my scowl. My people could have never afforded such luxury.

In months past, I would have crept closer to the table in Mascha's distraction and stolen slices of cheese from the tray. This time, I ignored my empty stomach and swallowed dutifully.

Play my part.

Bastian's gray eyes strayed to me. "What's this?"

"You remember Maralla." Mascha pulled out a chair for himself. "Please, sit."

Bastian only gaped. The first time I'd met him was the same night I'd slipped my binders, killed several guards, and nearly blown up Mascha's armory.

"Is there a problem, *amii*?" Amusement colored Mascha's tone.

"I—Well, isn't she—"

I lowered my head further to hide my smirk. *Ciir*, he remembered me.

"*Johtan Shasnaram*?" Mascha offered. He snapped his fingers and pointed to his feet. "Kneel, *rascha*."

I could have gutted him with that scabbing cheese knife.

My eyes closed against the urge, my calves tightening as if to anchor myself in place. This was a power move on Mascha's part—a demonstration meant to carry beyond these walls to other houses. By summer solstice, the entire country would know about the breaking of *Johtan Shasnaram*.

Ingenious, really. Though as I lowered myself to the tile, I hated him all the more.

Bastian collapsed into his chair with a huff. "Forgive me, Mascha. When you said the gala, I expected Scherazeme would attend you. The Chancellor will miss her performance."

"And Schera will miss the attention. But it is past time Maralla made her debut in the Chancellor's circle. I will entertain bids that night."

His brows edged higher. "You think she's ready?"

Though I kept my head down, I studied the jeweler from beneath my lashes. Disapproval etched lines around his lips. I flicked my gaze toward Mascha. If Bastian tried to talk him out of our arrangement...

"*Ciir*, she is ready."

Relief eased the pressure in my chest. I rested my palms on my thighs and flexed my toes. My knees began to ache, and I fidgeted.

Mascha's palm settled against my braids in warning.

My face twitched. I'd lasted this long without breaking his hand. I could last a few minutes more.

As if he could hear my thoughts, his fingers tightened in my hair. Then he traced a featherlight path from my crown to my nape, and gooseflesh erupted across my skin. Even more appalling were the moths that fluttered about below my navel. I flexed my abdominals to crush them.

Bastian crossed one ankle over his knee. "Mm. Well, I suppose I'll have something new to look forward to. I pray she's lighter on her feet in a ballroom than she is at market."

I stilled. News *had* traveled quickly.

Mascha withdrew his hand. "Fortunately, we won't be dancing. Not this year."

"But you dance every year. Why, it's my favorite part of the evening, watching you loosen up and enjoy something for once."

If the image of Mascha dancing was as absurd in reality as it was in my mind, it was no wonder Bastian looked forward to it. A savage killer lumbering through the fluid turns of the ii'senuu or surrendering to a partner with the passion and grace of the amaariana nearly made me snort.

A strained chuckle escaped my captor. "I'm sorry to disappoint you, *amii*."

"You have such chemistry with all your partners." Bastian shook a finger at him. "I swear, one of these days, you're going to get over your fear of marriage, and then the world won't know what hit it."

"There will be other events." Mascha tossed a square of cheese into his mouth. "Besides, entertaining bids and keeping the peace will be more than enough this year."

"Oh, pish-posh, don't be ridiculous. Without Ideghis there, House Amin won't cause any trouble. And the Yensmiirs, well, once you get the youngest one deep enough in his cups, he won't be able to stand, much less fight with the Verrisch twins."

"Bastian." Mascha drew out his name in warning.

"I think you should. At least one dance. You know how the nobles like their dancers." Bastian's smile turned mischievous. "Might even help you make the sale."

Mascha sighed and let his gaze settle on me.

I swallowed again. Play my part. Play my part, and don't meet his eyes. One of my fingers tapped of its own accord against my leg, and I pressed it hard into the lacy hem of my dress. He couldn't really be considering this.

"What do you say, *rascha*? Would you like to dance with your master?"

I'd rather run naked through a blizzard or stab myself with a serrated blade.

My gaze settled on the topmost button of Mascha's vest, and I attempted my prettiest smile. "Yes, Master, it would be an honor to dance with you."

"Marvelous!" Bastian clapped his hands like an overgrown child. "Now, we should make certain the Chancellor's orchestra knows some more traditional Syljian songs, and you can have your pick of dances…"

Mascha continued to study me as the human prattled on. A thin crease appeared in his forehead, as if he were working out a puzzle he couldn't solve. I lowered my eyes and fought the desire to close my hands around his neck.

I hadn't danced with anyone since before my mate died. The ii'senuu had been Nalerta's favorite, and sullying his memory with the likes of Mascha was enough to make me reconsider our plan.

A deep breath steadied me.

Thirty-six days.

Assuming I didn't kill him first.

Dinner passed by in a blur of "Yes, Master"s, curtsies, and wine. When at last Bastian took my measurements and departed, I wolfed down the admittedly lavish meal Mascha set aside for me and shifted my attention to my next move.

We returned to his quarters as a pendulus chimed the twenty-second hour. As soon as the chamber door closed behind us, I cut a path to his bedroom. Mascha stared from the doorway as I settled under his sheets and fluffed a down pillow for my back.

"What are you doing?"

I crossed my ankles and reclined against the headboard. "And here I thought you were a smart man."

His dark brows furrowed.

Poor thing. Apparently, I would have to scrawl it out for him. "If you don't see fit to provide me with a proper bed, I guess you'll have to spare yours."

Mascha sighed and shook his head. "I'm not in the mood for this, Maralla."

"If you think I give a shit what sort of mood you're in, you're mistaken."

"We settled this matter already." That earlier darkness seeped into his expression. "Get back to your cage."

"You can't detain a foreign power without cause. You're a host, not a jailor."

"I wouldn't suffer such an inhospitable guest." Mascha paced to the washroom and back, pausing at the end of the bed. He curled his fingers around the footboard, his grin as sharp as his axes. "If you intend to share my bed, then you will do so properly. Naked and writhing in climax."

He expected me to be disgusted, but I wouldn't fall for that again. I tossed aside the sheets and pulled my dress over my head. His grin faltered as I dropped the flimsy silk beside his bed.

"Fine." I spread my legs, surprising myself with how easily and unabashedly I managed it. One hand slid down my torso and came to rest in my white curls. "But I don't need you for that."

Astonishment usurped control of his face. I tipped my head back and coaxed myself to arousal with steady strokes of my fingertips. At first, my sounds of pleasure were made from pure spite, but as wetness and heat built in my core, I relaxed into the mattress. A genuine sound escaped me, and Mascha's gaze locked onto mine with a new intensity. He adjusted his grip on the footboard, shifted on his feet, and closed his fool mouth.

His scent enveloped me suddenly, forcibly, sending me careening into such an acute state of awareness that I recognized the musk of his arousal.

Worse, I *craved* it.

My heart rate spiked. Not even on raspaati, that infernal drug, had my senses been this sharp—had both my mind and body betrayed me. That meant...

No. I couldn't think of it. Nor could I back down while I held his full attention.

I cinched my eyes shut and summoned thoughts of Nalerta, of the carnal nature of his kisses, the way his mouth lingered on my breasts. I teased one nipple to a peak and arched into my hand. Pleasure lanced through me and turned fluid, effervescent. A sharp breath sounded from beyond the bed, but I bore down on that tender spot and pinched my other nipple, imagining my mate's teeth. I was back home in his arms, his body pressed against mine, his frost-white hair brushing my skin.

Eyes the color of spring lilac, a small scar on his lower lip. Ears that tapered perfectly, and a smile that warmed me even in winter. His laugh was burned into my memory, the same laugh our children had shared.

I forced aside the sting of grief and focused on the night we made Elliaana, our firstborn. My *oeloraati* had been overwhelming that cycle, my need for him consuming all thought and reason. Nalerta had joked the scent of me could make even the neighbors antsy. Still, his territorial growls when visitors came knocking had betrayed the effect it had on him as well.

My body clenched against a searing ache—a need as old as mortality itself. I abandoned my nipples and plunged three fingers as deep as they could go, imagining the tenderness between my thighs not as phantom injury, but as my mate's ferocity while he staked his claim.

Air rasped through my teeth. My lower back left the mattress as the world narrowed to that building pressure, that swift and unstoppable force straining at the confines of my awareness. Light exploded behind my eyelids, and a cry tore from me. Spasms gripped my fingers, and cold registered against my skin as I withdrew, still trembling.

Cloudy languor weighed me down. I opened my eyes to the gauzy canopy, for a moment not recognizing where I was. But the dark-haired figure at the foot of the bed drew my attention, and I clawed my way back to the surface to survey the damage.

I expected anger. Fury. But what I found in my captor was so much sweeter.

Mascha's breath heaved out of him, nearly as ragged as mine. Barely restrained desire smoldered in his gaze, and his white-knuckled hands clenched the foot-board.

A languid smile stole over my lips. He lowered his head as if to spare himself the sight of my victory.

He pried his grip free of the bed, turned, and left the room.

Chapter Nine

Mascha

I T WAS THE MOST erotic thing I'd ever seen.

Need roared through my veins. The tightness in my chest rivaled the ache in my trousers, and I fought for every breath to steady myself.

Countless times throughout my eighty years as Rorsch Hekkai had I demanded such performance from my partners. Men and women, both free and enslaved, had taken their pleasure in front of me, but Maralla was the first to take her pleasure *in spite* of me. Audaciously, unabashedly, not like the slaves who tried to hide their insolence. Not like the ones who wore steel because they couldn't control themselves.

She had disregarded my presence in my chambers—my own *bed*—as if she didn't fear me at all. No words could describe how that inflamed my soul.

I stormed down the halls to the slaves' quarters, Maralla's scent clinging to me like pitch. It bore the telltale aroma of a Syljian nearing *oeloraati*, and the urge to mate—to take what any slave should give freely to her master—made me dizzy.

Normally, *oeloraati* wasn't a concern. Most Syljians who were sent to me for processing were gone long before I had to implement herbs and oils to pass their cycles. I should have prepared for this. I should have known.

For too long, I'd considered claiming her. It would have been easy at the height of her passion. When she'd arched off my bed, when she'd thrust her fingers to the knuckles inside herself—gods, I grew impossibly harder thinking about it, as if I were a young man again, unable to resist my baser instincts. But I wasn't an animal. Not anymore.

The row of private rooms stretched before me. I reached my destination within moments, though with every step, my suffering grew. As I flung the door to

Scherazeme's suite open, I resolved to send Hasanthe into my chambers with the herbs to delay Maralla's triennial cycle. Silonas slay me, but I couldn't enter that room again until the slaves stripped every linen and coverlet free of that scent.

The door slammed against the wall, and I didn't bother to secure it behind me. Scherazeme strayed from her tiny washroom, owl-eyed, steam trailing in her wake.

"Master?"

"I have need of you, *rascha*."

I stalked toward her, and her entire body shuddered. She let the towel wrapping her torso fall. Her collar glinted in the candlelight. My hands closed on her waist; I pulled her close and breathed her in. Hints of lilac and jasmine flooded my senses. The scent of human arousal was more subtle and easier to ignore. It allowed me to reclaim the shambles of my control.

Beads of water meandered down her body in trails that my tongue soon followed. She melted into me as I lifted her, her thighs hugging my waist.

We fell in a heap on the mattress, my erection pressing against her heat through my trousers. She slipped the laces and reached inside. I gasped into her mouth.

"Master," she whispered. "May I taste you?"

It wasn't what I wanted. I needed her. Now.

My hand closed on her throat. "No. Tonight, you're going to scream for me."

Her surrender to me was absolute. "Yes, Master."

But first, "How do you make it—"

"*Kavvur*," she answered. "And *gheschal*. I know, Master."

"Very good." I straightened, kicking off my pants and discarding my shirt. "Turn over."

Scherazeme rolled onto her elbows and knees, ass in the air. I stroked her to wetness, fingers delving, until she pushed herself back into my hand.

"Please fuck me. Please."

"My good girl. I love when you beg for me." I withdrew my fingers and positioned myself. Her skin blazed as I gripped the back of her neck. "Say it again."

"Please, Master." Scherazeme trembled, but she knew better than to take pleasure that wasn't hers. "My body is yours."

Orderly, well-mannered obedience. *This* was how it was supposed to be. I pressed forward, and her body ceded to mine.

"You were made for me, *rascha*."

"Yes, Master."

"You will always give me what I want."

"Always, Master. Anything for you."

I breathed out, fully in control once more. "Good girl."

Pressure mounted. I pulled her back, back, back again, fingers entwined in her wet locks. Her head tipped into my grasp, and soft cries issued from her lips. I pressed between her legs so that every thrust forced pleasure, and Scherazeme buckled beneath my affection.

With an arm beneath her hips, I hauled her back up and thrust harder. "Arms, *rascha*."

She complied, folding both arms behind her. I held her wrists and returned my other hand to her apex. Her muscles clenched ever tighter as I thrust her face into the covers.

"Remember your manners."

She turned her head and rasped out her request. "Master, m-may I come?"

"Not yet."

I was close. So close. Each thrust provided that heady friction that sent lightning arcing into my loins.

"Master," she whimpered. "Please, I can't—"

"You can, and you will."

Her wordless acknowledgement quaked out of her, a frustrated sound of desperation and need. I bared my teeth, victory slashing through me like an axe. I knew her limits nearly as well as my own.

Skin slapped against skin, harder, faster—

"Now, *rascha*," I grunted. "Come on your master's cock."

Her scream rent the air, a crescendo that pushed me over the edge after her. My seed spilled in three forceful thrusts, filling her. Claiming her.

Scherazeme sagged against her bed, aftershocks turning her muscles to jelly. My throat burned with the exertion, and I withdrew from her to collect the towel from the floor. I glanced toward the washroom, where the tub of scented water had yet to be emptied, then abandoned the towel and summoned a trickle of magic from my earring. I poured my will into the water until it was steaming again. Then I lifted my slave and settled behind her in the bath.

Water sloshed over the side, and Scherazeme started, but I pulled her back to my chest by her hair.

"Leave it."

She giggled. "Good evening to you, too, Master."

I savored the pressure of her cheek against my chest. Her delicate fingers drew circles over my scarred pectorals as I used the soap to cleanse her shoulders. Avoiding the old burn scars along her spine, I worked the sponge down her back and let my knuckles skim the tattoos adorning her upper arm.

Scherazeme was a quiet companion, more introspective than most. I couldn't say whether it was an inherent quality or one instilled by her former master's cruelty. The man had been a middling-caste spice merchant, known for his quick deals and quicker temper. After witnessing the worm beat Schera bloody during a security deal, I offered to purchase her. Once her sale closed, a series of misfortunes befell his business, and he'd allegedly thrown himself off the Qetschel River Bridge rather than pay his exorbitant debts.

She sighed into me, and I wrapped my arms around her.

My conversation with Bastian returned to me, and a flicker of Foresight made me wince. "You're going to be angry with me."

"I could never."

Scherazeme sat upright, but she maintained protocol and didn't meet my eyes. More water lapped over the tub and splashed on the floor.

I touched her cheek to reclaim her attention from the mess. "I cannot take you to the gala this year."

She glanced up sharply, then away. "May I ask why, Master?"

Ever the portrait of Rillanese propriety, though the tremor in her voice betrayed her. She always looked forward to our summer performance. For the last seven years, she'd been my solstice companion. Each year, our dance stirred rumors that I might finally name a concubine. In the last two years, some even speculated I'd elevate her beyond that and take her as my first wife.

Even Scherazeme wished for it, or so the whispers among my slaves claimed. Thank Silonas she was too docile to suggest it herself. Too many men already requested her for deals, knowing how I favored her. I'd learned this lesson the hard way with Anelliiq, who had borne far too much abuse on my behalf. At least as a slave, Scherazeme could be made unavailable to the more aggressive nobles without fanfare or offense.

"I must take Maralla this year."

Lightning flashed across Scherazeme's face. "But, Master—" She clapped a hand over her mouth. If her eyes hadn't widened with horror, her outburst might have been amusing. Instead, it gutted me.

"Speak your mind, *rascha*." Here, in the quiet of the slaves' chambers, I could permit it. She deserved that much and more.

Scherazeme lowered her arm and her attention fixed pointedly on my chest. "We always go together, Master. We've been practicing all winter. It's not fair that I can't go when she's so... so..." She made a helpless gesture in the water.

I offered an apologetic smile. "Ill-tempered?"

She nodded.

"I suspect we'll see much better behavior after yesterday's market incident." As much affection as I felt for Scherazeme, I couldn't tell her the full truth. No slave was immune to gossip. "I plan to entertain bids for her that evening."

She started to pull away. "As you say, Master."

I caught her chin and forced lightness into my voice. "Come now, don't be like that." My lips brushed hers, and she leaned into my kiss. "Don't you miss my bed?"

"More than anything," she breathed.

"Well"—I nosed her head to one side and trailed kisses along her jaw, nipping when I reached her pierced lobe—"it seems to me an end to her processing is good for us all, yes?"

Scherazeme hadn't entered my bedroom of her own free will since I moved Maralla in. Something about the cage unsettled her, and I felt no need to pry.

She nodded again and reached for me, stopping a handspan shy of my chest. "Master, may I?"

"You may." I leaned back, bracing my elbows on the tub while she explored. Her touch lulled me, and I heated the water once more despite my wrinkled fingertips.

Once she'd had her fill, I pulled her to me and kissed her head before rising. The spilled water chilled my feet when I stepped onto the tile and offered my hand to help her out.

I wrapped fresh towels around us both before we left the washroom. Several lingering kisses later, I extracted myself, gathered my clothing, and left her room behind.

Hasanthe would still be awake at this hour, and he deserved at least a half-baked explanation for the state of Maralla's back. I could also put in the order for her herbs. From there, perhaps a visit to the kitchens to check on tomorrow's bread, and some late-night forms in the garden.

Something, anything, to keep me from the insufferable, intoxicating scent of the woman in my bed.

Chapter Ten

Maralla

A SCENT PURELY MASCULINE in nature woke me—drowned me—in its powerful musk. Wetness pooled between my legs, and I buried my face in the pillow, seeking more of that aroma. Foreign blankets draped my torso and wrapped me in warmth. The longer I lay there, half-dazed, the more the ache in my core grew.

A door opened, and something shattered against the floor. I bolted upright, and as Mascha's blonde-haired chamber slave and I stared at each other across the bedroom, last night barreled over me like the hooves of a thousand horses.

The slave, Catari, scrambled to pick up the broken crockery. My breakfast was scattered among jagged pieces of porcelain. Thick, beaded faelocks tumbled over her tattooed shoulders, and a white, embroidered kerchief cinched above her collar. In her haste, she cut her finger on a shard and gasped, promptly sticking the injury in her mouth.

I leaped out of bed to assist her, ignoring the dizzying burst of longing that came with leaving that scent. "Here, let me—"

Catari fell onto her backside, wide-eyed.

I shuddered to a stop halfway to the door, not because of Catari's overreaction, but because of the mind-blowing friction between my legs. I tried to take another step, and the ache combined with Mascha's scent turned my knees to butter.

Arousal slicked my thighs. I pressed my knees together, barely containing the howl of frustration building in my chest. All the signs were there: the heaviness in my breasts, the heat in my core, the fixation with male scent. I hadn't wanted to believe it last night; I'd hoped it had been my imagination. But even Mascha's reaction confirmed it: the onset of the most detested and euphoric six weeks I endured every three years.

Oeloraati.

No. No, no, no, the timing couldn't have been worse. This couldn't happen here. Not in the palace. Not in Rillion. I couldn't descend into my most vulnerable state in the most dangerous country in the world.

Catari opened her mouth to speak, then closed it. I focused on breakfast, curling my fists to tame the need for more friction, for more of that male scent on my skin. Spiced ullopie and fried eggs, the tang of citron juice and yellow slices of spike melon—they grounded me, allowed me to reach the shaking woman on the floor.

"It's alright," I said, crouching down. "I'll tell him I startled you. You'll not be punished for this."

"W-where is the Master?"

My sharp laughter pitched too high. Mascha hadn't returned to his chambers last night, and gods help me when he did. I'd been able to control myself on raspaati, but *this* was the real thing. "I don't know."

Catari's gaze darted toward the bed, likely drawing her own conclusions about what had happened last night. Her assumptions ate at me, but I'd agreed to this. If I wanted my freedom, *Johtan Shasnaram*'s legacy had to die first.

I'd slept like a queen in Mascha's bed, but he wouldn't allow me two nights alone in his room, much less the whole month before the gala. Not even self-respecting Nalerta could resist the pull of Syljian *oeloraati*, and I suspected the urge to mate wasn't something Mascha the Great Hedonist would deny himself for my sake. He would take his pleasure from me and feel no remorse about it.

Tingling heat pooled in my belly. I faltered in placing pieces on the tray and doubled over.

Mira help me, I might not regret it either.

"Catari, do you..." I moved just wrong and unwelcome pleasure seized my breath. "...does the kitchen stock wirethorn berries?"

Women in the north used them to dull their sense of smell during *oeloraati*. Their unpleasant odor also deterred some men.

"I can ask," Catari hesitated. "*Sadarah.*"

The word didn't register at first. I dumped the last of the crockery on the tray and sat back, letting the tiles chill my throbbing center. As Catari departed with the mess, I hung my head and pondered what I must have done to gain the title. Laughable that anyone would ever accuse *me* of being a lady.

I stared out the balcony windows. Mascha had posted more Aetherians out there to deter any residual hope of escape. As if to assure me of my new gilded cage, one of them marched by, green robes swishing, and disappeared around the bend.

The anteroom door opened and closed again, and several pairs of feet creaked through the library. White-robed Hasanthe entered Mascha's bedroom, flanked by three female slaves who immediately began stripping the sheets and drapery. Some sense of myself returned, and I rose to greet Hasanthe with the customary bow.

"Good morning, Master healer."

Hasanthe stopped short. "Good morning, *rascha*. How is your back?"

He smelled of grapes and sunbaked sand. Fortunately, neither sent me tumbling down the slippery slope of lust.

I folded my hands and kept my gaze low, considering whether I could persuade him to help me. "Much better today. Thank you."

"Good. Let's have a look." He twirled a finger, signaling me to turn. Though his scent didn't draw me like Mascha's did, his large hands on my back provoked gooseflesh as he examined my injuries. "Your master awaits you downstairs. You are to bathe and dress for market."

I swallowed hard. My condition would worsen over the next few weeks. I could only hope one of the vendors would sell wirethorn berries. The trouble would be persuading Mascha, who would surely delight in my misfortune then fuck me over a crate in the middle of the square just because he could.

Worse, some sick part of me would enjoy it.

A slave snapped a sheet to straighten its edges, and the heady burst of maleness nearly undid me. Hasanthe caught me as fire swept down to my toes and my knees gave way. His soft laughter reached me through the ringing in my ears.

"He has ordered a new regimen of herbs for you, too. You will consume them twice a day for one week."

I blinked fog from my vision. "Herbs?"

"Mm, yes." His smile was kind. "It should help pass your *oeloraati*."

The words rattled around in my mind for too long before they made sense. Pass my *oeloraati*. *Ciir*, of course, there were herbs that could pass a woman's cycle, but they were far too costly to obtain in the Northlands.

Another too-shrill laugh burst from me. This had to be some cruel joke. "I thought he'd prefer me pining for him like a bitch in heat."

Two of the slaves shot appalled glances at me. Hasanthe scowled and gestured to banish them from the room.

Once they were gone, he stepped closer and lowered his voice. "Mascha doesn't wish to sire a child with you." He set a parchment-wrapped package in my hand. "These should help curb the desire, but it'll take time for their full effect. You're not to couple with anyone until they're gone."

He went over his dosing instructions as I stared at the package. All my concerns, there and gone. It confused me more than it brought relief. Spreading his foul seed seemed just the sort of thing Mascha would do. Why the precaution now?

Hasanthe studied me. "I've known your master for many years, *rascha*. His methods may be strict, but he takes care of his own. That includes you for as long as you remain under his roof."

He meant as long as we were good little slaves who did what we're told. I crammed down the impulse to say it and bowed again. "Yes, Master."

The healer didn't look convinced. He sighed and pulled out a bottle of bathing oil, which he placed in my hand. "I will leave Odessa to assist you in dressing."

My brows furrowed. Slave skirts and midriff tops were easy to don without help. "That's not necessary."

One side of his mouth lifted. "I think once you see the outfit Mascha's chosen for you, you'll change your mind."

'Outfit' was a generous term for the scraps of silk and lace that draped my breasts. Mascha's Mautori chamber slave, Odessa, had wound my braids around my head to keep them from tangling in the silver chains tumbling down my back. White silk gathered at my waist and clung to my hips, while more chains jingled with tiny medallions at every step. I recognized Mascha's subtle jab for what it was. I might have even found his need to attach a metaphorical bell to my collar funny if I hadn't been in such a confusing state of mortification and arousal.

After a second, more successful attempt at breakfast, I downed the first dose of bitter herbs. Odessa layered my skin with rose oil and cool mint, then led me down the curving marble staircase to the foyer. She said little, but kept stealing glances at me. After fighting Mascha for so long, I'd become a curiosity to many of the slaves. I wondered if she was disappointed to see me fall.

Mascha waited at the foot of the stairs, his expression hungry. "She looks perfect, Odessa. Well done."

Odessa curtsied, only dipping her head half the usual distance to accommodate her horns. "My pleasure, Master."

She took Mascha's silent dismissal in stride and left me alone with my captor and the two slaves flanking the palace doors.

Tension sparked between us. Mascha stepped in close, and I braced myself for his overwhelming aroma. But he, too, had heavily masked his scent. It was faint beneath saffron and mint.

Surprised, my gaze darted up to his.

He ran his thumb along my lower lip—a tender gesture I couldn't shy from with other slaves present—and tipped my chin up. My heart feathered against my ribs, and my toes curled with mingled desire and revulsion. Our noses nearly touched before he leaned to one side, his beard brushing my cheek.

"Much as I would love to bend you over every surface in my palace," he said into my ear, "I thought this would help us stay focused on our agreement."

What should have disgusted me set every part of me ablaze. *Why?* I wanted to ask. Why not press his advantage while I was weak? Not that I wanted him to—I wasn't *that* far gone yet—but tactically, it didn't make sense. Why rearm his opponent when their arrows ran out?

"Come. I have business—"

Glass shattered. A scream tore through the palace.

Mascha whirled, placing himself between me and the sound. My fingers twitched closed around the phantom hilt of my sword, the spellbinders on my wrists stymying my attempt to summon it from the Aether. I peered around his arm.

A door flew open down the corridor to our left, and a peasant stumbled out. She fell in a heap of bloody skirts, a needle jutting from her neck. She flung it aside, then scrambled back to her feet. Her eyes alighted on us, her voice breaking.

"Help! Please help me!"

I started forward, but Mascha pushed me back. Incredulous, I shot him a glare, but he kept me pressed against his side, a vein bulging in his neck.

"Pox," he murmured, stopping me cold.

The woman shuffled toward us, sobbing and dragging one leg. Three open sores marred her cheek and chin.

Weeping pox. I'd heard Mascha's brother, Tasari, was working on a cure for the magically resistant disease. The pus-filled sores of pox victims quickly succumbed to fleshrot and poisoned their blood, leading to a swift but excruciating death. It was highly contagious, and the blight of any tropical city in the world.

Behind her, the same door opened again and Tasari strolled out, wearing a mask, gloves, and a white waistcoat splattered red. "Oh, Sahan, it's not that bad."

Sahan shrieked. The whites of her eyes flashed, and she limped faster, holding her skirts. "Please, *meschiir*, don't let him hurt me. Please!"

"You'll only make the serum work faster, running about like this," Tasari drawled.

My stomach threatened to upend its breakfast. Early in my captivity, before Mascha sequestered me in his rooms, rumors of Tasari's experiments passed through the slaves' quarters like ghost stories. I'd seen him get his thrills on Correction Day each week, when all the slaves who'd committed minor offenses were gathered in the disciplinarium to be whipped, but this was the first time I'd witnessed his more sadistic tastes.

I gripped Mascha's arm. "Do something," I hissed.

"Please, please, *meschiir*!"

Mascha's muscles went taut beneath my palm. "I can't."

"What do you mean, 'you can't'? Look at her. She—"

He spun, so close to me our chests touched. "*Kas hadem*. You forget yourself."

His command for silence only enraged me further. I opened my mouth, but Sahan's scream punched through me like a knife.

Tasari grabbed the woman by her hair and threw her against the wall. His laughter echoed off gleaming stone.

Mascha clamped down on my nape and pulled me into him. "That woman is dead already. You will follow me out the door, keep your eyes down, and don't look that way again. There is nothing you can do for her."

"*Meschiir! Meschiir!*"

Tears of fury stung my eyes, but I didn't try to push him away. If anything, I pressed closer to shield myself against her cries. "You scabbing coward."

He stiffened, then shoved me away. "Walk."

I squeezed my fists and trailed behind him out the door. Midmorning sun touched my skin, seabirds called, and the ocean's scent carried on the wind, but I couldn't savor any of it.

When we were far enough from the palace gates, I lifted my voice to be heard over the din of carriages, hawkers, and tourists. "Your healer's assessment of you seems generous."

Mascha's shoulders rose and fell twice before he pivoted toward a narrow alley between two sand-colored buildings. A beggar in tattered leggings looked up from a chipped plate of scraps.

"Out," Mascha snapped at him.

The beggar bared rotten teeth and squinted hard. He might have argued, had Mascha not stepped toward him and made the entire alleyway waver with ill intent. As hot iron overpowered the stench of sweat, the beggar snatched up his meager belongings, fell over himself twice, and scurried out of the alley.

Mascha shaped his magic into a shimmering black-violet veil and pulled it across the mouth of the alley. He turned back to me and clasped his hands, as if preparing to weather an unruly child's outburst. "Say your piece now, where it is safe, before you do something stupid."

"Hasanthe says you look out for those under your care," I seethed. "Either he's a fool, or you're a coward." *Or maybe it's both.*

"I cannot interfere with Tasari's work."

"Why?"

"Because the Deal-Breaker forbids it."

The gods-damned Deal-Breaker again. I scoffed. "Are you certain you're a free man?"

His expression darkened. "Tread carefully with your next words, Maralla."

I'd found another nerve, then. I edged closer and prodded it. "That's it, isn't it? He keeps the collar about your neck so tight, I'm surprised you can breathe."

"I wear no collar," he said through his teeth.

I matched his molten gaze. "Then you use him as your excuse for every terrible thing you do."

An unreadable emotion flickered across his face. He drew himself up. "Tasari has his tasks for our employer, and I have mine. We don't compromise each other's work, no matter how unsavory. It's the way of things."

Unsavory. As if committing vicious acts of brutality, raping women and slaves to seal business deals, and experimenting on those less fortunate could be summed up with a word as simple as 'unsavory.'

I shook my head. "That is an evasion. You're one of the most powerful men in this country, and you're telling me you can't stop your own brother from torturing peasants?"

Mascha stared at me as if confounded by the notion. He gaped for a full five heartbeats before tearing his gaze away. "It's not that simple."

I went after his hesitation like a hound on a blood trail. "Seems simple enough to me. If you wielded your influence the way you wield your axes, you could bring this entire country to its knees."

As the words slipped out, I pondered their wisdom, realizing too late their potential for instilling a tyrant with thoughts of grandeur.

Fortunately, Mascha didn't seem moved. He studied the walls rising on either side of us. The illusion behind me reflected in his eyes. "Are you finished?"

I blew an angry breath out of my nose. I hadn't even begun to say everything that should be said of him, let alone his gods-forsaken country. "For now."

"Good." He avoided my gaze and banished his spell with a wave. "The entire market will be watching you today. Stay one half-step behind me, do not speak, and keep your gaze down. Say you understand."

I let my arms fall and adopted the signature docile slave pose, envisioning all the ways I could disobey that directive. "I understand. *Master.*"

A muscle near Mascha's eye twitched, and I trailed him into the market once more.

Chapter Eleven

Mascha

My encounter with Maralla stuck with me long after we left the alley. Throughout my morning inspections, I let little infractions from the merchants' record books slip in my distraction. It gnawed at me over lunch, and during passing conversation I was dismissive to the point of rudeness. Even as I steered Maralla away from two public whippings that afternoon, I couldn't get that question out of my head.

Are you certain you're a free man?

It was preposterous, of course. There was a chasm of difference between employment and slavery. I lived more comfortably than most kings, and I could slake my thirst for every dark pleasure my heart desired on a whim. *Ciir*, I still had laws to abide, but everyone was subject to rules in a social hierarchy. That I luxuriated near the top of mine should have been proof enough of my freedom.

Still, I caught myself rubbing the smooth scar about my neck more than once.

Maralla couldn't see the full scope of things. A delicate balance existed within Rillanese culture, and the Deal-Breaker's machinations ensured order. Still, I couldn't deny that Tasari's place in that order remained a point of contention. I was the face of the Deal-Breaker's operation, but my brother handled the darker acts—those not even the Dasch'Kalliir would entertain. The assassins' code of ethics meant they preferred to kill swiftly or not at all, while orchestrating accidents, enfeebling key figures, and eliminating pockets of opposition all fell under Tasari's unprincipled authority. His use of peasants in his development of potions had never sat well with me, especially his most recent habit of deliberately infecting them with the pox in search of a cure. It just wasn't within my power to change.

As the sun began its descent toward the western horizon, Maralla and I approached the last stop on my rounds. She'd performed far better than I'd expected today, echoing my movements without fault, kneeling when instructed, and staying silent far longer than I'd believed possible. I hardened at the thought of rewarding her with pleasure when we returned home—something I would have done in the early days of her processing if she'd only allowed it. Gods help me if her *oeloraati* made us both receptive to such things now.

We climbed the steps to the shop door, and a bell chimed overhead. The smoky scent of leather enveloped us. Unzach's Leathercraft had seen many improvements of late. The Deal-Breaker's elevation of House Emisett beyond the middling caste was well underway.

"Mascha." Unzach Emisett II rose from the counter and bowed, a smile alighting on his clean-shaven face. "Silonas's blessings, *meschiir*."

"Blessings upon you as well. Is your father in?"

"I, um." His dark eyes betrayed his youth as they strayed toward Maralla. He cleared his throat. "No, I'm afraid he's taken ill. But if you're here for the tithes, I can assist you."

Before I could answer, he was already turning back to the counter. I waited until he'd retrieved the month's earnings and set the tithe box in my hands.

"Actually, there was another matter I wished to discuss with him," I said. "The Rorsch Hekkai cavalry needs new saddles and tack. I hoped he would be amenable to negotiations."

Emisett's mouth fell open. Certainly, he was aware of what such a sizable order could do for his family. House Emisett was new money, a rare and tenuous position in Rillion, and its members were easy to manipulate with the promise of social status.

Always eager to impress, Emisett II straightened. "We would be honored, *meschiir*."

"Excellent. Have him call on me at the palace once he's recovered."

Emisett's gaze strayed to Maralla again. This time, it lingered openly on her and his nostrils flared. Her scent, despite the heavy perfume, would be detectable even to some humans. "He's given me leave to negotiate in his stead. Just name a time this week, and I will accommodate."

Emisett shifted on his feet and wetted his lips. No doubt, he was already planning for Maralla to seal our deal.

I should have been pleased by how off balance she made him. Negotiations would lean in my favor if he was already thinking with his cock. But the thought of him bedding her provoked an odd tightness in my chest.

Possessiveness was to be expected. Biological imperative demanded I guard her for myself in her state. Once the herbs worked through her system, the feeling would pass.

"This week is booked, I'm afraid. We can schedule for the end of next week. Say, Saosday at eighteenth hour?"

Emisett's eagerness didn't abate. He bowed again. "I look forward to it."

We said our farewells, and I started back to the palace with that wariness still weighing on me. It would demonstrate Maralla's subservience if she sealed a few deals before the gala, as long as she didn't gut one of my guests in the process. I would speak with her about it later.

A flicker of Foresight caught my eye. I paused, tracking the Aetherial image of a familiar urchin boy darting from a fruit vendor's stall. The image stumbled, and citrons spilled from his pockets.

I turned, thinking better than to expose Maralla to the repercussions of the child's blunder. "We'll take the scenic walk home."

Maralla frowned, but kept her gaze down and adjusted course. We were halfway across the packed street when the merchant's voice cut above the crowd.

"Stop! Thief!"

Too late. I clenched my teeth, reaching for my earring and Maralla in the same motion. If I rifted us away fast enough—

My fingers closed on empty air.

Damn it. "Come, *rascha.*"

The sound of crates tumbling and the child's scream cut me off.

"After him!"

"Thief! Thief!"

Guards descended, and Maralla stood framed by the crowd that parted to avoid the fallen urchin. One of the boy's stolen citrons rolled to a stop by her feet.

She glanced back at me, conflicted.

I stepped toward her, wincing at the pattern of future images scattered through the Aether. "Don't."

Maralla swallowed visibly. The rasp of a sword being unsheathed snapped her attention back to the boy.

Foreboding lodged in my throat. I didn't want her to see this, not when she couldn't stop herself from interfering. I took another step, and another, hoping to close the distance before she bolted. All her Aetherial images coalesced into that one possible future as she worked through her options.

I seized her collar. "Maralla—"

The urchin scrambled to his feet, clutching three of the citrons, only to be struck back down by a Rorsch Hekkai in black and gold.

"Little rat." The dusky-faced man yanked the boy's hair. "I see the slut who raised you didn't teach you any manners."

Another guard seized his right arm. "Let's fix that."

As a third man brandished his cutlass, Maralla whirled on me. I braced for a blow, but stood dumbstruck as she hit her knees and clutched my legs. Her eyes brimmed with tears. "Master, please. *Tipori. Tipori daatahr.*"

Mercy. Mercy for him.

Phantom agony ripped into me. Her lance struck right on target, sending me back to that night years ago. Distant screams joined the swell of jeers and laughter.

The guards flung the boy over a barrel, stretching his arm across the wood. Upraised steel glinted in the sun.

Kaana'ruh ke'aave tipori.

I gnashed my teeth and shoved Maralla off me. "Gods damn you, woman. Stay here."

If she took this opportunity to run, I'd have to kill her. The thought whispered through me like smoke as I stepped toward my guards and projected all the power and authority I possessed into one word.

"Hold!"

Everything stopped.

The cries, the guards, the merchants, even the horses quieted. Men and slaves cleared a path as I strode to the center of the crowd. The guard with the cutlass lowered it, and the boy ceased his struggles against the other two men, staring at me open-mouthed.

He looked much the same as he had two days before, when Maralla had pressed her earrings into his hand and shooed him away. His face was layered with dirt so thick, it was impossible to tell the color of his skin. A scar sliced through one bushy eyebrow, and his cheekbones protruded sharply beneath clear hazel eyes.

My shadow fell across him, and I seized his jaw. "There you are, you miserable little wretch."

The guards shared curious looks. "You know this boy, Rorsch Hekkai?"

"I do." I released him and turned in search of the fruit merchant. "*Meschiir*, attend me."

Though he was shorter than I by a handspan or so, the merchant's tall crimson headdress gave him a false presence, which he attempted to salvage by swiping down his dusty robes. His gangly figure suggested a poor diet, and a map of wrinkles bespoke his years in the sun.

"Yes, milor" —he shook his head, recognizing his mistake—"er, Mascha?"

"How much fruit did the boy steal from you?"

"At least half a dozen citrons."

I nodded and withdrew a gold gran. "This should more than compensate for the loss."

The merchant took the coin, but he scowled and gestured at the boy. "This little pest has been all over the district stealing things from hardworking men. He should be punished to the full extent of the law."

I shook my head. "I'm afraid removing his arm is out of the question, *meschiir*. You see, the boy owes me a debt as well." I plucked a worn purse from the boy's belt and found—as I'd hoped—Maralla's diamond earrings buried among a handful of copper eighi. He'd likely found that no self-respecting jeweler in this quarter would buy pilfered gems from an urchin.

Sunlight caught the precious stones and threw rainbows across the merchant's face. After pocketing the earrings, I tossed the purse to the merchant as well. "And what I have in mind for him requires the use of both hands."

I smiled and let the men's imaginations do the rest, fully expecting their thoughts to turn toward rumors I'd started myself. Better they believe I was capable of such horrors than think I would spare a child out of weakness.

The fruit merchant's scowl warped into a fiendish grin.

"Very well, if it gets him off our streets"—he spat on the boy and feigned wiping his hands—"then perhaps some of your patrons will find a use for... parts of him."

The boy's struggle began anew. "No! No, let me go!"

I held the merchant's eyes, memorized his face. Indeed, some men preferred companions who had not yet come of age, and if this maggot was one of them, I would do everything in my power to ruin him. "I assure you, he will be put to good use."

Once I took hold of the boy's nape, I waved the guards away and summoned a rift. The black-violet void wavered before me as I sought out Maralla, still kneeling on the cobbles where I'd left her. Careful not to let my relief show, I beckoned to her. "Come, *Johtan Shasnaram*."

Gasps and whispers trailed her through the crowd. She kept her head down and ignored the lewd jokes and crude gestures. Demure and docile were her movements, though at their heart, a tigress lurked. Had anyone been foolish enough to reach for her as she passed, it was hard to say whether her claws or my axes would have removed their limbs first.

Spectacle aside, the plea she'd made for the boy had shown her hand. Maralla knew she could weaponize my nightmares.

Now I was in more trouble than ever.

The boy's name was Soltani, and he was very confused when I rifted us to my stables, rather than the slaves' quarters, and equipped him with a shovel instead of a collar.

Lord Naftalli's youngest son, Po, worked as my stablemaster, and I introduced the two as Po brushed down the last of the horses.

I didn't linger overlong. The boy was to work for me in exchange for three meals a day, a dry bed at night, and clothes befitting a man in service to the Rorsch Hekkai. Should he breach my trust or leave the grounds without Po's permission, I would remove his arm myself and cast him back into the streets. Soltani accepted my terms in stupefied wonder and immediately got to work mucking the stables.

As the sun set in glorious shades of scarlet and ochre, I collected Maralla from the corral gate and led her back to my chambers. I allowed her to disappear into my sitting room before trailing after her.

For all my skills with Foresight, I should have seen this coming. I'd been a fool to think her utterance of '*tipori*' and puzzling out another woman's importance to me would be the end of it. The question now was what to do about it.

She tossed her garment of chains and silk over her shoulder as I entered, and it thumped against the tile at my feet. Her scent wafted over me, the fragrant oils and her first dose of herbs having worn off. I closed my eyes against the surge of desire tightening my trousers. Gods help me, I had to focus.

"We need to speak," I told her as she drifted naked across the room to the table where my slaves had laid out a small feast.

"We do." Maralla nodded to the ensemble on the floor. "Chains don't make a comfortable outfit. You should raise concerns with your designer."

I blinked, then shook my head. "What happened today cannot happen again—"

"You did a good thing helping that boy," she cut in, collecting a plate. "I was impressed. And I don't think you'll regret it."

She spoke as if I were seeking her approval. As if she hadn't manipulated me into acting. My fingers curled. "I can't save them all."

"That's the tragedy, isn't it? If only you could speak to someone in power." She popped a grape into her mouth and continued loading her plate.

I stood motionless, staring at her. "You mock me."

Maralla smiled and turned for the divan, perching cross-legged on the center cushion. The scent of her arousal subsumed the urge to chastise her vulgar posture. I turned and built my own plate, attempting to ignore how my cock strained against my leggings.

"You're due for your next dose."

"What was her name?"

I paused, halfway to my seat. Maralla continued chewing. With lead in my boots, I made it to my chair and sat.

We ate in silence, the question left unanswered. Not even Anelliiq knew that story, and I refused to provide Maralla with further tools to destroy me.

Once she'd emptied her plate, she reached for the piccara board between us. Piece by piece, she built the playing field, then sat back, watching me.

I studied her, reluctant to prolong our interactions beyond the necessary. I'd taught many slaves how to play the strategy game over the years. Anelliiq was the best of them, and I enjoyed delaying my victories just to see how she reacted to new predicaments. I hadn't taught Maralla, however. I wasn't even aware she knew how to play.

With a sigh, I nudged my first sentry chip forward.

Maralla bested me in four turns.

I sat forward, eyeing how her soldiers caged in my monarch, and set my half-eaten meal aside. "How did you do that?"

Her eyes glittered. "Again?"

I stroked my beard, weighing the chances of emasculating myself against a greater opponent again. "You have an unfair advantage."

She tilted her head, and I nodded to her lack of dress.

Another grin pulled at the corners of her mouth. "You're saying you want an equitable balance of power?"

Her meaning wasn't lost on me. Rather than dignify it with a response, I rose and removed my shirt. She shifted on the divan, and her eyelids fluttered.

A thrill shot through me. Even dosing her with raspaati hadn't elicited *that* reaction. The knowledge that I could affect her during *oeloraati* as much as she affected me seemed to establish a momentary truce.

Resolving to take full advantage of that chink in her armor, I tossed my shirt over the chair and the rest of my clothing followed. Maralla's scent grew stronger, her breath quickening as she met my gaze. My lips twitched, though there was no hiding my desire now.

Hard as granite, every fingerspan of me blazing with need, I returned to my seat and reset the board. "Your move."

She reached for her soldier, a delicate flush staining her cheeks.

Chapter Twelve

Maralla

W E PLAYED PICCARA WELL into the night. Mascha's scent and mine mingled as the oils on our skin lost their potency. I choked down another dose of herbs and tried to ignore the heat lingering in my belly. The need to grind myself into the divan for any source of friction was one I couldn't surrender to under any circumstances. If I did, I wouldn't be able to stop myself from touching—or worse, trying to fill that aching void in my core.

Scabbing gods, I hated *oeloraati*.

At least with Nalerta, I could have allowed myself the passion of coupling, the rare submission to my mate as he fulfilled my baser needs. We could have enjoyed it together, even imagined the possibility of Mira's blessing upon us once more. Though a fourth child wouldn't replace the ones we'd lost, Nalerta and I had always wanted a big family.

But he was gone, and I focused on the pain of his loss to keep myself afloat in a sea of desire.

Sitting across from me, Mascha grinned like a dog with a bone. "Having trouble, Maralla?"

I'd been staring at the board too long. I reached for my fool and cringed as my gods-cursed arousal slicked the apex of my thighs. A whimper escaped me before I could bite it back.

My captor chuckled. "Normally, I would offer to assist you, but watching you squirm is almost as pleasurable as the act itself."

"Fuck you," I spat.

Tactless, but efficient.

His scent permeated my senses. His chiseled body was an annoyingly accurate rendering of a scarred god made flesh. My mouth watered at the thought of what his skin must taste like—

Appalled, I shook my head and moved my fool, only to realize too late that I had opened my monarch to his assassin.

His merciless gaze cut over my body. He reached down to claim his third victory in a row. "Only if you beg."

Fire exploded in my core. I tried to convince myself it wasn't anything more than fury. Still, I gripped the table between us as if rocked by a physical blow. Only during *oeloraati* would I find the idea of subservience arousing.

The herbs would take effect soon. This treacherous sensation had to pass.

Mascha slung an arm over his chair and leaned back, his cock standing proudly from a dusting of dark curls. It was all I could do not to stare.

But I remembered his advances while I'd been on raspaati. I remembered my resolve while I'd been caged in one of his infernal devices—the ones shaped to allow bodily waste through, yet block all reprieve from the artificial arousal he'd ordered Tasari to inject into my veins. I remembered who I was, and Commander Maralla Evallier of the Alliaansi Fourth Legion did. Not. Break.

The cracks in Mascha's composure became more apparent the longer I studied him. His fingers kept flexing behind his chair, visible in the shadow they cast on the floor. Though he appeared to lounge like a cat grown fat off milk, his abdominal muscles were coiled taut. His body quivered with restraint. A thin sheen of sweat glistened on his forehead, and not from the late spring heat.

I breathed a slow sigh and inhaled through my mouth. "I think I've already made it clear I don't need you for my pleasure."

His cock twitched, and the shadow of his hand stilled on the floor. "It was quite the performance. Perhaps you'll oblige me with another."

He parried well; I'd give him that. I smiled and echoed his casual sprawl, spreading my legs to call his bluff.

Mascha's breath faltered.

I reached down. "You want to see me come right here in front of you?"

He swallowed, his eyes flicking to my hand.

That silent confirmation seared me like lightning. The urge to plunge my fingers into my curls was almost irresistible. I flexed my thighs and cinched my toes to distract myself, taking heart in the bead of sweat that slid down Mascha's face.

My plan... I'd forgotten where I was going with this.

Pleasure sparked. I blinked away my hazy thoughts, only to find my body had betrayed me, and my fingers were already teasing circles around my center. A firm stroke coaxed a shiver from me. Another simultaneously relieved the pressure and stoked my desire for more.

"While you sit back, unable to use me for your own needs," I taunted. "Is that what you want?"

He straightened abruptly and leaned in. "That's exactly what I want. I want you to come for me right there on my couch while I do nothing to stop you."

His fervor jolted me back into my right mind like a strap to the back of my thighs. My hand stilled. I stared at him, uncertainty edging out my desire.

"Go on." Mascha's gaze sharpened. "Obey me."

Gods damn him.

I snapped my legs closed and stood so fast that my vision darkened. Reeling, I reached blindly for the piccara table and missed.

Mascha's arms closed around me before I hit the floor, but the impact of my body against his did more damage than cracking my knees against those fancy tiles ever could. The scent of him smashed my sensibilities into pieces.

Wetness coated my thighs. A choked gasp escaped me, and the weakness in my legs only worsened as my vision cleared. I looked up to find myself nose to nose with the king of slavers.

Mascha's skin blazed against mine. Everywhere our bodies touched sent my senses soaring. His eyes were the most stunning shade of violet, and they raked over my body with a possessive candor that both terrified and thrilled me. His erection pressed into my thigh with an insistence that ripped a whimper from my throat.

I should have been disgusted. I should have shoved him away.

Mascha spun with me until my back struck the wall.

Air burst from my lungs. He was moments away from demanding the one thing I'd long withheld from him, despite all his scheming, caging, and raspaati. This time, I might not have the strength to refuse him. That heady realization was like riding into battle without armor: liberating, exhilarating, and so incredibly stupid.

My lip curled. I needed to stop this. Especially with the risks of conceiving, fucking this bastard should have never crossed my mind. But the baser part of my brain was taking over, and reason withered on the vine.

Only a sliver of space remained between us. He held me with one arm around my waist, and the other bracing the wall. Dread and desire warred within me. *Oeloraati* could make even the gentlest man a force to be reckoned with, and Mascha was anything but gentle.

I didn't want him to be gentle.

The thought should have sparked such immutable rage that no power on Dessos could have snuffed it out. But I needed to quell the ache in my body more than I wanted to resist it.

Still, I wouldn't just give in. "So, this is how it is? Are you going to rape me now?"

Mascha jerked back as if I'd struck him. If not for the wall behind me, I might have fallen in earnest.

He searched my face, then retreated farther, a deep crease lodged between his brows. "No, I..."

Cooling air swept my skin in the wake of his sudden departure. I took a breath and shook out my tousled braids.

As quickly as his horror had appeared, it dissolved. "I would never take a person against their will."

My laughter was a whipcrack between us. "Idiot. You do it every day."

"How dare you—"

"Your slaves can't consent," I spat. Though each little movement still sent shockwaves through my core, the turn in our conversation was as bread to starving bellies, and I feasted on my rekindled anger to distract myself. "Not while you hold their very lives in your hands."

"In some households, that is true," he conceded, "but I have never forced myself on any of my slaves. Nor would I."

"No, you just cage them, drug them, and let them suffer until they beg you to make it stop." I stepped away from the wall, shaking my head. Of all his atrocities, how was *this* the subject that upset him? "Coercion is still rape, Mascha, no matter how you color it."

Truly, the notion seemed to stagger him. The storm clouds cleared from his expression and his gaze fell to the floor.

I turned away, ignoring the kernel of truth in his defense. Not once since I'd entered Mascha's palace had he forced himself on me. Considering I'd seen other masters rape their slaves in the streets for sport, I supposed that had to count for something.

I scoffed. Just because it could be worse didn't make his behavior any less deplorable.

Fervor still simmered low in my belly. I glanced between the wet spot on the divan and the path to Mascha's bedroom. If I didn't deal with these urges, there would be no sleeping tonight.

"It's better than the alternatives."

The gravel in his tone gave me pause. It was the same way he'd spoken of Soltani this evening. As easily as he'd provided that boy a chance at a better life, Mascha still claimed he couldn't save them all. Why couldn't he see how wrong he was?

I turned back, bracing for a fight.

Mascha stood framed by his costly possessions, the polished floor, the buttressed ceiling, looking for all the world like he'd lost something dear to him.

I shouldn't have let that soften me, but this hours-long state of arousal made my ire a slippery thing. The retort I might have lobbed his way died on my tongue. "What alternatives?"

He lifted his hands and let them fall. "I would rather use pleasure and denial than pain. I prefer not to leave scars if I don't have to."

The words weren't quite tinged with remorse, but they weren't defensive either. His desire had left him, and the tension eased from his shoulders. It could have been business sense—scarred slaves weren't as desirable—but I'd never heard that quaver in his voice before. It was like he actually thought what he was doing was merciful.

Tipori. Mercy.

Nevertheless, I steeled myself. "They still carry scars," I pointed out, far gentler than he deserved. "Even if you can't see them."

I needed to lie down, but I wasn't going near the divan again, and neither the chair nor the rug beside the empty hearth screamed 'comfortable.' I started for his bedroom, leaving Mascha to sort his own mess out. If I was lucky, he would storm out again and leave me in peace.

Of course, Silonas rarely favored me.

Only moments after I passed the threshold to his bedroom, Mascha entered behind me.

I'd once watched two feline chaagra posture for the right to rule a choice hunting ground outside my village. It was a blustery affair of raised hackles, bared teeth, and swishing tails. Mascha and I eyed each other similarly, standing at the foot of his bed. I was fully prepared to argue about the cage again. The only way he'd get me back in there was if he dragged me over and stuffed me inside it. I ignored the surge of lust that came with the thought of such rough handling.

Mascha looked toward the cage, then sighed. "You may share my bed. I won't touch you; I swear it."

I blinked.

A 'thank you' almost fell out of my mouth, but I caught it between my teeth. The bastard didn't deserve my gratitude for this modicum of decency. Still, I knew a victory when I saw one.

The silence grew awkward. Mascha finally crept past me to settle into bed, and I retreated to the washroom to relieve myself—in more ways than one.

Already, I could tell the herbs were affording me some semblance of poise. In any other *oeloraati* cycle, I would have never been able to leave that room.

I returned freshly sated to find Mascha sitting in bed, a tome in his lap. He'd read almost every night since my arrival—as long as he didn't have a noblewoman or a slave to tumble—and not once had I asked him about his literature of choice. I didn't plan to start tonight.

He'd left room for three of me on the other side, putting himself between me and the windows. Smart, if not overly cautious. I knew my best way home now was to cooperate.

Mascha ignored me as I climbed into bed. I was careful to keep as much distance between us as possible. I settled under the same sheet, facing away from him.

At least my climax in the washroom had dulled the effect of his scent. I'd come dangerously close to a grievous mistake tonight. Tomorrow, I would be stronger.

I had to be.

Chapter Thirteen

Mascha

I LAY AWAKE INTO the early hours, vacillating between fits of arousal and self-doubt. What started as a friendly battle of wills with Maralla had left me bloody, and I couldn't dig out the barbs of her assessment no matter how deep my blades of reason went.

Your slaves can't consent.

But they could. They *did*. I never forced them; I wouldn't. Maralla herself was proof of that. I rolled onto my back and tried to coax the tension out of my muscles. Around me, the subtle pinks and golds of dawn chased away the night, but they did nothing to banish the shroud over my thoughts.

As a slave, I'd been forced to take women against their will. It was for the Master's pleasure that his fighters entertain guests and further his breeding program. We were animals to him, even those of us who shared his noble blood, and I couldn't have denied his wishes without suffering far worse.

Not while you hold their very lives in your hands.

I squeezed my eyes shut. I wasn't like him. Mira help me, I was better than that.

When I became Rorsch Hekkai, I made it a point both to learn how to make sealing deals more enjoyable for my partners, and to perfect a new method of breaking slaves—one that didn't rely on violence. I had no stomach for whippings, not after I'd borne so many myself. Raspaati had been the answer. When my slaves associated my approval with their pleasure, they worked harder to earn what I denied them. It was cleaner, more humane, and it broke most of them in a fraction of the time.

Coercion is still rape, no matter how you color it.

I'd never thought of it like that before. Worse, I hated that she had a point. Just as I couldn't refuse the Master, the men and women in my care could only refuse me for so long. They only sought an end to their suffering, and while consent was given, it was as tenuous as if they'd consented under threat of punishment.

But I still had a job to do; I still had to break them.

I itched to move—to summon my blades and hurl myself into my forms until I collapsed. It was close enough to morning. I grabbed the sheet and tensed to rise.

Maralla murmured in her sleep.

I paused. Despite giving her the lion's share of my bed, she'd rolled closer overnight until she was only fingerspans away. Her heady scent lingered, and I could almost taste her on my lips. If not for our discord last night, the Aetherial images of us breaking furniture in our coupling might have come to fruition.

My cock stiffened at the thought, and I gritted my teeth. Under no circumstances could I sire another child. Nor would I take her when she truly didn't want me...

Forms. *Forms.* Silonas slay me, I couldn't think about this anymore. I made to rise again.

She grumbled something—a name?—and reached for me. Her hand pressed flat against my chest. "*Imaane'ruh.*"

Stay.

The command whispered into the quiet like smoke, but it swept through me like wildfire. I sagged back down, muddled by her easy authority. No other woman would dare speak to me like that, and any man who tried would have found his lungs ripped from his body.

It inflamed me all the more knowing her boldness wasn't just the product of sleep. I was familiar with the matriarchal culture of northern Syljians. The Master and my mother both had been fascinated by them. In the Northlands, women were warriors, leaders, scholars, even arcanists. They were so different from Rillanese women, who were barred from wielding magic, owning property, running businesses, or even making deals on a man's behalf.

I stared into the deceptive softness of Maralla's face, desire tugging at my loins. Her eyelids fluttered, and she buried her face in my ribs with a sigh.

Clearly, the order wasn't meant for me. She'd never spoken of a mate before, but it wasn't as if our constant contention allowed for small talk.

It should have been easy to push her away—to slip downstairs and clear my head before another trying day began. But a man could only go so long on paltry sleep, and at last exhaustion anchored me. I folded my arm closer to Maralla beneath my head, determined to stay true to my word. I wouldn't touch her. Tiior knew she already thought me a monster.

Her opinion shouldn't have bothered me. My eyes found the canopy above us and eventually drifted closed. I'd cultivated this persona for a reason, and yet...

It didn't matter. Truly. It didn't...

When next I roused, sunlight stained my vision red, and the call of gulls sounded shrill outside. A new weight rested on my chest. Another pinned my thigh. I cracked my lids to find stray white hairs tickling my nose. Maralla's sleep-tangled mane obscured her face, but there was no mistaking the sensation of her cheek pressed against my chest, her leg thrown carelessly over mine. Vanilla and rose barely masked her natural scent.

I lay still, uncertain whether my unwillingness to disturb her was more the reluctance to wake one's family cat or kick a Duerguardian cobra. My fingers ached to wrap around her, hold her closer, as I would have with any other man or woman who shared my bed. But the rarity of Maralla's closeness was somehow more precious.

And more lethal.

It meant nothing. I should extract myself before she awoke to see the position her dreams had placed her in. Before those deploring eyes opened and eviscerated me once more.

Maralla stirred, tightening her hold, then stiffened like a wolf that had caught the scent of another predator. She disentangled her leg first, slowly, as if not to wake me, and lifted her head. Her eyes met mine, darted to my arm still pinned above my head, then back to my face.

I rolled away and sat up, a curious knot lodged between my ribs. "Get dressed." I spoke into the space between my bed and dresser. "Today will be a busy day."

Svaronei would be here this morning to report on his interviews of the men at port. I still had a keallite cartel to dismantle.

The bed shifted, and I glanced over my shoulder. Maralla swung her legs over the opposite side. Her fresh scars reflected light in macabre stripes, and the knot in my chest coiled tighter.

Somehow, my own response steadied me. The Master had always reveled in the sight of such correction, but I didn't. I crossed the floor, the soft rug giving way to cool tile. I focused on the sensations to avoid any further constriction of my lungs.

"I thought you were someone else." Her voice carried a blunted edge that tore rather than pierced.

If there was one thing I'd learned from the arena, it was that jagged wounds always hurt more. My fingers closed on the diamond pull of my dresser drawer. "I know."

As I dug for a shirt, a shaky expulsion of air sounded behind me. Though I couldn't see her face in the mirror, I caught the flash of her fingertips as she wiped her cheeks.

Her pain was so raw and unexpected that something inside me pinched. Most slaves who were carried across the seas had families, and hopes of escaping and reuniting with them dominated talk on the slave blocks. It still twisted in me that I couldn't console them when those hopes inevitably came crashing down.

This time, though, I couldn't help myself.

"I know being apart from a mate isn't easy. You'll see them again soon."

It might have even been true.

She scoffed. "How could you possibly know anything about that?" Her eyes found mine again in our reflection. "You don't seem like the kind of man who falls in love."

I thought of Anelliiq, of Scherazeme, of those few other women and men whose heartstrings had the misfortune of tangling with mine over the years. Then I pulled the shirt over my head and turned back, adjusting one sleeve.

"No." The word came out less certain than I intended. "I suppose I'm not. But you have my sympathies all the same."

Maralla's lips parted, her brows caving into a frown. I avoided that scrutinizing look and busied myself hunting for trousers. When I returned to the bed, Maralla was still watching me. I gave her my back and sat to pull on my boots.

"No, I'm sorry," she ventured.

I paused in cinching the laces.

"That was... uncalled for."

My lips tugged upward. She apologized with as much grace as a new merchant paying his tithes for the first time. I straightened and let my smile bloom in earnest. "*Oeloraati* has softened you, I see," I teased over my shoulder.

Rather than scowl, she offered a rare glimpse of something other than derision. One corner of her mouth twitched up. "Don't get used to it."

"Believe me, I know better." I finished lacing my boots and stood. "Would you like breakfast?"

Her brows furrowed again, and it occurred to me I'd never asked her that question before. I took her confusion in stride and held her gaze, waiting.

Slowly, she nodded.

I dipped my chin—a gesture reserved for women of foreign powers. "I'll send for eggs."

A few hours later, I entered the palace gallery with Maralla in tow. She stayed one half-step behind me and to my right, maintaining both proper posture and poise—a feat I might have found impressive, if not for the fifteen-minute argument it took to get her there. I was starting to think she picked fights just to let off steam, like the volcanic fissures surrounding Mount Escha. And like Rillion's most tempestuous volcano, Maralla was both terrifying and beautiful in her fury.

If arguing with me was what she needed to pull this off, who was I to deny her?

Oil paintings adorned the walls, and sculptures of polished marble flanked the gallery doors. The paintings were largely landscapes—jungle floors, rolling meadows, and desert sunsets—with only a few portraits depicting the upper and ruling castes of Rillanese society. I saw enough of that already, and I'd purchased those pieces only to appease the snobbish patrons whose nepotism disallowed the appreciation of true art.

The sculptures, however, were my own commission. Each stood several spans high and depicted scenes of lust and love, respectively. The difference lay in how the man held his partner: tightly or with care; fingers grasping or sifting through his lover's hair; the expression leering with bared teeth, or softer with parted lips. The carnal nature of one juxtaposed against the sensuality of the other always inspired debate at parties. All but a few men seemed to miss the fact that the couple in each sculpture was the same.

I led Maralla to the sun-speckled atrium where Svaronei awaited me. A tray of untouched pastries sat on a low table, along with a sweating carafe of spike melon juice and two glasses. Farrah and Vassu lingered in the shadows, prepared to serve at the slightest wave.

The Aetherian Walker rose from a navy settee, sunlight shining on his oiled faelocks, and bowed. "Good morning, Rorsch Hekkai."

"Good morning."

Proving to the Deal-Breaker's man that the belligerent slave he'd been ordered to track down had been brought to heel was paramount. I'd spent half an hour lecturing Maralla on this at breakfast, and I tried not to hold my breath as I gestured for Svaronei to sit, and Maralla to kneel.

Both obeyed. I took my seat between them with no small lessening of tension in my shoulders. "What news have you?"

Svaronei reached for a pastry, eyes curious as he studied Maralla. "The silk wasn't on the manifest. We interrogated the portmaster, but he swears no involvement."

"Of course he does."

"Apparently he was ill that night." Svaronei crossed one ankle over his knee. "Said someone else stood in for him. One of Simmion's men."

My brows lifted. House Simmion had been on the Rorsch Hekkai's watch-list for some time. Lomov Simmion controlled several smaller ports both on Durgost Island and in Denna—the seedbed of our keallite epidemic. So far, we hadn't been able to pin the upper-caste lord with anything more nefarious than improper storage of saltpeter on his port-side properties, so *this* was a breakthrough.

I sat forward for the carafe, waving Vassu off before he could trace the path of his Aetherial image to the table. "Let me guess, you can't find this man now."

Svaronei shook his head. "All we have is a name: Kestra Hyanaro."

I didn't recognize it, but if this blight-sore was like all the other petty drug lords I'd crushed, I doubted he could lead us to the manufacturers of that vile substance any better than his Aether-addled clients.

Using the distraction of pouring juice to check on Maralla, I confirmed that she was still kneeling properly, palms on her thighs, before passing Svaronei a glass. "Lower caste?"

"Likely." He washed down the last of his pastry. "Want me to do some digging?"

"No," I decided after a moment. "We have a connection to Simmion now. We'll go straight to the source."

Svaronei leaned back, incredulous. "You're going to interrogate the lord of Simmion Estates?"

"Certainly not." I grinned, sipping from my glass. "I'm going to invite him for tea."

The promise of business would lure Lord Simmion in. From there, I could question him about his dealings at port, perhaps mention the name Hyanaro and see if it got him to sweat. If he suspected the Rorsch Hekkai were on to him, he would scramble, make a mistake, and then we could strike.

Svaronei shrugged. "Suit yourself." He glanced at Maralla again, wide nostrils flaring. "That one give you any more trouble?"

My humor vanished. Though Hasanthe's herbs were working—I could at least be around Maralla without wanting to rip her clothes off—it was obvious the human still sensed her, too.

"No. Her behavior is much improved."

"How much to bed her?" Svaronei licked his lips. "I imagine it's quite the experience."

I slid my fingers into her hair. Maralla's silent rage quivered through my palm. I dared not look at her, instead catching Svaronei's hungry gaze and holding it. *Johtan Shasnaram* would be a commodity—that was unavoidable—but not yet. Not before the herbs set in. Not while I could still protect her.

My voice became steel. "Another time, perhaps."

"Ah." The Walker shook himself. "Forgive me."

Whatever his assumptions were about the cause of my possessiveness, I didn't care to consider them. "There are four notable houses who specialize in the silk trade: Estille, Imaan, Korvio, and Baghara. I want reports on all of them, as well as increased surveillance on their dealings at market."

Svaronei cleared his throat. "Of course."

I made it apparent, with a tightening of my grip on Maralla, that it was time for him to leave. We rose together, and he bowed.

"Silonas's blessings, Rorsch Hekkai."

"Indeed."

Svaronei pulled saphyric energy from his casting chain, summoned a rift, and vanished.

I released Maralla, and she sagged forward, her white braids tumbling forward to disguise her face. Her shoulders rose and fell, and she braced herself with one hand against the floor.

I turned to the slaves still present. "Leave us."

"Yes, Master."

"Your will, Master."

Farrah curtsied, Vassu bowed, and both scurried out of sight.

I crouched beside Maralla and clasped her shoulder. "Are you alright?"

"Define alright." She shrugged me off with a growl and climbed unsteadily to her feet. I straightened again as she helped herself to the leftover juice and pastries. Maralla ripped a bite out of a blueberry tart and shook the rest at me. "If being alright is not getting my body loaned out to some scabbing creep who smells like onions and cheap whiskey, then by the gods, I'm fantastic."

Her honest tirade, coupled with the crumbs that flew from the pastry, broke loose the hook lodged in my spine. What fears I'd had for her mental state dissolved. I laughed.

"You think this is funny?" More crumbs flew. She grabbed the carafe and violently poured herself a glass. Juice sloshed over the rim and hit the table in bright yellow swatches. "Your country is so backward, I'm surprised you can't look down and see your own ass."

I held my sides and sank onto the settee, still laughing. Like a volcano, indeed. All this time, I'd tried to temper this woman. What a fool I was.

She carried on, spouting curses and drawing admittedly fair conclusions about my people's barbarity until all the pastries were gone. After chugging another glass of juice, she collapsed beside me and kicked her feet up on the table.

I didn't bother to chastise her. My ribs and cheeks still ached, and the lightness I felt was worth far more than any sense of propriety I'd tried to instill in her. Instead, I propped my legs up, too.

Maralla searched my face, only to shake her head at whatever she did or didn't find. "Why did you do that, anyway?"

I rested my arm on the back of the settee and let the sunlight warm my face. "Sealing deals is part of this ruse, but being a whore is not."

Our eyes met. For once, her expression was free of rage, and a passing curiosity folded her white brows inward. "That's surprisingly discerning of you."

"Until you leave my household, Maralla, you are my responsibility." I didn't reach for her like I wanted to, certain it would cost me a hand. Or worse. "We'll continue to follow Hasanthe's orders. You needn't worry about deals yet."

She studied me for a long time, jaw tensed. When she nodded, she said the last thing I'd ever expected her to say.

"Thank you."

Chapter Fourteen

Maralla

THE FIRST WEEK PASSED. Mascha and I settled into a rhythm where I played doting slave during the day, and he loosened up at night. We played piccara and drank wine, and he processed new slaves in other rooms to spare me the noise. The herbs worked their magic, and I no longer woke drowning in my own arousal, my thoughts muddied by dreams of Nalerta and scattered by the scent of the man sleeping beside me.

Mascha woke twice from nightmares of his mysterious woman, but I bided my time in broaching the subject again. With things more amicable between us, I wanted to preserve this balance as long as I could.

Even so, I didn't lose sight of what he was. The tightness in my freshly healed back might have lessened, but evidence of Mascha's cruelty still surrounded me: scars, whip marks, the occasional metal device. His household seemed to run on suffering, and yet so many of his personal slaves seemed content. *Content.* As if it were normal, this disgusting society that thrived on forced labor and sexual servitude. How anyone could condone business practices that reduced even the most powerful women to no more than a handshake with one's crotch was beyond me.

"Good morning, *sadarah*."

That was another curiosity. I turned from the railing and the view of the port as Catari stepped onto the balcony. I'd expected seeing me kneel at Mascha's feet, his hand in my hair, would have lessened the slaves' opinion of me. If anything, most of his household spoke to me with greater respect.

"Catari," I sighed, "how many times must I insist you call me by my name?"

"Apologies, *sa*—Maralla." Her cheeks flushed. "The Master has asked me to prepare you for your dance lessons. Will you come with me, please?"

I spared one last moment to savor the morning sunlight and fresh sea breeze before following Catari inside. Mascha was meeting with Lord Simmion today, attempting to glean more information about the undocumented silk and the keallite I'd stumbled upon in my last escape attempt. For curiosity's sake, I might have paid more attention to the details, but he and his Aetherian pig had spoken in Rillanese instead of the trade tongue that day, and my comprehension of their cock-gargling language was still crude at best.

Catari braided my hair after the Rillanese fashion—six long plaits that clung to my scalp before tumbling over my shoulders—and laced me into a boned corset and an impossibly short skirt. Then she led me downstairs to the ballroom.

If Mascha stuck to the traditional Syljian dances, I wouldn't need lessons, but he insisted I polish up my skills anyway. Apparently, his gala performance wasn't just Bastian's favorite part of the evening.

My slippered feet whispered across the polished wood. Wall-length blue drapery framed enormous windows that let in splashes of sunlight. Mirror-bright marble columns marched from one end to the other, supporting the vaulted ceiling.

I rolled my eyes toward the fanciful chandeliers. "He really doesn't spare a copper, does he?"

Catari gave me a curious frown but remained silent, as if such opulence and gratuitous waste didn't strike her at all.

Four slaves awaited us. Three held stringed instruments that looked like over-complicated viols, and the fourth wore a skirt of shimmering white silk and a bodice beaded with pearls.

Scherazeme was gorgeous; her floral tattoos accentuated lean muscle, and the angles of her jaw and cheekbones were worthy of a queen. Only the extensive burn scars across her back marred her beauty. I'd seen them many times before, but today they provoked a sobering rage that snapped me out of my complacency. What horrors Mascha must have put her through for her to become one of his highest-ranking slaves.

I folded my hands and offered a nod in greeting.

Scherazeme's dark gaze raked over me. "You've moved up in the world, haven't you?"

A prickling sensation skittered down my neck. I remembered too late Bastian's shock that *I* would be attending the gala, not Scherazeme. Apparently, one of Mascha's slaves didn't find me so awe-inspiring.

"It's easier to submit than to keep fighting him," I forced out. She paced forward, trying to threaten me with more posturing, and I sidestepped. "I... can tell you don't want to be here any more than I do. If you leave Mascha's instructions with the musicians, I can practice on my own."

"*The Master* has chosen the amaariana," Scherazeme hissed, as if his name on my lips were a curse. She signaled the musicians to play and shooed Catari toward the nearest wall. "If you know it so well, then keeping my promise to him will be easy."

"Your promise?" As if Mascha had given her a choice.

Scherazeme stalked forward and yanked me into position, her nails digging into my arms. She took the lead—the woman's position in the amaariana—and I stumbled through the traditionally male steps with my jaw cinched. Of course, the Rillanese would have bastardized my people's most intimate courtship dance beyond recognition.

Scherazeme's movements were precisely executed, albeit shaded by low-simmering fury. It was like the time I'd pissed my sister off only moments before she cut an arrow from my leg. I wasn't sure which encounter would end with less bloodshed.

Three spins later, she tugged me in close. Scherazeme's brows knitted and her eyes darted away from mine, but not before light caught the tears lingering at their corners. After fumbling through another series of steps, her muscles tighter with every turn, I began to suspect there was something more to her hostility than missing the gala.

When we whirled again, Scherazeme's steely expression finally slipped. "How did you do it?"

"Do what?"

Sunlight flashed across her face mid-turn, punctuating the return of her deadly glare. She guided me perfectly through an exchange of hands. "Don't play stupid. I know you must have done something."

My confusion only mounted. "I have no idea what you're talking about."

"You sleep unattended in his room." Scherazeme spun me once. "He gives you wine." Twice. "And he assigns you no duties in the palace other than warming his bed."

I had no clue what she was getting at. "He kept me locked in a cage for two months. I'm not sure what you think is happening."

She wrenched me to a stop, her breath on my cheek. "*Everyone* is talking about it." Something changed in her voice—a subtle desperation laced with pain. "They say he's going to keep you. That you're to be his concubine."

Realization dawned like the winter sun, devoid of warmth. "That's—"

He wouldn't. Mascha wanted me gone as much as I did. The only reason he lavished luxuries on me was to keep me contained.

"You misunderstand," I said. "He has plans to sell me. I don't care what the other slaves say. That's the whole reason I'm here now."

"He hasn't bedded me all week." Scherazeme's face crumpled further. "He always summons me, and he hasn't because of you."

Her grip tightened, and I twisted out of her hold. "I assure you, as soon as the gala is over, I'll be gone, and things will go back to normal."

She sniffled and wiped her face. Her despair confounded me.

"You know, I really don't understand you people. How you can care for someone who hurts you so badly—"

Scherazeme scowled. "The Master has never hurt me. He loves me."

This was insanity. She was absolutely scabbing insane.

Was this how Mascha made them all so docile? Did he have a mastermind skilled in memory alteration hidden away in his palace, or were his processing methods so effective that he could make them think what he did to them was love?

I couldn't, *wouldn't*, let this stand.

"He's a cruel and vicious man who hides behind a façade of charm and wit. Someone who loves you wouldn't have burned you like that."

Her scowl only deepened. "He didn't."

"He—" I paused. The trio of musicians stopped their playing, and Catari's teeth bared in a grimace. "He didn't?"

Scherazeme put one hand on her hip. "No. My old master did. The one he *saved* me from."

"He... Oh."

It was all I could manage. The other slaves shared knowing glances, clearly more familiar with Scherazeme's story than I. My cheeks warmed.

Her glower wavered, chased by a haunted look. "You have no idea what a cruel and vicious master looks like. If you pulled half the stunts you do with any other master, you'd be dead. Or sold to the mines."

I took another step back. I *knew* Mascha, and he was cunning, cold, and ruthless. But he was also the same man who'd caught me on the ship, killed three men in my defense, and carried me off to the healer rather than back to the post.

I didn't want to see what she saw. After all, the man who winced at '*tipori*' was the same one who'd whipped me bloody just last week. His palace slaves couldn't be trusted to give an accurate accounting of him. They were either too brainwashed to know any better, or they were coached in what to say to an unruly slave.

Still, he'd rescued a boy from mutilation simply because I asked him to. Sure, it should have been second-nature to protect a child, but Rillion carried different rules.

Any other slaver would have forced himself on me by now. He would have gladly accepted Svaronei's coin and allowed him full use of me. Mascha hadn't even taken advantage of me when I was out of my head with lust. He'd recoiled at the notion.

The more I thought about it, the blurrier that fierce image of him became.

"He takes care of his own," I murmured, studying Mascha's slaves. Catari cast a look at her feet. Two of the musicians nodded, while the third bit her lip and avoided my eyes. The heat in my cheeks crept into my ear tips. "You all have experiences like this?"

More nods.

Catari drew herself up. "I was a bed warmer before I came here. The youngest of twelve." She crept forward until she stood level with Scherazeme, who tucked her under her arm. "I was six when a patron asked for me the first time. Word got back to the palace that the brothel-master had allowed it. The Master brought me here the next day."

My stomach twisted. To be so young...

As if emboldened by Catari's confession, the raven-haired musician brandished his bow, revealing the two missing fingers on his right hand. "I was a slave to Lord Kortavian years ago. The lord ordered my fingers removed at a party after I made a mistake in my performance. Our Master stopped him—said if I could play again with only three fingers, he'd pay triple what I was worth to leave with me that evening." He shook his head. "I should have been terrified by all the things they say about him, but there was something in his face. Somehow, I knew I was playing for my freedom."

Freedom. And yet, he still wore Mascha's collar—a band of rose gold that complemented his bronze skin.

The second musician, an Aivenosian, looked between his companions and shrugged. "I was supposed to be executed for defending my sister from a nobleman. The Master bought us both instead." He gestured to our lavish surroundings. "We live better now than we ever did as lower caste."

He glanced at the last violist, but she shrank behind him as if her story was still too painful to voice aloud.

Scherazeme's expression softened. "Rillion is a cruel place." When she looked back at me, her eyes hardened with challenge. "We're lucky we have him on our side."

The former, I could certainly agree with. The latter was truer than I cared to admit. Mascha still allowed terrible things to happen, and I couldn't forgive him for that, but he also stood between me and Tasari. He'd spared my life when Rillanese law demanded he take it.

As consumed as I'd been by my dreams of escape, I'd thought little of these inconsistencies in Mascha's behavior. It was time to wake up and pay attention.

Maybe his slaves' loyalty wasn't as foolish as I'd thought.

"My apologies."

Scherazeme released Catari and placed her hand on my shoulder. "You're really not to be his concubine?"

I huffed a laugh. "No. I think his employer is expecting a generous return on his investment."

"Selling you at the gala will turn a huge profit." She looked me over a second time, at last without venom. "The nobles love slaves with artistic talent. They bring in deals just so wealthy men can fuck a famous poet or painter."

"And I imagine dancers get lots of attention," I said. Mascha's plan became clearer with each passing moment.

"He always gets bids for me after our performances, even though all of Rillion knows he'd never sell me." Scherazeme touched her chin, her expression thoughtful. "You're familiar with Syljian dance."

It wasn't a question, but I nodded anyway. I'd grown up practicing the fii'aalrio, the amaariana, and Nalerta's favorite, the ii'senuu. Even after the fall of Astenpor, Syljian arts were the one thing the sorcerers could never take from us.

"The Master always leads, so you'll have to get used to that." She signaled the musicians again. "You're good, but you're going to have to be better to generate bids." She offered her hand. "Let's get started."

Scherazeme walked with me down the palace corridors, past wall-length tapestries and paintings framed in gold. The humidity clung to my skin, and my frizzy braids were drenched in sweat. Schera fared little better, though she'd discarded her dress for a sheer slave's gown the moment she called a halt to our lesson.

Learning to follow in the amaariana was going to be much harder than I thought, but Schera's skill with my people's dance far exceeded many back home. It was rare to meet a human who knew both parts so well.

"Where did you learn to dance?" I asked.

"The Master taught me."

I couldn't help but lift my brows. "Really?"

Schera smiled. "He loves the arts. He's even hired tutors to teach us to read."

It wasn't illegal, but it was highly unusual. Educated slaves could be dangerous, even if they weren't trained in the sword.

"Vassu has been studying poetry as part of his palace duties," Schera went on. "The Master will have him recite at winter solstice."

"Our Master"—I nearly choked on the words—"enjoys poetry?"

"Why *Johtan Shasnaram*, I didn't think you could be surprised by anything."

"It's a new experience. I'm not sure I like it." Her teasing grin was contagious.

We passed through a door and crossed the airy mezzanine. The training yard lay below us, empty of recruits this late in the afternoon. Wind tossed my braids over my shoulders and carried the heavy scent of rain. Through a second door on the other side, rows of ornate arches and rooms lined the walls in either direction. Schera turned left toward the sitting room where I was to make an appearance for Lord Simmion. More smoke and mirrors, Mascha had said, to confirm the rumors we'd already set in motion.

"You know, he was like us once."

I side-eyed her. "Is this the part where you tell me he's not as bad as he seems?"

Schera's brows furrowed. "He doesn't talk about it much, but I can tell he pities us."

As if pity were a balm for wounds too numerous to count. I sighed and lifted my hands. "Then why doesn't he do something about it?"

Down the hall, two slaves stood flanking a pair of doors carved in flowery relief. The men nodded to Schera and one reached for a twisted brass handle.

Schera gestured for them to wait, then turned to face me. Her jaw worked as she searched for the right words. "A compassionate man who bares his neck among villains gets his throat slit here, Maralla. It's just how it is."

But it doesn't have to be.

A metallic crash stopped the words from leaving my mouth.

"You repugnant, louse-bitten cur!"

I flinched, drawing on my magic to summon Dawnbringer, then cursed the binders that prevented it.

From the other side of the wall, Mascha's young page, Raffi, stammered a response: "Ap-apologies, *meschiir*—"

Crockery shattered, and all three slaves in the hallway winced. My hackles rose as a low thud and a muffled yelp came from behind the closed doors.

"What a bumble-footed little shit your whore mother made you."

That had to be Lord Simmion. Chairs screeched, and Mascha's placating voice rode on the coattails of a snarl. "My deepest apologies, my lord. *Raschu*, clean up this mess—"

"I want the cretin whipped, Mascha. No lord should suffer such a gross display of negligence."

I was moving before Schera could grab my arm, my teeth bared at the absurdity. Raffi was one of the gentlest slaves in Mascha's palace. Whatever had happened, it was surely an accident.

"I assure you, the slave will be dealt with—"

"He should be whipped, I said! I've half a mind to see him to the post myself."

The slaves stopped me at the doorway, wide-eyed and waving their hands. All at once, the helplessness of the situation knocked the breath from me. I was supposed to be a slave. A broken, female slave.

"Maralla!" Schera hissed.

"Such a grisly task will not fall to you, my lord." Mascha sounded closer to the doors now, and I allowed Schera to pull me back. "You are above such things. I will see him whipped myself."

No. An icy stone settled in my stomach. He wouldn't.

I tugged against Schera's grip, but she pressed me back against the wall. My nails dug into my palms. If I charged to Raffi's defense, it would only destroy my image. It wouldn't spare him from the post at all.

The doors burst open, and the slaves posted there scrambled out of the way. Two figures stormed into the corridor—one familiar, one not.

Lord Simmion stood a few fingerspans taller than Mascha, his gray-dusted black hair tied back in a severe tail and left to fall across one broad shoulder. His navy cape swirled around polished boots, wrapping his legs as he pivoted toward my captor.

"See to it, then." His hooked nose tipped toward the ceiling and he swiped at a coin-sized stain on his silver vest. "And rest assured, if I find that swine Hyanaro, I'll alert the Rorsch Hekkai immediately."

"The Deal-Breaker thanks you for your attention to this matter."

Mascha snapped his fingers and the two slaves hurried to flank him, offering perfect bows to the pompous lord. I fidgeted against the wall. Schera stilled me with a finger to her lips.

"*Raschun*, see Lord Simmion on his way." Mascha threw a menacing look into the room. "This one is due for more processing."

The lord nodded emphatically, then adjusted his collar and stormed off down the hallway with the slaves trailing him. Without so much as looking at us, Mascha stalked back inside.

` Raffi's whimpered plea pierced me like an arrow.

All that talk of pity, all those stories of mercy, and now he was about to whip a slave for what I could only imagine was an honest mistake?

No chance in the Wastelands.

I shrugged Schera off. "It seems *the Master* isn't really much for compassion after all, is he?"

She winced, but didn't stop me this time. With the lord out of the way, no power in this world could keep me from stepping between Mascha and Raffi, slaves' gossip be damned.

Mascha's voice filtered out of the room, absent its bite. "Are you alright?"

My feet squeaked to a halt between the open doors, and I stared at the sight before me.

Mascha knelt on one knee beside Raffi, dabbing at the boy's lip with a kerchief. Raffi was shaking, and his white shirt was stained red. Beyond them, a tray of silver teacups and finger foods were scattered across the floor. A small tea stain marred the gray-upholstered divan behind them. More tea ran down the wall to my left and pooled amidst the remnants of a teapot.

"I'm so sorry, Master," Raffi sobbed. "I've disgraced you. Please, forgive me."

Mascha folded the bloody kerchief, then placed a clean side to Raffi's lip. "You've done nothing of the sort."

"But—"

"It was the lord's fault. That fool wouldn't know grace if it bedded his favorite wife."

Raffi's surprise reflected mine, his wide eyes gleaming in the light from nearby saphyrum lanterns.

I glanced toward Schera, who cast a cautious look at me before slipping into the room. I watched numbly as she began collecting the broken teapot.

Raffi cleared his throat and started to rise. "I-I should await you at the post, Master."

Before my protests could fully form, Mascha hauled Raffi up. "Never mind the post. We'll go see Hasanthe and tell him what happened."

Mascha's attention strayed to Schera. I took an involuntary step forward, and he seemed to notice me for the first time. Our gazes locked, and he cringed.

That little uncertainty drained all the anger from me. Surely he wasn't worried I would object to such subterfuge. Not for this.

His expression shuttered, and 'the Master' returned. I marveled at how easily he slipped that mask into place.

"Schera, Maralla, you'll both vouch for him. I carried out his punishment promptly, and he spent the rest of the day recovering in the infirmary."

Schera's response was immediate. "He passed out at the post, Master."

It seemed I was in on more than one secret, then. How many times had he sold this ruse since I'd been here? How many times had I failed to notice it?

I stepped inside the room and pulled the doors shut. When I turned back, Mascha was watching me. I dropped my gaze and hurried to right the tray and teacups. "It was gruesome, Master."

I took care kneeling in the short dancer's skirt, my movements caged by the corset. Cups *tinked* against polished silver, and for once I didn't consider the damage I could do with the cutlery. I reached for the cuts of sausage and smoked cheese.

The scent of iron stung my nostrils, and I looked up as Mascha's rift opened in front of me. He caught my stare again, his face lit by the glow of Aether. For the span of five heartbeats, we studied each other. I couldn't shake the feeling that the man before me was someone other than my captor.

At last, he pulled Raffi into the void and disappeared.

I knelt, staring at the place where the rift had snapped shut until the white-rimmed halo faded from my vision.

Could I dare believe what I'd just witnessed? Was our situation so similar, then, that Mascha's shows of brutality could be likened to my own performance as a slave? I *had* to play my part or lose my chance at getting home. If *he* was a man among villains, perhaps we were both one slip of a mask—one ill-timed outburst—away from ruin.

Which was he, then—a man or a villain? And why did it intrigue me so much?

I had three more weeks. What better way to spend them than finding out for certain?

Chapter Fifteen

Mascha

Kestra Hyanaro proved elusive, even for the costly scrying magic of the Rorsch Hekkai. Either the man was heavily warded, or Simmion had already killed him.

Morning sun heated my skin, and scents of hay and manure hung in the air. Only the sea breeze made today's visit to my stables bearable.

Lord Simmion claimed he'd severed his contract with Hyanaro several days before the silk shipment left the docks. Hyanaro was crooked, according to Simmion, and the lord believed he must have falsified his continued work as a port hand in order to take the dockmaster's place and smuggle the keallite aboard.

It was plausible, but the timing was too convenient, and I suspected Simmion's outburst last week had been purely diversion. The lord had deliberately tripped Raffi, affording himself the chance to storm out with all the affront he could muster. It meant little when he hadn't produced paperwork to prove Hyanaro's annulled employment contract until days after our meeting—long enough to have it forged.

I leaned against the corral gate and rested my chin in my hand, mulling over Svaronei's latest report. His inquiries with Hyanaro's closest associates had traced the drug smuggler back to a private mercenary unit hired by Lord Yamon Baghara's household—one of few houses in the silk trade. But I sensed more pieces missing to this mystery. Keallite took great care to manufacture, and neither Simmion's nor Baghara's men were known for their skill with chemistry.

"*Meschiir*, watch this!"

Dust flew as Soltani steered the silver-dappled mare around the ring. The former urchin tapped his heels, and the creature broke into a run. Horse and rider leaped over a board spanning two barrels, and Soltani's victorious shout carried across the yard.

I would never admit it to Maralla, but she was right about the boy.

"Very good, Soltani," I called. "What else has Po taught you?"

"Watch this!" Narrow-eyed, he stared down the next obstacle.

Soltani had taken to the horses like a fighter to the sword. Watching him now, cantering the animal about the ring, he looked a far cry from the grimy orphan I'd rifted in nearly two weeks ago. His freshly trimmed hair whipped about the tailored shoulders of his riding coat, and his grin exposed the gap in his front teeth. I would have to make an appointment with the barber-surgeon to install a gold replacement soon.

I planted one foot on the bottom rung of the fence while Soltani led the horse in a tight circle around another set of barrels.

A thick, accented voice tugged my attention to the side. "Axe Man going to ride today?"

My stablemaster hauled himself up two rungs to level with me at the fence. Posenka Naftalli was not a handsome young man. With an undersized jaw, an oversized nose, and squat, stubby legs, he was the only offspring of Lord Naftalli's who didn't engage in the house's political games. So much the better for me, because Po more than made up for his deficit in looks with raw intelligence. He was so shrewd in matters of business, in fact, that I often joked he was the only man whose wrath I feared more than the Deal-Breaker's.

Tension tugged at my cheek, half-smile, half-grimace. "And have the foul thing throw me again?"

Po snorted. "Is entertainment. Show Lefty what not to do."

'Lefty' was as much a prophetic reminder for Soltani as it was an endearment. His right arm would be removed if I had to carry out my initial threat, but if he'd already earned such a name from Po, the two would be thicker than thieves by year's end.

"I'm afraid I have to decline, *amii*."

I had no love for horses, and I preferred to keep my feet firmly on the ground. It was a mutual disdain, too. Turns out even the most docile creatures shied from the smell of Aether and blood.

Po elbowed my ribs. "Don't want to make a fool of yourself in front of your woman? Agh, can't blame you."

I lifted my chin toward Maralla, who was busying herself brushing down one of the older horses in the stable. "Why is that?"

"That one, the way she look at you..." Po puffed his cheeks and blew out a whistle. "She eat Axe Man alive."

"Astute little bastard, aren't you?"

"Is obvious. Axe Man like her, too."

Leave it to Po to pick up on the subtle things. In the days since Maralla and I had made our agreement, it was as if part of me had come alive for the first time in years. I lost more piccara games to her than I won. Her conversation, though aggravating, challenged me to see things from an outsider's perspective. And while I still desired her, I had come to appreciate her presence in my bed despite knowing I would never have her.

Each night, after all day kneeling at my feet, she made certain I knew her subservience was a charade only, and I was no more her master than I'd ever been. Her cutting glares and creative obscenities no longer annoyed me, but excited me. I still searched my rooms every night for weapons she might have hidden, and I was almost disappointed she hadn't tried to gut me in my sleep.

Po regarded me, both eyebrows raised. They edged higher when I realized I was grinning like an idiot. My laughter shook me head to toe.

Maralla's eyes met mine across the distance. Her hand slowed in the horse's mane, her brows furrowing. She'd been prone to more contemplative silences this week. We hadn't spoken of the morning she'd awoken nestled against my chest or the lie she'd caught me in to protect Raffi, but it was clear I'd become more of a curiosity to her than an opponent.

A ghost of a smile touched her lips. It echoed my own, as if we shared some private amusement. In a way, I supposed we did.

After another too-long pause, she went back to brushing the horse, and I cleared my throat. "I admit, I find her fascinating."

"Women are bad for business." Po tapped his temple. "Go right to a man's head."

"And you would know. Such vast wisdom for your meager twenty-two years." I nudged him. "Gods help us all when you stop wetting your cloutslings."

His expression pinched. "Agh! Axe Man see." His knuckles rapped my breastbone. "One day."

Po dropped to the ground with a crunch of sand and stuck two fingers in his mouth. His shrill whistle brought Soltani to the gate.

The boy's grin threatened to split his face in two. "Did you see, *meschiir*?"

"I did, indeed." I chuckled as he dismounted, then clapped my stablemaster on the shoulder. "You keep practicing—you'll sit that saddle better than Po before you know it."

I winked at the boy and turned for the palace doors. Maralla gave the horse one last pet and stepped into the midmorning light. Reason failed me at the thought of her sun-warmed lavender skin beneath my hands.

I shook myself. "Come, *rascha*. You'll attend me on the training grounds today."

Wooden swords crashed against shields and posts. The yard stank of sweat, and exposed arms and chests glittered with a film of sand. My men knew better than to heckle my slaves, but a few still took blows from opportunistic opponents when their attention strayed toward Maralla.

I smirked. Silonas slay me, but I knew that feeling.

One of my commanders excused himself from his conversation with a fellow trainer and closed with me beneath the mezzanine.

"Rorsch Hekkai." Catos bowed, pressing one gauntleted fist to his cuirass. Sweat streamed down his leathery brow and settled in the lines framing his mouth. "The heat rises."

I acknowledged his unspoken question with a nod. "Summer is nearly upon us. Move your exercises one hour earlier to prepare for solstice."

"Yes, *meschiir*."

"How fare the new recruits?"

Catos clicked his tongue. "I've seen better swordsmanship from one-armed boys. That one there"—he pointed to a man in the third row—"can't manage a parry to save his life."

"You've checked his grip?"

"First thing. Boy says his elbow pains him."

"Has he ever broken it or experienced severe injury?"

"I... didn't ask."

I frowned. "Take him to Hasanthe. Have him check for bone spurs. I'll handle the rest of this session."

Catos winced, likely sensing my displeasure. "Right away, Rorsch Hekkai." He turned to the recruit. "Lassero, attend me!"

My frown deepened as they departed. My commanders were supposed to put our soldiers' well-being above their performance, given that one could not exist without the other. In case Catos had forgotten this, I would assign others to monitor him in the coming days.

Another trainer approached me, this one with a recruit needing more instruction in ripostes and advances.

I nodded toward a nearby bench and bade Maralla sit. "This won't take long," I promised.

Half an hour later, I called a halt to the practice and dismissed the men early. At some point, I'd discarded my vest, and my shirt clung to me in sweaty patches. My trousers bore dusty stains, and a small stone had lodged in the sole of my boot.

The cacophony of returned equipment, relieved voices, and shuffling feet faded as I toweled off my face. When the last man left the training yard, Maralla rose, expression incredulous.

I glanced around for stragglers. "What is it?"

She folded her arms. "Is that really how you train your men? No wonder they're so easy to kill."

The Rorsch Hekkai were one of the most elite fighting forces in the world. Stormy indignation arose, but I hesitated in bringing it to bear. It was Maralla's signature tactic to provoke me to insecurity. Not to mention, she'd killed four of my men during her takeover of my armory in her first month at the palace.

My eyes narrowed. "Explain."

"None of them worked on footwork at all while they practiced. Footwork is the foundation for good swordplay, and yet only two of the lot seemed to have any idea what they were doing." She looked me up and down. "Even yours could use some work. I thought you were supposed to be a Champion."

A tactician and a commander in her own right. Only now did I truly take it in. The set of her spine, the self-assuredness, the faint definition of muscle returned to her since her confinement at sea. She met my gaze, standing mostly naked in the shadow of my palace, and dared chastise me for the rust I'd collected on my form.

I'd never wanted to kiss her more.

Heat gathered in my ear tips and I turned away, feigning embarrassment. The glint of steel in a nearby weapons rack caught my attention.

I crossed the packed sand and chose a pair of swords from the rack. After checking their balance, I returned to Maralla and offered her the lighter blade.

"Alright, Commander, you have my attention. Show me what you can do."

Her jaw went slack as she took the sword. She glanced around, but there was no one to see us. "With live steel?"

"What's the matter? Afraid you'll cut yourself?"

Shock drained away as quickly as it had come, and she glowered at me. "Maybe I'll take the opportunity to run you through."

If my grin grew any wider, my lips would surely reach my ears. "I suppose if you do, you can try to make the same agreement with Tasari. I don't expect he'll be as forthcoming, though."

Maralla regarded me, then looked the sword over and hefted its weight. She spun the sword blade-down and rested the point between her feet. "Fine, but I want armor, too."

Gods, I loved her fire.

"Not a chance."

Her glare returned. "It's only proper."

"I'm not that ignorant, Maralla."

"I hardly see how you think this is a fair fight. You have the advantage of wearing real clothes. At least allow me a shirt and trousers."

It wasn't an unreasonable request. I pointed with my sword to a bin full of spare linens. "If you find something in there that fits, it is yours."

She eyed me suspiciously, then stalked away to sort through the fabric. A few minutes later, we stood in the sunlight facing each other, her oversized shirt knotted behind her back. The trousers fit loosely about her legs, and she'd chopped over a handspan off the bottom to accommodate her stature, but an extra span of rope pulled them snug at her hips.

"Should you wish to up the stakes," I said, basking in the wildness of her appearance, "I'm willing to make another deal."

She matched me step for step as we circled one another. "I'm listening."

I tipped my sword up. "First man to draw blood chooses dinner and the activity for this evening."

"*Any* activity?"

"Within reason, of course." I let my eyes linger suggestively.

Maralla's gaze sharpened. "Deal."

When our swords clashed for the first time, I couldn't help but laugh. My mirth seemed contagious, too. Her teeth flashed in a feral grin as we traded blows and danced our way across the yard.

Right away, I could tell she was an accomplished fighter. She used her speed and smaller build to her advantage, never allowing our swords to lock and pit my strength against hers.

Her footwork *was* impeccable. Twice, my Foresight predicted moves that my eyes didn't see, so quick and well-balanced were her movements. She whirled, white braids flying, every bit the warrior queen. Had she been at her peak, allowed to train during her enslavement, she might have stood a chance at besting me.

Steel rang against steel, our feet scuffed the sand, and my breathing grew ragged. Maralla fought until her sword arm flagged, and I pushed the advantage with my greater endurance. Stepping inside her guard, I locked our hilts together and spun the blade out of her hand. Her sword hit the ground three paces away, and I leveled my weapon at her throat.

"Yield."

Face flushed, she stared up the blade's length and lifted her hands.

Without warning, her Aetherial image split in two.

A feint to the left and a roll for her sword, or a blade-grab and a bold dip beneath my sword arm. Either motion wouldn't rob my victory, so I stepped backward and let her real intent play out.

Both images converged again, too late for me to react. Maralla tackled me to the sand.

I let my sword fall and seized her shirt, rolling with her. She thwarted my first pin and my second, sand caking our skin and sweat soaking our clothes.

Another split image coalesced: her lips crashing against mine, or a throat-chop that would gain her the upper hand. I raised an arm to block the blow, certain the kiss was another ruse.

Maralla stilled.

She was straddling me, thighs snug against my hips, her mouth only fingerspans from mine. Her braids tumbled around me, caging me in shadow. Uncertainty stayed my next move, and my grip tightened on her waist.

Our chests heaved in uneven time. My heart threatened to crack my sternum in two. She leaned closer, and I swallowed. I couldn't smell her *oeloraati* anymore, but her heat pressed against me, and desire coiled in my abdomen.

Her palm slid up my chest, fire trailing in its wake. Her other hand splayed flat in the sand beside my head. My stomach fluttered, and my mind reeled at the impossible reality unfurling before me. I wanted her. I wanted her badly.

She brushed her nose against mine, and her amethyst eyes closed.

Our mouths collided. Her lips devoured mine, claimed them, as if they could never belong to anyone else again. She arched into me, and my arms slid around her, pulled her closer. I couldn't draw breath enough to resurface from the storm she summoned inside me. Gods help me, I hoped I never did.

Her command of our kiss left me trembling. I ceded to her, parted my lips for her tongue, seeking, begging for more.

Her teeth sank into my lower lip. A cry burst from me, the pain so sharp and unexpected that my eyes watered. I recoiled, tasting blood.

First-drawn blood.

Maralla sat up, mouth swollen, grinning victoriously. She was still panting for air, but her eyes were clear of heady elation. "It seems the evening is mine, Mascha."

I couldn't even find it in me to be angry. I forced myself to my elbows, licking blood from the wound. Words failed me twice before I managed, "You sly woman."

Surprise lit her face. "In all fairness, you should have had me."

"Nevertheless, the terms of the deal are met." I tried to wipe my brow free of sweat, but only succeeded in smearing sand across my forehead. Maralla's grin widened, and I chuckled to work loose a sudden tightness in my throat. "Name your prize, Commander."

She lingered astride me while she considered, her touch forge-hot against my abdomen. I avoided drawing attention to her closeness, bewildered by the pleasure it brought me just to have her near.

I banished the thought. Po was right; I was losing sight of my objective. I couldn't get close to her. I had to get her out of here.

"We'll have boiled crab and braised sprouts for dinner." Maralla's head tilted. "And afterward, you'll take me swimming."

Both reasonable requests. I dipped my chin. "As you command."

Chapter Sixteen

Maralla

Ocean surf pounded the coastline to an unsteady beat. Saltwater chilled my feet and pulled sand from beneath me with every step. Light reflected off the whitecaps in shades of orange and red, but it wasn't the sunset I kept coming back to.

It was the slaver wading barefoot in the waves beside me.

Ever since Schera's revelation and the incident with Raffi, I'd paid more attention to Mascha's interactions with others. He wore his cutthroat persona for nobles, merchants, and new acquisitions, while his softer side came out around his personal slaves.

But the man he was with me no longer fell toward either extreme. He was witty, playful, and genuinely seemed to appreciate my opinion. Mira help me, the way he'd laughed in the stables today reminded me of Nalerta. My mate had never sat a horse well, either, and Mascha endured his stablemaster's ribbing with grace.

I couldn't help thinking I was seeing the man behind the illusions. I'd never admit I liked what I saw.

We had the palace beach to ourselves, apart from the stray seabird or mosaic turtle. Though Hasanthe had healed Mascha's lip, I'd caught him touching the spot a few times over dinner, and again while he'd watched me swim.

I hadn't expected him to respond to my kiss that way. Surprise, lust, aggression—those I'd prepared myself for. I hadn't expected passion or tenderness. Least of all, surrender. I almost felt bad about ruining it. Never mind that the taste of him, the warmth of his lips, the press of his tongue still lingered.

A wave broke against my thighs, dousing the heat that might have otherwise swept through me. "Mascha."

He blinked three times in rapid succession before looking at me—the tell I'd come to know as his Foresight lending ghostly predictions of the future. I sucked in a breath, but his gaze darted away before I could form words.

"Schera says your lessons are going well."

They weren't, actually—I still couldn't get the follower's steps of the amaariana to flow properly, despite nearly a week of practice—but the distance in his tone made me hesitate. It was the first time he'd spoken since the sun began to set. He'd been quieter than usual at dinner; now I sensed that silence was something more than distraction.

I relented with a sigh. "She's a great teacher."

"She is."

More tightness. Further retreat. I didn't know if he could hear sound with his Foresight, or if he'd just intuited my intentions by what he'd Seen. A vein in my temple throbbed as I considered whether his clairvoyance of my apology was good enough.

Surf thundered down the beach. Birds called overhead. A distant bell rang across the water, but the silence between us was louder still, and it made me squirm. I summoned my courage again, determined to loosen whatever knot had tangled between us. "Mascha, I'm—"

"House Emisett will be here tomorrow evening." He cut me off with a pointed look. The Master surfaced once more. "I suspect he'll request you seal any deal that results."

Heat flared in my chest, but not because of my so-called duty. I was prepared to fuck my way to freedom if I had to; it was the loss of his candor that stung.

Last week, Mascha had blocked three requests for me while the herbs sped my *oeloraati* along. Once the risk of conception had passed, he'd reminded me with each visit that any deal could require my presence. His guests thus far had chosen their own favorites instead, but my evening would inevitably come. When it did, he cautioned, I should perform enthusiastically, or the rumors surrounding the breaking of *Johtan Shasnaram* would come undone.

But this wasn't about House Emisett at all.

I'd thought kissing him would be as meaningless to Mascha as kissing a slave or sealing a deal. Instead, he seemed to be rebuilding the walls that once stood between us. We'd established a truce of sorts while I was battling my desire, and he hadn't used it against me, then. With a wince, I realized I'd crossed a line today using his desire against him.

I shouldn't care. I should think he deserved to experience his own brand of manipulation. So why did it bother me?

I steeled my spine and reached for him. "I'm sorry."

He wrenched his arm away. "Don't."

"Is that supposed to frighten me? You should know by now that doesn't work."

"*Kas hadem.* You forget yourself." Black anger pooled in his expression, his face half-silhouetted by the sun. "I've obviously been too lenient with you."

No *way* was I going to deal with this surly bluster again. I stepped closer, fighting against the waves that tried to force me back. "I didn't know that kiss would mean as much to you as it did."

"It meant nothing."

His denial patched the crack in his armor, though the weakness lingered. Instinct urged me to strike at the spot again, but I still needed him on my side.

Holding his molten gaze was akin to walking on coals, but I endured the heat. "All the same, I'm sorry."

He scoffed and spun away, muttering something unintelligible in Rillanese. I let him stalk partway back to the beach, an odd pressure mounting in my chest. I was losing him, and while a part of me insisted the slaver's feelings didn't matter, a greater part recognized a man trying to insulate himself from further pain.

I had to do something. I had to get the witty, playful Mascha back.

Another wave crested my thighs. I scooped water off the whitecap and launched it across the short distance. It struck Mascha's lower back.

He slowed, but didn't stop.

I did it again, slinging an armful that fanned his rolled trousers.

He pivoted, lip curling.

I lobbed the third scoop at his face. He spluttered around a roar and rubbed his eyes. Once he recovered enough to stare at me, I grinned in challenge and bolted.

Surf and sand robbed me of speed. My tired muscles screamed, hindered by our swordplay, but I labored through the waves until I reached the water's edge. Mascha stood a few dozen paces from me, his mouth hanging open. He took a careful step toward me, and I bolted again. Feet slapping the sand, wet braids flying, I tore down the beach, only turning back when a less hurried set of footsteps sounded behind me.

No less confused, but no longer scowling, Mascha slowed, watching me like he'd never given chase to someone for amusement before.

With a pang of sorrow, I realized he probably never had.

"*Rascha—*" he began.

I darted back into the water, forcing out a cry somewhere between a laugh and a scream.

Shells dug into my soles and fish scattered. I tripped on a piece of driftwood buried in the sand and went down with a splash. Salt burned my eyes, and sand scored my knees as I fought to regain my feet.

"Maralla," Mascha called. He waded back into the surf, brows furrowed. "Laangor's blight, what's gotten into you?"

I spat water and splashed him as he approached. "Certainly not you." I side-stepped his grab for me. "Unless you can catch me first."

Before he could overthink it, I slapped more water into his face and dove under the waves. I surfaced several spans farther out, hoping the incentive would enliven him. Inevitably, it meant giving in to something he'd tried for months to get from me, but that was the language they spoke here. It was the only apology I knew for certain he would accept.

"Come on, Mascha," I taunted. "Come and get me."

He started toward me with the slow implacability of an avalanche, his powerful thighs parting the water. Tingles rippled through me—a thrill that set my body alight like *oeloraati* come again. I stepped backward, and my knees turned to butter. He fixed me with his predatory gaze and dove fully clothed beneath the waves.

I'd always thought I was a strong swimmer. Mascha was much stronger. He cleared a third of the distance in three powerful strokes, and I dove in a panic to reclaim the lead.

I made it back to shore before he snagged my dress. I twisted away and laughed. His face finally split into a cautious grin, and he gave chase in earnest.

He caught me easily, wrapping both arms around my waist. We hit the dry beach in a heap, his torso pinning me as I sank to the wrists in flour-fine sand. My laughter carried down the shoreline, followed by his more reserved amusement as he rolled me onto my back. I bared my teeth and hooked my heels around his thighs.

Sand rained down in sheets. His hair dripped onto my collarbone and his wet clothes pressed into my skin, his eyes searching mine. I tilted my head up in silent offering. When he hesitated, I grabbed him by the nape and pulled him down.

His mouth lavished mine with earnest hunger, and I met him with all the passion he'd poured into me this afternoon. He tasted of sea salt, fine wine, and tropical fruit. Even beneath the smell of the ocean, that distinctly male scent caused my legs to curl more tightly around him. His arousal ground into my center, and my sharply expelled breath lent him encouragement. He arched into me with a moan that traveled across my lips.

Just as he'd surrendered before, Mascha ceded his mouth to me, and my tongue brushed his with unwavering demand. Fire erupted in my belly, and my eyes closed at the force of it.

The truth of my desire became clearer the longer we kissed. I could tell myself this was just an assurance that Mascha would adhere to our agreement, but with every brush of his tongue, the ache between my thighs grew.

For who he was, for what he did, for how he held me captive, I still hated him. This was only to keep things amicable between us. I couldn't lose sight of that.

I hiked up the obscenely short hem of my dress and broke our kiss. "Your prize, Mascha."

A rumble passed through him. One sandy hand came to rest on my hip, and his beard brushed my chin as he captured my lips once more. Patient and unhurried were the kisses he placed along my neck, but his voice was strained.

"Not here."

My brows tensed. I gazed up at the stars brightening in the twilight sky and sifted my fingers into his hair. I hadn't coupled with anyone since Nalerta. Under the stars had been our favorite place. A sudden sting pinched my eyes shut, and my throat tightened.

Mascha was right. It couldn't be here.

Cool air and shifting sand reclaimed my attention. Mascha pulled back, frowning. "What is it?"

Something more than lust arose within me—a need for closeness, a longing so acutely painful that it stole my breath. I swallowed against a stone three times before I could speak. "Take me to bed."

After another moment of scrutiny, he rose and summoned a rift. Aetherial wind slashed sand across my arms and legs. Mascha lifted me gently and stepped through the misty black void to his balcony. The travel left me reeling.

I touched his face as he carried me into his bedroom, trying to gauge his mercurial mood. He offered a weak smile, then set me down on the tile. Mascha slipped the wet straps of my dress off my shoulders and let it fall.

"Come." He took my hand. "You'll not go to bed covered in sand."

Gleaming marble reflected fading light across the washroom floor. Mascha summoned more magic, and the sharp, metallic odor of Aetherial flame quickly gave way to the scent of burning wood. Once he opened the tap, he turned back to me and paused again.

In three strides, I crossed the floor to divest him of his clothes. The wet fabric fell in a pile, and I stepped over them as I put my hand on Mascha's chest. He let me guide him backward into the water, where, finally, whatever reservations he'd been entertaining seemed to wash away with the sand.

Steam rose around us. For once, I let myself explore his expanse of chiseled muscle, marveling at how he shuddered beneath my touch. His palms slid around my waist, coming to rest gently, not possessively, on my lower back. My fingers traced one of many old scars across his chest.

I looked up at him, and when our eyes met, I saw only a man, not a villain.

Mascha's dark hair fell in wet locks around his face, and droplets glistened in his beard. He studied me as if I were a complex equation, his head lowering until I could feel his breath on my lips. I pressed him flat against the wall and lifted onto my toes to kiss him.

In some ways, I needed this as much as he did. Over a year had passed since I'd sought a man's touch purely for comfort. Nalerta had always known what I needed before I could voice it. We'd been married so long, I'd taken all that easy contact for granted.

Mascha touched my cheek, drawing my gaze back to him. He didn't speak, but that subtle crease in his brow returned.

I threw myself into our kisses, cupping his face, stroking the points of his ears. He released me only long enough to retrieve the soap and lathered every part of my upper body with care. When he paused below my navel, I took the bar and pressed his hand lower in silent demand.

He obliged me, fingers seeking, deepening our kisses beneath the shower stream until I could no longer hold myself upright. Mascha turned with me, bracing us against the wall as his fingertips spun pleasure. Before long, I was panting, gripping his shoulders, crying out as my climax nearly sent me to my knees. Mascha held me to him, then kissed me as if I were the most cherished woman in his world.

Scabbing gods, it was intoxicating. I could see why Schera and the other palace slaves doted on him now. If he could make anyone feel this special, it was no wonder they vied for his attention.

The reservoir ran dry too soon, but we took our time leaving the steamy washroom. He slicked my skin with rose oil and wicked moisture from my braids with a towel.

He takes care of his own.

The healer's words provoked a new ache in my heart. Mascha's careful focus, that intense set to his brows, the patience in his movement. He took care of his own, true, but who took care of him?

Little more than two weeks separated me from the gala. Nineteen more days of servitude. Only a few more to close the sale, and from there I would plan my freedom. Life for Mascha would go back to normal, and he would likely forget about me in his long line of processed slaves. We would both get what we wanted. Still, as he cupped my cheek and planted a kiss on my forehead, I couldn't help thinking he seemed lonely.

His erection was still half-hard between us. I reached for him and leaned up to catch his mouth. Mascha returned my kiss, but extracted himself even as he stiffened against my palm.

My brows shot upward. I pulled back. "What's wrong?"

"If you don't—" His voice broke, and his throat bobbed once. "I would just like to hold you tonight, if it's all the same to you."

His request gutted and flattered me all at once. It was rawness, vulnerability, and need all wrapped in one delicate package. That he sought such comfort with me confirmed what I suspected. Even surrounded by loving slaves and clamoring nobles, Mascha was as alone in this wretched country as I was.

The walls between us crumbled again. I wouldn't refuse this chance to see more of the man behind the mask.

I held out my hand. "*Tipori*?"

He took it and let out a shaky breath. "Please."

Chapter Seventeen

Mascha

I GATHERED MY WHIP from a ring on the wall and hooked it onto my belt. Tasari hefted his leather satchel. "You're going to like this one. Vhedja says she fought him the whole way."

Impatience quickened my step. Vhedja had come to call much too early; the sun had not yet risen. Extracting myself from Maralla's arms to deal with this disruption had been the hardest thing I'd done in years. "She's a relinquishment?"

"From House Akaaris. Enghal said she bit off one of his men's fingers." Tasari giggled like an ingrate. "Didn't like the way he touched her, I guess."

That sense of autonomy didn't come from native-born stock. She must have come from overseas. "Her name?"

"Raenara."

"Brogrenti? We don't see many of those."

He shrugged. "She's exotic. You know how the men love red hair. Her papers say she sold for almost fifty thousand gran."

"To House Akaaris?" I didn't hide my surprise. "Enghal doesn't have that kind of capital."

Tasari lifted an eyebrow. "You think it's dirty money?"

"It very well could be." Funds like that were always worth a second look, especially to ensure they had filtered through the Deal-Breaker's tithe collection channels. "Have our clerks send for an audit."

"I'll put it on my list."

We walked side by side down the curling staircase, where sounds of muffled rage carried up from the foyer. Vhedja waited there, seated atop a large wine cask from which the screams came. I limbered my back and cracked my neck. The sooner I subdued this new acquisition, the sooner I could get back to bed.

Tasari set his satchel down and leaned against the balustrade. Hasanthe shuffled in from a side corridor, still collecting himself from sleep. I studied the Aetherial images my Foresight presented me and readied my whip.

"Alright, Vhedja," I said. "At your leisure."

Vhedja hopped off the barrel and shoved it over, dumping the contents onto the floor.

Raenara was a mass of flaming curls and freckles, fair skin, and ample breasts. Her left eye was swollen, and her back was crosshatched with welts nearly as red as her hair. Her snarl echoed off the walls, and she wasted no time before bolting.

I snapped my whip outward and caught her ankle. She fell with a yelp and a long string of Brogrenti curses. Her fingers dug at the coiled leather to no avail. I stalked closer.

The sight of her struggle twisted something inside my gut. My boots squeaked to a stop as if I'd been yanked by a lead. I curled my fingers tighter on the whip, but for the first time, I couldn't force myself past the sensation—the knowledge that, within a week, my near-perfect record of breaking slaves would snuff out this woman's autonomy like wind to a candle.

Normally, the thought bolstered me. Normally, I could reason that my methods were more humane than violence.

Coercion is still rape, no matter how you color it.

My arm trembled.

Tasari and Vhedja were watching me. Hasanthe shifted on his feet.

I couldn't delay any longer. "Raenara, stop this nonsense. You are in the palace now. There is no hope of escape."

"Caelyn curse ye, ye pompous shitelicker!"

Her accent was a novelty. That was an insult I hadn't heard before, at least. Reclaiming the air of indifference that would see me through this exchange, I forced a smile. "You've a colorful vocabulary, I see. But by week's end, I guarantee I will put that mouth to better use." I extracted my whip from her ankle, and she shot to her feet again. Her ice-blue eyes darted from me to Vhedja to the entrance, clearly weighing her chances.

When she ran the second time, I channeled saphyric energy, dipping my will into the flow of Aether. With one hand, I shaped my slave-binding and snared her in bands of black mist. She went down hard, arms pinned to her sides, thighs pressed together.

"I know you are angry." I kept my voice calm despite my own disquiet. She bucked against my magic, and the tremors of her struggle rippled down my outstretched arm. I paced toward her and crouched down. "The gods have cursed you with a cruel fate, but this need not be so unpleasant."

Raenara spat at me. I caught the moisture with my free hand and smeared it across her face.

"There are simple rules in my home," I continued. "You will be assigned duties, which you will do without complaint. You'll be respectful of other slaves and my staff, and you'll attend me and my guests whenever I wish it. Most importantly, you will not take any pleasure that is not explicitly given. Your body is mine now, and you'll not take what doesn't belong to you. Say you understand."

By the time I finished administering my usual speech, Raenara was quivering with rage. "Laangor will have yer entrails."

I stroked her cheek, more for show than a desire to touch the poor wretch. "Not before you break, *rascha*." I coiled my whip and returned it to my belt. "Hasanthe, shave her and fit her with steel."

"Yes, Mascha."

I hesitated, then pressed on, banishing my uncertainty with one decisive swallow. There were too many eyes on me already; I couldn't deviate from protocol twice. "Tasari, give her a double dose of raspaati. We'll see how long her ill-mannered behavior lasts."

"With pleasure, brother."

A double dose would be even more torturous. I steeled myself against the urge to withdraw the command. This was a proven method, stimulating desire and barring the slave from their own pleasure. Normally, I wouldn't cage them right away, instead opting for raspaati only and dragon pepper oil on their hands to stay them from touching. But I needed her obedience quickly.

She began to struggle again as Tasari approached with his satchel. He knelt and pulled out a vial, a piglet's bladder, and a cured quill.

As he filled the bladder with liquid raspaati, the whites of the woman's eyes bulged. "W-what is that? Ye can't—"

"But he can," I snapped. "Let this be your first lesson, Raenara. You are subject to my will." I fed the slave-binding a slow stream of magic to keep it strong. "Beyond these injections, you will only be harmed if you disrupt my household. I assure you, you *want* to please me. The alternative only leads to suffering."

Tears glistened in her eyes as I rose from my crouch. Tasari drove the quill into her arm, and she cried out.

The churning in my gut redoubled, and I turned away. But I already had one unruly woman drawing the Deal-Breaker's ire. Every move I made was weighted now.

"Vhedja, kindly escort my new slave to the infirmary for her fitting." As the Aetherian hauled the bound woman up, I beckoned to Hasanthe. "Assign her to Emmi for palace etiquette, and have Raffi draw up a list of chores. I'm hosting House Emisett this evening, so I'll check on her tomorrow."

Hasanthe dipped his chin. "Your command, Mascha. Oh"—he stopped me before I could retreat to the stairs—"we received a bird from the Deal-Breaker's emissary. Saarach wants an update on Maralla."

I bristled, surprising myself with the burst of protective fury. "Tell him she will be auctioned at the gala, and that I anticipate a hefty sum. That should appease the whoreson."

If Hasanthe was taken aback by my vehemence, he knew better than to mention it. "As you wish."

I took the stairs two at a time, and when I was out of sight of the foyer, I rifted the rest of the way to my chambers. Careful not to make a sound, I slipped inside and locked the door.

In my bedroom, Maralla's soft snores eased some of the tightness in my shoulders. I paused, studying the gentle curl of her fingers in the moonlight, the soft rise and fall of her chest. The warrior's runes across her nose, forehead, and chin normally lent to her fierce appearance, but with her lips parted and white eyelashes brushing her cheeks, much of her intensity had abandoned her.

She was so beautiful, and I was indeed a fool.

I discarded my whip, stripped down, and climbed back under the sheets. Maralla murmured something into her pillow, and I resisted my desire to pull her closer. This ceasefire masquerading as intimacy was too fragile to carry forward into morning, but I'd have been lying if I said I didn't long for it. She was everything my slaves weren't: stubborn, irascible, maddeningly perspicacious. A moment of unguarded affection from her felt more valuable than gold.

As if she sensed my attention lingering, Maralla groaned and rubbed one eye. "...time is it?"

"Almost dawn."

"Ungodly hour." She grumbled again and, with her eyes still cinched shut, pawed her way back onto my chest.

Too stunned to move, I lay there staring at the canopy until she shrugged my arm around her with a violent jerk of her shoulder. Despite my misgivings, I grinned into her braids and surrendered easily to that demand.

As I drew circles over her ribs with my fingertips, Maralla slipped her palm over my heart. Its beat was still elevated from my dash up the stairs, but it stuttered at her touch.

"More nightmares?" she asked.

Shame shuddered through me. I couldn't taint this moment by telling her where I'd gone. It was easier to lie, to preserve this illusion of the man I could be with her.

"*Ciir.*"

She sighed and nestled deeper. I expected that to be the end of it.

"It wasn't your fault."

My breath hitched. Distant memories of blood, pain, and death tumbled into my mind.

It was. It was my fault.

Maralla pressed her hand more firmly against my chest, as if she might rise.

I swallowed and tightened my grip on her. "Go back to sleep."

For once, she didn't argue. Maralla relaxed, her body draped over mine, and I pressed a kiss to the top of her head. There was another hour, at least, before sunrise.

Another hour for me to convince myself she was anything but mine.

Chapter Eighteen

Mascha

Striking the deal with House Emisett didn't take long. The merchant arrived early with three slaves and both of his younger sisters in tow. Each slave toted sample saddles and tack, which Po and Soltani tested in the corral. Once they'd agreed on their preferences, Emisett and I haggled to a price and drew up the contract. Then we retired to the red hall for dinner.

"I assume you've been watching the very public dispute between the Ideghis and Amin houses." Emisett sipped his wine and sank a little more in his seat. He crossed one ankle over his knee. "What do you make of it, *meschiir*?"

I held out my glass to Maralla, who stood at my right shoulder. She poured wine while I considered my response. I'd not been watching, in truth. My focus for much of the past two weeks had been split between Maralla and finding Kestra Hyanaro. Moreover, Wali Amin's attempts to discredit Neborov Ideghis V only served one purpose for me: ensuring Ideghis was nowhere near the Chancellor's palace on the night of the gala.

"Lord Amin raises a good point," I said, thinking back to my meeting with Wali and Anelliiq. "Too many mines under one house's control creates a monopoly on the trade."

Emisett's gaze sharpened, every bit the businessman seeking a morsel of gossip. "You agree with Lord Amin, then? That House Ideghis already holds too much sway in the saphyrum market?"

I sensed the trap before it sprang shut. My bias could heavily influence public opinion, and I would not be maneuvered into making enemies with either of the strongest houses in Rillion. "I prefer to let the trade commission handle it. They can conduct a full review of Neborov's assets and determine if the sale would be detrimental to consumers."

The merchant thrust out his lower lip. He glanced toward Vassu and Farrah as they cleared our third course, then leveled with me again. "A pragmatic answer, as always."

I chuckled. "Don't look so disappointed."

"I admit, I was hoping for a more passionate response." He gestured around the lavish dining room. "With your influence, I thought you'd take a more active stance in matters of trade and politics."

Maralla had said something similar not long ago. I set my glass on the table. "The trade commission and the senate do a fine job of handling those affairs. My focus is on domestic security and maintaining peace."

He tipped his glass toward me, then drained the last. Maralla stepped forward to refill it. Emisett's hand strayed between her legs.

I stilled.

"I suppose you do have the nobler task." His fingers trailed up the inside of Maralla's thigh. She kept her eyes low, as a fully processed slave should, and didn't bristle as she had in the past. Even so, I found it hard to breathe. "I heard about the ship you captured in the channel. Keallite is a monstrous thing."

"Indeed."

Maralla poured the last of the wine into the merchant's glass and stood poised as he stroked the back of her knee. Her dress attached to the front of her collar and plunged down her midline, leaving her breasts bare.

Emisett pinched one pert nipple and grinned. "Do you like that, *rascha*?"

Maralla's face twitched. "Yes, *meschiir*."

"You are a pretty one."

I tore my gaze away and forced another sip of wine. It wasn't unusual for guests to fondle the slaves after a deal had been struck. I usually engaged in such behavior myself, but all three of Emisett's male slaves knelt untouched beside the hearth, and his sisters quivered like fawns missing their mother.

Emisett licked his lips. "You know, I heard a rumor the other day at the port that might be of interest to you."

Vassu placed the main course—butter-seared dove and herbs—in front of me. Farrah likewise served the merchant, but he paid no mind to the delicacy, nor the dark-eyed beauty who delivered it.

I picked up my cutlery and lifted a brow, feigning nonchalance. "Are you going to keep me in suspense, then?"

If Emisett's hand strayed any higher up Maralla's skirts, he risked losing it.

But no, this was the ruse. I couldn't stop him no matter how badly I wanted to. My teeth scraped my fork, and the rich meat turned to ash in my mouth.

Emisett leaned forward. "House Akaaris has had several shipments from Eidosinia over the last few months, totaling over two hundred barrels of pure Cintoshi spirits."

That seized my attention. Cintoshi spirits in small quantities weren't suspicious, but large volumes of the potent liquor were used in the refinement of keallia flower—the main component in keallite production.

And Enghal Akaaris had recently purchased an exotic Brogrenti slave worth far more than the audit of his accounts suggested he could afford.

"Where did you hear this?"

"I overheard sailors from the *Ruby Red* talking. They said Akaaris must be a fool to pay for four round trips through the Straits."

How had my men missed this? How had *I* missed it? Our security measures were supposed to catch repeat shipments like this. That meant someone at the port had intentionally overlooked it.

Just as they had overlooked the silk crates.

Several houses of note dealt in the silk trade, but only one, House Baghara, was friendly with Akaaris. Baghara also had connections with both Hyanaro and Lomov Simmion.

Their operation took shape with only a little conjecture. House Akaaris likely made the keallite, then transferred it to House Baghara for packaging inside their silk shipments. House Simmion assured swift passage out of port and redirected any cargo searches at the ship's destination.

With this new information, I didn't need Hyanaro in order to demand a full search and seizure of all three estates. Once I finished sealing this deal with Emisett, I would have Hasanthe send a bird to Saarach. I needed the Deal-Breaker's approval to send Rorsch Hekkai into three separate houses, but I had no doubt I would get it.

I inclined my head and returned to my dinner. "The Deal-Breaker thanks you for this information."

Emisett finally reached for his cutlery. "You know I aim to please."

As he sliced into his dove, Maralla retreated to my side, and a knot loosened between my ribs. I breathed easier through the main course until Emisett's glass ran dry again.

Deeper into his cups now, Emisett made a brazen grab for Maralla's backside. She tensed, her gaze straying to the knife beside my plate. I started, then redirected the movement to adjust my seat when the Aetherial image of Maralla stabbing the man in the throat faded.

"Come here, you delectable thing."

Emisett pulled Maralla onto his lap, oblivious to his peril. She gasped, and the new bottle of wine nearly slipped from her fingers. He extracted it and set it beside his untouched dessert.

His teeth sank into her neck, and I curled my fist under the table. Sour heat built in my stomach as I picked at my cherry custard. Gods, I'd cautioned Maralla repeatedly about this, and here I was, fingerspans away from losing it. Both Emisett's sisters shrank further in their seats, as if they could sense my ire.

"Your Master is a lucky man, little *rascha*."

Maralla ceded to him with each nip along her collarbone. Her head tipped back, and a moan left her. The sound struck a flat note inside me, reverberating with the wrongness of it.

"You'll please me well tonight, won't you?"

"Yes, *meschiir*," she breathed.

This wasn't her. This wasn't the savage warrior woman who had commandeered my armory, my bed, my—

I stopped myself from following that thought to completion. This was her duty, the farce in which we'd agreed to act. But Silonas slay me, her performance was too convincing. I couldn't bear it.

Emisett claimed one of her nipples in his mouth. Maralla whimpered again, and the merchant's buoyant laughter made me bristle. Heat blazed through me, and I took hold of my dinner knife.

I remembered her pained expression on the beach last night, the unshed tears she'd tried to hide in the shower, how she'd offered herself to me to placate my ill temper. The woman I knew would have never done any of that, and now the thought of this whelp's cock inside her, of her riding him, of her forced compliance, threatened to undo me.

It shouldn't have. This was the way of things. Women were made for business in Rillion.

Not this woman.

I slipped the blade beneath the tablecloth and pressed it hard into my palm. Pain slashed through me, and blood welled. I dropped the knife and shoved my chair back, the squeal of wood masking the sound of steel hitting tile.

Emisett looked up as my shadow fell across him. His flicker of outrage dissolved into unease. "*Meschiir*?"

I reached under Maralla's skirts and clamped down on her womanhood.

She started, whirling on me. "Mas—"

"You're bleeding, *rascha*." I leveled one of my sternest looks on her and painted her nethers with a single firm swipe.

Maralla stared so long at my bloody fingers that Emisett responded first.

He shoved her off him and blanched at the few spots I'd left on his trousers. "Bleeding Wastelands!"

"My deepest apologies, *meschiir*." I reached for a napkin, feigning disgust, and rounded on Maralla. "Filthy *rascha*. Get out of my sight."

Mouth gaping, Maralla stumbled away from me. Her confusion easily passed for fear. "Apologies, Master."

"Another delay will see you whipped. Out!"

Maralla flinched and, with one last incredulous look, fled the room.

I stood with the napkin balled in my fist, keeping pressure on my wound. My distaste was easy to refine as I regarded Emisett's sisters, shivering in terror at my outburst. Neither could have been older than thirteen—much too young, but too many men believed if a woman was old enough to breed, she was old enough to do business. These two clearly had little experience with either. I used Emisett's preoccupation with his trousers to dismiss them. "You two, Farrah will show you to a room. I have no need of you."

They whimpered their compliance and left in a flurry of scraping chairs and swishing skirts.

I turned to Vassu. "Send for Emmi."

"Right away, Master."

As he hurried away, I shook my head and turned to Emisett. "Please, accept my apologies, *meschiir*. Her courses were not due for several days. I'll have Emmi attend you; she is one of my best personal slaves."

"My clothes—"

"Will be laundered and ready for you by morning."

The merchant quieted. "Thank you, Mascha. I-I'm certain this was just ill-timed." He gathered himself up. "Did my sisters displease you?"

"They are lovely, *meschiir*, but I couldn't possibly claim such fine flesh after this embarrassment." I nodded toward the three men by the hearth. "I would take one of your slaves, should you find that acceptable."

What began as unease drained into understanding. His face softened. "It is more than adequate, of course."

I appraised the slaves, then selected the only one who didn't tremble at my approach. "This one will do."

Emisett came to stand beside me. "Xagoras. A fine choice."

I ran my thumb along the slave's lips. "He has lovely features."

The door opened behind us. Emmi curtsied a greeting and drifted to the merchant's side. Her silk slip left nothing to the imagination.

"Mira's mercy," Emisett breathed. He cupped her face. "Aren't you exquisite?"

Ever one for flattery, Emmi's cheeks darkened. "*Meschiir* is too kind."

The napkin in my hand had soaked through. Before I engaged in further intimacies, I needed Hasanthe. "*Rascha*, take our guest to my finest suite and show him your best hospitality."

"With pleasure, Master."

As Emmi led the merchant away, he seemed to forget his grievances. I looked down at Xagoras and caressed his jaw. "I'll be back for you shortly."

Chapter Nineteen

Maralla

Mascha didn't return to his rooms until after the leather merchant left the next morning. I spent much of the evening puzzling out what had happened. My courses only came once every three years, but they always directly followed my last week of *oeloraati*. When they didn't come this time, I'd thought the herbs must have prevented them. Then I supposed they could have simply delayed them, but I'd experienced no pain or discomfort, and there was no sign of further bleeding once I'd scrubbed the area clean.

I didn't know how he'd done it or why, but there was no doubt Mascha had kept me from bedding Emisett last night. Not that I wasn't grateful not to be drooled on and humped by that eager dog—I just didn't understand.

Mascha strode into his chambers without acknowledging me. I trailed him to his study, where he dropped the sealed contract on his desk.

I leaned against the doorframe. "Why did you do that?"

"Do what?"

"*Saonis miraar*. You don't play stupid well."

He seemed content to ignore me, suddenly distracted by the ledger on his desk.

I folded my arms. "Mascha."

"What?"

His tone was bitter. Annoyed. It heated my blood.

"Look at me."

He scoffed. "You're giving me orders now?"

"You wanted me to play this farce. Why would you risk sabotaging our plans?"

Finally, Mascha looked up, his characteristic scowl taking root. "You thought about stabbing him at dinner. I wasn't going to chance sending you to another room with him."

Damn his scabbing Foresight. "I think about stabbing you all the time, and yet you still wake up every morning."

Though I meant it in jest, Mascha winced. "I know." He leaned against the desk. "You'll not attend me for any more deals. It's too risky."

"What's risky is faking my courses while I'm sitting on another man's lap." My voice rose. "Really, Mascha, what were you thinking?"

The insufferable man glared down at his ledger. "I wasn't."

"You—" I stopped.

The confession had fallen from his mouth, and it took several heartbeats for me to process it. His behavior had become increasingly erratic over the last few days. He'd been shy about touching me, quicker to yield during our disagreements, and more prone to staring when he thought I wasn't looking. A sinking feeling settled in my stomach. It was almost like...

No. He couldn't have.

I cleared my throat. Started again. "You—"

"I allowed my emotions to influence my actions," he cut in. "It was a mistake. One I won't make again."

This couldn't be happening. I'd heard of captives feeling affection for their captors, but this was so much worse. I shoved away from the doorframe, struggling to find my voice. "You aren't thinking about reneging, are you?"

"No. I would never." The fierceness in his response stayed my spiral into darker thoughts. He sucked in a breath. "This changes nothing between us. The safest place for you is a world away from me."

I had no idea what to say to that. Here I was, standing with the man who'd drugged me, coerced me, whipped me, and enslaved me for half a year, and I was struggling not to go to him, to comfort him. But that would only make this worse. I tried to project my intentions so his Foresight would pick them up. If he knew I'd thought about it and refused, maybe that would make the inevitability of my departure easier to bear.

"I'll assign you to your own room."

That news should have elated me. Instead, it hit me like a quarterstaff to the chest. "You said the slaves would talk."

Why was I fighting this? Scabbing gods, what was wrong with me?

Humorless laughter rasped out of him. He sank into his chair. "I don't care. Let them talk."

He was falling apart before my eyes. It should have brought me satisfaction to see such misery from my captor, but all I could think about was how he'd held me in his arms two nights past. How he'd kissed me that evening on the sand. How his killer's hands softened against my skin. My chest constricted at the memory.

"It's just *oeloraati*," I reasoned. "Lingering possessiveness." It wasn't love or affection. "Gods forbid another man play with your toys."

The moment the words left my mouth, I regretted them. Mascha's mask slipped further. He squeezed his eyes shut and went so still, the gods themselves might have stopped time.

The rawness of his pain was like glass in an open wound. I recoiled from it and snapped my mouth shut. Even if there was a sliver of truth to what he felt, I was leaving soon. There was no future for us.

That the thought even came to me was another problem. I squared my shoulders against the redoubled ache between my ribs. He was right; separate beds would serve us both. "Should I still attend you in the evenings?"

Mascha scoffed and pinched the bridge of his nose. "No."

I steeled my spine and refused to acknowledge his answer as rejection. "Then I'll await your summons. And if anyone requests *Johtan Shasnaram* for a deal again, you can't interfere."

He lowered his hand. "See Raffi after you've met with Schera. I'll send your new room assignment over shortly."

"Thank you."

Mascha's jaw worked awhile before he reached for his ledger. "Dismissed."

The subtle hardening in his tone should have made me feel better. If he was going through all this trouble to keep me at arm's length, surely he wouldn't change his mind before the gala.

I turned and strode out of his study. But all the way down the stairs and through the palace, another feeling burrowed into my spine. It left me aching and restless throughout my lesson with Schera. I couldn't focus on the timing or the steps.

It was the sense that I'd just lost something important, and I hadn't known its value until it was gone.

My new room was a private suite with a dedicated washroom and a study in addition to a central living area. Tomes filled a low bookshelf, and cotton sheets wrapped the soft mattress. There were no windows, but the suite was clean and spacious—even bigger than my sister Orowen's apartment, which she and I had shared for years before I met Nalerta.

Despite its comforts, I hated it.

Only a few years separated me from my younger sister. Since I couldn't remember a time before Orowen was born, I'd always had someone to help fill the silence. We were always off on patrol together, hunting Chaos priests or fighting sorcerers. I longed for the feel of Dawnbringer in my hand again, for the pulse of magic in my veins. Palace life fit me poorly, and I was even more ill-suited for being alone.

Even when Mascha kept me in his cage, I'd still had the company of chamber slaves flitting about. Here, every little move I made seemed loud and obtrusive, like I was disturbing a tomb.

When a knock came at the door, I nearly launched through the ceiling.

"Maralla?" Schera's voice.

Grateful for the distraction, I snapped a tome of poetry shut and hurried to let her in.

"I just heard the news." Schera looked around the room, then perched on the edge of my bed with a smile. "Why didn't you tell me we were going to be neighbors?"

I sat beside her. "I didn't know."

Now that I was allowed among them again, Schera and the other slaves had lost many of their reservations about me. The young ones, Catari and Odessa, often asked for stories from battles I'd led. Farrah and Vassu inquired about northern cuisine—though they'd been devastated when I told them what a terrible cook

I was. Schera showed interest in Syljian culture and how my northern brethren differed from those here in the south.

We'd danced together only an hour or two before, but she was already freshly bathed and dressed in luxurious cotton. If not for her collar, it would have been hard to believe regal Scherazeme was a slave.

"You're sure you haven't gotten sick of me yet?" I asked.

"As long as you don't stomp on my toes in here *and* the ballroom, I think I'll be fine."

Beneath her sunny smiles and friendly banter, however, lay a deeper curiosity. She fidgeted with the hem of her skirt and brushed the dark waves from her face too often to pass for nonchalant.

"Is something on your mind?"

"It's just, well…" She turned toward me. "You said the Master planned to sell you, right? Everyone's wondering why he assigned you a room for a palace slave."

I couldn't believe *everyone* already knew about my reassignment. Palace slaves were even worse gossips than soldiers. I decided on a half-truth. "The Master doesn't want me to share his bed while I bleed."

She frowned. "He's never cared about a woman's courses before." Then her gaze narrowed, turning mischievous. "That's only for squeamish merchants who can't stand the sight of blood."

If rumors were candlewicks, this whole palace would go up in smoke.

I forced a chuckle. "It was embarrassing."

"It happens. I started mine once during relations with the captain of the Chancellor's Guard."

My eyebrows shot upward. When she dissolved into further laughter, I couldn't help but follow suit. "Leave it to the Rillanese to redefine the phrase 'messy business.'"

"Oh, it wasn't business. He took me at a gala a few years ago. My performance got him all riled up, and he was too impatient to wait to get home to his wife."

She spoke so irreverently; I couldn't mask my shock. "He raped you at a gala?"

"No, no. The Master was there. He approved it."

As if that made it alright. All at once, the reminder of who Mascha was and what he did to people for a living hit me. Even if some of it was a ruse, even if he insulated his slaves from the worst of it, he was still part of the problem.

My disgust must have shown on my face. Schera reached up to tuck a beaded braid behind my ear. "I didn't mind. He likes to watch."

Except last night, when he'd looked ready to tear the leather merchant in half. My brows crept inward as I studied the way her cheeks darkened and her gaze grew distant. Mascha may have rescued her from a worse fate, but couldn't she see that what he allowed other men to do to her was still repellent?

"You think you love him."

"Of course I do."

And you think he loves you. It was a fae tale to outlive the ages.

Too aware of what had happened the last time I'd questioned Schera, I bit my tongue. Perhaps he *did* love her in his own broken way.

Pushing the subject wouldn't help foster our tenuous friendship. Besides, there was this nagging sense that I was missing something. Mascha could have convinced any of his women that what the Rillanese did wasn't a mockery of love. He could have taken a dozen wives and concubines to elevate his status, yet he chose to be alone. Even his friend Bastian had commented on the oddity. If Mascha truly feared companionship—feared marriage—there was a reason.

Tipori daatahl.

Mercy for her.

"Schera," I ventured, "do you know who he dreams about? The woman in his nightmares?"

Her eyes blew wide, as if I'd spat in Mascha's morning tea. "You must never ask the Master about that. It is forbidden."

"Forbidden? Why?"

"It's not for us to know." As if to punctuate her statement, she stood and turned for the door.

"Was she his lover?" I *had* to know. I couldn't explain why. "Is she why he won't take a wife or concubines?"

Schera rounded on me. "Do not speak such lies. He *will* take a concubine, if not a wife."

And it would be her. The words left unsaid hung like a threat between us. I folded my hands in my lap and looked down. Though it irked me to appear cowed, it was the only way I could stop myself from pointing out the fallacy in her assumption. If Mascha refused to speak to someone about his past—if it haunted him so much that he would rather shut people out than admit he had demons—then he would never have a future with anyone.

Not that I should care.

Schera's fists balled. "You'd do well to forget you ever witnessed those nightmares."

"You're right." I rose from the bed and walked her to the door. "Will I see you at dinner?"

When I didn't press the issue, some of her ire drained away. All the slaves ate dinner in rotating shifts based on sleeping arrangements. If Schera and I were neighbors now, we would share the same mealtime.

She let her posture relax. "I usually dine with Emmi and Farrah. You're... welcome to join us."

I pulled the door open for her and nodded. They would want to hear what happened, eager for any crumb they could spread around, but at least I wouldn't be alone. "I'd like that."

Chapter Twenty

Mascha

The Deal-Breaker's approval for the search and seizures came the following morning. It was accompanied by further evidence from Vhedja and Svaronei that something was amiss in the Simmion, Baghara, and Akaaris households. They'd found more mercenaries guarding portions of Baghara Estates, and Lord Simmion had just made a new investment in the local shipyards. However, their financial reports revealed no means to fund these expenditures. Trade ledgers also confirmed Enghal Akaaris had received four deliveries of manure recently, despite having no presence in the farming business. Keallia was a hungry flower, however, and it needed much in the way of fertilizer.

By sunset, raids on all three houses were underway. To keep my mind off Maralla, I went with them.

Rorsch Hekkai stormed the upper-caste district in waves of black and gold. Aetherians rifted onto estate doorsteps, flanked by lesser arcanists weaving light sigils into protective shields. With the bulk of resistance expected at House Baghara, I chose to lead the assault there.

Four significant structures made up Baghara Estates. I divided most of my men between three of them—the ones most likely to have the evidence we sought—and took only three soldiers with me to the estate house. Surprised staff and terrified slaves scattered as we burst into the candlelit foyer.

I seized the collar of the nearest slave. "Bring me Lord Yamon Baghara."

"Y-yes, my lord. Right away."

I curled my lip at the title and thrust the slave away. He stumbled off down a corridor, catching the wall for balance.

Foresight flickered, and Trennon Baghara, the lord's eldest son, swept into the room seconds later. His outrage skipped confusion and dissolved immediately into horror. He stumbled backward and tripped on his own robes.

"Guards!"

"Your guards will die if they draw steel against me, *Meschiir* Baghara."

The waifish lad steadied himself on a nearby chair. Like a cornered dune kitten, he bared his teeth. "You have no right. I command you—"

"I suspect, then, you know why we're here. Show us to your silk stores, or we'll tear this place apart to find them."

"Show them, son," a wizened voice said. Lord Baghara strode into the foyer, adjusting his tunic sleeve. Graying hair framed heavy jowls and a hawkish nose. He eyed me with open distrust. "We have nothing to hide, Rorsch Hekkai."

"Then you won't mind our intrusion." I turned partway toward him to deliver my decree, still keeping the son in my peripheral vision. "By order of the Chancellor, House Baghara is to be searched, and any contraband or illicit substances related to the refinement or distribution of keallite will be seized. You will attend us as we search, my lord."

Trennon looked about to protest, but his jaw snapped shut at his father's glare.

As he led us out the back door and into a courtyard paved with flagstone, the shadows of at least twelve mercenaries sidled up around the low stone walls. My men fidgeted, but I didn't summon my axes. Private mercenaries were far cheaper to hire than my Rorsch Hekkai for a reason; they posed little threat to us.

Baghara approached a small warehouse at the end of a stone path and beckoned us inside with a smug narrowing of his eyes. Right away, I knew there was no keallite here, but a search would allow the others time to scout the rest of the estate unimpeded.

The slaves quieted when we entered. Some paused in their work of rolling silk bolts around wooden forms, while others worked faster and didn't look up.

I nodded toward the workbenches. "Search them."

While my men tore apart the silk stations, I perused the closets, chests, and crates.

"Nothing here."

"Nor here."

"These are clean, too, Rorsch Hekkai."

I replaced the lid to a waist-high crate and turned back to Lord Baghara.

The man's expression was that of a child who'd just consumed the last pastry; not even a paddling could usurp his victory. "You see, Mascha? There was obviously some miscommunication."

Svaronei strode through the door behind him. "Found it." He held up a parchment-wrapped package. "In the grain storage under the floor."

Trennon paled. "That's not— You must have—"

"Perfect timing, Svaronei." I fixed Lord Baghara with a cold stare. "This is your chance to divulge any further locations of illicit substances. If you name any of your associates, I will ensure the courts are more generous in your sentencing."

Lord Baghara stared open-mouthed at me, then at the door three spans away. I didn't need Foresight to guess his intentions.

"You can scurry into the night and order your men between us." I strolled through the wreckage from our search. "But if you make me chase you, I *will* track you down, and when I find you, I will cut out your entrails and use them to hang you over the Scarlet Fountains."

The lord's breath grew shallow. "That's savagery."

I grinned. "*Ciir.*"

Aetherial mist wrapped around father and son, swirling into images that foretold their next moves. Lord Baghara's likeness spun for the door. Trennon's image lunged toward Svaronei. A plume burst in behind them, morphing into broad-shouldered mercenaries.

I threw out my arms and channeled magic. Rifts split the air above and below my hands. Black mist poured from the tiny fissures and solidified into Furyborn and Bloodletter—twin battle axes made infamous by their time in the arena.

Lord Baghara's poise shattered. He spun in perfect mimicry of his image. "Guards!"

Trennon collided with Svaronei, and the Aetherian snarled. I stalked forward to meet the first of the mercenaries funneling through the door.

Fervor danced across my skin. I didn't need magic for this. Years of training and instinct guided my movements. The first man raised his sword against me, met Furyborn's blade, and died with a gaping hole in his neck. A second man threw a razor-edged star that whispered past my ear. He took Bloodletter to the calf and fell screaming before my boot crushed his windpipe. The third and fourth faltered in the doorway, their eyes ringing white as their companions shoved them forward to their deaths.

Movement in the corner of my eye and a flash of mist; I brought Bloodletter up. It caught the projectile just as I realized my mistake. Trennon had wrestled the package from Svaronei. It met my blade and exploded, coating me in a fine layer of white.

I shuddered as the familiar citrus scent flooded my lungs. Gritty powder clung to my lips and lashes. Despite decades of sobriety, I could only fight the impulse to lick the substance from my mouth for a few heartbeats. Time seemed to dilate as the heavy dose of keallite awakened my senses for the first time in nearly a century.

The Master used to dose me before every major fight. It made me faster, stronger, more aggressive. With my Foresight and mastery of Aetherian magic, I became death incarnate.

Even as the horror of what I was about to become lodged in my chest, I leveled my gaze at Trennon Baghara and laughed.

"You fool," I spat, the sound of my own voice chilling me. My vision sharpened and my heart rate quickened. Magic surged through my veins. "You've destroyed yourself."

I looked to Svaronei while I still had reason, though already my hands itched for action. "Evacuate the estate."

Svaronei backstepped, eyes wide, as if he could sense the storm inside me building. Once I reached the top of the high, I wouldn't know friend from foe. But for now, my enemies stood before me, hesitating. My inhibitions crumbled like a castle made of sand.

With a roar, I lunged through the powdery haze, and bodies parted. Blood sprayed my hands and face. My axes swung, and men died. It was no fight I brought these mercenaries, but butchery. Even with the keallite quickening their impulses, these men were no match for my enhanced Foresight.

Three mercenaries approached on light feet, two with swords and one a spear. The Aetherial image of their steps played out two full heartbeats before we engaged: a sword slash to my left flank; a sword thrust to the right; the spear would pierce the space I would step and skewer my lower back. The first swordsman would regroup with a sweeping cut to my knees, and the second would take my head.

I chopped off the first swordsman's arm at the elbow and stepped into the blow from my right. Bloodletter locked with the second man's sword. The spearman paused at the first man's scream, giving me the opening I needed. Using the swordsman's resistance for balance, I kicked the spearman in the knee and hammered Furyborn's haft into his skull. The second swordsman bared his teeth and disengaged, swinging at me twice before I buried Bloodletter in his thigh.

By the time I cleaved Trennon Baghara's head from his shoulders and resummoned Furyborn in a cloud of mist from Lord Baghara's corpse, only torchlight and a sliver of moon lit the grisly scene littering the courtyard. Men lay broken on the flagstones, some with their lungs pulled from their backs. I'd blacked out for a moment, and I struggled to recall when I'd left the warehouse. Blood drenched my shirt and trousers, none of it mine.

At least, I didn't feel injured. I felt invincible.

Screams tore through the night. A man rushed me. I might have known him, but there was little left of me that cared. I was a savage in the ring again, bred for blood and chaos, living for the high, for the destruction. For the pleasure of killing.

I rose from the man's body, bits of pulmonary tissue stuck beneath my nails, his broken ribs scraping my wrists. With no more corpses to be made, I turned my attention to the structures around me. The symbols of power, of privilege, of slavers under whose heels I had scraped and groveled and bled. Aether bent to my will and I brought them down, sinking them in yawning black chasms that split the ground. Stone hewed from stone until all the saphyrum beads I carried crumbled to dust, their magic spent.

I hit my knees and vomited black bile, limbs shaking. My entire body was drenched in sweat. Darkness edged out the hazy firelight, and only vaguely did I acknowledge the high had left me. I was on the way down, and the well of despair opened wide to swallow me. I clawed at the walls of my mind as if to slow the fall.

Are you certain you're a free man?

No. No, I wasn't.

If you wielded your influence the way you wield your axes...

Of course my last thought before I blacked out would be of Maralla.

"Well done, Mascha," Saarach cooed. "The Deal-Breaker is pleased."

I didn't remember returning to the palace last night. Hasanthe said I did so under my own power, but my limbs were so shaky and weak this morning, I didn't see how it was possible.

"You have made a fine example of these treacherous houses."

I looked up from my tea. Saarach's pompous smirk swam in my vision. The light streaming through the window drove spikes into my eyes. I growled. "Raenara, the drapes."

"Yes, Master."

My title came easily from her lips. She rose from where she knelt at my feet, her red hair tumbling over freckled shoulders. The scent of her persistent arousal nauseated me.

Saarach placed his untouched glass on the table. "May their names die with them."

Their names.

I frowned. More missing pieces from the night before. I remembered killing Baghara and his heir, but they shared a name. I sensed Saarach meant something more. "Akaaris and Simmion fell in the raids as well?"

The messenger gave me a curious look. "Why, yes. Svaronei says you beheaded them yourself."

I blinked several times, trying to remember leaving the Baghara estate.

"Do you not recall?" Amusement colored his tone. "I understand it was quite the spectacle."

Memory loss wasn't uncommon after keallite use. I'd won dozens of fights and stumbled off the sand with no idea what had happened. But destroying three notable houses? Just how much keallite had I inhaled?

My temples throbbed, and I scrubbed a hand over my face rather than answer the cankerous boil. A twitch began in my left thigh. The incessant ticking of the pendulus keeping time in one corner threatened to drive me mad.

"I suppose it is of no consequence. Now, the Deal-Breaker wishes for you to seize their remaining assets and send their women and slaves to the auction blocks in Epillon. The proceeds will go to securing our ports."

Raenara returned to my side, bringing that scent with her. I leaned away and breathed into my tea. "Consider it done."

Anything to get this snake-skinned vermin out of my palace. Pain thrummed through my skull, and my heart fluttered. Silonas slay me, but a half-dose of that wretched dust would rid me of all my symptoms in a matter of—

No.

My fingers curled tighter around my glass. 'Just one more' always led to another, and my addiction held no power over me anymore.

Saarach withdrew a scroll. "In addition to the security you've already assigned, he has made some suggestions."

They were demands, not suggestions. I took the scroll and broke the seal. With the drapes drawn now, it was too dark to see, and squinting increased the pressure at my temples. I nearly cast the scroll aside in frustration, but one phrase caught my eye.

"Rift wards. On every ship?"

"Yes." Saarach's smile could have sweetened vinegar. "The Deal-Breaker proposes that any ship to dock in a Rillanese harbor should be equipped with a rift ward to deter smugglers."

And escaped slaves.

This was going to be a problem. I pulled out a bead of saphyrum and summoned light.

Increased patrols, inspection of every crate and barrel, a cap on the size of boxed cargo. With every new guideline, the odds against Maralla's escape grew, until I could no longer see a way out of port for her. At least, not on her own.

I sat back. "He's going to need a lot more than three upper-caste estates to fund these changes. The wards alone will cost a fortune."

"Ship captains or their respective agencies will be responsible for the wards. We will only need a small force to ensure they are installed properly. As for the rest, long-term costs can be mitigated with higher levies on arena winnings, business transactions, and luxury imports." His smile slipped. "Really, Mascha, you are a numbers man. Work your magic with the ledgers. I know you will make him proud."

Ciir, and ensure Maralla never left the country alive.

"I will do as he suggests." My jaw seized on the words, and I prayed it wasn't evident in my voice.

These new security measures addressed a longstanding problem with the drug trade in my country. They truly were a boon in every respect but one. If I could delay their implementation for a few months, perhaps that would give Maralla enough time to escape.

"If there is nothing else"—I forced myself to sift my fingers through Raenara's hair, and she whimpered—"this one is due for more raspaati."

As expected, she broke protocol to meet my gaze. "No, Master. Please. I've been good. Please, no more."

"Eyes down," I snapped.

Raenara mewed in abject misery, her need so heavy I could almost taste her. Regret pierced me for leaving her in this state for so long. Maralla was right; it was just as inhumane to take from them what they wouldn't give without raspaati, but in this, I could not show mercy. Not if I was to keep up appearances. Not unless I wanted to impart more scars and enact more violence on innocents.

My stomach churned, even as my mouth watered for that sweet taste of citrus.

Saarach chuckled. "I'll leave you to your work. Good day, Mascha."

Chapter Twenty-One

Maralla

Faking my courses was a challenge among the female slaves. I had to deflect more than one offer to wash my linens, and I started wearing the infernal things to keep up appearances. And while the slaves' willingness to provide me with company warmed me, I grew bored of the constant rumormongering within a few days.

"The new girl broke yesterday," Emmi told us at breakfast one morning. She giggled. "The Master had her bent over the desk in his study."

I paused in my chewing, certain if I swallowed, it would come right back up. The last time I'd seen Mascha was the day he'd assigned me to a new room. Apparently, he'd been too busy killing nobles, ransacking estates, and ferrying innocent women and slaves off to the capital to spend much time here.

I'd seen Raenara with Emmi, though, and each time, the poor girl spent the length of our encounter pawing at her cage and grinding into her seat. I remembered that desperate need for friction, the pressure of that metal against my skin. For a human like Raenara, who had never experienced true *oeloraati*, I couldn't imagine suffering that overwhelming need for the first time at his hands.

I'd been a fool to think my comments on his methods would change anything. My fingers tightened around my fork.

"I lost my bet to Vassu. She lasted longer than I thought. What was it? Six days?" Farrah twirled a dark curl around her finger and made a face at the sweet rolls on her plate. "I think I added too much cinnamon."

"Seven." Schera pushed her half-empty plate away. "He'll tire of her soon."

Emmi gave Schera a long-suffering look. "You know he's expecting an influx of slaves from those other houses."

"She just misses his bed. Poor Schera, so many new toys for Master. He'll have no more come for her."

"Shut it, Farrah." Schera lobbed a sweet roll at the kitchen slave's head.

"Oh, don't be such a sour citron." Emmi plucked the sweet roll from where it had fallen and took a bite. She spoke as she chewed. "They won't be here long. I bet the Master will have men lining up for a bid on Lord Simmion's daughters."

My stomach rolled. That a group of slaves could titter about three entire houses falling overnight to the whims of one man said more about the cutthroat climate of Rillanese politics than any tome ever could. How I'd thought for even a moment the mighty Mascha could be a better person was beyond me. Scabbing gods, I had to get out of this place.

The rumors of him piking noblemen's bodies outside the market square returned to me. I'd have hoped for less barbarity, given that the square was frequented by women and children. I followed Schera's lead and shoved my plate away.

"I heard Lady Akaaris might be among them."

"And Baghara's three concubines."

I'd heard enough. "You've all been to the summer gala before. What's it like?"

Three pairs of eyes settled on me. They shared incredulous glances, as if they couldn't believe I'd want to talk about anything else.

Emmi's brows furrowed. "It's like any other party."

"Except bigger," Farrah added.

"And way grander." Emmi went doe-eyed. "If you see the Chancellor's steward, Maralla, you must take in every detail and report back."

Farrah sighed. "Oh, yes. He's beautiful."

I studied what remained of my breakfast. These two weren't going to be any help with planning, or even distraction, this morning.

Schera rolled her eyes. "Just stay close to the Master, and when it's time for your performance, remember to smile and pretend you enjoy it."

I seized the opportunity to leave. "Can we start our lesson a little early?"

"Sure."

Emmi feigned a gasp and covered her mouth. "What's this? Farrah, do my eyes deceive me?"

I rose from the table, intent upon ignoring her.

Farrah's grin was absolutely feline. "Leaving early for lessons. By the gods, Emmi, I think *Johtan Shasnaram* is nervous."

Emmi fell into Farrah's lap, cackling. Farrah nearly toppled out of her chair, and they both dissolved into hysterics. My face warmed.

I wasn't nervous. Not really.

Despite the heated glare Schera spared for our companions, her lips twitched. "You're both insufferable." She took my arm. "Come on, Maralla."

"One, two, three, four. One, two, three…"

I shuffled across the ballroom floor, hand in hand with Schera. As usual, she took the female lead in the amaariana while I followed along with the traditionally male steps. I stumbled more times than I could count.

Finally, after I tripped on *her* feet, Schera called a halt. Likely sensing my frustration, the musicians avoided my gaze and drifted toward glasses of watered ale and plates of fruit.

"You're distracted," she said. "Just relax."

"You can be honest," I groused. "I'm getting worse."

"It's normal to be nervous."

"I'm *not* nervous."

Her thick brows arched toward her hairline.

"I'm…" I rubbed my face. I wasn't nervous. I'd performed hundreds of dances in front of my people before. I led soldiers into battle and gave speeches before the masses. I could present before foreign powers and negotiate treaties that affected us all. "It's just…"

What was it, anyway?

Behind me, a door opened.

"*Raschan.*"

Then it struck me. It wasn't nervousness that had been eating at my guts for the last few days. It was anger—fiery, low-simmering anger smothered by layers of ash that Mascha's appearance stirred like a boot kicking up coals. After all he'd done, after how I'd let his little kindnesses blind me—

Schera lit up and dropped into a curtsy. "Good day, Master."

I stifled a growl and turned.

"Good day, Schera."

My annoyance spiked higher at that smooth baritone, that kindly smile, as if he hadn't just killed dozens of people and enslaved several more. I fixed him in my gaze and tried to convey all my disappointment, fury, and distrust with a single look.

"Master."

Mascha stopped short.

Calculations ticked away behind that intelligent stare. Though his eyes didn't glaze over with Foresight—yet another disappointment, since he likely didn't See the kick to his chest I considered for good measure—he did give me a wide berth on his way to Schera.

She melted as he cupped her cheeks and kissed her.

"Master, you'll ruin your shirt. I'm all sweaty."

"You are most beautiful covered in sweat," he purred.

She giggled, and I turned for the fruit tray before I gagged on my own tongue.

Chunks of spike melon and orange slices filled the tray. Ripe sickleberries and prickly-skinned aghavi accompanied a bowl of sweet yogurt. I distracted myself by piling a plate.

Mascha extracted himself from Schera's lips. "I'm afraid I need to borrow your student."

I paused in peeling an aghavi.

"We were just finishing up." Disappointment soured Schera's tone.

Dread and curiosity warred within me, but I refused to look at Mascha even when he cupped my shoulder. His beard brushed my ear tip and lightning shot down my spine.

"Come, *rascha*."

My jaw ached from clenching so hard. Only the promise of impending freedom kept me from throwing my entire lunch into his face. A rift opened beside us, and whistling wind tugged my braids toward the black void.

"You may strike me if you wish," Mascha whispered, "but only once we are alone."

He didn't wait for my surprise to fully register before tugging me through the rift. I stumbled into the corridor outside his chambers. Most of my food had been sucked off my plate and lost to the Aether.

So much for lunch.

Mascha led me inside his anteroom and locked the door. As he turned back to me, the urge to accept his offer proved too tempting to ignore.

My open hand connected with his cheek, and a satisfying sting blazed through my fingers. The rest of my fruit splattered on the floor. Mascha's head snapped to one side, teeth bared in a grimace. I braced myself for barbed words or razor-edged anger, but he merely rubbed his jaw.

"We have a problem," he said.

"Damn right, we do." Hitting him once felt so good, I thought about doing it again.

"You'll only get one of those. The..." Mascha glanced at the trail of crimson sickleberry juice on the floor. A tremor shuddered through him, and an odd twitch seized his right hand.

I frowned.

"The Deal-Breaker"—he winced, curling and uncurling his fingers—"has issued orders to tighten port security. I tried to delay certain edicts, but others have already pushed through the senate. Once you escape your new master's estate, you'll need help getting out of the country."

He outlined the new measures and those that would be instated within a few months. The wards, the customs checks, the cargo restrictions—he laid it all out before me as pressure mounted in my chest.

"Is there anyone I can contact who can assist you?" he asked.

Aon'In was over four months away by ship and another two to three months over land without enemies harrying the journey. Without Conduits or Walkers, it would take over half a year to deliver a message there. Not even the strongest masterminds I knew could send a telepathic message across that distance, and psionics were illegal in Rillion, anyway.

No matter how hard I tried to stop myself from sliding into despair, my hope for freedom slipped through my fingers like sand.

"Not unless you've an arcanist you trust to send to Aon'In or Kuma'Kiir," I said, shaking my head. "No one could get here before the ward requirements are in place."

"The Deal-Breaker owns both Walkers I know." His hand twitched again. He held it behind his back and lowered his gaze. "I wouldn't trust any of the Conduits not to betray us. A coded message sent that far north might draw suspicion."

The words he wasn't saying pierced me like an arrow and sank all the way to the fletching: I was trapped.

With no one outside to pull me from the jaws of Rillion, I would languish here as a slave for the rest of my life.

Numbness overtook me. My pulse pounded harder and harder between my ears until it matched the tightness in my chest. I looked down at the plate I still held, and hurled it as hard as I could at the wall. Ceramic shattered.

"Maralla—"

I whirled on him, thrusting a finger into his chest. "*This is all your fault.*"

Rage surged through me, so hot and biting that it registered as cold before I broke into sweat. I clawed at my collar as the same nauseating sense of confinement and helplessness I'd felt on the slave ship barreled over me. "You should have let me escape when I had the chance."

Mascha reached for me. "Maralla, listen to me—"

But I was beyond listening. "You treacherous, craven mongrel. Where was your Foresight for this?" I planted my weight against his chest and shoved hard. "Where's all your wealth and power now, Mascha? Why couldn't you stop this?" I shoved him again. How little he moved only inflamed me further. "Your word is as worthless as your honor!"

Mascha allowed a final shove before grabbing my wrists and pinning me against the wall. "Listen, you gods-damned infuriating woman—"

I tried to thrust my knee into his groin. He blocked me with his shin, and I howled my fury into his face. "I hate you!"

"I know." Mascha grimaced. "I know you do, but I still need you with me in this. I'm going to make it right. Do you hear me?"

He might have been speaking an ancient tongue for all the sense he made. Mascha of the Rorsch Hekkai wouldn't risk his reputation or defy his faceless master for me. I slipped a hand free and went for his eyes. He ducked my slashing nails and pinned my wrist above my head. Mascha leaned down, his face so close to mine I could have bitten him. Anticipating the move—because of course he did—he shook me once and pressed me harder against the wall.

"I'm going to help you," he growled. "I'll find a way."

His chest rose and fell against mine in rapid succession. The thundering of both our hearts reverberated through my rib cage. My eyes closed against the sting of betrayal, of wanting so desperately to believe him. He put on such a front; I couldn't tell what part of him was real.

I turned my head and struggled in vain to get my arms free. "You don't mean that."

"*Ciir*, I do." Mascha released my wrist and took hold of my chin, forcing me to look at him. "You don't belong here. I see that now, and I'm going to get you out."

Spasms wracked the arm holding me, and he retreated with a wince.

I leaned against the wall, trying to breathe reason and logic back into my body. The beat of his heart so close to mine still resonated through me. I touched my chest and choked on a sob.

Mascha paced the anteroom, flexing his fingers, and when he paused to rub his hip, it seemed the tremors wracked his leg too. He caught me watching him and turned away.

"What's wrong with you?" I asked, more to fill the silence than because I truly cared.

"It's nothing."

"You need a new title. Might I suggest, 'King of Poor Evasions'?"

Mascha snorted. "Only if you call me 'Your Majesty.'"

"As if you need a bigger head." Wearily, I slid down the wall and sat, knees drawn to my chest. "You should see Hasanthe."

"I'm afraid he can't help with this."

Hasanthe was a skilled enough healer; he could handle a few nerve tremors. I considered other conditions with similar symptoms, recalling from a list Orowen used to cite before every difficult case. Unfortunately, I wasn't well-versed in the art of healing.

"What is it, then?"

Mascha hesitated. Silence stretched so long between us, I wasn't sure he'd answer. He turned, studying me as if he feared my reaction. "I was exposed to keallite during the raids."

It threw me.

He was once a pit fighter. One of the best in the world, according to the stories. It didn't take much to puzzle out the connection. I rested my wrists on my knees.

"You were addicted once."

"*Ciir.*"

"Does it always make you twitch like that?"

Mascha shook his head. "It was a heavy dose. Lord Baghara's son threw a package at me and it exploded."

A whole package. Just the tiny plumes from the silk pouches on the ship had been enough for me to experience some effects. "It seems counterintuitive to arm your enemy with a performance enhancer."

A frown creased his brow. "I suspect he was hoping I would overdose." Mascha resumed his pacing and raked a hand through his hair. "Instead, I came un-hinged."

Anger sparked again, albeit weaker this time. "You murdered three entire hous-es."

I expected nonchalance and arrogance. I expected him to gloat about how the destruction was justified. But the look Mascha gave me was nothing short of devastated.

His jaw worked around words long in coming. "I don't remember any of it."

I might have scoffed, but for that look. "You mean it all bled together, like a battle frenzy?" It was common enough; I'd even experienced it myself.

"No. I mean I blacked out. I remember fragments, but as far as I knew, I never left Baghara Estates."

"Who says you did?"

"Saarach."

My lip curled. That creepy bastard could do the world a favor and swallow nails. "He was there?"

"No. He said my men saw me behead the lords of the other estates. I confirmed it with the Aetherians assigned there." Mascha staved off another tremor and rubbed his face. "The only thing I remember clearly was telling Svaronei to evacuate Baghara Estates. I knew what was coming, and I didn't want innocents to get hurt. But I went back and found corpses." Mascha blinked several times. "Far too many corpses."

I drummed my fingers against my shins, then rose. All the rumors of that night painted him as a ruthless monster, cutting down everyone in his path. That was the image he nurtured for the public to see. A savage clad in silk.

But a savage didn't express remorse—didn't tear up over lives lost. Mascha might have been a killer, but gods knew I'd done my share of killing, too.

Was I seeing *him* again? Or was this a mask he wore for me?

I remembered Raffi, Soltani, Schera, all the slaves who claimed he was more than what he appeared, and at least in that moment, it was hard to hate him like I wanted to.

I stepped into his space.

He started to pull away, but I seized his arm. "I could use some fresh air. Will you walk with me?"

Chapter Twenty-Two

Maralla

"I thought about what you said," Mascha told me as we walked the corridors of the palace, past slaves who deferred to him with bows and curtsies.

He and I had spoken little. I was too busy kicking myself for whatever half-brained plan I'd embarked on since leaving Mascha's chambers.

I caught his gaze, my brows furrowing.

"About raspaati," he clarified.

He must have sensed my lingering disquiet over Raenara. "I noticed you hadn't taken it to heart."

"I agree with you. The method is flawed at its core."

I scoffed. "You have a funny way of showing it."

"I don't have a choice."

He grimaced, as if my scowl was akin to a slap in the face.

Sunlight spilled across my skin as he led me into the northern courtyard, where green foliage dotted with red and purple flowers greeted us. Beyond, down the same cliff face I'd climbed weeks ago, lay the channel and Mascha's private beach. He nodded to the guards at the gate, then led me down a long, winding path to the sand.

Once we were out of earshot, he continued, "If Tasari and the Aetherians believe I am compromised, you will be, too. They'll report me to the Deal-Breaker, and he'll remove me from power. Now, more than ever, we cannot afford mistakes. I needed Raenara to break quickly, and I refuse to cause her physical pain." When I side-eyed him again, grudgingly admitting to myself that his logic made sense, he forced a self-deprecating smile. "There's only space for one unruly woman in my career."

I shook my head. He was as guilty of perpetuating the same backward thinking as all the pompous lords in Rillion. I tried my best to believe it.

A compassionate man who bares his neck among villains gets his throat slit.

I could detest his use of raspaati all I wanted, but he was at least trying to find alternatives to violence in a society that positively reveled in it. Maybe he really didn't enjoy it as much as he wanted others to believe. If that was true, he didn't belong here any more than I did.

"It still doesn't make it right."

"I know." Mascha's attention strayed to the horizon, his expression etched with remorse.

I sighed. If this was the mask, then the gods fancied me a fool.

Our footsteps crunched on sandy gravel, down staircases slick with moss, back and forth across the switchback carved out of rock. As I'd hoped, Mascha's mood improved with every step we took away from the palace. He cast off the smoke and illusion of his villainous aspect. Without the suffocating mantle of power over his shoulders, the darkness plaguing him retreated like shadows from the light. By the time we reached the bottom of the cliff, he was just a man again.

Saonis miraar, had I actually missed this side of him? What in Mira's name was wrong with me?

"I noticed you had fewer guests this week." I toed off one silk slipper. Warm sand caressed the sole of my foot. "Is it normally slower around solstice?"

Mascha leaned against a boulder and tipped his face toward the sun. "Mm, no. It's usually very busy."

My second slipper joined the first, but I paused in retrieving them. "Mascha."

"What?"

I folded my arms. "Don't 'what' me. You know what."

He opened one eye, then closed it, one corner of his mouth lifting. "I've no idea what you mean."

"I thought we agreed you wouldn't interfere if someone else requested me."

"We did." He bent to retrieve my slippers. "So, I postponed all my deals until after solstice."

His possessiveness was almost sweet in an annoying sort of way. "Didn't you parade me about the market specifically to drive interest?"

I tried to take my slippers from him, but Mascha feinted the handoff and held them high above my head. I stared, and he grinned like a devil.

"*Ciir*, but withholding you makes you a commodity in the eyes of covetous men." He wiggled the slippers just out of reach. "And, at least until week's end, *I* am your master, so I get the final say in who beds you—oof!"

A solid punch to his gut brought the slippers lower, and I plucked them from his grip. "I can carry these, *Master*."

Mascha doubled over, playing up the pain in his stomach. His voice came out strained. "Finally, the respect I deserve."

Genuine laughter spilled from me. He straightened, beaming at last, and I took his offered arm. We strolled down to the water through powdery sand. Light glinted off waves that lapped at our feet.

Tension eased from my muscles the farther down the beach we traveled. I hadn't forgotten the news about port security, but I didn't let it sour this rare moment of peace. Mascha had helped so many others, and he took pride in keeping his word. I would put my faith in him and pray the man I saw now wasn't the mask.

"You could come with me, you know." I marveled at how easily the suggestion rolled off my tongue.

He laughed. "I'm afraid I'm ill-suited for snow. The cold tends to shrivel things."

"Vain man. Mira forbid you look any smaller than you are."

"How dare you. I'll have you know I was bred with my endowment in mind."

"A mind fond of practical jokes, maybe." I would never admit it, but the man *was* impressively endowed.

"You wound me." His voice trembled, but his eyes glittered. "What a cruel woman you are."

My whole face hurt from smiling as we waded deeper into the surf. The water crested my hips.

He tsked. "Those poor soldiers under your command must suffer terribly."

A larger wave nearly swept me off my feet. Mascha grabbed my waist to hold me upright. But when the wave passed and he made to withdraw, I caught his elbow and turned until our chests touched.

"I'm serious." I searched his face. "The Alliaansi need fighters like you. The Sorcerers' Guild wants to wipe our kind out in the north. You could find purpose there, fighting beside us, training troops—without slavery, misogyny, or deal-making to weigh you down." My palm slipped inside the laces of his shirt. "And you wouldn't have to pretend your heart is made of stone."

Gooseflesh erupted beneath my touch. His eyes squeezed shut, and a tremor passed through him. It was hard to say whether it was from the drug.

Mascha carefully took my wrist and pulled it away. "It's a lovely thought."

My chest tightened. "It could be a reality."

His unspoken refusal hurt, but I should have expected it. Mascha was still leader of the Rorsch Hekkai. He was one of the wealthiest and most powerful men in the world. He could have any man or woman he wanted, and he wouldn't give that up to go live in squalor and mud.

He touched my face. Shockwaves trailed across my lips in the wake of his thumb, and when he cupped my cheek, a tide of longing rose so potent and deadly that I risked being pulled out to sea. I forced it back and pushed him away. Finally, with distance between us, I could think clearly again. It had been a stupid thing to suggest, anyway.

Still, his touch lingered like the echo of his heartbeat.

I must be going mad.

Waves crashed. I waded out until the water rose to my ribs. Cold bored into me and I stared north, savoring the wind's bite that reminded me of home.

Warmth closed in behind me. I stiffened, intent upon ignoring him, but Mascha pressed his palm to my abdomen and pulled me back against his chest. I shouldn't have allowed the affection, the closeness, but senselessly I ached for it.

"I made a deal many years ago." His silky baritone rolled over me. "When I joined the Rorsch Hekkai, the Deal-Breaker promised me I would lack for nothing, and once I proved myself an asset, I would live better than the richest kings."

My head came to rest on his collarbone. With nothing better to do with my hands, I rested them on top of his.

"But I had to agree to two things. The first was that I could father no heirs. I couldn't claim a child conceived from any deal, and any children born to my women would be sold as fighting stock or breeders."

Breath shuddered out of me. Why would anyone agree to sell their children? I started to turn, appalled, but he held me tighter to his chest.

"The second," Mascha went on, "was that I would remain in Rillion and work for him until my death."

His hold didn't loosen. Waves rocked us back and tangled my dress around his legs.

"I know it probably seems strange to you that I would agree to such a deal. But as a newly freed slave, already used to such conditions, it didn't seem so bad. At least, not until much later."

My eyes fixed on the northern horizon, across the channel, on the tiny speck that was Epillon. Understanding and horror warred within me. Mascha kept all his personal slaves on a regimen of herbs to prevent conception, but I'd learned it was frowned upon to provide such herbs to wives. Should a free child result from a sealed deal, it was considered a blessed contract, and the mother's spouse or closest living male relative had first rights to claim the child.

Sour heat filled my stomach. "That's why you won't take wives or concubines. Because they're required to bear children they can't keep."

"*Ciir.*"

My lips parted. Everything he did, every move he made, was somehow meant to protect the ones he cared about. The man didn't even whip his slaves except as a last resort. Why had it taken me so long to see it?

Mascha's breath caressed my ear tip. When I looked over my shoulder, he cleared his throat and blinked furiously. "There are other reasons, too. I'm sure you can imagine I've made many enemies, and a Lady of the Rorsch Hekkai would be a target for those men. She would be obligated to seal every deal for me unless someone made a special request—normally considered a slight upon my honor."

I knew a seal of flesh required an equal exchange, but I hadn't thought about the ramifications if a man had only one wife or concubine to close deals with. Laangor's wrath, what a horrible existence. "But as slaves, their burden is shared with others of their station."

"Exactly."

Mascha allowed me to turn this time, and the waves pushed against my back.

He looked into my eyes. "You see, it's not that I wouldn't consider going with you. It's that I can't."

My throat tightened. "But you can. To the Wastelands with that deal. It was a bad one."

"No one defies the Deal-Breaker and lives, Maralla. His Aetherians would hunt me to the ends of the world." He brushed my temple. "It wouldn't be safe for you."

I wished I had more ground to stand on, but he knew his employer better than I did. It had taken nothing for his Aetherians to find me on a ship weeks ago. Mascha wasn't the type to live the rest of his life with a wardstone in his pocket. And he was right; if the Deal-Breaker's men found him with me, they would take me as well.

Doors were closing all around us, until there was only one path forward. I would leave, and he would stay, and we would never see each other again.

It shouldn't have bothered me, but it did. I couldn't help the sense that he wanted to be more than what Rillion had made him.

A spasm shook Mascha's arm, and he winced.

I swallowed hard. "You alright?"

"*Ciir*. It should pass with time," he said, though his note of uncertainty didn't inspire confidence. A seabird cried overhead, and Mascha tracked its flight, flexing and relaxing his hand.

"Do you—" I stopped myself, then shook my head. The gala was less than a week away now. I wouldn't spend the next eight days pining for company alone in my room. Not when I could have this side of him a little longer. "Do you have plans tonight?"

He regarded me curiously. "No."

"Well, you do now."

Chapter Twenty-Three

Mascha

Something Maralla said clung to me like a burr all evening. *It seems counterintuitive to arm your enemy with a performance enhancer.*

I slipped into the breezy night, sparing one last look at the woman in my bed. Maralla lay wrapped in my sheets, her frosty mane spilling over her perfect breasts. One arm curled beneath her head, and the other settled in the space I'd left. She stirred, stretched, and turned over.

I timed my departure between guard patrols, noting the weakness in my security with no small humor. For now, at least, it would serve me well. I could address it in the morning.

Rifting would have saved me time, but the light from the spell would have drawn attention. Word couldn't get back to the Deal-Breaker where I was going. Nothing could give him reason to suspect.

Hood drawn, I pulled from a saphyrum bead and wrapped the eddies of Aether around me. To an untrained eye, an Aether Cloak would appear only as shadow, fully obscuring my passage through the city. I crossed the balcony and climbed three stories down the stonework to the courtyard.

Though I'd revisited the destruction at Baghara Estates two nights ago, I'd neglected Akaaris or Simmion Estates for fear of what I would find. I would rectify that mistake tonight, and put my misgivings to rest once and for all.

Maralla was right. It didn't make sense to dose an enemy with keallite, especially one who'd once made a career of killing. Even a lethal dose would take time to work, and any man exposed to it would have several hours of enhanced skill before the drug took him. Anyone in the keallite trade would know that. So, either the lord's son had grievously underestimated me, or he'd gotten exactly the reaction he wanted, and just hadn't expected to be caught on the backswing.

Only essential traffic was permitted in Durgost's streets this late at night. A group of Rorsch Hekkai guards stopped a wagon in front of me. I ducked behind a cobbler's shop and pulled the misty Aether tight. The guards exchanged a few words, checked the driver's papers, and sent him on his way.

Akaaris Estates was half a league from the edge of Baghara Estates, with Lord Belfahr's lands between them. Another oddity—Belfahr's holdings had suffered no damage. Under keallite's influence, I couldn't always distinguish friends from enemies; I surely wouldn't have known one man's estate from another.

Avoiding Belfahr's guards, I strode along the property line between his lands and Akaaris's vacant plot, seeking signs of entry. Moonlight illuminated rows of sweet-smelling orange trees laden with young fruit. I could have passed through here that night, but a deep stream cut through the ravine on Belfahr's side. I tried to recall whether my stockings had been wet when I awoke the next morning, but the memory proved elusive.

There were no breaks in the densely packed branches of the hedgerow at the border. Not even the flowerbeds had been disturbed.

A Rift Bend from Baghara's land into unfamiliar terrain would have been a death sentence in a blackout state. Even Silonas didn't favor me enough to stop an exit rift from opening into a wall or a tree and sending me careening back into the void. I would have needed a Walker like Svaronei, with the finesse to guide me among deadly obstacles. Assuming he could get close enough to me without losing his head.

Something else that didn't sum up—before the fight started, Trennon Baghara had leaped toward Svaronei. An untrained whelp with no weapon on his person had lunged *toward* one of the most well-trained arcanists in the world. Not only had he lived through that encounter, he'd also managed to wrestle a package of keallite from him and attack me with it. I knew Svaronei's abilities. He would have never allowed it.

Unless he'd wanted it to happen.

But why would he want me to lose myself in a keallite-addled frenzy and cut a warpath across the estate? Across *three* estates? Simmion's property was farther off still. That meant another rift. Another impossibility. But I'd spoken with

Svaronei and Vhedja about that night. They assured me I'd killed the lords myself, and they had no reason to lie.

Grass whispered underfoot. Stables and outbuildings lay in piles of broken timbers. The estate house was farther up the road, half its front entry littering the veranda. Most of the dead would have been burned in mass pyres by now, and the corpses of the lords and their heirs had been mounted on pikes surrounding the Scarlet Fountains. The wreckage, however, would take more time to remove.

Dried blood spattered the stairs to the slaves' entrance, and the door hung off its hinges. My fingers brushed the telltale signs of an axe through the wood. I closed my eyes and tried to remember, as if touching the evidence could call the memory forth.

But there was nothing.

My breath left me in a slow sigh, and I braced myself for what I might find inside. I dispelled the Aether Cloak and summoned light, holding the saphyrum bead in my fist to dim its glow.

More blood and broken crockery lined the corridor. Enormous cracks split the walls. The stench of fear lingered—an amalgamation of stale urine and sweat. I kept moving, through the kitchens, through the dining hall, through a sitting room, where a new stench suffused the space.

I knew that smell as intimately as I knew my mother's face. When the slaves came through looking for corpses, they'd missed one.

Part of me shied from what I was about to see. Instinct demanded I turn around, let the dead lie, and take away from this experience only the sight of the bloodstains, the rubble, the corpses piked around the fountains.

A greater part of me demanded I see my victim's face.

She lay beneath a broken armoire. I lifted the heavy pieces from her and set them aside. Bloody foam had leaked from her nose and mouth, and bloat distorted her features. Her neck bulged around her silver collar. Bone jutted from a wound near her clavicle—the killing blow from an axe.

I pressed my fist to my mouth and stepped back. A sound broke the silence, and at first, I didn't recognize it as having come from me. My eyes stung and my body trembled, but still I forced myself to look upon the child.

I hadn't considered there would be children among the innocent dead. It was...

Gods, it was unforgivable.

Mira condemn me for what I'd done.

My knees buckled. My knuckles ground into my brow, my stomach heaved, and my abdominals contracted with shuddering sobs. By the time my tears slowed, the light from my bead had begun to dim, and drawing breath was like raking knives down my throat. I mustered the strength to lift my gaze, but exhaustion pressed me to the floor.

"I'm so sorry."

The child, of course, didn't respond.

A crushed scroll lay caged between her fingers. A final message, I guessed, for when time ran out and the killing began. It was tied with twine and soaked with blood. I carefully extracted the scroll from her and read over the hastily scrawled message.

'The Deal-Breaker knows.'

Gooseflesh crawled across me. I could feel all the fear and urgency with which the words had been written.

My eyes found the axe wound again. The bone had sheared clean through except for the last half-fingerspan, which had splintered before it broke—a familiar pattern burned into my memory from countless arena matches. A pattern I vowed never to see again on one so young.

All the peculiarities of that night tugged at me. The keallite, the lord's heir, Svaronei, my losing control and having no memory of murdering a child—

You have made a fine example of these treacherous houses, Saarach had said. *May their names die with them.*

It seemed like an overstatement, the more I considered it. Keallite was a blight upon us all, but even the highest castes were known to use it. That Baghara, Akaaris, and Simmion had found a way to profit on the substance didn't equate with the destruction of their houses.

We'd collected enough evidence; the courts would have ruled in our favor. Heavy sanctions would have been imposed on the offending estates, their production and distribution equipment would have been seized, and they might have bled themselves dry within a few years without making some drastic alliances.

Instead, it appeared I'd been dosed with keallite, Walked from estate to estate, and strategically set loose to kill them all.

It sounded like conspiracy.

It sounded like madness.

The Deal-Breaker knows.

Something more was going on.

Treacherous, Saarach had called them—a strong term for a keallite ring I'd flushed out within a matter of weeks. How likely was it that something else had necessitated their swift removal from the board?

An ominous weight settled inside me. There was no way to prove I'd been intentionally dosed, but the more I contemplated it, the more likely it seemed. The more I *needed* that to be true, or else this was all my fault. I would have never agreed to destroy these estates without due process from the courts.

But if it was true, if I'd had my autonomy stripped from me by the Deal-Breaker's machinations, then I possessed even less power over my fate than I'd thought.

I tucked the scroll inside my cloak and said a prayer to Baosanni for the dead. The child deserved a proper pyre, but I couldn't grant it without attracting attention. I would order slaves to begin clean-up work at dawn, and they would discover her then.

My knees shook with the effort of rising. I'd seen enough of my own bloody handiwork to last lifetimes, but I still had one last estate to visit before daybreak. If there were any more clues that might guide me to a greater plot behind this butchery, I had to find them.

Chapter Twenty-Four

Maralla

I WOKE UP ALONE.

Night still held the city in thrall, and moonlight bathed the sheer drapery adorning the bed. Mascha's place beside me was cold. The blankets slipped from me as I sat up and scanned the room. It was too early for him to practice forms, and no sounds came from his washroom.

Something was wrong. I felt it like an itch in my limbs, an ache in my spine.

A shadow fell across the balcony doors. One of Mascha's enemies, come to exact revenge. My pulse spiked. I searched for an improvised weapon, grabbing the tome from the bedside table. I slipped out of bed and let the darkness shroud me as I crept toward the door.

The shadow vanished. A silhouette with pointed ears and shoulder-length hair took shape, and my relief swept through me. I lowered the tome.

Mascha banished the Seal on the door in a flash of black-violet and entered quietly. He held a stack of books under one arm.

I stepped into the moonlight, naked, and managed a smile. "You were about to get a book corner to your throat."

He stiffened. I couldn't see his face, but the way his shoulders bowed shoved my prior sense of unease back to the fore.

"Everything alright?"

"Back to bed." The command came out strained, and there was no conviction behind it.

Something was *very* wrong.

I stepped closer, brows furrowing. "What is it?"

His voice cracked. "*Please*, go back to bed."

I might have listened, if not for the realization that he wasn't just asking me. He was begging. He didn't want anyone to see him as a man with a weakness. I hesitated, torn between pressing this advantage, using it to get under his skin, and allowing myself to show the compassion I sensed he desperately needed.

I shouldn't care. He was a slaver. But the last time he'd cried in front of me, I'd refused to go to him and regretted it. I wouldn't make that mistake again. The tiles chilled my soles as I closed the distance.

He backed away. "Maralla—"

"No." I seized his face, forcing him to look at me. "Don't do that. Don't shut me out."

He dropped the stack of books and grabbed my wrists, teeth bared in the meager light. His fingers dug into me with bruising force. "You are right to hate me."

They were my words, lobbed in anger and reflected back at me, but the agony rolling off him was so much worse than their sting. To see him hurting like this brought me no joy or satisfaction. It ate at me like acid.

"Don't lose sight of why," he spat.

I shook my head. "I don't hate you, Mascha."

"You should."

"Well, I don't."

"Then you're as much a fool as the rest of them."

An answering heat arose in my chest. Slaver or not, whatever battle he was facing, I couldn't let him do it alone. But simply asking him to let me in would get me nowhere. I hardened my expression as if facing down one of my errant soldiers and kept my grip firm.

"Tell me what happened."

He scoffed. "I don't think you really want to know."

"I wouldn't have asked if I didn't. *Tell* me."

"Fine. *I killed a child.*"

Cold speared the fire in my muscles. He tore my hands away and retreated, leaving me frozen as he paced the room, clutching his head.

I turned to him, still trying to make sense of his words. "Tonight?"

"No. When I blacked out—when I destroyed those estates." He sucked in a breath. "There is no greater evil than this."

Only in this Chaos-touched country would that news console me. "You weren't yourself."

"I killed her!" He rounded on me, eyes glistening. "I buried my axe in her little chest and she bled out on the floor."

And it was tearing him apart. Mira help me, I didn't know what to say. If he'd really blacked out, he'd probably killed more than one. In war, accidents happened, and though there was no assuaging the guilt, it was at least easier to counsel a soldier who'd made a bad call. But this...

"Do you remember it?"

He shook his head, sagging to the bed with his face in his hands. "I tried, but I couldn't."

I stepped closer until I was within arm's reach. "Would you have killed her if you had the choice?"

His head snapped up, and he glared at me over his curled fingers. "Not in a million gods-damned years."

"I didn't think so." I shoved his hands aside and tipped his chin until his fiery gaze met mine again. Beneath all that anger, heartbreak etched itself in every line of his face. My chest grew heavy, as if his grief were a physical force pressing on me. "You were under the effects of a very powerful drug, Mascha. I imagine it's like raspaati." I couldn't help the jab, and I didn't regret it even when he winced. "I'm not saying you shouldn't grieve or be angry. What I *am* saying is that choice was taken from you. This was as much an accident as any other."

"It was no accident." He waved toward the books scattered on the floor. "He wanted this to happen."

I hesitated, though I didn't have to ask who 'he' was. The Deal-Breaker was the crux of every wretched scheme in Rillion.

Mascha tried to turn away, to hide the single tear that slipped down his cheek. I caught his chin and forced him back.

"Stop that," I snapped. At his owlish look, I wiped the tear and scowled. "You'll not hide this from me."

He sat in stunned silence while I unfastened his cloak, my mind made up. Dark fabric pooled around him. I ran my palms across his shoulders, and a new awareness of the man before me sent a rush through my limbs.

Mascha wasn't used to others taking care of him. Not like this. His need to resist me coiled the muscles beneath my hands, but words alone were no consolation for the travesty he'd experienced. There was only one language that might reach him in this state. If we could lose ourselves in each other for a little while, then maybe his soul-crushing despair would ease, and he might feel better in the morning.

When I reached for the hem of his shirt, he caught my wrists again.

"What are you doing?"

"Let go."

I stood between his knees, my stare unwavering, until he obeyed. I pulled Mascha's shirt over his head.

Bare swells of muscle captured the moonlight, and faint shadows pooled in those chiseled valleys. Small cuts peppered his skin, but my gaze didn't linger on them.

"Remove your boots, then stand up."

I stepped back and waited. He watched me warily, and I said a silent prayer to Delvin that Mascha would take my word as law.

As he bent to unlace his boots, I closed my eyes and breathed out. In the near-seven months I'd spent with Mascha, I'd learned so much about him. I knew the sound of his breath and the cadence of his footsteps. I knew the pattern of scarring on his torso, the subtle crease in his brow when he was thinking, and the pair of dimples in his lower back. I could trick his Foresight into seeing double, and I could predict to within a few seconds when his patience with my little annoyances would run out.

But the most important things I'd learned came only from the last few weeks. I knew how sensitive his ear tips were, and how he liked when I took control when we kissed. I knew the sound of his heartbeat—a strong, steady rhythm beneath my ear—and I knew how firmly to wrap my arm around him when that rhythm changed and the nightmares threatened.

Most of all, I understood how Mascha protected those he could from a system that would otherwise crush them. I knew now that his most unsavory traits were merely for show, that beneath his coarse exterior existed a man who only wanted to live his life in comfort and peace. Yet, if the Deal-Breaker had his way, he would strip Mascha of what little compassion and temperance he still possessed.

He wasn't Nalerta. He could never replace the mate I'd lost, but Mascha was more than just a slaver, more than Rorsch Hekkai, more than the master of this palace. It staggered me, knowing in my heart that I would remember him long after I left this country behind me.

He rose from the bed, and I reached for that rhythm within his chest. Elevated though it was, the turmoil that only moments ago threatened to undo him began to ebb in the wake of my instructions. Quiet curiosity filtered in beneath his furrowed brows.

I kept one hand pressed over his heartbeat; the other claimed the laces of his trousers.

"You don't have to—"

"*Kas hadem.*" I lobbed the Rillanese demand for silence gently but firmly back at him, lifting my chin until our noses nearly touched. Our breaths mingled, and my lips feathered over his. My own heart was racing, and tremors of heat pooled in my belly. "Let me do this for you."

With a solid tug on his laces, our mouths met and his trousers loosened. He grabbed my waist and pulled me closer, so that I had to maneuver around him to shove the fabric off his hips. He stepped clear and hoisted me into his arms. I wrapped my legs around him and went to war with lips, teeth, and tongue.

He broke away with a gasp. "I can't ask this of you."

"You're not." I pulled back, stroking his ears with my thumbs. "Do you want to stop?"

"No, but—" Conflict warred in his eyes. "You shouldn't feel obligated."

I understood what he needed then. I kissed him again, long and slow, taking control. "I don't feel obligated." I punctuated the statement with another kiss. "You are not my master." My hands sifted into his hair. "You never were." I arched into him, and he shuddered. "And you never will be."

"You are a goddess," he whispered, trembling, turning with me toward the bed.

My back struck the plush blankets. His hungry kisses stole under my jaw, down my throat, between my breasts. I heaved a sigh as he seized my leg in one hand and splayed his other fingers over my chest.

White-violet magic rippled outward from his touch, dancing with the moonlight on my skin. A cool lightness caressed my neck. I touched the space where my collar had been, marveling at his silent reassurance. He claimed no ownership over me, and I came to his bed of my own free will.

Mascha knelt between my legs and stared back with an intensity unrivaled by the staunchest warriors. "I would worship you."

He lifted my legs over his shoulders. His beard tickled my thighs, and more heat spilled into me. "Give me pleasure, Mascha."

He shivered. "As you command."

With gentle fingers and expert tongue, Mascha redefined devotion. My toes curled against his back, thighs clenching his ears. Waves of sensation crashed through my body. I seized his hair and arched into him, craving more. My inner walls squeezed his fingers, and the moan that left him traveled into my core.

He came up for air, lips gleaming, his fingers still buried inside me. "You taste divine."

I laughed breathlessly. "I didn't say you could stop."

His mirth came out broken, riding the edge between a sob and purest relief. The sound brought a rush of warmth to my eyes. He went back to work with renewed vigor, grinding his tongue to the rhythm of his hand. My cries filled the room.

I was so close. He seemed to sense it and thrust harder, tongue lashing me relentlessly. Pressure built as I arched off the bed. His free hand gripped my backside, holding me to him. A growl punctuated his determination. The knowledge that I would come for him, one way or another, was a heady one.

Just this once, I surrendered to him.

Stars exploded behind my eyelids. My climax stormed through me like thunder. A cry tore from me, then another, and a third broke in my throat as Mascha kept the pressure on, circling, stroking, lavishing me with his tongue. Such exquisite torture could have lasted moments or lifetimes, but it wasn't until another stronger climax broke over me that his movements slowed.

I lay there dazed, muscles shaking. My breath couldn't fill my lungs fast enough. Mascha kissed a lingering trail up my torso until he reached my breasts. I held him to me, shivering when his mouth claimed first one nipple, then the other. When I could finally form words again, I ran my thumbs over his ear tips and spoke into the silence.

"Kiss me."

"Your will, goddess."

A smile threatened. "Careful. I might get used to that."

"Maybe you'd prefer queen?" His nose brushed mine. "Or empress?"

"Hm." I chuckled. "I think I prefer goddess."

Mascha caught my lip between his teeth. "Goddess it is."

I lifted my head to meet his kiss, then threaded one leg through his. With firm pressure against his chest and an insistent tug of my heel, I rolled with him until I was on top. Messy braids tumbled down my back, and my fingertips skated his length. He twitched, letting out a groan of need, but made no demands. Though my thighs still quivered from his attention, I rolled my hips forward as if he were already inside me.

"What shall I call you?" I grinned as I curled my hand around him.

"Helpless," he offered. "Stricken. Besotted."

My noncommittal hum rebuffed all three. I thought long about it, stroking him until his breath grew labored and his powerful figure writhed beneath my touch.

"Tipori."

Eyes that had grown heavy-lidded refocused through a haze of desire. He frowned. "Tipori?"

I nodded, more to myself than to him. *Ciir*, for the way he protected his own, Mercy was a good name for him.

Mascha pushed himself up and captured my chin. Though I kept possessive hold of him between us, he studied me with a scrutiny that could have put the most learned scholars to shame. A maelstrom of emotions flickered across his face, too fast for me to name every one.

But then he was kissing me again, and it didn't matter anymore.

Urgently, passionately, he kissed me, until I was dizzy with need and reeling from lack of air. He held my waist, my hips, my thighs, as if to stop himself from touching me would be the death of him.

I plunged one hand into his hair and rose onto my knees, positioning him at my center. My forehead rested against his as I sank onto his length.

"Gods, woman." Mascha traced my jaw with his lips. "What are you doing to me?"

My fingers tightened in his hair as I tilted his head up. "I'm taking you away from here, Tipori." I offered a smile at his hesitation. "Just for tonight."

Longing and devotion softened his expression. "Alright. For tonight."

Fully in control of our movements, I began the work of coaxing pleasure from him in earnest. Chest to chest, arms bracing his shoulders, I captured his mouth and brushed my tongue against his lips. He surrendered to me with a sigh, hands splayed across my back.

Sweat coated my skin. It dried on my brow and collarbone as Mascha blew cool air over me. I bared my throat to his kisses, and he obliged me with a fervor that forced my eyes to close.

He slipped his hand between us and found my center once more. With every roll of my hips, he ensured I felt that sensation against his fingertips. I whimpered my need, and his teeth bared to the moonlight in a smile both enchanting and victorious.

"Are you going to come for me again, goddess?" he teased.

Forget his history in the arena; his *stamina* was the thing of legend. I shifted just enough to take the pressure off that sensitive spot. "You first."

His laughter resounded through the room. He stole a kiss and repositioned, chasing that sensation threatening to send me over the edge. "Together?"

My brows tensed in a faltering attempt to understand how such a thing could be so well-timed. Curious, I nodded. "Together."

A predatory spark alighted in his gaze. "Hold on to me."

He gave me a little time to wrap my arms around his neck before flipping me onto my back. Still inside me, adjusting his hand, Mascha took over. He blinked rapidly once, eyes glazing, then blinked again, and some of my whimpers turned to broken laughter.

Foresight. Of course.

With a subtle movement of his fingers, he stroked me from a new angle while he thrust. A shockwave of pleasure scattered like chain lightning through me. My gasp became a cry as he thrust again, and again, each time like a saphyric flare going off in my core. Mascha's rhythm was exactly what I needed, perfectly paced to undo me.

"*Saonis miraar*," I breathed, clinging to his shoulders. "Mascha, I'm—"

"I know," he panted. "Come with me."

His movements lengthened and his eyes closed. As he filled me with a final, solid thrust, my entire world splintered apart. My awareness became no more than fragments of moonlight awash in pleasure and heat. Only my hands, anchored against Mascha's shoulders, kept me from dissolving into the Aether itself.

I was still breaking, still spasming, when Mascha sagged to the mattress and tugged me close. He brushed my hair from my neck and planted featherlight kisses along my jaw.

"Thank you for this," he whispered. "It is a memory I will cherish."

True mastery of my quivering limbs felt hours away, but I managed to turn and settle deeper into Mascha's arms. He tucked my head beneath his chin and held me tighter. His heartbeat lulled me and his scent enveloped me in a sphere of comfort.

And for the first time in seven months, I didn't think about leaving him.

Chapter Twenty-Five

Mascha

"Marvelous." Bastian adjusted a wayward string of jewels and circled Maralla again. Dozens of golden strands hung from her new collar and flowed between her breasts. Each glittered with tiny diamonds like water in the sun. A matching skirt of chains settled low around her hips and shortened gradually as it wrapped from left to right. "Truly a masterpiece."

I leaned to one side of my high-backed chair, swirling my wine and subtly shaking my head as Maralla eyed the sharp tools on Bastian's belt. Outside of the jeweler's view, she rolled her eyes, and her Aetherial image gave me a crude gesture.

"She is," I agreed, my gaze never leaving her face.

Bastian guffawed. "I can't believe this is the same woman they called *Johtan Shasnaram*. You have done wonders with her."

In my mind, I could almost hear Maralla laughing. "She presented quite the challenge."

Ignorant of his own peril, Bastian reached out to stroke Maralla's temple. She shivered, but didn't recoil, and I made a conscious effort to appear amused. This was good practice for us both, in truth. My tailor, Frahtziir, had already visited this morning to make the final adjustments for my solstice attire, and he'd spent long minutes afterward ogling Maralla and fondling her breasts. Tasari had also stopped by earlier to offer lewd commentary before announcing he was leaving for Epillon early to shop for supplies.

There would be much more of this to come at the gala this evening. Best to desensitize her now, while I schooled myself in keeping my head.

Bastian studied her, then gave me an odd look. "Will you keep her?"

I stilled.

Perhaps he sensed my fondness. Maybe I'd been careless about my lingering glances. However he'd intuited my desires, nothing could come of them. Gods help me, I wanted to keep her. If she could be happy with me, I would keep her for all time. But she didn't belong here, and I would sooner see her freed than force her to contend anymore with Rillanese politics.

I sipped my wine and set my glass aside. "No, I'm afraid not." I rose and collected Bastian's payment from a side table. "This one wasn't meant for me."

Bastian hefted the coins and eyed me with a knowing candor. "I beg to differ, my friend. To hear the nobles talk, she is your crowning achievement. And to be truthful, you are getting older. Isn't it time you chose a wife?"

I lifted a brow. "This, from a man who has never taken a wife or had children? Maybe my preferences better align with yours."

"If that were true, I'd know it. Besides, where I come from, wives are a chore. They learn to expect things." He made a face and gestured dismissively. "You know, respect, quality time, that sort of thing."

A laugh rumbled out of me. "Gods forbid."

Still, the jeweler didn't relent. He pounded my shoulder. "But you, Mascha, are a Champion, and *leader* of the Rorsch Hekkai. Why, you should have three or four wives and a dozen children by now."

I forced a smile. Rather than assure him I did indeed have several dozen offspring out there somewhere, I steered him toward the exit. "I don't need that sort of distraction any more than you do, *amii*. Now, if we're finished—"

"On the contrary," Bastian argued as I opened the door for him, "I think it's just what you need. You've been too comfortable for too long here in this dusty old palace. Imagine what fine, strapping boys the two of you could make together."

"Believe me, if the Deal-Breaker saw fit to provide me a wife, he would." I wasn't about to explain my true reservations to Bastian. I shot a sideways glance at Maralla and gestured for her to remain here while I escorted the jeweler out. "Seeing as how he hasn't, I can only assume it's not part of his plans."

Bastian pursed his lips, grudgingly allowing me to usher him into the corridor. "Well, perhaps the old boy is busy. Tiior knows he can't be everywhere at once."

I chuckled. "Debatable."

The Deal-Breaker's network of agents and spies was so extensive, a man couldn't move about this country without encountering one. By design, my employer made himself unreachable, even for those who worked for him directly. It was even likely the man who had placed my Freedom Wager eighty years ago was not the same one I answered to now.

"You know, if you actually showed some initiative, I'm sure he wouldn't refuse you." Bastian's chiding continued until we reached the foyer. A pair of slaves opened the doors for him, and he finally relented with an indignant huff. "I just don't see what you're so afraid of."

I clapped his arm, then offered my hand. "Have you met Lord Belfahr's wife?"

The grin that broke across his face was half-grimace. "A crude but acceptable point." He clasped my wrist. "Pleasure doing business, as always, Mascha."

"Always." I returned the gesture. "Will I see you this evening?"

"Mm, you know I wouldn't miss it." Bastian leaned in conspiratorially, his grip on my wrist tightening. "Plus, I'm looking forward to your first dance with your future bride."

I laughed and shoved him out the door. "Get out of here. I've other business to be about."

"Yes, yes, of course you do."

"Until this evening."

The doors closed behind him. I turned from the entrance, brows furrowing, and made my way back to the sitting room where I'd left Maralla.

We'd practiced our dance a few times this week, but my preoccupation with the note from Akaaris Estates and the secret ledger books I'd found in Lord Simmion's study made our attempts counterproductive.

The Deal-Breaker knows.

Simmion's ledgers had revealed financial exchanges with dozens of lower-caste and middling-caste houses, most of whose leadership had disappeared or died recently from accidents or mysterious illness. The treachery Saarach had spoken of became clearer with each name I investigated from the list.

One name stood out from the rest: the as-yet-unaccounted-for Kestra Hyanaro. Every ledger page, every correspondence pertaining to Simmion's lower-caste dealings contained either his name or his initials. Not only did Hyanaro seem to have his hand in every facet of the upper-caste lords' keallite business, but there were other ventures too: weapons, lands, food, education. Hyanaro had even been paid a handsome donation for something labeled 'urchin initiative.'

It seemed rebellion was brewing in the lower echelons of Rillanese society, and I'd just cut the wings off a newly hatched dragon. The keallite trade had been the rebels' main source of funding, and my personal involvement in the raids had both circumvented the courts and allowed the Deal-Breaker to crush Hyanaro's strongest supporters in one swift blow.

I'd always thought of myself as the wielder of the axe. It sobered and horrified me to realize I was merely the axe instead.

Maralla greeted me with a scowl and gestured toward the costly jewelry. "You really expect me to go out in this?"

I appraised her at length, deliberately taking in every curve and plane until her annoyance with me became a tangible thing. "*Ciir.*" One corner of my mouth lifted. "And try not to kill any of the guests while we're there. It may be hard to sell you if you do."

"He was asking for it." She folded her arms. "They all were. Especially that bastard brother of yours."

"Bastian is a good man." I collected the wine I'd left unattended. Out of habit, I dumped the rest of the fine vintage in a nearby house plant before retrieving a clean glass and an unopened bottle. "Though Tasari, I will not dispute."

I uncorked the wine and poured a glass. Maralla crossed the space and took it from me, her sharp gaze daring me to protest. Rather than rise to the bait, I filled another glass.

"To freedom."

A shadow fell over her face. She studied my raised glass, then frowned into hers.

My humor faltered. "What is it?"

Furrows lined her brow, but she eventually lifted her eyes and offered a weak smile. Crystal rang between us as she raised her glass to mine.

"To freedom," she said.

We sipped our wine, but the shadow lingered in her expression. She retreated to the empty hearth, chains swaying, giving me a full view of the scars on her back.

Sorrow bit into me. Free though Maralla would be, the evidence of how I'd harmed her would forever remain. How fitting—how terrible—that her memories of me should match my legacy of pain and blood.

I set my drink aside. We hadn't coupled again since that night, but she'd spent every one in my arms, as if seeking refuge from the world outside my bedroom. My duties to Raenara and the new slaves had suffered as a result, but I didn't care.

I'd felt this recklessness once before with Anelliiq. This all-consuming need to be beside her, to kiss her and hold her. It was how I knew I had to complete Maralla's sale as soon as possible. I would put her on the fastest ship in the West Aivenosian and ensure we never saw each other again.

Maralla sighed and hugged one elbow, the top of her wine glass visible beyond her arm. I hesitated in going to her, referencing my Foresight for how she might respond to my touch.

Only one image formed. My heart stuttered at how passionately her misty image kissed me. It was desperation, longing, and acceptance. It was affection, hope, and trust.

I saw it now. That feeble smile, her hesitation, the lingering look into her wine… No. No, this couldn't happen. If I simply refused to act, it should vanish.

Maralla placed her glass on the mantel and turned. Fire kindled in her gaze. "Tipori."

Exquisite agony nearly sent me to my knees. She could have called me anything, yet she'd chosen that. Though she couldn't understand its significance, it was like she could see the man I was supposed to be.

I stepped toward her, lest I stumble. "Goddess."

Maralla traced her misty image across the space and leaped into my arms, palms seizing my face. Our mouths locked, and I didn't know if I should push her away or pull her closer. Chains and gems dug into my abdomen; her strong thighs wrapped my waist. I held her backside and parted my lips for her tongue, even as the sensible part of me tried to resist.

"I still have business—"

"Damn right you do." Her tongue traced the length of my ear.

I shivered. "What would you have of me?"

"All of you."

Rose oil and jasmine overwhelmed me. I carried her to the nearest table and laid her down. Her chain skirt scraped the wood, and I fumbled for the clasp to remove it.

Svaronei would be here soon to Walk us to the capital, but Vhedja was busy overseeing the distribution of Rorsch Hekkai security, and Tasari was stocking up on supplies. We had time.

I stroked her to wetness, then entered her carefully, my fingers circling that spot. This was about her pleasure, not mine. She might wear my collar, but she wasn't my slave. She never had been.

Maralla bared her throat to my kisses, her nails biting into my shoulders as I moved inside her.

"Say you'll come north."

Whispered words, full of yearning, caressed my ear. I drew back with a wince, bracing my weight against the table. "I can't—"

Her expression turned fierce. "Lie to me, Tipori. Tell me you'll find a way."

Breath abandoned me when I realized what she was really asking. I never gave my word unless I was certain I could honor it. But as I held her smoldering gaze, content to let her fire consume me completely, I set that conviction aside. She needed me to cut her loose from the last rope tethering her to Rillion. If I couldn't be the man she thought I was, then I would be the axe.

I captured her mouth with mine. She hooked her heels over my thighs and pressed me deeper. As I resumed my task of pleasuring her, I pressed my forehead to hers and lied so well, I almost believed it myself.

"I'll find a way north. You have my word."

Chapter Twenty-Six

Maralla

The last time I'd set foot in Epillon, the Iceborn raiders had just unloaded me from a cargo hold smelling of fleshrot and death. Out of a hundred or so taken from the battlefield near Sessia, an ocean away, roughly half of us remained. We were starved and sick, infested with parasites, and covered in body fluids—many not our own—but I'd managed to stash enough saphyrum inside my orifices before our capture to have some strength left. I'd sent the first slaver who'd touched me above deck overboard with a broken nose.

I'd just stolen a hairpin, picked the lock on my spellbinders, and set fire to an entire slave block when I met Mascha for the first time. He'd been amused by my attempts to break through the rift wards. He promised me I would soon be spreading my legs for him on sheets worth more than my price tag.

I would never have expected to return to this gods-forsaken city wearing his collar and leaking his seed. Worse, I'd never expected I wouldn't be angry about it.

Svaronei dumped us out of his rift far away from the port. At least I wouldn't have to relive the horror of the docks.

I was still reeling from the Walk over when we reached the palace gates. Gleaming metal twisted into elaborate whorls, and vicious spikes adorned the tops. Two pairs of purple-clad guards waved us through, each leering at different parts of me as we passed.

Mascha's plan to draw others' attention certainly worked. Even the gardeners paused in their tasks to gawk at me in my ridiculous attire. The only way it could have been more ostentatious was if I'd worn jeweled slippers instead of silk-topped leather.

Turrets capped with elaborate domes marched away from the palace doors in both directions. The midday sun gleamed through arched windows and scattered shadows across sculpted reliefs of dragons guarding the veranda. For all its gaudiness, it was less intimidating than Mascha's palace. Either I was growing desensitized to the way the Rillanese threw away their wealth, or the Chancellor's abode didn't have the same reputation as the infamous Rorsch Hekkai's.

I trailed Mascha and Svaronei through the entrance, failing to keep my eyes low as I took in the four-story chandelier falling like rain down to the first floor. Banners made of shimmering fabric lined the path, each one bearing the seals of the most powerful houses in the country.

Svaronei's boots squeaked across polished tile ahead of us. I stopped short when the light caught a vein of blue-green in the stone.

Saonis miraar.

Saphyrum. The floor was laced with saphyrum.

Fury alighted in my chest. It swept outward to scorch me all the way to my fingertips. I'd endured many decadent displays in Rillion, but this...

This was worse than wasteful casting, worse than using it as a light source, worse than wearing it as jewelry. My people *died* for lack of what these bastards trod on every day.

Slaves and guards bustled through the foyer, some eyeing me as I stood staring at their feet. Mascha made it several more paces before turning back.

I'd lost my youngest child to saphyrum sickness. Supplies had been running low that year and maintaining the pregnancy had been hard. Declaan was born at fifteen months—three months earlier than any Syljian babe should have. He'd been a feeble boy, prone to breaking bones his body couldn't heal. My sister's magic had been his only saving grace, but even Orowen couldn't sustain him forever. The sickness had taken him shortly after he turned five.

A nauseating blend of bile and tears arose.

Mascha retraced his steps. Though his warmth steadied me, his words cut deep. "It's beautiful, isn't it, *rascha*?"

"It's an extravagance." I choked on the words. "Master."

Play my part. Play my part.

He touched my face, wiping away a single tear with his thumb. "Come. The Chancellor awaits."

I'd never discussed my people's plight with Mascha, but he seemed to understand. After he greeted Chancellor Aggasar Hassiim and confirmed the placement of both the palace guards and his Rorsch Hekkai forces, he drew me away to a private suite and Sealed the door.

"I've heard stories about what it's like in the north." Mascha stood behind me in the ornate mirror. Diamonds and gold thread adorned his white doublet and glinted in the sunlight. "How Syljians suffer."

I studied our reflection and how perfectly regal he looked. Like a king, gods damn him, and I—powdered, primped, and bedazzled—his consort. I barely recognized myself. If not for the runes on my face, I might have accepted this as my new reality. I might have cast aside all hope of returning to my people—to the mud, snow, and rock where I belonged.

I scowled at my facsimile in the mirror. I wore furs and leathers, not silk and jewels. I was a warrior, a commander, not a simpering display piece for men to ogle and fuck as they saw fit.

"We should end this farce quickly." Turning to him, I added, "My people need me."

He nodded, contemplation creasing his brow. "Would your Alliaansi be amenable to anonymous donations?"

My first inclination was to scoff—of course a Rillanese man would expect any problem could be solved with money—but I bit my tongue.

"What do you mean?"

"I own a private mine down by Naskatam that produces more saphyrum than I need." He smoothed my eyebrow with his thumb. "Normally, I sell the excess or use it in trade, but it wouldn't be missed if I sent it north instead."

"You..." My voice broke. "You would do that for us?"

"For you, *ciir*. It's not much. Perhaps a few dozen barrels every quarter."

A few dozen *barrels*? I shook my head, disbelieving. "Mascha, that's more than some of our mines make in a year."

"Then consider it yours."

My breath labored as I considered how much difference that would make to so many lives. "Thank you."

How was this the same man I'd met seven months ago? How had he retained so much of his compassion despite this gods-cursed country that would sooner grind its subjects into dust than lift a finger to help those less fortunate? They didn't deserve him. Not the Chancellor, or the nobles, or least of all the Deal-Breaker.

"It will have to be discreet. I cannot embroil Rillion in a foreign war."

Overcome, I wrapped my arms around his neck and kissed him. His warm hands closed on my waist. The diamonds on his doublet scraped my skin as I pressed myself flush against him.

Mascha grinned against my mouth. "Careful," he mumbled. "You'll start something I intend to finish."

I bit his lip in defiance, then pried myself away. "Such pretty promises you make."

The first guests arrived as the pendulus chimed nineteenth hour.

I paused in the corridor behind Mascha's right shoulder. He glanced around a sculpted archway, observing the silk-and-jewel-bedecked nobles and slaves who filtered into the palace. His security directed them between stone sculptures, through curtains of purple velvet, and into the glittering ballroom beyond.

"Remember," he said, turning to me, "you're here on display for all of Rillion to see. Keep your eyes down and be silent unless someone asks you a direct question."

"I know."

He hesitated. "Any potential buyers will fondle you at length and openly. You must let them."

I'd heard all this twice before. I could still feel the tailor's hands on me, and the last thing I wanted was to be reminded of it. "I *know*."

"This is important, Maralla." He glanced around the corner again, then pulled me into a small alcove and cupped my cheek. "If you insult someone here, it could mean your life. Say you understand."

I reached up to tug his beard. "I understand."

"Good. With Silonas's fortune, I can make a deal for you tonight and close within the week." Our noses touched briefly, but when Mascha straightened, his mask slipped into place once more. "Are you ready, *rascha*?"

I clasped my hands and lowered my eyes. "Yes, Master."

"Then come."

Chapter Twenty-Seven

Mascha

As we approached the line of guests, I spared a glance behind me to ensure Maralla was following at an appropriate distance. Her jewelry caught the last rays of sun and set off a dazzling display across her lilac skin. Catari had styled her hair in the current Rillanese fashion. Ornate braids and beaded ribbons coiled around her head before tumbling down her back.

I looked away, lest the sight of her leave me breathless.

Our appearance from the side corridor caught the attention of Chancellor Hassiim's guests. Instantly, conversation shifted to the new slave at my back.

Everyone knew processing slaves was my specialty. Maralla would be coveted not only for her beauty, but also for my exceptional training of her. Even if I'd come to agree with Maralla's condemnation of raspaati, I couldn't deny its results. My slaves loved me for what I could give them, and feared me for what I could take away. It was a system that had only failed me once in over sixty years.

That failure had just hit the market, and based on the long line of men whose ravenous eyes made my skin crawl with possessive fervor, I wagered she would sell within hours.

There was a small chance her escape might come back to haunt me. But given my reputation, it was more likely to cost her new owner prestige and status instead. The man's competence and estate security would be called into question, and no other man worth his coin would do business with him again.

I considered which of the houses in attendance might be in the market for an exotic beauty. I eliminated any men who paid handsomely for Rorsch Hekkai security, houses I didn't wish to see suffer such a loss, and any families the Deal-Breaker favored. That left four potential names: Ommun Zaff III, Doneev

Sattar VI, Andalah Imiir, and Po's father, R.S.J. Naftalli. Smaller houses all, but with enough capital to pay what Maralla was worth. I would see to it that one of them took her home.

Uttered words followed us all the way to the curtains:

"Good evening, Mascha."

"What a beauty she is, *meschiir*."

"Greetings, Rorsch Hekkai."

"You've outdone yourself this time."

"That's *Johtan Shasnaram*!"

I returned the greetings when appropriate and slowed to catch the eye of the handsome young lord who had spoken Maralla's epithet. I winked at him and smiled.

As we entered the bustling ballroom, the lord's neighbors pounced, demanding all he knew about *Johtan Shasnaram*. By twentieth hour, gossip would reach the farthest corners of the palace.

Though the night was young, over a hundred guests already roamed the space. From the crystal and silver adorning the tables to the stained glass back-lit by saphyrum lanterns, the room was awash with light and color. High columns stood thicker than Aivenosian oaks and supported balconies crafted from saphyrum-laced stone. Mirrors were strategically arranged around the ball-room, creating the illusion of infinite space.

I gave the room a thorough sweep, searching first for anyone who might bear symptoms of the weeping pox. It was in these close gatherings that the magically resistant disease seemed to thrive, and until Tasari or another alchemist could manufacture a cure, only vigilance and quarantine stood between us and economic ruin.

Next, I paid close attention to things that might trigger my Foresight: certain places, like near the buffet or the dessert tables where rival houses often congregated; certain people, like Wali Amin, who enjoyed assaulting slaves and complaining about the service; and certain passageways where illicit deals might go awry and lead to stabbings. Misty images formed, but I Saw nothing beyond ordinary squabbles in the immediate future. For those few that appeared not to resolve themselves without incident, I signaled three Rorsch Hekkai guards and directed them to new locations to deter those conflicts. I would check again throughout the evening.

I glanced over my shoulder. "Are you hungry?"

Maralla kept her eyes low. "Yes, Master."

I made for the buffet, striding right to the front of the line. I slipped in between Lord Rehmund Belfahr, his gristly old wife, and their youngest daughter, Syleese.

Belfahr sputtered. "Now, just who in the Wastelands do you think you—"

I took hold of the daughter's shoulder and pressed close. "Pardon the intrusion, *sadarah*."

Her tawny skin erupted with gooseflesh. Her dark eyes peered out from a mass of beautiful black curls, and she swooned against me. "You are a welcome intrusion, Rorsch Hekkai."

"Mascha!" Lord Belfahr hurried to press a plate from the stack into my other hand. "Apologies, my friend. I didn't recognize you. How is business?"

The nobleman's clumsy attempt to disguise his contempt failed spectacularly. A smile tugged at my lips.

"Busy as always, my lord." I turned to the buffet and began loading my plate. "Has the new security at your estate been satisfactory?"

Old Belfahr's face pinched like a dried fig. "Oh, yes. Your men are just as promised." He fumbled for something more to say as we moved down the line. "After that keallite scandal next door, I've a mind to purchase another regiment. It's truly a shame Yamon and Enghal sank so low."

"Indeed." I plucked two dinner rolls from the buffet. Rumors surrounding the raids had reached outlandish proportions and brought me no closer to finding Kestra Hyanaro, but it was best to let them run their course. I made a show of eyeing Syleese before smiling at her father. "I'm certain we can come to some arrangement."

Belfahr hesitated. The lord was still cross with me for demanding that Syleese seal his last security deal rather than either of his older, empty-headed daughters. He'd even filed a complaint with the trade commission, claiming I'd overstepped my seal of flesh by taking her before her impending nuptials. But even the mighty commissioners wouldn't meddle with the Rorsch Hekkai.

He snatched a glass of wine from a passing slave and cleared his throat. "Perhaps with a reduced fee?"

Unfortunately for Belfahr, I recognized the endeavors of a man trying to rise above his station.

I popped a cherry tart into my mouth and chewed, keeping my expression steadily impassive. That was all the intimidation the little man needed. While the lord of Rehmund Resorts floundered with his unseemly request, I passed my heaping plate to Maralla, who waited behind me with a line of other slaves. Then I took Syleese's face and kissed her firmly on her lips. She leaned in, sighing into my mouth. When I pulled away, she remembered her manners and her heavy-lidded eyes slid off mine.

"I'll see what can be done, provided this one seals the deal for you again." I stroked her cheek, looking aside to Belfahr, who knew better than to bristle at how Syleese melted like tallow in my hands. "And pending an audit of your accounts."

Belfahr paled. "An audit, my lord—"

"I am no lord." My grip on Syleese tightened, and she whimpered. "We have been over this before."

"M-my apologies, Rorsch Hekkai." Belfahr's eyes darted to his daughter. He bowed low—a movement made awkward by the plate he held. "Forgive me."

My grin slid back into place. I released Syleese and steadied her plate. "Good evening to you, *sadarah*."

Syleese flushed. "Good evening, *meschiir*."

With a final nod to Lord and Lady Belfahr, I returned to Maralla, who stared pointedly at my plate. Her lips parted, then closed as I strode past her. She fell in behind me.

I found a vacant table in one corner, took the food from Maralla, and gestured for her to kneel beside me. Slaves were not permitted to sit at the table, nor were they allowed to eat from the buffet. However, they could consume what their masters didn't eat—a practice to ensure little went to waste. The less food wasted, the fewer peasants would rummage through the palace trash later.

Maralla knelt, and I slipped her a bite. Her pouting lips and shadowed eyes betrayed her mounting anger.

"What is it?"

She shook her head and kept her eyes down, but I knew her moods well enough now. If she didn't let something out, she might explode.

"Tell me."

"You play your part a little too well."

Though she didn't raise her voice, its bite sank deep. I sat quietly, picking at the vegetables on my plate. "You knew what to expect."

"*Ciir*." She fidgeted with a gold strand in her lap. "But it's still hard to watch how despicably women are treated here."

I was only acting as the nobility expected me to, but now wasn't the time to reassure her. Under the guise of watching Aetherial eddies come and go, I noted not for the first time how free women and slaves looked so much alike: hands clasped, eyes downcast, adorned with fake smiles or none at all. Some of the free women spoke to their men, but most remained silent. They were bartering tools in Rillion; the prettier they were, the more likely a man could seal a deal with them.

Yet the most intelligent, perspicacious people I knew were women I'd bedded, and I preferred their company over most others. To see them languish in a system that sought to grind their entire gender into the dirt—it *was* despicable.

I'd been at the bottom. I knew the horrors of slavery as well as anyone. It was why I tried to make my slaves' lives better. If I was to protect them, I had to protect myself, and deviating publicly from Rillanese expectations would see me removed from power immediately.

"Rillion has been this way for hundreds of years." I looked down at Maralla. "It is simply the way of things."

"You're content with a centuries-old system of oppression that has caused you and so many others such immeasurable pain?" She shook her head in disgust. "I'm disappointed in you, Tipori."

The words ran me through.

If you wielded your influence the way you wield your axes...

I wasn't content with it. I hadn't been for years, and yet I'd done nothing.

"Well," I told her, "if you think of a way to change it before you leave, I'm all ears."

"Don't patronize me," she spat, glaring at the floor.

"I'm not." I offered her a dinner roll as I contemplated my next words. "You're right. I have enough influence here. Perhaps I can be a catalyst for change."

That *did* make her break composure. As she looked up, I looked away, ensuring our eyes didn't meet.

It was a good thing, too, because a flash of Foresight afforded me a glimpse of a rail-thin Rillanese noble striding toward us through the sea of tables. A few moments later, the man appeared. He wore a silver-embroidered doublet and matching trousers. His bushy brows turned up at the corners, and a braided mustache framed his thin lips.

I rose and locked eyes with Ommun Zaff III. The man faltered when he realized my full attention had settled upon him.

"*Meschiir* Zaff," I said. "I was just thinking about you."

Zaff was in his late twenties, but he had the spine of a man much older. In the time it took to close the gap between us, he managed to regain his wits. He grasped my wrist, his voice steady.

"Good things, I pray." His eyes betrayed his intentions as they slid toward Maralla.

I squeezed his wrist in turn, pleased the gossip had reached him so soon. House Zaff had lost some social status recently with the announcement of his mother's retirement from deal-making. Zaff III had yet to marry, and Mira had only blessed the family with boys. He must have gleaned what renown he could reclaim with the purchase of *Johtan Shasnaram*.

"Good things, indeed." I released him. "What can I do for you?"

"I think you already know." He thrust his chin toward Maralla. "Is she for sale?"

"I'm accepting offers."

"May I?"

"Certainly. Rise, *Johtan Shasnaram*."

Maralla rose smoothly, still holding the dinner roll in one hand. I took it from her and placed it on the table.

"She is papered, I assume?" Zaff grasped her chin. Her eyes slipped away from his.

"*Ciir*." I clasped my hands. "All my slaves are papered and guaranteed free of parasites and disease upon delivery."

Zaff's hand roamed over the golden strands of her collar, down to her naked chest. Maralla stood unmoving and impassive, selling her ruse flawlessly.

"How old?"

"One hundred and fifty-nine."

Zaff nodded. "Syljian longevity. They live to—what, three hundred?"

"Four hundred, if properly maintained. The extra years should, of course, be reflected in her bid."

Nodding again, Zaff's fingers skimmed across her belly. He walked a slow circle around her and squeezed her backside, pausing at the sight of her scars. "I heard she gave you some trouble."

My face twitched, but I fashioned it into a smile. "She wasn't named *Johtan Shasnaram* because of a docile temperament, *meschiir*. But as you can see, my methods just needed more time with this one. The healer assures me the scars will lighten with age."

"They will decrease her value."

"I don't think so." This time, my grin was genuine. So predictable, these young ones. "Those are the product of the last beating *Johtan Shasnaram* took before she was broken. They may mar her beauty some, but the legendary moment they represent is something special."

Zaff stared long at me. Then he laughed—a deep, jovial laugh. "So, it is true what they say about you. You really could sell the boots off a peasant."

I continued to smile.

"Alright," he said. "Two hundred thousand."

Maralla's eyes went wide. It was an exorbitant offer for any ordinary slave, but much less than she would sell for at auction. Her offer price must reflect her worth *and* the convenience of outmaneuvering the competition. The last thing I wanted to do was draw the Deal-Breaker's attention to a suspicious sale.

"Two hundred." I inclined my head. "I'll keep that in mind, *Meschiir* Zaff, and notify you by evening's end if yours is the most substantial offer I receive."

Zaff bowed, accepting the subtle rejection with grace. "You honor me with your time, Rorsch Hekkai."

"Likewise." As the man moved off, I returned to my seat. "Kneel."

Maralla knelt, and I passed the dinner roll back.

"Two hundred thousand?" she hissed when she was safely hidden below the tabletop. "And you turned him down?"

"Patience, Maralla." I scanned the room again for pox marks or the flickering haze of future trouble. "This is a dance all its own."

"You're just trying to get the most money out of me you can."

I dispatched Svaronei to the ballroom entrance, where a fight would break out between two arcanists sometime in the near future. "In a way, *ciir*. The price must be convincing, or it will draw my employer's ire. Believe me, that's the last thing you want."

Maralla fell silent, nose pinched as she chewed the buttered bread.

The din of conversation swelled to a crescendo, signaling a shift in the night's entertainment. Feet shuffled and chairs squealed as the attendees found their seats. Right on schedule, the Chancellor appeared. He wore his royal headdress with matching violet robes, and walked flanked by both palace guards and my Rorsch Hekkai.

With His Excellency's summer address imminent, I swept the room again, relocating Vhedja and two more guards. Then, still keeping an eye out for trouble, I settled in to hear the Chancellor speak.

Chapter Twenty-Eight

Maralla

THE NEXT BASTARD WHO pinched my nipples or grabbed my ass would get one of those pretty forks through his scabbing hand.

I caught only a few words from the Chancellor's speech as he prattled on about his great country. Dinner passed by in a blur of intrusive inspections and gawking eyes. Business, as usual, was conducted in the trade tongue, so I didn't miss a single crude remark. Mascha flaunted his arrogance with such flair, I had to remind myself repeatedly that it was a mask.

When the slaves cleared the dessert plates and the first couples whirled onto the dance floor, Mascha pulled me into a side room.

"Leave us," he barked at the three men who looked up from pleasuring each other when we entered. One of them scowled and started to protest, but his companions had enough sense to silence him and drag him out.

"The orchestra will play our piece after the Dennian waltz." Mascha eyed the dancers outside, then closed the door. His brow creased. "This dance will largely determine how high your price goes."

As if that mattered to me. "You put way too much stock in this. They're already salivating out there. Just pick one."

"It's not that simple."

"It never is with you."

"The Deal-Breaker expects—"

"You don't have to tell me again." I folded my arms. "The Deal-Breaker expects a tidy sum for the woman stolen from her home and shipped down here to spread her legs for a bunch of bloated, self-obsessed men whose sense of entitlement far outsizes their cocks."

Mascha blinked. He glanced around the empty room before a smile cracked his façade. "Do you feel better now?"

I did, actually. Some of the pressure in my chest had bled off with my outburst. Still, I wouldn't deign to confirm it. "Not by half."

"Hm." His grin widened.

"It's not funny."

A hearty chuckle spilled out of him. "*Ciir*, goddess."

I didn't know if I should slap him or laugh along. My lips twitched upward, but I fought the movement back. "Gods damn you."

He closed the gap between us and kissed me. A rush of lightness made me dizzy. I tipped my chin up and leaned into him, only marginally annoyed by how I relished the possessive warmth of his embrace.

"I know what we practiced," he murmured against my mouth, "but I want you to lead our dance."

I broke our kiss. "What?"

"We've fumbled every time we've attempted it together." He brushed my temple. "So, I want you to lead. Do what is natural to you, and I will follow."

The amaariana was a traditional courtship dance, with the lead asserting dominance over her partner. It hailed from former Syljia and lived on in the Northlands, where a Syljian man took his woman's last name. But here, a statement like that was risky.

"Won't that go over poorly?"

"You are *Johtan Shasnaram*." Adoration softened his violet eyes. "They've seen you kneel long enough."

"But they expect my subservience. Do you even know the steps? What if—"

Mascha stifled my concerns with another kiss. He cupped my cheeks and pressed his forehead to mine. "We're going to war, Commander. You know what to do. Just let instinct guide you."

The last notes of the harp rang out across the ballroom. I stood at the dance floor's edge, behind Mascha's right shoulder, awaiting the perfect moment to seize the night.

Scabbing gods, I hoped he was right about this.

A familiar melody drifted over the crowd. The abrupt shift from formal and courtly to soft and sensual took some nobles by surprise, but others grinned in appreciation and grabbed their partners once more.

Mascha had explained that his performance was never scheduled, exactly, so much as taken. He assured me if I commanded the same presence in the ballroom as I did on the battlefield, the crowd would part for me.

A natural break in the dancers formed. With a deep breath in, I stepped out of Mascha's shadow and strode headlong into the gap. Cries and gasps trailed in my wake. Nobles shied from me in an ever-widening circle. I spun back toward Mascha, who placated the loudest dissenters with a wave and a reassuring grin.

Hundreds of eyes settled on me. With my pulse pounding in my ears and static arcing across my skin, I beckoned him closer.

Shocked murmurs rippled outward. The music picked up, and Mascha paced with the beat into the space I'd cleared for us. He took my hand, and I led him in a wide circle, ending with a spin that brought us nose to nose.

Then, the king of slavers dropped to one knee at my feet.

The crowd recoiled. Dread writhed in my stomach. It was part of the dance, *ciir*, meant to represent the beginnings of courtship—the male's recognition of his mate as greater than himself—but Mascha kneeling for his slave was a scandal of legend. I glanced to the side, where men glowered and women stared.

This wasn't going to work. This was going to ruin everything—

"Eyes on me, *Johtan Shasnaram*."

Mascha's voice carried, setting the nearest men at ease. As my gaze found his, I caught on to his game and my shoulders sagged.

A ruse within a ruse, I marveled. Our dance would sell the illusion of *Johtan Shasnaram*, but Mascha's quiet correction reassured the nobility he was still in control.

I played up my shaky response. "Apologies, Master."

"Just as we practiced." He winked. "Now, start again."

I obeyed and pulled Mascha to his feet. My mate chosen, the courtship begun, I threw us into the music with a series of turns and spins that cleared the floor completely of other dancers.

Our bodies flowed together, one step into the next, like ribbons on the wind. Mascha answered every move I made with flawless precision. He danced in the same way he kissed me, with passion, urgency, and eagerness. His body responded to mine with the same devotion as when we coupled, as if he truly thought me divine. I could have been anywhere else in the world with him, the music drifting over us, soft light glinting off his hair, and our dance might have felt like true courtship.

Nose to nose once more, I caught the subtle glaze of his Foresight and grinned. "Cheater."

He laughed breathlessly. "You are so beautiful. I just can't wait to See what you do next."

My skin flushed. I led him into another set of spins as I choked down my emotions and focused on new intentions. Ones so outlandish and insane that they couldn't be anything less than right.

I whispered into his ear: "Do you See me, Mascha?"

His steps echoed mine. He blinked three times and focused on me with clear-eyed wonder. "I See you, Maralla."

It was a part of the dance Schera's lessons had trimmed out—the pinnacle moment of the amaariana that brought the story of courtship to its completion.

With swift footwork and a subtle exchange of hands, I surrendered the lead to him—a move that represented acceptance of a marriage proposal, the man's lead symbolizing the promise of protection and support for the life the couple would build together.

My feet left the floor as he spun with me, gripping my thighs. I extended one leg and wrapped the other around him. I cupped his face as our lips met, then he set me down and flung me into a triple spin that I embellished with a cartwheel. Mascha stalked across the floor and stole me back into his arms.

Our steps slowed, lightened, as the music wound down. He lifted me a final time, and the feeling of weightless submission liberated me fully from all thought.

Mascha dipped me on the last note to thunderous applause.

He held me motionless, his fingers tracing my throat down to my breasts. My heart hammered beneath his palm and sweat rolled down my face. I stared up into the stained-glass murals, panting, until Mascha tugged me upright and plunged both hands into my braids.

His kiss drowned out the overwhelming reception of our dance. It drowned out everything but the taste of his lips, the scent of his skin, the strength of his body against mine. I couldn't get enough. It was more than survival that held me to him. It wasn't a ruse or an illusion or any agreement that lifted me onto my toes and placed my palms on his chest. It was pure, carnal, and true.

Saonis miraar, was it love? Even after Nalerta, after I was so sure I would never feel this way about anyone again?

Mascha broke away with a ragged breath, his smile sheepish. Gods, even his ears had darkened. I returned the look, even as I cursed myself. Cursed us.

I remembered that day in his study when he sent me away to ease the pain of my leaving. Now it seemed he wasn't the only one whose stupid heart was about to break.

Chapter Twenty-Nine

Mascha

After we showcased Maralla's skill and beauty on the dance floor, men from dozens of houses assailed us. She endured twelve more inspections and I received nine enthusiastic offers, but only one was from an intended target. Lord Naftalli wasn't interested, and Doneev Sattar VI had been embroiled in a friendly argument with Wali Amin for the last half-hour. Fortunately, Andalah Imiir held the highest bid so far. With his promise of five hundred thousand gran, I could be patient.

I was entertaining another offer from a merchant when a familiar, jewel-encrusted figure swept into view. The merchant inspecting Maralla slunk away without a word.

"Mascha, you rascal, that was delightful!" Bastian clapped my wrist and beamed.

"Good evening, Bastian." I returned the greeting, my face warm from the wine I'd consumed to dull my possessive urges. "You look positively cutthroat in black, *amii*."

He squeezed my shoulder, sparing a glance at his onyx waistcoat. Obsidian buttons flashed in the light, and silver lapels flanked the jeweler's heavy sapphire pendant. More silver dusted the corners of his eyes, and his eyelashes were stained a complementary shade of blue. He dismissed it all with a shake of his head. "Nowhere near as dazzling as you and your lady. By Mira, I've never seen anything so spectacular." He leaned in, shielding his mouth. "And quite clever, I might add."

It had been a risk, letting Maralla lead our dance, but between the Aetherial flashes of us stumbling as we did in practice and her temper mounting with every wayward hand, it had been the right course.

"You flatter me."

"Flattery well deserved. Why, this must be your best performance yet!" His exuberance drew sideways looks from other guests. He stepped toward Maralla and cupped her cheeks, his prior fear of her ostensibly lacking. "And you, sweet girl. I saw you out there, breathing life into old Mascha's dead heart. Such a fine match shouldn't be sold, no, no, no. You must insist he keep you."

Maralla's cheeks darkened. She let her eyes dart toward me, as if uncertain whether to respond.

I saved her the indignity and laughed. "You're incorrigible."

"With good reason." He shook a finger at me. "I have a sense about these things."

"Is that so?"

"Call it jeweler's intuition. You let this one go, and I'd bet my entire enterprise you'll wish you hadn't."

Another man entered my peripheral vision, his attention split between Bastian and Maralla. Sensing his hesitation, I cut Bastian's ribbing short. "Well, as tempting as that bet is"—I nodded toward the new arrival—"I do have business, *amii*."

"Yes, yes, business. Hmph." Bastian scowled, but he allowed my gentle shove toward the buffet. "But don't say I didn't warn you."

He wandered off, muttering to himself, and I held on to my fleeting mirth for the next man who stepped up to assess Maralla. I greeted the young noble as all the others, but when he made it clear his only interest lay in fondling a noteworthy slave, I shooed him off.

Apparently, just in time.

"*Tipori*."

The orchestra masked her voice, but Maralla had my full attention in an instant. Her hands, though still clasped, had begun to lighten at the knuckles. I took one of them in mine and uncurled her fingers. My thumb brushed over her palm, where her nails had carved crescent-shaped grooves.

She twitched as a pair of noblemen meandered past us. One gestured crudely to the other and both men laughed. A tremor passed down Maralla's arm.

She was starting to unravel. I performed another sweep of the area with my Foresight, gestured a handoff of the floor to Tasari on a nearby balcony, and started for a corridor off the main room. Only a few greetings followed us down the hall and into the rose garden.

It was akin to stepping into a fae tale. Drunken laughter filled the air, discarded clothing littered the cobbled walkways, and merry couples and trios romped in the grass, engaging in all manner of fornication as Maralla and I strode past. Stars and torches lit the night, and the spray of fountains turned to shimmering mist on the breeze.

I found a quiet space far from the garden entrance. Sheltered between two dark hedgerows threaded with climbing roses, it was the least likely place we would be seen. When we reached the end of the row, where the sounds of Rillanese hedonists were easiest to ignore, I took her hand again and pulled her down to sit on a stone bench.

Maralla closed her eyes and breathed. "Thank you."

"It's almost over. You've done your part well."

Maralla scrubbed her free hand over her face. "Gods, I hope it works."

I stroked her knuckles, considering our next move. Gossip should have reached Sattar by now, but he hadn't glanced our way all evening. Either he wasn't interested, or he was biding his time, waiting to see how high the bid would go. But that was time Maralla didn't have.

"I'll take Imiir's offer. It should be adequate enough."

The declaration seemed to ignite something between us. "*Adequate*?" She wrenched her hand away. "Half a million gold is simply adequate to you?"

I didn't need to see the misty images that Foretold the consequences of Maralla losing herself here. Even secluded as we were, sound could travel beyond the hedgerows and draw all manner of guest, guard, and slave to witness a spectacle. And gods help me, I couldn't be forced to whip her again.

"Lower your voice," I warned.

Her scowl turned molten. All the anger she'd been bottling up throughout the evening seemed to erupt at once. "Do you know how many *years* I could feed all the orphans in Aon'In with five hundred thousand gold? How different their lives would be?"

I cringed, though I was no less aware of the tremendous excess with which Rillanese nobility lived. I thought of Soltani, how he flourished under my care, the joy he found in my horses, and how simple it had been to turn his entire life around with a few hundred gran.

Shame burrowed into me. "Quite a few, I'm sure. But Maralla, you must be calm."

I might as well have been trying to tame a thunderstorm.

"Instead, your people use it to buy a single gods-damned slave. And for what? Wetting your cocks on a whim? Showing off what pretty toys you have?"

"Business." It always came down to business.

Maralla rose from the bench and paced the cobbled path. Three full circuits lightened the set of her shoulders, but her next words bit deeper than a whip woven with glass. "Tell me, Mascha. What's so appealing to you about owning someone else's body? Breaking someone's will?"

I could have lied and said there was no appeal, that I abhorred the practice as much as she did. But the truth was, my ability to inspire fear and command obedience gave me power—a power I craved, for it was the only thing separating a slave from a free man.

Are you certain you're a free man?

A young slave with an axe wound in her chest came to mind. How easily my choices—with her, with Raenara, and Maralla—had been stripped from me.

She stalked forward and grabbed the sides of my face. "You don't have an explanation, do you?"

Because I enjoyed it. Because I reveled in that moment when the most stubborn of slaves broke, and my will finally usurped theirs. It was too much like in the arena, when I tore a man's lungs from his back and held them up for the crowd to see.

"I..." Breathing was suddenly like sucking air through wet linen. I could try to play it off, pretend I was an honorable man, but I wasn't. I hadn't been that man for most of my life. My hands tightened into fists. "I do it because I'm a monster."

Maralla searched my face, her expression losing its dagger-sharp edge. "You really believe that?"

"I do." The hedgerows closed in around me, and distant screams clawed at my awareness. Pressure built in my chest—constricted my throat. "I'm as much a monster as any other noble in that ballroom."

She pressed her forehead to mine. "You don't have to be."

A bitter laugh escaped me as I pulled away. "I don't have a choice." I rose and ran a hand through my hair.

"Yes, you do. You've already proven you have a choice. You play the villain so people will fear you, but that's not the person you want to be."

I lifted my face toward the stars. "You just don't understand."

This was the way of things. This was how I had survived so long in a place that devoured weaker men whole. Instinctively, I pulled on my saphyrum, and the image of hedgerows and cobbles wavered in response.

"*Tipori*," Maralla said, and I winced. She closed with me, her body heat at my back. "Mercy. You beg for it in your sleep, but not for yourself. For someone else. *Tipori daatahl.*"

The ripple around us became a tremor, then a full-cresting wave in the Aetherial Wall. My chest heaved, the hot-iron taste of magic coating my tongue. I turned to her. "*Don't* do that."

"Why? What are you so afraid of?"

It was a violation to bring *her* into this. What had happened to her was not a campfire story. It was a tragedy of my own making. "You will forget you ever witnessed those nightmares."

"Who was she?"

"*Stop!*"

An explosion of saphyric energy burst from me, through the Wall, causing the hedgerows to wither and roses to blacken. It broke over Maralla, and she shuddered. Beyond our place in the garden, sounds of revelry paused.

Slowly, subdued chatter resumed, moving deeper into the garden. I balled my fists to regain control.

"Was she your lover?" Maralla softened, but she didn't relent. "A sister? Or a child?"

Two stray tears fell. "No."

"Tell me, then." She stepped closer and placed her palm over my chest. "What makes a trained killer cry in his sleep?"

My resolve eroded beneath her touch like sand before the tide. A growl forced its way between my teeth. I could no more deny the effect she had on me than I could stop the sun from rising.

Maralla led me back to the bench. I sat stiffly, throat aching. Her fingers traced small circles over my wrist.

"Please, Mascha," she said. "Let me in."

Her request was so earnest, her expression so concerned, but I'd never shared that memory with anyone. I didn't even know where to start.

"Tell me her name, at least."

I couldn't. Shouldn't. But Maralla had already gotten through my guard. My reluctance was less the need for discretion than the reflexive grasp of that memory. A name lingered on my lips, clinging like the last drop of rain on a leaf.

"Evora."

"Evora," Maralla echoed. "That's beautiful." She continued those slow circles over my wrist, my palm, my forearm. "Who was she to you?"

"She..." My gaze fixed on the cobbles. Maralla's touch grounded me, though my breath hitched. "She was my mother."

Maralla rested her head against my shoulder, fingers still tracing paths beneath my sleeve. "What was she like?"

It felt as if she were prying my grip from my only remaining weapon long after the battle had been lost. Once this story began, I knew there would be no stopping it.

"She was Syljian. Born a slave here in Durgost." Tears stung my eyes, but I blinked them back.

"Tell me more."

I gave in slowly, implacably, until the words began to fall like rain. "She worked as a midwife in the Master's house. She excelled at it, too, and loved teaching the art to others. At one time, I knew more about childbirth than I did gutting a man."

Maralla smirked. "What else?"

I took a moment to gather my thoughts, the tension in my face receding. "She was humble and kind, but perceptive as well. She always knew when I was about to get myself into trouble."

"Did she have Foresight?"

"Mm." Something I'd always wondered. Foresight was so rare a gift, I'd never known another soul who possessed it, but it could be passed from parent to child. "I suspect she did, but she would always deflect when I asked."

"As mothers do," Maralla chuckled.

One corner of my mouth lifted, but fell soon afterward. "She hated violence, especially for how it changed people. It didn't matter how hard the Master worked me each day. She expected me to be a gentleman the moment my feet left the sand. '*Kaana'ruh ke'aave tipori,*' she always said."

Remember to have mercy.

Maralla laced her fingers with mine. "A noble endeavor."

I squeezed her hand, grateful for her silent comfort, her steady presence. "She never wanted me to be a pit fighter. She wanted better for me than the life of a slave in the ring." After another calming breath, I rested my cheek atop her head. "I never knew anything else while she lived. But she was always an advocate for me, often to her own detriment."

Night filled my hesitation with chirping insects, the splash of a fountain, and distant music. Maralla pressed closer when a cool wind ghosted through the withered roses.

I wrapped my arm around her, swallowing hard. "When the Master announced he was sending me to the arena, she went to him, begging him to reconsider. I think she saw what the pits did to me, and knew the arena would be much worse. Of course, he refused her."

The details became blurry after that. I'd only heard about their exchange from another slave who'd witnessed it.

"The rumor was that she attacked him." My jaw clenched. "I can't say for certain what happened, but I know what came next."

My nightmares. I recoiled from the images seared into my memory. The echoes of terror and rage I'd felt that night made me shiver.

Maralla lifted her head from my shoulder. "Tell me."

I was already here at the precipice—the moment that had made the boy my mother loved into a bloodthirsty savage. Why was I telling her this? Why couldn't I stop it?

"The Master dragged her below." My voice came out strangled. I swallowed a stone and fought to breathe evenly. "He tied her to a post. Then he released his fighters and bade us all have our way with her."

Maralla's lips parted. I couldn't look at her—couldn't watch that growing horror usurp control of her expression.

"I was twenty-five. Barely a man and untested against so many." I stared down the path, and the hedges came alive with shadows. Unfocused images of bodies breaking and blood spattering sand. Screams tore through me afresh, and my teeth bared in mounting anger. "I killed eight of them, trying to get to her, but by the time I pulled the last man off her, it was too late. In their lust, they'd torn her apart."

"That's horrific, Mascha." Maralla's grip tightened, and her attention strayed into the darkness as if she could see the apparitions, too. Her mouth set in a contemplative frown, then she looked carefully at me. "He really expected you to—"

"No. He knew I wouldn't harm her." I straightened. "Her death was my audition. The Master had investors posted in the mezzanine overlooking the yard. They paid my entry fees for the arena, and he sent me away the next day. He hadn't even burned her body yet."

"Gods, I'm so sorry."

My voice broke. "She shouldn't have defied the Master for me. She should have known better."

"She loved you." Her eyes glistened. "For some of us, there's little we wouldn't do for those we love."

"It's a shame love couldn't save her."

The venom in my voice didn't frighten her.

"But it could save you."

I scoffed and extracted my hand from hers. "I don't need saving."

"You've amassed your fearsome reputation by spilling blood and inflicting pain. You push away anyone who might care for you so you don't appear weak or flawed like the rest of us. But for all your power and prestige, you still can't find peace. Why do you think that is?"

That knowing, self-assured tone grated. I hadn't told her these things to be interrogated. I shouldn't have told her anything at all. "I find peace knowing I'll be rid of your haughty mouth soon."

It was a lie, and we both knew it.

To her credit, Maralla didn't snap in return. She remained steadfast, a mountain against a gale. "I think you can't find peace because you know you were meant to be a better person. The sort of person Evora would be proud to call her son."

In any other situation, I might have laughed or answered with some scathing retort, but my feelings for Maralla disallowed both. There was so much blood on my hands. So much suffering. If my mother could have seen me now, she would be appalled by what I'd become. Not only had I failed to save her that day, I'd failed her one wish for me, too. No matter how much I tried to be anything else, I was a murderer. A Champion. My very name had been appropriated into the Rillanese language: *mascha*—death.

A word still chanted in the arena before every suspenseful kill. Still screamed by spectators whose great-grandfathers had been children when I'd perfected my signature blow.

I remembered the massacre in Yamon Baghara's courtyard. The bloodstains all over those estates. The child.

I looked away. "It's too late for that."

"No." Maralla claimed my chin and forced me back. "Change always begins with a decision, no matter how small, to do better. To *be* better. I see how you care for others. I see *you*, Tipori. You can't hide from me."

She tugged me down by my beard and kissed me. Her gentle affection cascaded through me like hope—a pure sensation that pushed back my darkness and drowned my remorse in a shockwave of pleasure so sweet, so perfect, it could only be love.

Gods, I loved her.

I broke away with tears on my face, certain I would suffocate under their weight. "I can't be who you think I am."

Maralla tucked a lock of hair behind my ear. "Then why bother helping me at all?"

She didn't wait for a response. Cool night air encroached as she rose. I caught sight of the gruesome scars on her back. Scars I'd given her.

"Maralla."

She turned, the diamonds on her skirt and collar gleaming. Her voice caressed my ears like the softest silk. "*Ciir?*"

I struggled to find the right words, then drew a breath and just let the thought fall out of my mouth. "I want to be better. I'm just not sure how."

Maralla's smile set my world spinning again.

"Well, you're off to a good start."

Chapter Thirty

Mascha

I ESCORTED MARALLA BACK inside, pleased to see the gala hadn't become a free-for-all in my absence. We paused under the archway leading into the ballroom, and I scanned the crowd for trouble. My attention settled on my half-brother.

Tasari nodded to me from the main entrance. He shouldered his crossbow, preparing to retreat to his post on the southern balcony, but I motioned for him to remain. I had business, the gesture said, and I wanted eyes on the floor while I settled up.

I swept the ballroom again, this time not for the flicker of future events, but for the linen-clad titan that was Andalah Imiir. He sat at a table not far from the buffet. A palace slave sat on his lap, and a second one rubbed his broad shoulders. His bright smile cut through his black beard as he pulled the girl on his knee closer. His green waistcoat hung unbuttoned, exposing a scar from an old sword wound that trailed beneath his shirt.

I glanced at Maralla, who sold her obedience without fault. Our last few nights together were at hand. The sooner I shook on this deal, the sooner I could get her home.

Movement caught my eye as we stepped out of the archway. I glanced that way and stopped so abruptly that Maralla collided with me. A paralyzing chill shot down my spine.

Standing before the door to the Chancellor's antechamber, speaking to the Chancellor himself, was a tall man in his late thirties. He was attended by six beautiful Syljian slaves dressed in jewelry as artfully crafted as Maralla's. The man himself was a picture of wealth. A crown of platinum medallions, gold chains, and blue-green saphyrum beads ringed his oiled scalp. He wore a black formal tunic cut with violet, and the capelet slung over one shoulder bore the embroidered pick-and-hammer sigil of House Ideghis.

The Master's house.

"Who is that?" Maralla whispered.

My tongue stuck to the roof of my mouth, and I found myself cast like a stone into the depths of my Foresight. I Saw Ideghis V—the Master's great-great-grandson—holding Maralla's face in his hands. He was appraising her with a favoring eye, stroking a thumb over her runes. He spoke to her as if from a distance or underwater. I couldn't make out what he said.

Fury and fear jolted me back into the present. I gasped and reached for the archway to steady myself.

"Master?" Maralla's hand rested on my forearm.

I had to get control of myself. Shaking away the lingering haze of Foresight, I placed my hand over hers and pulled her back into the shadow of an alcove.

"That," I whispered back, fussing with the diamond strands of her collar, "is Neborov Ideghis the Fifth."

Recognition sparked dread in her amethyst eyes.

"One of the most powerful houses in the country," I elaborated, "and a breeder of Syljian slaves."

Maralla licked her lips. There was a flash of uncertainty before she steeled herself. "I take it his security is as good as yours?"

"He wasn't supposed to be here." The words tumbled out in a rush, as if the answer to her question went without saying. I knew firsthand how impenetrable Ideghis Estates' defenses were, both for intruders breaking in and slaves breaking out. "He was supposed to be in Tahamel, negotiating for a new mine on the southern coast."

"Apparently not." Her voice was numb.

Self-directed anger surged through me, but I forced it aside. I had to think rationally. "We have to move quickly." My fingers still threaded through the dozens of golden chains, even though they lay perfectly against her chest. "I have to shake on the deal with Imiir before Ideghis learns of you. I have to protect you."

Maralla closed her eyes, and her expression steeled before she opened them again. "I'll follow your lead."

The trust she put in me made my oversight that much worse. If I could only leave her in the hallway or banish her to the garden—except slaves not of the household could never be left unattended, nor could I leave the gala with her and let her go to auction. It was only a matter of time before gossip reached Ideghis. If he missed her tonight, he would be watching for her in the days to come. He might even call on me at the palace.

I steeled myself as Maralla had. Her warrior's calm was a thing to behold, and I drew inspiration from it. She was counting on me; I couldn't let her down.

With a glance around the corner, I ensured Ideghis was still speaking with the Chancellor. I looked the other way, toward Lord Imiir.

"Come."

Quickly, quietly, I slipped into the sea of tables, weaving through gala guests and slaves that floated like driftwood into our path. Maralla kept pace with me, a shadow at my right hand.

She was safe. She was safe with me.

I nodded toward the few greetings I received, never breaking stride. We were halfway to Imiir when a nasally voice called my name over the din.

Now, of all times, Doneev Sattar VI would try to get my attention. When I slowed to look, the lord was rising from his chair beside Wali Amin, beckoning me over.

"Boil-faced toad," I muttered to myself, holding up a hand partly to acknowledge him, but mostly to stop the man from calling out again.

My attention darted toward Imiir, still eight tables away. Like a climber's piton coming loose, or a sailor's knot slipping, I felt my chance to settle up quickly pulling out of reach. Ripples of Foresight cascaded over the ballroom. To ignore Sattar would cause its own disruption, drawing more attention to Maralla. To make the man wait would be inexcusable to my employer, especially if he planned to offer more for Maralla than Imiir had. With Epillon's most powerful family sitting beside him, I truly had no choice.

I changed course with a growl.

"I was afraid you'd left, Mascha," Sattar drawled as we approached. As he took a long pull from his ebony pipe, Sattar's beady eyes strayed to my right, looking Maralla up and down. His lips parted, billowing smoke and exposing a mouthful of crooked teeth. His blackened tongue skated out along their pitted edges. "I heard the Little Giant offered you half a million for your newest acquisition."

"Indeed, he did. Good evening, Lord Sattar." I nodded to Wali Amin and spared a glance for Anelliiq and her two sons. "And you as well, House Amin."

"Always so proper. Impressive for a savage," Wali Amin slurred. The jackal-faced nobleman pounded the table three times, shaking the glasses and startling the younger, scraggly-haired boy seated beside Anelliiq. "You see, there, Damiir? Even slaveborn half-breeds can become men if they try hard enough. You still have a chance."

The boy, who couldn't have been more than thirteen, hastened a glance at me before returning to the napkin on which he'd been scribbling. "Yes, Father."

Wali sat up straighter. "Boy, look at me when I speak to you."

Both Damiir and his mother flinched. Anelliiq regained her composure quickly, but her son paled three shades as he met his father's angry stare. When Damiir's attention strayed from the napkin, Wali's older son, Fausch, snatched it up and began to read it.

Fausch sneered. "Poetry, Damiir?"

"Give that back!"

Damiir lunged for the napkin, and I seized my opening. "I was just on my way to settle up with Lord Imiir. If you'll excuse me—"

"Wait just a moment." Sattar put a hand on my arm. "I would like to inspect the girl as well."

It took everything I had not to break his gangly fingers. The ichoru dealer had grown confident in his new friendship with Lord Amin. Sattar was likely using it to jockey for higher status. If I hadn't been in such a hurry to end this encounter, I would have put Sattar back in his place as I had with Belfahr. I fixed him with a glare, and he quickly removed his hand.

"Make it fast, my lord. I won't keep a committed buyer waiting."

"Of course, of course. It will only take a moment."

Sattar pulled from his pipe again, labored to his feet, and shuffled toward Maralla. He yanked on her hair, forcing her chin up. I looked away—lest I act on the impulse to break Sattar's hands—and used the opportunity to locate Ideghis.

The Master's heir was right where I'd left him. I watched him as Sattar went about his inspection. When Ideghis shook the Chancellor's hand, bidding him farewell, I slid my attention back to Sattar with a renewed sense of urgency.

He was in the middle of torturing one of Maralla's nipples. He circled around to give her backside a firm slap, and when he came round again, he pinched her other nipple. I imagined all five of those digits removed at the knuckles before I fed them to my hounds.

"A little waifish for my taste." Sattar put the pipe to his lips and blew acrid smoke into Maralla's face. She recoiled, provoking his wheezy laughter. "Hard to believe this little thing gave you so much trouble. Unbreakable. Ha!"

Wali guffawed. "I bet Fausch could break her. He likes the little ones, don't you, boy?"

The older Amin boy grew tired of keeping the napkin from his brother and tossed it over his shoulder. While Damiir went to retrieve it, Fausch grinned and leered at Maralla. "Yes, Father. The smaller the slave, the tighter the fit."

I'd endured enough. "If you wish to make an offer, Lord Sattar, you may do so now. Otherwise, I will be on my way."

"Why the rush, Mascha?" Sattar teased. "Are you worried the Giant will wise up and change his mind?"

"You waste my time." I turned to leave.

"Alright!" Sattar called, too loudly, his true desire unmasked. "Alright, you win. No more games." When I turned back, still glowering, Sattar winced and looked at Wali. "What do you think, my friend? Is her story worth six hundred thousand?"

Wali leaned back in his chair. He pulled out his own ichoru pipe and began packing the stringy brown herb. "Only if it's true."

"It is." My tone was clipped. "The scars tell it plainly enough."

"Yes, I suppose those are some magnificent scars." Sattar tapped his chapped lips with his pipe. "I expect a full recounting of the tale before the goods are exchanged."

"You will have it." My relief swept through me like an autumn breeze, but I kept my expression hard. Maralla would escape this toad easily. Ruining Sattar's name would only bring me joy after this. I held out my hand. "We are agreed, then—"

As I spoke, Sattar and Wali both paused, their attention drawn to something behind me. Wali's face twisted, and his eyes narrowed to slits. A creeping sensation worked its way up the back of my neck.

"*Johtan Shasnaram*," a honeyed voice purred. "Oh, Mascha, she is a vision."

Gods damn it all.

My fingers curled like wilted petals. With an icy void yawning open in my chest, I turned to face Ideghis V.

"Lord Ideghis," I forced out. "Good evening. I am surprised to see you here."

The man's hooded brow cast a shadow over his eyes as he stepped forward. For a split second, it seemed I was looking into the Master's face, so similar were their features. His chestnut skin was unmarked, and his neatly trimmed beard and mustache were isolated to his chin and upper lip. Sculpted cheekbones and a strong jaw completed Ideghis V's regal bearing, but I knew beneath that handsome façade existed a killer of unmatched cruelty.

Keen amber eyes regarded me, his smile deceptively warm. Ideghis extended his hand. "I wouldn't miss the Chancellor's summer gala."

I stepped toward him and took his wrist in a too-firm grip. Though I made it look incidental, my move forward forced Maralla back, away from Ideghis and the Syljian entourage flanking him. She hovered at my right elbow—safe, at least, for the moment.

"I heard you were in talks to acquire Aegren's last saphyrum mine," I ventured, as if discovering how Ideghis managed to make it from Tahamel to the capital so quickly would change anything.

"The negotiations settled early." Ideghis released my wrist. "We close a week from Saosday."

Wali rose from the table, glaring at his rival. "I suppose that means the cost of saphyrum will be going up, now that you've cornered the market."

I didn't need Foresight to know how quickly things could escalate between these two. Even though my goal was to sell Maralla this evening, I couldn't forget my true purpose here was maintaining order.

"I'm certain Lord Ideghis will price his goods accordingly," I said. "The trade commission monitors global pricing on saphyrum for a reason."

"The trade commission should have never allowed the sale," Wali argued. Despite his round belly, he was of a height with me, but still shorter than Ideghis by several fingerspans.

Ideghis lifted an eyebrow. "I will certainly abide by the commission's recommended price adjustment. Aside from that, I've hardly cornered the market. Naftalli and the Ohanis brothers own the rest."

"As if you don't have all four of them wrapped around your slimy fingers," Wali snarled.

"We have common interests, only," Ideghis replied, his voice as smooth as silk. "But I didn't come over here to bicker with you. Mascha, would you kindly introduce me to the lovely woman behind you?"

Before I could respond, Wali snarled again. "The slave is spoken for. You're too late, Neborov."

I never thought I would be relieved to have Lord Amin on my side. "It is true, my lord. Sattar submitted quite the generous offer, and I have accepted."

Amusement flickered across Ideghis's face. "Is that so?" Without turning, he spoke a Syljian command to his slaves, "*Vaash'ruh.*"

All six knelt in unison, heads bowed, hands resting on their thighs. The familiarity prickled my skin. All the way back to Ideghis I, the family's Syljian slaves had been trained to move in perfect synchrony with the Master. But in tight spaces where such movement wasn't feasible, they would be left to kneel for as long as the Master required.

Ideghis slipped around me, past Maralla, to stand before Sattar. "Doneev," he said, "I understand your contract for the farmland south of Denna is ending soon. Has your family paid the lease to cover next year's operation?"

Sattar looked up at Ideghis, his pipe going slack in his jaws. "What are you up to, Ideghis?"

Wali growled.

For once, I shared the sentiment. "I understand your grievances over missing out on the bid, Lord Ideghis, but no threats will be made over it."

Glancing over his shoulder, Ideghis gave me another charming smile. "I have no intention of making threats, Rorsch Hekkai. Only informing Lord Sattar that I am prepared to contribute to next year's contract price, should he wish to remain on Ghor's land."

"He's not going to rescind his offer to buy your favor," Wali snapped.

Sattar, however, seemed to like the idea of Ideghis buying *his* favor. The void in my chest grew wider as the little worm took his pipe from his mouth.

"How much are we talking?"

"Two hundred thousand."

Wali gaped, recognizing as well as I did what Ideghis was doing. Two hundred thousand was over half the cost of Sattar's yearly lease on the land he used to grow his crops. Lessening the financial burden at the beginning of the year would allow greater investment in the crops overall, leading to greater yields and more profit by harvest time—all over a slave who would otherwise cost him triple that, with no assurance of profit.

Sattar jabbed the air with his pipe. "Make it three."

Ideghis's smile never wavered. "Three, it is."

Sattar spared a glance at Wali—who looked ready to burst from his new ally's treachery—then his eyes found mine. "I'm certain you understand. I'm sorry, but I must retract my bid."

"I understand." *Cowardly little maggot.*

Likely sensing his welcome at the table had been rescinded as swiftly as his offer, Sattar excused himself, giving Wali a wide berth as he retreated.

Once the merchant was gone, Ideghis cleared his throat. "Well, it does appear your slave is available once more." He reached into a pocket and produced three shining rubies. Winking, he pressed them into my palm. "I promise to make it worth your while."

Numbly, I pocketed the gems, envisioning Ideghis as a broken smear on the Chancellor's ballroom floor. "I should hope so." An Aetherial image of Lord Amin spiraled out of control beside me. I waved toward a less hostile part of the ballroom. "Shall we?"

"A private room, perhaps? You remember how my family prefers to do a thorough inspection, free of distractions."

How could I forget?

The urge to kill had not been so strong in many years, but I fought it down. Ideghis was one of the Deal-Breaker's most favored patrons, and he occupied the topmost tier of Rillanese nobility.

"Certainly. The Chancellor should have a room to spare."

"Excellent." Without glancing toward his slaves, Ideghis uttered another Syljian command. "*Drest'ruh.*"

The mixed retinue of men and women, adorned only in gold, platinum, and diamonds, rose and fell in line behind their master as two orderly rows of three. I started toward a side corridor with Maralla one half-step behind me.

She'd fooled many lesser houses so far, but Ideghis would be trickier. I wished I had a way to warn her of the things to come, but there was nothing for it. She would either sell her performance to this man, or she wouldn't.

I said a silent prayer to the gods on her behalf.

Chapter Thirty-One

Maralla

Their eyes were dead.

Ideghis's slaves moved with dancers' grace and each had a courtesan's beauty, but they were little more than husks. No glances passed between them. No emotions showed on their faces. Statues would have been more lively as they trailed behind their master. With a sinking feeling in my gut, I realized why they unnerved me: they were adornments for the slaver, no different from the crown on his head or the rings on his fingers.

Even more harrowing—I couldn't find a single scar on any of them. It was as if their souls had broken long before their bodies had.

My heart ached for them.

I didn't dare catch Mascha's eyes as he stopped before a door and pulled it open. By now, I recognized the signs of his discomfort: that austere expression, his formal posture, the neutrality in his voice.

We were in trouble.

"*Vaash'ruh.*"

The command came again, and a chilling uncertainty passed through me. Though it wasn't meant for me, Ideghis's voice was so compelling I could have sworn it was laced with magic. His slaves lined the wall, knelt, and turned to stone. I shivered.

Mascha beckoned us into the lavish guest room. I scanned the space as if it were an enemy campground. A round table and four chairs sat in one corner, opposite a matching cherry armoire and full-length mirror. Sheer red drapery and white linen sheets complemented the golden four-post bed. The one other door led to a tiled washroom.

No windows. No weapons unless I improvised. A shattered mirror could slit a throat. Drapes could strangle. Chairs could bludgeon and break bone. I had options.

And I had Mascha.

The door shut behind me and I turned. Thank the gods his slaves had stayed outside. Some of my dread eased.

"I was so sorry to hear I'd missed your performance." Ideghis regarded Mascha with a wistful smile. "The amaariana is such a beautiful display of submission."

I fought the urge to bristle. Only a slaver would equate my people's most intimate and complicated dance with such a simple exchange of power.

Mascha stood with his feet shoulder width apart, hands clasped. "It is one of my favorites."

"I pray you'll honor me with a private presentation sometime. It is rare to see an unaltered version here in the south." Ideghis's dark eyes shifted to me. Two of the medallions near his ear flashed in the light like drawn blades. "But where are my manners?"

He started forward, lifting his arms as if to embrace me. His hands cupped my face, and I rooted my feet to the floor. I wouldn't shy from this scabbing viper, no matter how high my hackles rose.

"Oh, what perfection you are." His thumbs stroked my cheekbones. "I have not seen such beauty in all my years as lord. What is your name, little one?"

I closed my eyes, trying not to scowl at his saccharine tone. Of course I knew which name he wanted, but I spoke the name the masses had given me instead. *"Johtan Shasnaram."*

Warm laughter greeted my defiance. "Your real name, *neime.*"

Neime.

It was like he'd stabbed me.

I sucked in a breath. It was a word I hadn't heard since I'd kissed my sister goodbye before Sessia. A term of endearment reserved for the closest friendships. I couldn't bear to hear him say it again.

"Maralla."

His smile sharpened. I would have given my left big toe to strike that smugness from his mouth.

Ideghis examined my jaw. "I can tell by your facial structure that at least one of your parents is from the north."

In any other circumstance, I would have snorted. There was no way for him to glean that from looking at my bone structure. It was an easy guess, considering most Syljians once lived in the north. Maybe I would've been impressed if he'd been more specific—

"Vale's Hollow, perhaps?" Ideghis walked his fingers down my neck like Orowen did when she was checking for swelling. "Or were you from the capital?"

Apparently, there was something to it. "Vale's Hollow."

"Hm. Fine bloodlines from the vale—many strong with magic." He turned my head and felt along one ear point. "What is your family name, Maralla?"

"Evallier."

Ideghis paused and studied my face again. "As in Commander Evallier of the Alliaansi Fourth Legion?"

A prickling sensation swept down my nape. Not even Mascha had been familiar with the Syljian leadership in the north. The Iceborn didn't bother to keep track of their prisoners' names. It wasn't until after I'd taken over the palace armory that Mascha had pried deeper into where I came from. "Yes."

Ideghis turned to him, eyes wide. "Did you know this?"

Mascha stepped closer, nearly level with the man. "*Ciir.*"

"What fortune." The slaver's fingertips brushed my warrior's runes. More urgently, he asked, "You were born with these, I pray?"

I nodded, unable to swallow the sand in my throat.

"What a fascinating tale they tell." Ideghis tapped three separate runes. "Dauntlessness. Persistence. Leadership."

He could read runes.

Scabbing gods, the art of reading warriors' runes had been abandoned with Astenpor over a century ago. Only a few Syljian historians still lived who possessed the knowledge. Big surprise, our gods-given personality traits mattered less when we were starving.

"No wonder she gave you so much trouble," he said to Mascha. "I take it you kept her apart from your other slaves to prevent a revolt?"

Any man or woman Mascha had bedded in the last few months would have seen my cage in his bedroom. Any slave he'd processed before our agreement would have known. Word would have gotten out. That had to be how Ideghis knew.

Cracks appeared in Mascha's neutral armor. "The possibility crossed my mind, *ciir*."

"She could certainly rally the masses." Ideghis took my chin and tilted my face up to his. I was careful not to meet his gaze. "I have heard stories of you, Commander Maralla Evallier. You are a living legend among your people. A true inspiration." The honesty in his smile disarmed me. "It is an honor to meet you."

In the beginning, I'd used my anonymity to my advantage. I'd made sure Mascha and the rest of his minions underestimated me. I couldn't use that tactic now. My stomach rolled with anxiety and anger.

I didn't know how to respond, so I fell back on Mascha's instructions and remained silent.

"Let me see your eyes," Ideghis commanded.

My gaze met his smoothly, effortlessly. I took him in, from the thin lines around his cruel mouth, to his pitiless, soul-black stare.

Beside him, Mascha winced.

Ideghis began to smile again. "*Johtan Shasnaram*, indeed," he mused, his voice soft. "Mascha has overlooked a few things, hasn't he?"

Too late, I realized what I'd done. A broken slave would have possessed an intrinsic urge to avoid a slaver's gaze. I should have hesitated. It was a mistake. A grievous, irrevocable mistake.

His fingers dug into my jaw. Darkness surfaced in his expression. "Hasn't he?"

I glanced aside to Mascha, uncertain. His mask cracked further, revealing the simmering rage beneath. He pressed his mouth into a line and gave me a stiff nod. Part of me hoped he would snap and tear this man apart.

I looked away. "*Ciir*."

"Better," Ideghis crooned. "Though I'm afraid we've a long way to go before you are truly presentable." His thumb skated over my lips. "Open."

I did, tensing as Ideghis inspected my teeth. Mascha mouthed a single word: *steady*. Gods knew he probably Saw my desire to bite down, and what trouble that would cause. I fixed my gaze on his doublet, anchoring myself to him.

He took care of his own. Just play my part.

My mouth snapped shut as soon as Ideghis moved on.

He examined my shoulders and arms, paying particular attention to my manacles. "Slips her binders, I see." He touched the locks, welded shut. "That would be her Evasive rune. It's a wonder you've kept her this long."

"The early days were difficult," Mascha agreed through clenched teeth.

"Your work with her is exceptional, all things considered." Light pressure on my wrist accompanied another command. "Turn."

Only Mascha's presence beside Ideghis allowed me to give this fiend my back. I would have never allowed an enemy such an advantage otherwise.

Ideghis gathered my braids over my shoulder and carried on his one-sided conversation. "It's a shame your mother was a slave, Mascha. If you'd been born a free man, you would have excelled in the family. Ah..." He caressed the scars striping my shoulders. "The Endurance rune. One of my favorites." His hands slid over my backside, down my legs. He stopped above the back of my knees and straightened. "I suspect she has atrophied some with captivity, but that is of little consequence." He spun me back around to investigate my hips and lower abdomen, tracing the faded scars there. "You've children, Maralla. How many?"

Ideghis was a breeder of Syljian slaves, Mascha had said. I couldn't deny his assumption with the evidence right in front of him. But maybe I could make myself less appealing. Maybe he would have no use for me if I appeared incapable of the task he desired me for.

"None living." My breath caught on the words. For once, I didn't hold back the storm of grief. I weaponized it.

Elliaana with her fiery temper and a dusting of white freckles across her nose. Rysios with his father's cleft chin and gentle voice. Declaan with his frail limbs and trusting, gap-toothed smile. I drew upon their memories and sharpened each one into a blade capable of piercing the dragonhide armor around my heart. Pain bloomed outward in searing waves that stung my eyes and crushed my lungs.

Mascha's look of devastation blurred in my vision.

"Mm, I see." Ideghis stroked his chin, his hunger and amusement dissolving into quiet contemplation. "How many have you lost?"

"Three."

"To violence? Or illness?"

"They were late term losses."

His hand stilled in his beard. "Such tragedy."

I sniffed and wiped at my cheeks. The distant orchestra filtered through the walls to fill the silence.

With a deep breath in, Ideghis's expression lightened and he made a shooing gesture. "To the bed, then. Let us finish this."

Made impulsive by my grief, and unsettled by whatever manner of 'thorough inspection' he meant to give me, my fists balled at my sides. Mascha shifted in place once, twice, drawing my attention to the subtle thrust of his chin toward the bed.

But I delayed too long.

As swift and unyielding as the Straits of Fate, Ideghis surged forward and seized me by the throat. I chopped his wrist on reflex, the blades of my hands closing to disengage his grip. Ideghis snarled, and horror brought my retaliatory strike to a stuttering halt.

Saonis miraar. What had I done?

I let his stinging backhand connect with my face. Light exploded and I tasted blood. As I staggered from the blow, Ideghis grabbed me again and forced me back. My legs struck the bedframe, and I tumbled into the mattress. His shadow loomed over me as he bore down on my throat. Pressure built inside my face, and my ears pounded with every racing heartbeat. My vision wavered, and the scent of magic stung my nose.

Mascha swam into view above me, his thunderous rage rolling through the Aether. "Ideghis—"

The slaver lifted an arm to stay him. That he had enough power and social status to do so, rather than burst into bloody mist, was a harrowing realization.

"That warrior's heart must still be tamed, I see." Ideghis let up enough to allow me small sips of air. "In my house, Maralla, touching a free man without his permission earns ten lashes. Failure to follow an order promptly earns another five. If I must repeat myself, both punishments will be doubled, and I should kindly inform you I use a barbed whip on my slaves. Say you understand."

Scabbing monster. I would smash his face in with a table leg. I'd carve out his heart with a salted spoon. But right now, all I wanted to do was breathe.

"I understand."

"Good. Now be still." Ideghis released me. "Mascha, a chair, if you please."

Drapery the color of blood hung over my head, an ominous shade that matched the spots in my vision. Wool filled my ears and muffled the sound of Mascha's footsteps.

You have no idea what a cruel and vicious master looks like.

Schera was right; I'd had no idea. The lifeless eyes of Ideghis's slaves returned to me. Such statuesque poise wasn't natural. They were living ghosts.

He knew me too well. He knew my runes, my military background, my family origin. If he could keep Mascha in line with no more than a look, what would become of me?

I couldn't go to this man. I couldn't. There had to be a way to stop this.

Ideghis appeared once more at the side of the bed. He'd taken off his outer tunic and rolled his sleeves to the elbows, exposing forearms corded with lean muscle. He rubbed his hands together as if to warm them and smiled down at me.

"Now, let's see what we have, shall we?"

Chapter Thirty-Two

Mascha

It took all the willpower I had not to open a rift and hurl Neborov Ideghis V into it. In the time it took for me to retrieve a chair and place it by the bedside, I'd contemplated over a dozen ways to end him. He might be warded against misting, but not even the most expensive wards could stop an axe to the face. Neck bones were fragile things, and with one solid twist I could sever his spinal cord. Not to mention all the creative ways I could stab, flay, and dismember him with the dagger in my boot.

But I couldn't kill him. No matter how badly I wanted to, a fate worse than death awaited me if I upset the Deal-Breaker's hierarchy and killed the wicked swine right here in the Chancellor's guest room. Too many people had seen us enter, and if I was removed from power before I got Maralla out, she would never make it back home.

Maralla went deathly still. Ideghis leaned over her, his fingers massaging her breast for tumors. There was nothing sensual or lecherous about it, and after a time, he moved to the other side. He felt along her abdomen, expertly prodding as a healer would. Both Ideghis I and II had once done the same to all their prospective slaves.

I tried to lessen the tension in my body by stepping closer, hoping to catch Maralla's eyes. The most invasive part of Ideghis's inspection was nearly upon her. More deadly thoughts crowded in as the slaver's hands worked lower. He examined her thighs, her ankles, the tips of her toes, until there was only one place Ideghis hadn't touched.

"Open your legs."

There it was. The one command Maralla had never obeyed for me. No matter how much raspaati I used, no matter how long I kept her caged, she had refused me. But if she refused Ideghis now, she would be forced, and I had no desire to breach her fragile trust.

One second became two, and then three.

Please, Maralla.

It was as if she'd heard my silent plea. Maralla's feet slid apart, wrinkling the white sheets. I could finally breathe again; my eyes closed against the dizzying rush of relief.

Ideghis beckoned to her. "Slide down this way, *neime*. Don't be shy."

She followed his gesture until she rested with her toes curling around the bedframe. Her fingers made crater-like impressions on either side of her hips.

When Ideghis touched her beneath her patch of coarse white hair, Maralla and I both stiffened. I studied her face as she stared into the red canopy. Her expression crumbled into the same dissociative mask I'd witnessed on hundreds, if not thousands, of slaves.

I prayed it was an act. Artful Mira, let it be an act.

Her eyes squeezed shut as Ideghis pushed two fingers inside her and felt about her lower abdomen. He pressed downward from the outside.

Maralla whimpered, and I contemplated tearing him apart.

"Shh, it's alright," Ideghis cooed, his voice carrying that magical compulsion. "*Besaav'ruh.*"

Be at peace.

Warmth and soothing vibrations traveled through the Aether. For the first time in decades, I didn't fight the blanketing effect. I needed a level head, and I couldn't negotiate if all I wanted to do was bury my axes in my enemy's back and crush his lungs with my bare hands.

Maralla's breathing slowed, and the tautness in the sheets lessened. Ideghis's internal inspection was over in moments, but it felt like whole minutes had passed before he removed his fingers and withdrew a handkerchief.

"Everything seems to be in order." He wiped his hand, then patted Maralla's knee. "With the saphyrum shortage in the north, you must have Mira's blessing to have conceived at all. Rest assured, you won't face such challenges here."

Ideghis rose and tucked the handkerchief into his pocket. "She will do for more processing, but I find her very satisfying overall. What is the current bid?"

I tore my attention away from her. "Five hundred thousand." The Deal-Breaker wouldn't allow me to arbitrarily refuse Ideghis the sale, but a mistake in the contract could prolong closing, or a sudden illness could keep her in my care a little longer.

"Five hundred? Is that all?"

Something in his voice roused me. I frowned. "*Ciir.*"

The slaver laughed. "Oh, my friend, you might as well give her away at that price. No, no, no." He tapped my chest and pointed at Maralla. "You don't realize what you have. With the right stud, this one will bear a Champion, I guarantee it." Ideghis paused. His brows furrowed as he looked back at Maralla. "The two of you together. Your features are a perfect complement to hers."

The thought of breeding Maralla for the Master's heir finally severed the head of the snake writhing in my stomach.

"No."

Ideghis blinked. "Why—"

"You're out of line, Ideghis," I growled. "I don't provide stud services."

Ideghis wore his slack jaw openly. I went to Maralla, blood burning in my ear tips, and pulled her upright. She gave no resistance and remained still as death while I straightened the golden strands of her skirt and collar.

The momentary silence, however, was simply that. "If I have offended you, Mascha, you have my sincerest apologies."

My fingers stilled. "You propose the duty of a slave to a free man. No meager apology will amend such an outrageous suggestion."

Ideghis lifted placating hands. He even had the wherewithal to look apologetic. "Of course, how callous of me. Your history is bound to provoke some reservations over this sort of thing. Perhaps, if I phrase it better?"

Time itself seemed to slow as I glowered at him.

Ideghis laced his fingers together. "I am prepared to offer you one million gran for the slave, provided you bed her to seal all future deals House Ideghis makes with the Rorsch Hekkai."

The bastard. The conniving son of an oathbreaker. With expertise worthy of the Master himself, Ideghis had turned his slight into a reasonable request. A generous offer.

To be truthful, it was more than generous. I couldn't remember a female slave in all my years who had sold for such a price. The extra time and investment I'd dedicated to her would be justified, and the Deal-Breaker would be pleased. But if I agreed to this deal, Maralla wouldn't escape him. With only a few moments of study, Ideghis had used her runes to pick her apart like a crow feasting on carrion. He would be well-equipped to continue processing her, perhaps eventually breaking her in earnest.

I couldn't let that happen—wouldn't—any more than I would condemn another of my children to die in the arena.

Latching on to his slight, I said, "I choose my own women. I'm sorry, but I must decline your offer."

The feigned softness in the slaver's face eroded into cold, calculated anger. "Don't be a fool. You won't get a better offer, not even from the Chancellor himself."

I stepped toward him, placing myself between Ideghis and Maralla. "Good evening, *my lord*."

Ideghis took a matching step backward. His anger flickered into fear, but with several audible breaths in and out, he drew himself up and thrust a finger at me. "You will regret this, Mascha. The Deal-Breaker will hear of this. Mark my words."

"Get. Out," I snarled.

Ideghis stormed out, slamming the door behind him. The orders he barked at his slaves carried down the corridor. Those poor souls would bear the weight of his fury, but there was nothing to be done for them. I had more immediate problems.

I closed my eyes and focused on regaining my composure. It was some moments before I found my voice. "Maralla—"

The moment our eyes met, her expression caved. She let out a single broken sob. I sat beside her and opened my arms. She threw herself into me, and my heart constricted so hard it might burst. I stroked her hair over and over as she cried into my chest.

"It's alright."

The lie tasted sour. I gathered her into my lap and rested my chin atop her head. For long minutes we sat that way, my arms caging her in as if to protect her from the coming storm.

"You're safe."

But she wasn't, and neither was I.

It was a mistake crossing Ideghis. Saarach would come knocking within the next twenty-four hours. He would demand an explanation for my offense against the most powerful house in Durgost. He would force me to take the deal and pay costly reparations to make amends. Maralla would be sent to Ideghis, and the Master's family would have me once more for breeding stock. Ideghis would win.

"You're safe now."

There were still a few options left to us. I could try to close with Andalah Imiir tonight, before the Deal-Breaker caught wind of Ideghis's offer and demanded I take the better deal. I could approach one of the other bidders, but then I would really be in trouble, and it was likely a deal with an inconsequential house would be broken.

The last option available was the simplest one, but it came at the highest cost. I would lose my position, destroy my reputation, and possibly wind up a slave or one of Tasari's test subjects myself. But as Maralla clung to me for comfort, shaking so violently she might come undone, I decided none of that mattered. If I could do nothing else, I would be the man she believed I could be.

I would set her free.

By the time we had composed ourselves enough to rejoin the gala, Andalah Imiir had already departed.

Mirrors and glassware shivered as the very Aether responded to my frustration. I swallowed the taste of iron. Guests shied from me and my guards regarded me with alarm. I scanned the crowd, but none of the other bidders met my eyes. My knuckles cracked with the force of my clenched fists, and a throbbing ache took root in my temples.

They could smell the blood in the water. Ideghis's outburst seemed to have subdued much of the fanfare, and only those deep enough in their cups not to notice his departure still appeared jovial.

I glanced at Maralla, whose submission no longer seemed forced. Her shoulders slumped, and she moved as if a hundred years of silt had lodged between muscle and bone.

This had gone on long enough. I had to get her home.

Svaronei was nowhere in sight. I refused to linger long enough to track the Walker down. We would take the ferry back to Durgost.

I started to signal Tasari, but Aetherial mist flickered in the corner of my eye, and Fausch Amin's drunken slur rose above the din.

"I don't care what Lord Swineface said. That louse promised her to me, Father." Across the room, Lord Amin's oldest son stood between his mother and younger brother, holding an empty wine glass and swaying on his feet. "She was supposed to be *mine*."

This again. Fausch Amin had been one of Syleese Belfahr's suitors before her engagement to Tennsel Verrisch. Unsurprisingly, Lord Belfahr hadn't chosen the malicious boar for his youngest daughter, and Fausch still hadn't the grace to accept defeat.

Such squabbles were beneath me. I growled and readied a motion for guards to give a warning, but my gesture stalled as the next black-violet image formed.

And what are you going to do? I remembered Anelliiq's challenge, weeks ago when I'd asked about her scar. *It was within his right.*

Lightning struck my core. I started for the Amins' table. Maralla followed a pace behind.

"Sit down, boy," Wali snapped. "You're an embarrassment."

Fausch reached for the closest bottle and missed his glass, spilling wine all over the tablecloth. "This is all Mother's fault. No one wants to bed a withered crone."

Change always begins with a decision, no matter how small...

Scorching fury burned me from within.

Anelliiq winced, but she caught the bottle when it slipped from his grip. "Fausch, my love, I think you've had enough to drink."

Three paces. Two.

"How dare you—" Fausch began.

One.

My shadow fell across Fausch as he followed the path of his Aetherial image. Before his knuckles connected with his mother's cheek, I caught his wrist and twisted.

Fausch crumpled to his knees with a cry, his glass shattering.

He bucked, trying to free himself. I held him fast, almost to the point of bone snapping. His wide-eyed parents made no move to protest. The ballroom fell silent.

"There will be no violence at the Chancellor's gala, Fausch Amin." Steady though my voice was, I twisted his arm a little more.

"I'm sorry. I'm sorry!"

"Apologize to your mother."

"What—agh!"

He howled, and bone creaked beneath my grip.

"Apologize." Part of me hoped he wouldn't. "Now."

"I'm sorry. I'm sorry, Mother. Sands' curses, let go!"

He dropped into the puddle of wine. I crouched beside him and seized a fistful of his hair. Onlookers craned their necks to peer over the table.

I wrenched him close, his cheek pressed against mine. "Let me be clear, lordling," I whispered. "I'm quite fond of your mother. In fact, I consider her something of a friend." My hold on his hair tightened. "And I don't like when people disrespect my friends."

The whites of his eyes bulged. Wine-sour breath puffed out of him, and his body quivered like a plucked string.

I raised my voice so his father might also heed my warning. "So, unless House Amin wishes to make an enemy of the Rorsch Hekkai, I suggest you do not raise your hand to her again. If you do, I will hear of it, and you will find your contracts with me become prohibitively expensive. Do you understand?"

Fausch licked his lips and attempted a nod that made him wince. "Y-yes, Rorsch Hekkai."

"Good." I rose, my boots squeaking in the wine. "Now, *Meschiir* Amin, you've upset the Chancellor's guests. I'm afraid I must ask you to leave."

"Mascha, that's hardly—" Wali attempted.

"It is necessary. He is free to wait outside the palace grounds until you depart, or my guards will escort him home. The choice is yours."

At my gesture, two of my men hauled Fausch up. He shrugged them off and swiped at the wrinkles in his britches. With a stiff bow to his father and a glance at me, he stumbled away, my guards trailing behind him.

I looked down at Anelliiq. She forgot herself in her astonishment and stared back, as if she were working out a piccara move she hadn't seen coming. Her emerald eyes darted toward Maralla, two steps behind and to my right.

I bent to collect her hand and kissed her knuckles. "Enjoy the rest of your evening, Lady Amin."

Chapter Thirty-Three

Mascha

It was well past third hour when we left the Chancellor's gala. The coastal wind caressed my face, and water lapped at the ships looming like enormous beasts in the harbor. I spent too long studying them, contemplating whether I could strong-arm a captain into taking Maralla out of the country immediately. But the Deal-Breaker's newest laws extended the nightly curfew to bar all but local ferries and fishermen from leaving port at night.

Aside from that, the nearest foreign port was over a week away by sea, and Maralla was spellbound, nearly naked, and covered in thousands of gran of metal and diamonds. The risk of harm to her was too great.

We boarded the ferry out of Epillon in silence. As soon as the ferryman brought us within Bending distance, I rifted off the boat and into the palace. Weariness seeped into my bones, and a thick band of pain pulled taut across my eyes.

My rift closed behind us, and I spared a look at the woman for whom I'd just done the unthinkable. The last of the Aetherial winds tussled her hair, and moonlight caught in the snowy strands. She hovered like a shadow at my right shoulder. I waited, expecting her to remember herself and snap her gaze upward, but she only stared at the floor.

Damn Ideghis. Damn this place, and damn the Deal-Breaker for putting her in this position. I turned and caught her jaw. She gave no resistance as I pressed her chin upward and swept aside the stray braids falling into her face. Her eyes closed, but not before I caught the subtle gleam of unshed tears. A docile mask held her features in thrall.

I knew that look.

No. No, I couldn't bear this. Not with her.

"We still have options." I cupped her face. "Don't you dare give up."

"What more is there?" Her voice trembled. "You said you had to sell me tonight, or I'd go to auction. He'll be there waiting for me."

"I'll send a message to Lord Imiir accepting his offer. I can couple it with an apology that I didn't catch him before he departed." I reassured her as much as I reassured myself, as if her survival had become analogous to mine. "At the very least, tying up the sale in disputes will buy us time."

Her entire body shook with her indrawn breath. "Thank you for trying."

Defeat rang in every syllable, and for the first time in decades, I was at a loss for what to do. I stroked her rune-covered cheeks. "Keep playing the game for me. I'm going to fix this."

I didn't know how, but I *had* to fix it.

The senate's swift enactment of the Deal-Breaker's suggestions was almost offensive in its efficiency. Arcanists had already woven the first rift wards on our navy ships, and all the harbormasters had received an influx of soldiers and slaves to assist with cargo checks. Maralla couldn't go by sea unless I owned every man on the ship.

Rift Walkers capable of traversing such distances were rare even in Rillion. Rarer still were Walkers whose loyalty didn't lie with the Deal-Breaker. I couldn't trust any of the Rorsch Hekkai with her. Not when any man under my command could be a spy.

No matter what happened, I would rather kneel before Ideghis myself than see her wearing his collar. A wave of nausea tightened my grip at the thought.

If it pained her, she didn't show it. A sad smile turned up the corners of her mouth. "I believe you."

Her soul-weariness opened a hollow in my gut. "Come." I tried to force lightness into my voice. "Sunrise will not be kind to us."

I led her back to my chambers and incanted the lanterns to a soft glow. Maralla stood in my bedroom, arms folded around her middle. The distance between us stretched wide, even though I was only spans away.

I tossed my doublet aside and closed with her. She started at my touch, and I pulled back with a wince. "What is it?"

Maralla swallowed hard and squeezed her eyes shut. "I can still feel his hands on me."

I would kill him. I would break him into pieces one body part at a time, starting with his fingers. "A shower, then?"

She nodded.

In the washroom, I summoned magic to light the fire beneath the reservoir and adjusted the flue. I hesitated before turning back to Maralla.

I hadn't Aether-bonded the metal in her gala attire, so I couldn't dismiss it like her normal collar. But I remembered how hard it was to accept physical contact after such a violation.

"I'll have to touch you to remove those."

Finally, a spark. Her eyes flicked upward. "I want you to."

My relief lifted the weight from my chest. I would have swept her into my arms that second, but I held back. "Are you certain?"

Her melancholy eroded. She stalked toward me and seized my shirt. One hard tug brought my mouth crashing down on hers. She turned with me and pinned my back against the wall.

Hungry, demanding kisses assailed me. A moan forced past my lips.

"Maralla, we shouldn't." I knew what she was doing. I was also intimately aware of the crushing despair that would follow. "You'll only feel worse in the morning."

"I know what I want," she snapped.

"But—"

She jerked back as if I'd struck her. Then her expression crumpled. "Please, Mascha. Get his hands off me."

Gods, this woman. How could I have let this happen? I should have stopped him, should have—

But now there was nothing to be done. Nothing except obey her demand. I gathered her to me and reached for the clasp of her skirt.

"I want you to touch me," she repeated between kisses. "Make me forget."

I growled into her mouth as I fumbled with the clasp. The scent of her reigned over me. Jasmine and rose, with underpinnings of vanilla. That scent would haunt me for the rest of my life.

More kisses. Her body pressed flush against mine. I wanted my hands on her supple curves, but this Chaos-sworn clasp—

The chain skirt snapped, showering the washroom in diamonds and gold. I'd deal with Bastian's ire later. With my victory over the skirt in hand, I tore off her collar and lifted her by her thighs. Maralla wrapped her legs around my waist, and I strode fully clothed into the shower.

She groped for the tap and wrenched it open as her teeth laid claim to my lip. Water drenched her hair, her back, my sleeves and trousers.

"Make me forget, Tipori."

"As you command."

I lowered her feet to the floor. She watched me through heavy-lidded eyes as I kissed my way down her front, cupping her breasts, rolling her nipples between my fingers. My tongue circled her navel, and then I knelt before my goddess and drew her thighs over my shoulders. With her body pressed against the wall, her backside in my hands, I buried my face between her legs. She cried out for me and arched hard against the tile. I bore down on her with single-minded intent, relishing the way she pulled my hair.

I couldn't remember when the water stopped flowing, or when the ache in my jaw began. I focused only on the heady taste of her, that musky feminine scent, the way my cock throbbed with desperate need, and how my work on that tiny bundle of nerves made her come apart in my arms.

"Inside me," she panted, pawing at my shirt. "Make me come again."

"*Ciir*, goddess."

The ferocity in her eyes as I undressed was reminiscent of a tigress hunting her prey. My sopping clothes joined the diamonds on the floor. Chest heaving, I surged forward and stole her off her feet once more.

We barely made it to the bed. Steamy tiles made for poor purchase, and only the rug saved me from tumbling the last span onto the mattress. Maralla smothered my gasp with her mouth. Her tongue plunged deep and conquered mine. She shoved me onto my back, and I ceded to her, shuddering as she grabbed my cock and positioned me. My need was so great that when she sank down, it pulled a cry from me. Her eyes flashed with triumph.

I was hers. Gods help me, I was hers, and I would never be the same again.

Her hips rolled, and molten pleasure flooded my abdomen. She leaned down to capture my lips. I held her head, her back, her waist as she kissed me. Wet braids tumbled over my superheated skin. Her palms fit flush against my pectorals.

"Come north with me," she whispered, brushing her nose against mine. "Please. Say you'll come."

I couldn't. I couldn't go, no matter how badly I wanted it—wanted *her*. I couldn't, not if her people needed saphyrum. Not if I didn't want to live the rest of my life on the run. Not if change for Anelliiq, for Schera, for Emmi, for all the women and slaves of Rillion had to start with me.

"Come with me."

"I will," I lied. My fingers grazed the scars on her lower abdomen as they made for her center. "I'll come with you."

I positioned my knuckles so she could grind against them with every thrust. Her muscles flexed in perfect synchrony, braids tumbling over her shoulders and tickling my sides. She kissed me like her entire world had narrowed to this moment. As if, while our bodies were entwined, our very souls could speak to one another.

As if she were saying goodbye.

I love you, I almost said. The words hung on the tip of my tongue. *With everything I am, I love you.*

But I swallowed them down. I wouldn't tie her to me—to this place—that way. "I'll come with you."

If that was the reassurance she needed, if that would keep her from hesitating when it came time for her to leave, then I would lie for her.

I love you, and I will set you free.

Maralla's body clenched around me. Her rhythm grew more erratic as she climbed toward her peak. "*Saonis miraar,*" she gasped.

Gods above, indeed.

Bathed in the soft glow of saphyrum lanterns, we moved as one, driven by a fervor both carnal and magnificent in its simplicity.

Maralla came with a choked cry. I wrapped my arms around her and took up the rhythm as she climaxed. With her breasts brushing my chest, her lips sealing over mine, I drove myself to the top of some unfathomable precipice.

And threw myself over it.

Chapter Thirty-Four

Maralla

In some ways, the detached nature of Ideghis's inspection had been worse than if he'd taken me by force. Pain and violence made sense to me. Injuries could heal. Long ago, I'd managed to salvage my self-worth after a brutal attack by four enemy soldiers. To cope with how they'd assaulted me, I'd forced myself to think of it the same way I thought of being stabbed.

But the sensation of that emotionless touch lingered. Objectified me.

I'd never felt more like a slave.

It was a feeling no healer could fix, and so when I woke the next morning in Mascha's arms, I still felt dirty. I slid beneath the covers and roused him with my tongue.

Mascha's look of mingled confusion and astonishment was a sight for the ages when he came to with his hand on the back of my head. He seemed to understand what I needed, and once his pleasure strained at the confines of his skin, he poured all his affection into our coupling until my screams echoed off the stone.

He didn't bother to dress when he left me to draft his message to Andalah Imiir. After sending it off, he returned to bed with renewed hunger and devoured me until my body was thoroughly spent and quaking.

It was an hour past sunrise when he finally collapsed beside me. The press of his skin had long overcome the phantom feeling of those dispassionate hands, and he further banished it by planting lingering kisses at the base of my neck. His teeth grazed my shoulder. I shivered, still floating on aftershocks of euphoria. His fingers skated over me in lazy circles, his palm coming to rest over my lower abdomen.

The placement was comforting in its possessiveness. My fingers laced with his.

"I'm going to send extra saphyrum north with you." Mascha's voice coaxed me back from the edge of sleep. "For you and your mate."

An intense surge of longing forced the breath from me. "That's…" The story I'd given Ideghis returned to me. My grip on Mascha's hand tightened. "That's not necessary."

"But it is. It's imperative that you have adequate saphyrum, especially in the last half-year of pregnancy—"

"Mascha." I turned in his arms and touched his face. "I lied to Ideghis about those losses."

The crease in his forehead vanished. "Clever."

I scoffed. "Maybe if it had worked."

If it could have deterred Ideghis from placing a bid at all, we wouldn't be floundering for the last few minutes of peace before the storm. I could sense it building as surely as the tension in Mascha's muscles each time a noise sounded outside his bedroom.

"For the future, then," he said. "Tiior knows I've kept you from him long enough."

Scabbing gods. His desire to care for me, even after I returned to the mate he assumed I had, moved me in a way I couldn't explain. "My mate was called beyond Baosanni's Gate last year."

Speaking the words aloud was easier than I'd expected. I'd had a long time to wallow in my misery on the slave ship. I'd even wished for death at the bottom of my despair, only to find myself again in defiance of the men who sought to bring me low.

Mascha's face fell. "Forgive me. I thought—"

"You couldn't have known." I stroked one of his dark eyebrows, then moved on to the gentle taper of his ear. "Sorcerers ambushed us outside one of our northern villages. They'd been treating with the Iceborn raiders for an alliance." The tightness in my throat worsened. "Nalerta… caught an arrow that was meant for me."

"Nalerta." Mascha acknowledged my mate's name as if paying his respects. He hesitated. "What of your children?"

I swallowed against my emotion. If I didn't get this out fast, I'd be a blubbering mess before I could finish. "Two of our children went with him during the attack.

Our daughter, Elliaana, took a blade dipped in frost viper venom. Rysios was killed by a fire savant. The youngest, Declaan, perished the winter before, after years of battling saphyrum sickness."

There was a depth to Mascha's expression I hadn't seen before. His eyes glistened, and his voice quavered. "You have my condolences."

He swiped at a stray tear on my face. I burrowed into his arms and pressed my forehead to his chest. Though my safety was as much an illusion as Mascha's villainous persona, I took comfort in his strength. For a little while, I would let myself believe he would find a way out of this for us.

We dozed in a tangle of limbs until well past tenth hour, when the inevitable knock came at Mascha's door.

"Master?" Catari called. "*Meschiir* Saarach has requested you."

Mascha's baritone rumbled beneath my cheek. "I'll receive him in the great hall."

Catari's footsteps retreated while we delayed a few moments more. The scent of hot iron leaked from Mascha as he pulled saphyric energy and summoned Aether. Cold metal coalesced around my neck.

"Come." His gentle kiss stole my breath. Then he pushed us both upright, still holding me close. "He'll expect to see you as well."

The great hall was even more ostentatious than Mascha's ballroom. Its windows formed a circle of stained glass behind a carved dais depicting a pride of lions at leisure on the Marillinoni savannah. A black marble throne stood atop the dais, cushioned with red velvet pillows. We approached the throne from a side entry, Mascha's doublet and my dress a match of lilac and silver.

Catari, Vassu, and Raffi all hovered near the main entrance. Raffi manned the door, while Vassu held a tray laden with wine and cheese. Catari's look of relief when we entered suggested Saarach unnerved her as well.

Without acknowledging the Deal-Breaker's messenger, Mascha placed one of the pillows beside the throne and gestured for me to kneel.

I kept my eyes down, but from beneath my lashes, I watched Saarach fluff himself up like an incensed cockatriin at the base of the stairs. A slight, then, to have a slave kneel for comfort rather than service, while the emissary was forced to stand. The image of Mascha plucking the man's metaphorical feathers provoked a smirk that was hard to hide.

"I hope you have a good reason for interrupting such a beautiful morning, Saarach." Mascha lowered himself to his throne, looking every bit the king, with a jeweled band of platinum across his forehead. His fingers settled into my unbraided hair. I didn't have to fake the shiver that traveled down my spine.

Saarach's graying eyebrows lifted. He dabbed at his face with a kerchief. "I would be more concerned if I were you. He is upset, Mascha." The half-blood enunciated every word. "And you know what happens when the man is upset."

"I will not apologize for it." Mascha's fingertips continued their steady sifting through my hair. "The lord's request was outrageous."

"That is hardly an excuse. Bedding the same woman each night is what one does in other parts of the world. You Rillanese are a spoiled lot. And for a million gran? You know you must take the deal."

"My choice of flesh will not be stripped from me in any deal, regardless of contract. I've already sent word to Lord Imiir, accepting his more reasonable offer."

Saarach's expression remained unnervingly impassive. "That message was intercepted three hours ago."

Sickening dread nearly shattered my composure. That message had been our last hope. Now nothing stood between me and Ideghis. I fidgeted despite my attempts to remain calm. Mascha's palm rested flat against my head as if to steady me.

"You will take the deal for one million and bed the slave at her new owner's behest," Saarach said. "The Deal-Breaker has deemed both conditions nonnegotiable."

The slightest tremor in Mascha's arm betrayed his disquiet. I squeezed my eyes shut, silently begging him to force the issue. Surely, he could do something. Anything.

Those dead-eyed slaves haunted me. I couldn't, wouldn't, let that become my future.

"To further salvage your image," Saarach continued, "he expects you will sponsor Keizai in the next fight and make an appearance in the Chancellor's box as a former Champion."

It was like watching a lion being cornered at the circus. I'd heard of Keizai, Ideghis's current pit-fighting sensation. Rumors claimed he was some relation to Mascha—a grandchild or a nephew some number of generations removed.

Mascha withdrew from me and gripped the stone arm of his throne. "He wants to remind me of my place, is what I'm hearing."

"The arrangements for the fight have been made. You are to deliver the slave to Ideghis Estates by tomorrow morning."

I stiffened.

Tomorrow morning? No other deals of this magnitude would have closed so soon. There was no way we could orchestrate a way around port security with so little time.

"I will counter Ideghis's offer." Mascha's possessive grip returned to the back of my neck. "I will pay our employer double to take her as my first wife."

My mouth fell open. Across the hall, Catari gasped.

It took everything I had not to break protocol and look up. Two million gran to make me his wife. Thoughts and emotions stormed through me—admittedly not all negative ones. I would be a free woman, able to travel with him. It would mean bedding men on his behalf, but if it bought us time to work out my departure...

Ciir, this could work. And with my *oeloraati* recently stymied, it would be years before the next one came about. I would be long gone by then.

Maybe with more time, I could convince him to come with me.

A sharp barking sound issued from Saarach's throat. It was so cold and uncanny that I barely recognized it as laughter.

"Oh, Mascha, you can't possibly be serious."

"I am." His nails bit into my nape, and I went rigid as a cat held by its scruff. "She is of more use to me as a Lady of the Rorsch Hekkai. It will be well worth the time and resources I've dedicated to her processing. The Deal-Breaker should find my terms agreeable."

Saarach cackled again. Icy foreboding prickled the hair on my arms.

His amusement cut off as abruptly as it had begun. "It is as he expected, then." He turned toward the other slaves. "Leave us."

Vassu and Raffi didn't hesitate. Catari glanced sideways at me before pulling the door closed after them. She would go to Schera and tell her what she'd just heard. It would be all over the palace—gods, all over the scabbing city—before sunset.

My breath was coming too fast. I leaned into Mascha's touch to slow my galloping heart. Now wasn't the time to consider the likelihood of his jealous lover's retaliatory strike.

Saarach dabbed at his face again, then smoothed his perfect lapels. "This woman's recklessness has influenced you beyond reason. You will not reward a slave as wild as she with freedom only a month after nearly costing you everything, nor will you seek to undermine a noble house's generosity."

"I wasn't aware my gold weighed any less. Our union will bring more profit than a sale to any noble house. Take word of my decision—"

"He has spoken, Mascha," Saarach cut in. "I suggest you do not test him further. Our master doesn't want your gold. He wants your loyalty—a commodity I would hate to inform him is in short supply."

Loyalty. More like slavery.

Saarach lifted his chin. "May I deliver your acquiescence to his terms?"

I dared a glance up, because really, what did I have to lose?

Thunderous fury tightened Mascha's face. He'd tried—gods, he'd tried—but unless he was willing to defy the Deal-Breaker's orders, even two million gran wasn't enough to save me. I would be sold tomorrow morning and kept as breeding stock, like a prized mare or an exotic animal.

Mascha's hand relaxed. I fought the urge to pull away as he brushed my hair, his touch a silent apology. The sense of betrayal I felt wasn't fair to him, but it burned me nonetheless.

I couldn't do this. I just couldn't do this anymore.

Mascha gestured dismissively, as if I was of little consequence. "I will deliver her tomorrow."

Saarach bowed. "The Deal-Breaker thanks you for your prompt attention to this matter."

"I'm sure he does. Leave me, Saarach."

"Good day, my lord—"

"Don't. You know better."

The bastard smiled. "My apologies. Farewell, Mascha."

Saarach departed, leaving us alone in the great hall. Mascha leaned forward, rubbing his temples.

I wasn't foolish enough to think I could best Ideghis on his own terms. He would make no mistakes in my early days to allow me to get the lay of his estates, nor would he leave me alone long enough to find weaknesses in his security. He'd keep me in chains from the start.

I shuddered. The scent of rose oil and leather morphed into the stench of fleshrot and death. My eyes closed and my body betrayed me, rifting me back to the floor of a ship and the press of metal rubbing my skin raw.

There had to be some other solution, some other avenue we hadn't yet explored. Maybe we'd overlooked something. A disguise, an illusion, a bribe—this was Rillion, for the gods' sakes; it shouldn't be that hard.

But no, the Deal-Breaker had already waylaid Mascha's deal with the other nobleman and avoided diversion by cutting my transfer down to a matter of hours.

With Mascha's counteroffer denied, there was only one other way out of this. Only one way I didn't wind up like the rest of those pitiful wretches enslaved to Ideghis.

"Kill me."

The words slipped out before I could balance their weight on the scales of possibility and consequence.

Mascha stilled. He looked over his knuckles at me. "I beg your pardon?"

"You heard me." I stared back, unblinking, each passing heartbeat tempering my resolve. I wouldn't be wrapped in chains again, no matter what. "If you must send me to Ideghis, I would rather die."

Something sparked in Mascha's gaze. He straightened and reached for his earring. A dark, translucent dome twined around the dais as he called Aether to shield us. After sweeping the great hall, eyes glazed with Foresight, he returned his attention to me.

"You're not going to Ideghis Estates."

"You've an idea?"

"*Ciir.*" He studied me, his expression one of hope and determination in equal parts. "But it's going to take the best performance of your life."

I set my jaw and straightened my spine. "Tell me what I have to do."

Mascha reached down and brushed his thumb against the crude welds keeping my spellbinders closed.

"First, we need to see the jeweler."

Chapter Thirty-Five

Mascha

"YOU'VE GONE AND LOST your damned fool head," Bastian declared. His bewilderment might have been amusing if it didn't fill me with dread. After he'd struck off Maralla's irons and replaced them with silver binders inlaid with amethysts, I'd invited Bastian into my sitting room for a drink. With a Silencing spell in place and no interruptions in our Foreseeable future, I'd laid out my plan.

"It would only be for a few days," I insisted. "Just long enough for me to arrange her transport out of the country."

"No, no, absolutely not." Bastian waved his hands as if to ward me off. "I don't want to get mixed up in your quarrel with Ideghis."

I'd known it was a long shot. Bastian was a pragmatist, always careful to ensure he owed no loyalty to any of the Rillanese houses. He took great care to remain neutral in matters of state, always paid his tithes to the Rorsch Hekkai in a timely manner, and even paid extra to insure his business ventures against bad deals.

He was my first choice when I'd considered where to hide Maralla. At the very least, Bastian wouldn't report me. After all, to do so would bring us both to the forefront of a scandal of legendary proportions.

"Your estate would be the last place anyone would look, *amii*."

"Your confidence doesn't inspire me in the least. What if your plan fails and the Deal-Breaker's Aetherians come looking for her?"

"I can ward one of the rooms to shield her from divination. I just need a few wardstones."

Maralla stood at my right elbow, holding an opened bottle of wine. Bastian glanced up and motioned to his half-empty glass. She filled it immediately and stepped back.

"It's not really her safety I'm concerned about," Bastian said. "What of my business? My estate? My—"

"I cannot let her go to Ideghis," I cut in. "I know what he's capable of. Believe me, no one deserves that fate."

Bastian threw his hands up, painted nails flashing. "He has hundreds of slaves, many you've sold to him yourself! And yet, you would defy a direct order for this one—" He stopped, looking between us. Then he grinned. "Oh, I see." He snatched his wine from the table and sat back. "Now it all makes sense."

"What makes sense?"

Bastian regarded me over his glass, blue eyes shining as if he were privy to some inside joke. He crossed one leg over his knee.

I didn't bother to hide my annoyance. We had only hours to make this work. "Spit it out, then."

He rested his drink on his upraised ankle. "Have you told her yet?"

"Told her what?"

"That you love her."

"That's..." *beside the point*, I nearly said, but the words caught in my throat. Blood warmed my face, and I became painfully aware of Maralla's eyes on me as she broke protocol in front of our guest.

"It's true, isn't it?" Bastian's expression softened. "Why else would you risk your entire livelihood for a slave?"

My jaw tightened. Maralla already suspected how I felt, since that day in my study weeks ago, but I still refused to say it aloud. I couldn't risk it changing anything between us. "I won't see her suffer as I did."

Bastian's focus shifted to Maralla. "What of you, my dear? How do you feel about your master?"

She had no ready response. Her mouth opened and closed twice before she set the wine on the table.

I tried to save her the embarrassment. "It doesn't matter how she—"

Bastian held up a hand to silence me. "Be honest," he prompted her.

Instead of speaking right away, Maralla touched my wrist. Gooseflesh swept over my arm.

"I see him clearer now." She spoke without subservience, but with a quiet confidence that rang with pride.

I dared not look at her, lest my emotions betray me. Instead, I silently implored Bastian not to take this any further. Only pain could come of it.

The jeweler's knowing smile still clung to his lips. "It's a brave thing he does for you, defying his employer. Foolish, certainly, but also brave."

"I know." Maralla lifted her hand from my wrist and slipped it beneath my chin. A gentle, insistent pressure forced our eyes to meet. "I want you to come north with me."

Silonas slay me, was she trying to rip my heart out? "Maralla..."

"My people need men like you." Her fingers brushed through my beard. "I think it would be good for you."

If Bastian's smile got any wider, the corners of his mouth would touch his ears.

"Your people need saphyrum more than they need men." I pulled away so I could think more clearly. "I can't send them what I have if I leave."

"We can find another way." She lowered herself to her knees beside my chair so we were eye-to-eye. "Come with me. You hate it here; I know you do."

I didn't, in truth. There were certainly parts of it I could do without, but the power I wielded here—the fear I inspired—was as much a drug to me as the Master's keallite had once been. The thrill of negotiation, the satisfaction of matching wits with some of the greatest minds in the world...

"It's not that simple," I told her. Despite the game we played, despite how I lied my best for her in our most intimate moments, the fact remained that I couldn't just leave.

Frowning, Maralla put her hand over my wrist again. "You are still a slave, Mascha. Maybe not to your old master, but certainly to your current one."

I scowled. "I answer to no master."

"Maybe not by name. But your employer certainly has you twisted around his fingers. You may not wear his collar, but you are still bound to him."

Her accusation stirred a font of anger inside me, but I couldn't deny there was truth in what she said. I rubbed the smooth scar where my collar had once been.

The Deal-Breaker knows.

How easily he'd used me to crush his opposition that night. He'd stolen my autonomy and used me to cut down anyone who dared defy him—and too many who were simply in the wrong place at the wrong time. I would remember the face of the child I'd killed for the rest of my life.

I might have built the Rorsch Hekkai into an empire over the years, but I wasn't the one with true control of it. His spies were everywhere, undermining me whenever it suited him. I couldn't even wed without the Deal-Breaker's approval now. My children would be forever slaves to his system.

And I with them, if I didn't act.

"He forces you to obey for fear of what will happen if you don't," Maralla went on. "You want to rise against him, and trust me when I say that feeling will only grow with time."

Except, I already knew that feeling. I'd felt it in the pits. I remembered the urge to disarm my trainers and turn their whips against them. By the time I'd entered the arena, that urge had become a roaring inferno. To keep me compliant, the Master had imbued my collar with magic and ordered my overseers to shock me whenever my attention strayed from my training or lingered too long on a weapon that wasn't my own. The pain had reminded me of my place.

Now, the same thing was happening all over again. The Deal-Breaker's demand that I return to the arena as a display piece was proof enough. He knew I'd never return of my own free will. I'd stepped out of line by denying Ideghis, and I was being shocked back into compliance.

"Let yourself be free of him." Maralla tightened her hold on my wrist. "Come with me."

If I went with her, I would be hunted, and that would endanger Maralla's escape. I couldn't jeopardize her chances by going with her. And it wasn't in my nature to run when a powerful foe threatened me. I met my enemies face-to-face and destroyed them.

I'd already resolved to undermine the Deal-Breaker by freeing Maralla. If I could get her out, it would prove the man was not omniscient. Perhaps this was my chance to start pinpointing the crime lord's weaknesses. Once I toppled him, no one would stand above me. No one would enslave me ever again. I could abolish the practice entirely. I could be the difference, not just in Soltani's life, but in the lives of thousands.

Such subterfuge would take time and planning over many years. I would have to be patient.

Maralla and Bastian were watching me. I considered sending Bastian away so Maralla and I could speak privately, but I'd already shown my hand. This was my chance to prove I held the right cards.

With a glance in Bastian's direction, I placed my glass on the table and took Maralla's hand in both of mine.

"I have to stay. I want to change things and make Rillion better." Reaching up, I touched the runes that Ideghis had identified as Dauntlessness and Persistence. "Especially for its women."

She leaned into my touch, closed her eyes, and nodded. When she opened them again, they blazed with pride. "Then that's what you should do."

We both looked at Bastian, then. He still sat with one ankle crossed over his knee, glass in hand. His expression had lost all of its prior humor.

"Will you help us, Bastian?" I asked. "Please."

After several moments of silence, he brought his glass to his lips. "You know just how to twist a man's arm, don't you?"

Relief swept through me. "Does that mean yes?"

Bastian finished off his wine and set the glass down with a deep, throaty chuckle. "Yes, my friend. Of course I will help you."

Maralla bowed her head, her voice thick with emotion. "Thank you, *Meschiir* Clairmont. I promise you won't regret this."

Another smile crinkled the corners of his eyes. "Seeing the way he looks at you, it is worth the risk."

I extracted myself from Maralla and rose, rounding the low table. Bastian rose as well, taking hold of the crease near my elbow. I repeated the gesture and tugged him into a tight embrace.

"I will never forget this."

Bastian laughed again, wrapping his free arm around me. "I know you won't." He pushed me away, but kept hold of my elbow. There was mischief in his expression as he reached up to pat my cheek. "I intend to remind you every chance I get."

I laughed. "I would expect no less."

Bastian released my elbow and returned to his chair. "Now," he said, all business once more. "Let's discuss this plan of yours."

Chapter Thirty-Six

Maralla

W HILE MASCHA SAW BASTIAN out the door, I followed his wordless dismissal and headed down the halls to the slaves' quarters. Wariness and curiosity followed me. Down every corridor was another slave who looked at me like I'd won my own Freedom Wager. It staggered me how fast Mascha's announcement had traveled.

What wouldn't have traveled was Saarach's denial of Mascha's request to make me his wife. If this new plan was going to work, we couldn't allow the knowledge that Mascha favored me to spread beyond the palace. We needed to fabricate a new rumor—one the slaves could confirm when Saarach returned to investigate the sudden and suspicious death of *Johtan Shasnaram*.

Muffled voices carried from inside Schera's room. I hesitated, knuckles poised to knock. Mascha trusted Schera with our secret, but he'd cautioned me on the number of unknown spies the Deal-Breaker had inside his palace. I braced myself and rapped the wood three times.

Emmi opened the door. "Maralla." Her surprise gave way to a scowl. "Shouldn't you be warming the Master's bed?"

Her tone was as cold as northern winter. I glanced beyond her at Farrah and Catari, who flanked Schera on her bed. The dancer's eyes were bloodshot and her cheeks were puffy. She glared at me and dabbed her nose with a kerchief.

Remorse lodged in my chest. Aside from my dance lessons and pointless conversations over my hair and clothing, I had barely seen any of them since I'd returned to Mascha's bed.

They deserved better than that. I knew how this looked, and of course they all felt the betrayal. I had to crush this misunderstanding before it could fester.

The anger in Emmi's dark eyes sobered me, and I twisted the hem of my silver gown between my fingers. "I need to speak to Schera."

Her scowl deepened. She opened her mouth, but I hastened to explain before she could refuse.

"It's not what you think. Mascha's not marrying anyone. Saarach refused him."

Catari gaped, but the others' faces only darkened.

"The Master, you mean." Ever one for propriety, Schera rose and stalked across her suite. She shooed Emmi away to take hold of the door herself. "If I'd known belligerence and disrespect were what he wanted, maybe he would have made me a wife, too."

My sigh was half-growl. "He doesn't want a wife. Not when she would bear children she can't keep."

Their confusion made me wince. Too late, I wondered if the deal with his employer was a secret, too.

Farrah's brows furrowed. "What do you mean?"

"For the gods' sakes, haven't you ever wondered why a man with every woman in the nation at his disposal doesn't have children? They all get sold as slaves." It seemed so obvious now that I kicked myself for not making the connection sooner. I looked back at Schera. "He's trying to spare you that pain."

She looked from me to the other women in silent conference. Her white-knuckled fingers relaxed on the door. "Why would he suggest wedding you, then? You said he meant to sell you."

"He did." I tried for a pointed look to reiterate my need to speak with her alone. "But circumstances changed."

Schera folded her arms and made no move to dismiss her friends.

My frustration mounted. We didn't have time for this. If I had to settle for all these women being complicit in our deception, I would have to levy my intentions with careful truths. "Ideghis wants..." Gods, I couldn't even say the words without choking on them. "Ideghis wants me for his breeding program. He demanded Mascha act as a stud as part of the bid. Our Master refused, but the Deal-Breaker has ordered him to take the offer."

Finally, their collective ire faltered. Farrah looked like someone had pissed in her bread dough, and Catari and Emmi recoiled open-mouthed.

Schera proved a quick study. She frowned. "He was trying to stop the sale by wedding you."

I swallowed, uncertain whether that knowledge would work in my favor. After all, if Mascha had succeeded, it would have afforded me a position on a whim that Schera had coveted for years. But my survival was at stake, and it wasn't like he couldn't take another wife.

"Yes."

She glanced up and down the corridor, then seized hold of my arm to tug me inside. My surprise blurred into unease as the women gathered around me and conversation turned toward House Ideghis.

"You're going to be alright," Farrah said, squeezing my shoulder.

"Just do everything he says," Emmi agreed. "Don't give him any reason to be cross with you."

Catari shivered. "And don't ever sass him. He burns his breeders' feet if he can't whip them."

"Catari!" Farrah scolded.

"Well, he does! Or else they kneel on a bed of rice—"

"Stop it. That's not helping." Schera glared at her, then guided me to the bed to sit. "Don't let them frighten you. Ideghis has been known for kindness if you do your best to please him. They say he favors those who bear strong sons."

I thought of Mascha's mother, Evora, and how she'd met her end at the behest of Ideghis's great-great-grandfather. For once, I let myself be well and truly shaken. A laugh bordering on hysteria burst from me. These Rillanese had a warped sense of kindness.

"We'll all pray to Mira on your behalf," Emmi promised.

I shook my head. Feigning trepidation wasn't necessary; all the horrible feelings I'd been stuffing down since my inspection came rushing back.

"This can't happen. It can't." With four of the palace's leading gossips all in the same place, I could allude to Mascha's plan as if it were my last desperate attempt to escape. "I'm not going."

Schera brushed my hair from my cheek. "No one defies the Deal Breaker, Maralla. Not even the Master."

How easily she accepted that as fact. No person deserved to hold that much power over others.

Farrah knelt and cupped my knee. Emmi sat on my other side and hugged me. I took the kerchief Catari handed me and scrubbed my eyes and nose.

No more words were offered. Their pitying looks said enough, as if I were no more than a tracking hound tugging at my leash and strangling myself with my own collar.

The familiar scent of hot iron wafted into the room, and Aether flashed through the crack under the door. I wiped my face again and balled the kerchief up. Schera released my other hand and turned as her door swung open.

When Mascha entered, Catari and Emmi dropped to their knees beside Farrah and bowed their heads. Schera paused in sliding from her bed to study me. Another frown creased her brow.

I didn't move. Schera didn't either.

"Good evening, Master."

"Evening, Master."

The chorus of greetings was met with a discerning sweep of Mascha's violet eyes. His dark brow quirked at Schera's defiance. He addressed the women on the floor.

"Out."

I envied how easily he could dismiss them. Scabbing gods, I missed my post in the north.

He stepped aside and folded his hands as the women complied. Once the door closed behind Emmi, he reached for his earring and called forth that veil of Aetherial Silence.

Schera shifted beside me. The whites of her eyes gleamed in the candlelight. "Master?"

"Peace, Schera. It is only a precaution. I have something very important to discuss with you."

She stared long at the inky swirls of magic twining around us, the dome muffling all sound outside its reach. "I'm at your service."

"What we discuss here will not leave this room." Mascha lowered himself to one knee in front of her and took her chin. "It will endanger you, so if you don't wish to take part, you are free to say no. You'll not be punished for it."

Her eyes slid off his like a proper slave before they snagged on mine. Conflict stormed across her face.

I nodded once, hoping to encourage her. She sucked in a breath so deep it lifted her shoulders. Resolve sparked in her expression, like a new warrior having struck her first solid blow to an opponent.

She looked Mascha full in the face. "What would you ask of me, Master?"

The corners of his mouth lifted. His attention flicked toward me before settling on Schera once more. "I need you to come to bed with us tonight. Make it known that I've commanded you to perform with Maralla one last time before she is sold to Ideghis. Tomorrow, you will report everything you witness to Saarach, down to the moment we leave my chambers. You will scream for help as loudly as you can, but the guard posted outside won't reach us in time."

Calculations ticked away behind Schera's eyes. If she'd been under my command in the Fourth Legion back home, I'd have demanded she accept a role as one of my junior tacticians.

"You're going to—"

Mascha pressed his fingers to her lips. "I will not have you involved in any more of this than necessary. We just need a witness whose testimony can placate the Deal-Breaker. Can you do that for me?"

She fidgeted with the folds of her skirt. It took so long for her to formulate an answer, I thought she might say no.

Schera spared another glance between us. Her hands began to shake in her lap. I considered reaching for them, but stopped myself. This had to be her decision, unguided by Mascha or me.

She wetted her lips and made a valiant attempt at sternness. "I would ask something in return."

Mascha blinked, and I cracked a smile as his most docile and obedient kitten bared her claws.

He shot me a warning glare, though his eyes glimmered with amusement. "Name it."

"I want..." Her courage faltered. She wrung her hands and swallowed twice. "I would be your wife."

I expelled a slow, silent breath against the tightening in my chest. It was the most logical course, after all.

Mascha's humor crumbled. "Schera..."

"Or your concubine," she hastened to say. "And I can still take herbs in secret if you don't want a child."

He would need someone here for him when I left. I clung to that knowledge and did my best to shove the prickly sensation in my chest down.

Mascha cupped her cheeks. "Even as a concubine, you will be subjected to terrible men. I can offer others of similar station now, but if I elevate you beyond it, that protection goes away. Even more men will demand you, and there will be no one to share the burden."

It was like watching the tide turn. Schera lifted her hands to encircle Mascha's wrists. He allowed her to pull his arms into her lap and interlace their fingers. "I accept the risks. Master, I have been loyal to you for nearly ten years. I deserve to stand by your side as something more than a slave. I'm stronger than you think. Please let me prove it."

"You are a lioness." His smile was wistful. "Is that truly what you want? To be my concubine?"

"More than anything."

He took her wrists in turn, a gesture reminiscent of making a deal. "Then in exchange for your aid, I will make it so."

She threw her arms around him. "Thank you, Master. Thank you."

I averted my gaze and distracted myself by studying the lazy eddies of Aether surrounding us. I was under no illusion that Mascha would have a change of heart and come with me, but I didn't expect this confirmation of it to sting so much.

A warm palm touched my knee. I cleared my throat and found them both studying me. For Schera's benefit, I hardened my expression. We would all get what we wanted this way. It was for the best.

"Come. We have other preparations to make." Mascha squeezed my knee and rose. He looked at Schera as I shoved to my feet. "Attend me in my chambers after dinner. Tell Emmi and the others nothing of your new status. I'll announce it later."

"Your will, Master."

The dome dissolved around us, and a rift split the Wall with his flippant gesture. He kissed Schera long and deep, then pulled me into the Aether.

Chapter Thirty-Seven

Mascha

Dawn had just broken over the horizon when Scherazeme's scream of terror echoed through the halls of my palace. "Help! Somebody help! She's gone crazy!"

I stalked down the corridor after Maralla, attempting my most menacing stare. Three slaves were cowering in an alcove near the stairs; they shrank further as I summoned my axes. "I tire of this game, *rascha*," I growled. "Put that down before you harm yourself."

Maralla brandished the iron poker she'd stolen from my fireplace. She swung at me with all her might, following her Aetherial image. I stepped into it, lifting my axe too late to stop the blow. The point slashed across my chest, and blood gushed down my torso.

I staggered. Maralla ducked around the corner, out of sight of a slave-binding. I snarled for effect and spun toward Scherazeme, who stood frozen in the doorway to my chambers. "Call the guards. Now!"

"Yes, Master." Scherazeme darted away, but she would find the men difficult to rouse after their late night of carousing and wine cut with poppy milk.

Axes in hand, I stormed after Maralla and took a deliberate turn away from her before doubling back. She needed distance to reach the ground floor before me. I counted to thirty, then made certain I rifted away in full view of Odessa and Catari.

Maralla's howl of fury greeted me as I stepped out of the rift. She slashed at me as if the poker were a sword.

I blocked it with Bloodletter. "Stop this!"

She disengaged with a snarl, eyes flicking toward the pair of male slaves who'd stopped dead in the corridor. Beyond them, the rising sun spilled across the foyer.

I chopped the flat of Furyborn down toward her shoulder, narrowly missing her as she spun out of reach.

"You only delay the inevitable."

"*Iithe'ruh caezo, ashaan*," Maralla snarled through bared teeth.

Eat shit, half-blood.

She swung the poker again. Iron met steel with a resounding *clang*. I shoved her hard through our joined weapons, and Maralla went sprawling.

I paced toward her and winced, glancing down at the blood slicking my skin. I banished Bloodletter to the Aether and freed one hand for a slave-binding. But before the mist could form its damning black bands, Maralla kicked upward, just shy of my groin.

I exaggerated the pain and doubled over. My binding dissolved into mist. Maralla leaped to her feet and dashed down the hallway. The two slaves tried to dive in opposite directions out of her way and collided. She leaped over them and kept running, the poker swinging in her hand.

"Maralla!"

Feigning a slow recovery, I glared after her and slashed open a rift. Maralla reached the foyer as a second shimmering rift materialized a few spans in front of her. I plunged my hand into the Aether and *pulled* at the fabric of reality behind it. My vision warped into streaky lines for an instant. Then I was beside her, taking the tip of the poker to my abdomen.

"Agh!"

I seized her throat. She tore the poker out and went for another jab. Pain teasing red into my vision, I hurled Maralla across the foyer. She landed hard and choked on a gasp, the poker clattering across the tiles.

Both entry slaves cowered beside the doors. I stalked forward, blood seeping into the waistband of my trousers. Another rivulet trickled from a cut over my eye, and I tasted copper from the split in my lower lip.

"That is the last time you defy me, *rascha*." I kicked the poker toward the stairs and grabbed her by the hair. "Fifty lashes—"

Maralla spat blood at me. I jerked back, and she struck the nerve near my elbow. Pain spiked hot from wrist to shoulder. My fingers went slack, and she shot toward the doors.

Still nursing feeling into my hand, I drew back with my other arm and threw Furyborn. Both entry slaves dropped to the floor and covered their heads. The axe sailed end-over-end and cracked blade-first into the seam between the doors, sealing them against her retreat.

Maralla whirled and hissed at me.

As I prepared another binding, my attention flicked toward the far corridor. The commotion should have reached every corner of the palace by now, but there was no sign of movement from the man we needed most to make this work.

My teeth clenched. I knew he was here. I'd made certain of it.

Black-violet bands coalesced in the air. I didn't have to pretend at distraction; my injuries truly made casting more difficult. Maralla dodged the bind and dove for her makeshift weapon. I abandoned my magic and tackled her.

We struck the floor in a heap. She sank her teeth into my arm, snarling into my torn flesh. I struck her twice, forcing her to let go. As we grappled, the movement I'd been waiting for finally caught my eye.

Tasari.

My half-brother sauntered down the hallway from his quarters, a predatory smile staining his lips. When he reached the mouth of the corridor, he leaned against the threshold and folded his arms.

Sitting astride Maralla, I clamped my hand around her throat. "Brother," I said. "Go get your box of toys. This one would like to play your favorite game."

Maralla screamed, her face contorting around her swollen eye and lower lip. "You bastard! Don't even think—"

I squeezed harder and cut her off. Her nails dug into my wrist.

Tasari regarded us coolly and tilted his head. "While I do love to hear her scream," he said, soft as silk, "I should remind you she is no longer yours."

Rage alighted in my core. Of course he would choose this moment to show restraint. "She is still mine until delivery," I growled.

Tasari didn't move. "Ideghis may not take kindly if we mutilate his new acquisition."

Maralla's skin deepened to a sickly maroon. Her grip on my arm loosened. I eased up to allow her a ragged breath. She squirmed under my weight. A tear leaked down her cheek and into her ear.

I fought against the sourness in my gut, the disquieting sense that I'd gone too far, and attempted my best mocking smile. "I won't do any permanent damage." I wiped the moisture from her face. "Just a little parting gift. We don't want to send him unprocessed goods."

"Ideghis will—"

"I didn't ask for your opinion." This time, my anger was real. "Do as I say."

Where most other men would have trembled, Tasari only rolled his eyes. "Fine. I'll be right back."

While Tasari slipped down the corridor to his rooms, I stuffed down my unease and took in the state of our surroundings. The two entry slaves had risen to their feet and now stood eyeing the axe embedded in the doors. Down the corridor through which Maralla and I had come, the pile of limbs pressed into the rug had cleared itself up.

At the top of the stairs, Raenara's Aetherial image turned the corner seconds before she appeared in earnest. She paused and stared at me, then dropped her gaze to the basket full of linens in her arms.

"Bring a towel, *rascha*," I commanded. While her eyes were still downcast and the other slaves were distracted, I reached into the leg of my trousers and withdrew a small scalpel. "I'll need something to mop up the blood."

"Yes, Master."

"You're a monster," Maralla seethed. She began her struggle anew, making a grab for my throat. I caught her and pressed the scalpel's handle into her palm, forcing her arm back to the floor.

"Stay down," I spat. Gods help me, even in these direst of circumstances, I could still marvel at her fire.

She held my stare with convincing fury. I let more of my weight settle over her, crushing her. When she finally looked away in grudging submission, her fingers closed around the scalpel and disappeared beneath the white braids haloed about her head.

Raenara hurried down the stairs, rushed a curtsy, and offered a towel. I took it and dismissed her with a wave.

Tasari returned as the slave hurried away. "That one would do well with the Amins." He set his leather satchel next to Maralla's head. "Wali likes those red-haired girls."

I snorted. "His older boy would tear her apart."

"Fausch is a half-wit."

For once, I agreed with him.

Tasari bent to flick one of Maralla's dark nipples. "Are we doing this right here?"

"Why not?" I forced a grin. "When we're finished, perhaps you can borrow her for a few hours."

Tasari scoffed and knelt on one knee to unclasp his satchel. "*Now* you let me have her? After all this time? She must have really pissed you off."

As Tasari began pulling out vials of various colored liquids, sniffing at each one and then dismissing it, I sat back on Maralla's hips, letting my hand stray to her sternum. When Tasari withdrew the vial of sky-blue liquid I was waiting for, I pressed my palm flat against her belly. Her eyes darted toward the vial in Tasari's hand at my signal.

Frost viper venom was an expensive commodity this far south. Native to the cold climate of the Eidosinian Northlands, the frost viper didn't thrive well in Rillion, and its venom broke down within a few days in the heat. Even harder to find was the antivenom for that particular snake. Tasari was the only man in the country with access to both. By blackmailing an old arcanist and making a costly investment with a Duerguardian inventor, he'd found a way to house a live snake in a cold cell in his bedroom.

Tasari used diluted drops of venom to immobilize his test subjects in lieu of rope. He liked it especially because it could be absorbed through the skin and took effect within seconds. A full dose taken internally could freeze a man's heart within minutes.

He placed the venom beside the rest of his potions. Tasari frowned into the satchel, turning it on its edge. Metal instruments clinked against one another as he dug through them. "I Im."

I feigned a frown. "What is it?"

"My antivenom is gone."

On cue, Maralla shrieked and shoved herself off the floor. She buried the scalpel in the muscle of my neck. Pain exploded. I roared and rolled off her, clutching the handle.

Maralla lunged for the venom.

"No, no, you don't." Tasari made a grab for her. She hit the floor with him lying half on top of her. The vial skittered across the tile.

He pulled her hair until her back arched. She screamed again, clawing at his fist. I plucked the scalpel out of my neck and used the towel Raenara had provided to apply pressure to the wound. Pushing myself to my feet, I searched the foyer for the venom and found it in a shaft of morning sunlight. I gritted my teeth. We *needed* that vial.

Still clutching the wound, I paced toward Tasari and presented the scalpel. "Someone's been in your things."

Tasari growled and took the instrument. He tugged harder on Maralla's hair and held the bloody blade to her throat. "Little thief," he hissed. "Just what did you think you would accomplish?"

"Chaos curse you, pox-addled swine!"

Maralla writhed beneath him. The movement caused her sheer white skirt to ride up her hips. Tasari adjusted to sit astride her thighs and pressed in with the scalpel, grinding his crotch against her exposed backside.

"I think I'll have her now, if it's all the same to you, Mascha."

"Be my guest." I turned away from the desperation welling in Maralla's eyes. I tried to ignore the growing pressure in my chest. Tasari's lust was just the distraction we needed while I amended our plan.

"No!" she cried. "Gods damn you! Get off me!"

Tasari set the scalpel aside and began unlacing his breeches, one hand still tangled in her hair. Maralla continued to protest while I strode across the floor to retrieve the venom. I kicked it back toward the satchel, where it slid to a stop a span from Maralla's hand.

Eyeing the rest of the collection, I recognized another liquid: Tasari's own creation, a golden serum called Agony, made to amplify the feeling of pain. I plucked it out of the pile.

"Use this." As I spoke, I let my eyes flutter closed. I dabbed again at the wound and stared at the mess on the towel. "I think she nicked a vein."

"You should see the healer. I'll take care of her." Tasari called over to the two entry slaves, "*Raschun*, help Mascha to the infirmary."

"I'm fine." I shook my head as if to clear it and offered the vial again. "Make her suffer."

Maralla's look of shock and betrayal speared me like a lance. I couldn't explain it to her with a simple glance. I could only pray she would forgive me if this had to go that far.

A smile made of pure malevolence spread across Tasari's face. He took the potion. "As you wish."

He uncorked it with his teeth and spat the stopper into his open satchel. Maralla snarled and renewed her struggle. Her lips sealed shut when he brought the vial to her mouth.

"Drink," Tasari ordered.

While they were locked in their battle of wills, I nudged the venom closer to Maralla with my foot. I was careful to keep it on the far side of the satchel, away from the slaves' view.

"Open your mouth!" Tasari leaned forward to better position the vial at her lips.

Maralla shook her head and thrashed harder. With the pressure of his body lifted from her legs, she threw an elbow backward into his ear with enough power to knock Tasari sideways. His potion splashed against the floor. Maralla dove for the scalpel and stabbed it into his arm.

He grabbed for her, but she kicked him in the jaw and spun toward me. I dropped the towel beside the satchel, then looked sharply down and back up, praying my silent instruction was clear.

She swiped at me and lunged for the venom. The scalpel sliced the back of my hand so cleanly that it took a full two heartbeats for pain to register. By the time blood began to pour out through the split flesh, Maralla had uncorked the container and downed its entire contents.

"No!" The word echoed in the open space. I stalked forward and backhanded her hard enough to make her stumble. "Baosanni take you! What have you done?"

Maralla shook with manic laughter, holding the vial between her forefinger and thumb. "I told you I wouldn't be going to Ideghis."

"The antivenom." Tasari stumbled back to his feet and shook her. "What have you done with it?"

The vial shattered on the floor. Her toes were already turning blue. "I'll never tell."

"Check the slaves' quarters." Time wasn't on our side. I summoned magic, and my first rift split the space between us. The second rift would spit us out upstairs next to the infirmary. "I bet she has an accomplice. One of the maids, perhaps."

The bluish hue was creeping up Maralla's legs. I lifted her in my arms, unnerved by how cold her skin already felt. Her laughter took on an eerie quality as the venom worked its way through her.

"You'll never find it." She settled into me. "You lose, Mascha."

"We'll see about that." Tasari bolted off to the slaves' quarters.

Her eyelids were growing heavy. Maralla's head rested against my shoulder, her body pressed against the flask of antivenom hidden in my pocket.

Holding her tightly, I stepped through the rift. Aetherial wind snapped at my hair and streaky lines of black-violet dissolved into a pair of ornate doors. I kicked them open. "Hasanthe!"

Emmi and Charice started.

"H-he hasn't returned from the market, Master," Charice stammered.

Emmi regarded Maralla with widening eyes. I hid my satisfaction behind a scowl. I'd given the healer a long enough list of errands to keep him out until dusk.

I placed Maralla on the closest infirmary bed. The women started forward, but I held up a hand. "I need frost viper antivenom."

They exchanged a look. "We don't have any, Master," Emmi said. "Only Master Tasari has access to—"

"Tasari left his supplies unattended. The antivenom was stolen." Maralla's eyes were glassy now, and her lips were blue. I needed every possible witness removed immediately. "Charice, organize a search." To Emmi, I said, "How long will it take to make more?"

She looked between my boots and Maralla's still form. "It's too late, Master—"

"We have to try. Get moving. Now!"

The women nearly tripped over each other trying to flee my wrath. As the door closed, I pulled out the antivenom, uncorked the flask, and pressed it to Maralla's lips. We were nearly out of time.

"Swallow," I instructed, massaging beneath her chin.

She coughed weakly on the liquid. Some of it trickled down her cheek.

"Come now. Do as I say." I rubbed her throat more insistently. "Maralla!" Her unfocused eyes stared past me. I shook her. "Don't you dare. We're so close."

Panic constricted my throat. No, no, we had it all planned out. This was supposed to work—it *must* work. I forced her mouth closed around the antivenom and slapped her.

She blinked once. One long swallow later, she went still.

I held my breath, waiting.

But nothing happened.

The strength left my legs. I sagged to my knees beside the bed. I couldn't have been too late. Surely, I hadn't. "Please, Maralla."

I slid my hand into hers. My breath quickened against the sting of tears. I squeezed her fingers, as if I could drag her back from whatever precipice she stood upon. The first tear fell, followed by another. I shook my head and kissed her knuckles.

"Come back, *neime*."

Chapter Thirty-Eight

Mascha

S AARACH TSKED. "THIS IS most unfortunate."

I stood with my hands clasped behind my back, staring into the flames. Smoke towered over the inner courtyard and stung my eyes. The slaves who'd been closest to Maralla surrounded the pyre and watched in stunned silence as the shrouded body burned.

Saarach glanced toward Scherazeme, who huddled close to my side. "Why did you not report her outburst to your master sooner?"

The firelight reflected off the tear streaks on her cheeks. "I thought nothing of it, truly. She was prone to acting out."

"Indeed, she was." I spoke carefully, lest I betray my emotion. I looked toward the Deal-Breaker's messenger. "None of my slaves will be punished for their failure to inform me. This was my fault."

The results of Saarach's investigation had yielded everything I'd hoped. His interviews of the entry slaves and Tasari confirmed that Maralla had dosed herself with frost viper venom. The venom, after all, possessed a unique odor that was impossible to mistake or replicate. Scherazeme had reported our dispute in my chambers, as well as the failure of the guards to intervene in a timely manner. Odessa and Catari supported Scherazeme's testimony, and Emmi and Charice both confirmed Maralla's condition when we'd arrived in the infirmary.

What they hadn't seen was my rift down to Bastian's waiting carriage and back. How I'd exchanged Maralla—bleary-eyed and still recovering—for the body I'd taken from a graveside in the Slicks. The pox, for once, had worked in my favor.

"You are not entirely to blame." Saarach minced his words as if the admission tasted sour. "Tasari's misplacement of his belongings allowed much of this to transpire."

"Even so, I was her master. I accept full responsibility."

He studied me with discerning eyes. "The damage we'll suffer from this incident remains to be seen, but I suppose it is considerably less than an escape would have caused."

I held his gaze and slipped my arm around Scherazeme's waist. She turned her face into my chest.

"It sends a message." I pulled carefully on the saphyrum pendant beneath my shirt. Aether rippled around me as if from barely restrained fury. "The only escape for a slave is death."

Saarach nodded. "An acceptable outcome. The Deal-Breaker will expect a formal statement from you to that effect." He swiped at a dusting of ash on his yellow robe. "You will also reimburse House Ideghis for the loss of this sale from your private coffers. The money he has already sent will remain in the Deal-Breaker's accounts."

I opened my mouth for an argument, then closed it with feigned reluctance. "Fair penance," I said through my teeth.

It was more than fair. I would have paid a dozen times more to assure Maralla's freedom.

"Make certain this does not happen again."

"I will not allow it."

Saarach clicked his tongue. "Mm, yes, I suspect you won't"—he turned to leave—"if you know what's good for you. Good evening, Mascha."

The threat lingered between us as his silhouette disappeared into the fading sun. My lip curled, and a tremor passed through my left hand. I was a mongrel on a long lead. A lion in a gilded cage.

The Deal-Breaker had made a deadly enemy by denying me Maralla as my wife. I was more resolved now than ever to be the man's undoing. If he thought Kestra Hyanaro's little rebel faction was a problem before, I would see them rise to shake the foundation of this country and ensure true change in Rillion.

But first, I had to put Maralla on the fastest ship back to the Northlands.

In my periphery, Soltani swiped at his nose and clung to Po, who made to shrug the boy off before relenting and patting his shoulder. Emmi sobbed into Farrah's arms, and Catari wrung her hands against the pleats of her skirt. Scherazeme sniffled and lifted her face from my chest. She stared into the flames, shaking her head as if still disbelieving. Much as I cared for them all, the loss of *Johtan Shasnaram* had to seem real to everyone.

For all the world knew, Commander Maralla Evallier was dead. Now we had to keep it that way.

She would be safe at Bastian's for a few days while I found an appropriate ship. A disguise was the easiest way to get her through port security, but it wasn't without risks. I planned to cut her hair and paint her face, but a woman traveling alone would still breed suspicion, and a pureblood Syljian as beautiful as she would draw eyes no matter who she was.

What I wouldn't give for an illusionist's magic. But the new wards at the larger ports would nullify such spells even if I could find someone trustworthy enough to cast them.

I cleared my throat and extracted myself from Scherazeme. "Raffi."

My page rushed to wipe his eyes and hurried over. "Yes, Master?"

"Cancel all my appointments for the next two days. I'm not to be disturbed."

Raffi bowed. "Your will."

"Master?" Scherazeme's dark eyes brimmed with uncertainty. "Shall I accompany you?"

Her concern was scrawled all over her face. I stepped into her space and tilted her chin up.

"I will send for you soon." I pressed the softest of kisses to her forehead, then lowered my voice so only she could hear. "I just need time."

The worry lines around her mouth faded. "I will wait, of course."

"Thank you." My thumb skated across her lower lip. Then I lifted my voice to the rest of the slaves. "Take tomorrow off to grieve if you must. On Mirasday, I expect you all back to your duties."

Subdued assent murmured across the courtyard.

A log crashed down on the pyre, sending up a shower of sparks. I turned my back on the flames and strode for the palace doors. Every moment counted now.

Chapter Thirty-Nine

Maralla

BASTIAN'S HOME IN WESTERN Durgost was only an arrow's flight from the sea. It wasn't safe for me to venture outside the suite he'd set aside for me, but at least I had a view of the sunset through the sitting room's glass doors. If there was one beautiful thing about this wretched country, Caelyn had seen fit to paint the sky with brilliance. Only with the ash clouds of Mount Eisekii in the north—the way light scattered off the haze and brought the sunsets alive with color—had she done it better.

I turned from the rays sprawling across the sea and the sheer cliff face walling off the estate grounds. It was nearly time. I drifted past the makeshift bedroom and into the tiny foyer, where a set of double doors opened into a high-walled, tropical garden. Wet heat greeted me and stone scraped my bare feet as I walked along the path to the fountain. It was part of Bastian's private sanctum, and the only entry was through his own suite on the opposite side. He assured us what few slaves he possessed would be discreet if they found me here. It was a risk we chose to take only for lack of options.

I perched on the fountain's edge, and within moments, the scent of Aether signaled Mascha's arrival. Anticipation jolted my heart into my throat.

Light from his rift flashed across the flowerbeds. It had been three days since we'd faked my death, and Bastian had finally confirmed that tomorrow morning, I would be going home. I should have been overjoyed—*was* overjoyed. Except for one thing.

"*Iiren'norvaa*," Mascha said in greeting.

Even before the rift closed, I was in his arms, kissing him. If I only had until dawn to convince him, I wouldn't waste a second. "Come with me."

"I will." His grip on my waist turned possessive, his kisses hungry. "I am."

It was a game we'd played until now, but this time his lie only fueled my desperation. I knew he wanted to change things, knew it was for the best that he stay to make things better, but...

"I'm serious. I want you with me."

Our foreheads met, and I wrapped my arms around his neck. His harder planes steadied my softer curves, which had grown thicker these past weeks with all the fancy wine and lavish food. He cupped my face with such gentleness that tears sprang to my eyes.

I didn't want false promises. I wanted *him*, gods damn me. He'd done so much for me—*risked* more than I could have ever asked of him to set me free. Whether my desire was insanity or not, I couldn't deny my heart any longer.

"I'll be right behind you," he said. "There are some things I need to finish here first."

"Liar."

He didn't deny it. He swept me up like a storm, and I wrapped my legs around his waist. My back struck the soft grass, and my fingers raked into his hair. I pulled his mouth to mine.

"I've arranged for the first shipment of saphyrum already," he panted, tugging my blouse off my shoulder to reach my collarbone. "It should reach Brynn before winter."

The subtle reminder of one of the many reasons he couldn't leave quieted me as I palmed his length between us. My people needed that saphyrum more than I needed him all to myself.

"Tell me you'll be there to accept it." Mascha slipped the laces of my trousers and found my center with ease.

"I..." I gasped and arched into his touch.

There was an alternative I hadn't considered. It required me to give up a part of who I'd always been. But with the saphyrum shipment headed north and a promise of more every quarter, I'd done more for my people here than I could have on any battlefield. *Ciir*, wars with the sorcerers were inevitable. My people needed commanders to lead them. But we couldn't exist at all without saphyrum, and I could ensure that supply continued.

"What if—"

"No." He jerked back, eyes glazed. "You can't."

Scabbing gods, his Foresight was unnerving sometimes.

"But—"

Mascha kissed me, and I ceded to his affection.

Our lips were still locked together when he started shaking his head. "It would never work. The world thinks *Johtan Shasnaram* is dead. You'd have no allies, nowhere to stay, nothing to fight for." His voice was strangled, mirroring the ache in my throat. "You have to go. You have to be free of this place. Promise me."

A tear slipped from his face and landed on mine. He cradled my cheek and stared at me with such longing and misery that I might have done anything for him in that moment.

It was too much. It was all too much. "Mascha…"

"You can't hesitate tomorrow. *Promise* me you won't."

"I promise." My lip trembled, and the weight of that vow threatened to crush me. Tears slid across my temples, and he wiped them away. "Give me pleasure, Tipori."

"*Ciir,* goddess."

I helped him out of his vest and shirt, committing to memory the feel of his scarred chest beneath my palms. His beard brushed my neck, and his teeth claimed my ear, provoking gooseflesh that forced my eyes to close.

The cooling night air lapped against me as he rid me of my trousers. I discarded my blouse into a nearby bush and lay back against the grass. Then he was on me again, teeth grazing my nipples, expert fingers seeking me out. When he plunged to the knuckles inside me, a cry left my throat and my nails bit into his shoulders.

The light from my suite threw shadows over us. The fountain's mist coated my skin, and glistening droplets caught in Mascha's hair. I grasped his nape, and our noses touched. His hand kept up a steady rhythm that had me writhing for him in moments.

When I couldn't bear anymore, I shoved him onto his back and ripped at the laces of his leggings. He kicked them off, and they went flying somewhere over the stone path. His palms skated up my thighs to my waist, and I held his gaze as he filled me.

Those violet eyes drew me in, set aglow from ambient torchlight and the rising moon.

I love you.

The ache to say it arose, and I opened my mouth, only to find his fingertips pressed to my lips.

"I know," he whispered. His expression twisted with agony. "Please, don't say it."

Tears welling, I nodded.

Mascha pushed himself upright and pulled me to his chest. He kissed me with all the passion and love we couldn't convey with words. "I'm going with you."

A sigh shuddered out of me. "You're coming with me." I let the lie ease the vise around my heart.

It was the first time I'd made love under the stars since Nalerta. In little more than a month, Mascha had awakened feelings in me that I'd forgotten about in the darkest hours of my grief. It seemed I'd done the same for him. Even if we couldn't be together, we would be better people for the time we'd shared. I would leave tomorrow and keep my promise.

I could only pray I wouldn't spend the rest of my life wishing I hadn't.

Chapter Forty

Maralla

Mascha fussed with my unruly curls for the fourth time in an hour. The infernal paint disguising my runes made my face itch, and all the sap keeping my hair at bay filled the jeweler's carriage with a spicy stench. I batted at Mascha's hand.

"For the gods' sakes, stop that."

Mascha chuckled. "Apologies, Commander."

Beside him, Bastian swayed with the motion of the carriage. "Careful you don't lose your fingers, my friend."

Though Mascha's hood shrouded half his face, the roguish bend to his lips was on full display. It was a crime against mortals everywhere for him to be that handsome, and he knew it.

I swallowed the emotion crawling up my throat. I would allow myself to feel it later, once Rillion was out of Bending distance, and an ocean stood between my head and my heart.

I rubbed my wrists where my spellbinders had been. Though I still wore a collar for my safety—lone women caught without one in Rillion often disappeared, only to show up later on the underground slave blocks—it was easily unclasped and threaded with beads of saphyrum so pure and white, they would pass for pearls under all but the closest inspection. The heady zing of magic in my blood would calm as soon as I reacquainted myself with it. After over a year wearing spellbinders, my skills with magic had atrophied. Fortunately, I should have plenty of time to practice before I needed it.

We trundled along the road to a tiny port outside Durgost. The ship Mascha had arranged would carry foodstuffs down the Durgostian Channel to Naskatam before resupplying and striking out over the Khestian Ocean. It avoided the treacherous Straits of Fate to the northwest, but it wouldn't carry me all the way home. Once the ship reached Aivenos, I would use the coin Mascha had provided to buy passage to Brynn or Aesin—neutral cities on the Northlands' eastern coast. Iceborn pirates controlled those waters, but I had enough money to bribe a transport and live comfortably along the way.

I snorted, regarding Mascha across the carriage. As he tilted his head and studied me in turn, I wondered if living comfortably would ever have the same meaning again.

My home in Aon'In was a four-room cabin that Nalerta and I had built with our own hands. It wasn't luxurious, but it hadn't needed to be. We'd lived there for over twenty years, and despite the harsh winters, the cramped quarters, the leaky roof, I'd never wanted anything else.

But could I live there without him? Without our children?

That thought stuck in me like a fisherman's hook, and I couldn't dislodge it no matter how carefully I worked around its barb. Going home meant returning to my sister, to our friends, to my post, to all the people I'd longed to see again. It also meant returning to that cabin. It meant going back to the place where Nalerta and I had reared our children. It meant standing beneath the first tree Elliaana had ever climbed, seeing the pond where Rysios had once hunted frogs, visiting the temple where Declaan had eventually succumbed to his sickness—

My fingers dug into my palms. Their memories would be everywhere, ready to flay me alive around every corner.

I swallowed my grief and sat straighter. I would sell the place if I had to. Start over elsewhere.

"Almost there." Bastian peered out from behind the silk drapes. A shaft of morning sun speared through. He let the curtain fall and left me blinking. "Are you sure you want to go through with this, my dear? You could—"

"Bastian," Mascha warned.

"What? You know, I suspect if you make her leave, you'll regret it for the rest—"

"Enough."

Mascha's cutting glare made Bastian's jaw snap shut. The jeweler patted his knees and glanced about the carriage, then adjusted the folds of his robe.

I reached over to squeeze his thigh. "Thank you for everything, *Meschiir* Clairmont. I owe you a debt I can never repay."

Bastian's ring-bedecked hand closed over mine. "No debts necessary, Lady Evallier. It was an honor to be of service. Besides, I'll have more than a few favors to call on at the palace now." He winked one kohl-lined eye and sat back, looking pleased with himself once more.

Mascha scoffed, but mirth returned to his features. He elbowed his friend in the ribs, and Bastian whacked him with the folded fan on the seat between them.

I felt lighter by the time the carriage rolled to a stop. Mascha pointed out the window toward the ships lining the docks.

"*The Messy Pantry* is the three-masted ship there with the pantheon star on its mainsail." He handed over my boarding pass and pointed toward a small thatch-roofed shack beside the boardwalk. "You'll stop at the harbormaster's station there and check in. He'll direct you to the gangplank when it's time to board. Just keep your head down and speak to no one unless spoken to."

I knew the drill. "And if he asks why I'm traveling alone?"

"You were visiting relatives in Johrfallen, but your uncle fell ill and you had to return home to Aivenos early. His name is Demiitrii Bernaan."

The same name appeared three times on my paperwork. I nodded and eyed the last hatch that stood between me and freedom. The moment had finally come, but I didn't feel any elation at the prospect of opening that door.

I should have. I should have wanted it with the vigor of fire to kindling, a child to parchment-wrapped sweets. But once I left this carriage, I couldn't look back. I could only go forward to the lonely future that awaited me on another side of the world.

I thought of Orowen, of her exuberant hugs and her incessant mothering despite being the younger of us. How we'd both break down and cry the moment we saw each other again.

It was almost enough.

So many things would have changed during my absence. My command would have been filled by now, any hope of recovering me set aside. Those who might have grieved for me would have moved on, remembering me only in fleeting moments. If they remembered me at all.

I looked into Mascha's eyes, and the pain there took too long to dissolve back into his stoic mask. Could I truly leave him like this?

Don't hesitate.

I couldn't stop the parchment from falling to the floorboards. I couldn't stop myself from leaping across the space, straddling him on the bench, and seizing his face in my hands. The sting in my eyes and the ache in my chest were only alleviated by his kiss, his scent, his touch. When at last I ripped my mouth from his, it was like tearing out a part of me and leaving behind a jagged wound that would never heal.

"You're coming with me," I breathed.

He clutched my body against his. "I am always with you."

The wrongness I felt in lifting that latch was only the product of my captivity. I was like a timid foal, long confined to a stable, braving the open air for the first time.

I had to go. I didn't belong here.

I leaned in for one last bruising kiss before climbing off him to gather my things. As I wiped my face, I dared a glance at Bastian, who was watching me with an expression I couldn't place. I nodded to him, and his frown reverted to a smile.

"Farewell, my dear."

"May the gods favor you, *meschiir*."

Certain one more look at Mascha would destroy me, I opened the hatch and slipped out onto the gravel road. Each step away from the carriage was easier than the last. The road to war felt much the same: the longing, the denial, the fear—a hundred thousand refusals littering my path until only duty and survival remained.

Sea wind peppered me with ocean spray and sand. All around me, sails snapped, crewmen shouted, and boards creaked. I passed slaves whose eyes never met mine and Rorsch Hekkai whose eyes lingered too long. Before I knew it, I'd reached the harbormaster's station, and one leg of the laughably short journey to the boat was behind me.

Still, something didn't feel right.

I steeled myself and carried on, presenting my pass to a middle-aged man with a crescent scar on his cheek. He looked me over so long that my pulse began to pound in my ears.

The harbormaster said something in Rillanese, but I only caught a few words. I shook my head and spoke in the trade tongue. "I'm sorry, I don't understand."

He sucked his teeth and said in garbled Trade, "Ain't safe traveling without your"—he glanced at the boarding pass—"uncle, is it? What's your business here, girl?"

I was old enough to be this sorry human's great-great-grandmother. Through several measured breaths, I passed along Mascha's false story.

It seemed to mollify the man. He stamped my papers and passed them back. "Dock twenty-three, up the boardwalk there."

His gesture was less than helpful, and most of the signs were coated with peeling paint. I ignored them and headed for the ship with the twelve-pointed star. No one stopped me.

I hovered at the gangplank, watching slaves load cargo onto *The Messy Pantry* in the haphazard way one would expect with a ship so named. It was comical enough to make my lips twitch, but inevitably, my attention strayed back to the carriage still sitting atop the rise.

It made sense for him to wait until the ship set sail, but part of me... wondered. I fidgeted with a saphyrum bead on my collar, drawing the path of a rift with my eyes. It wasn't too late. I could make it if I tried.

No.

Not when I was this close. Not after I'd promised him.

"Excuse me, milady?" The smooth tenor came from the gangplank behind me. A human wearing a yellow waistcoat and a rapier descended to the dock and bowed. Not for the first time in my life, I wondered why Mira had to make the humans so tall. "Have you clearance to board?"

I studied the star insignia on his breast. It wasn't a military symbol I recognized. "Are you the captain?"

"First Mate Ozley Gerrander." He peeked over my stack of papers, then smiled. "At your service, Lady Bernaan."

I liked him already. "Just Kaara, please." It was the name on my boarding pass, anyway.

"Ah! Forgive me." He offered me his arm. "May I show you to your room, Lady Kaara?"

The teasing sparkle in his eyes was unmistakable. I glanced between him and the water flanking us.

His blond eyebrows quirked. "If you're thinking about pushing me in, I'd ask you to at least wait until we're farther out to sea. The channel stench is hard to wash out, you understand."

Mascha's hand was scrawled all over this man. My smile bloomed in earnest. I took his arm and let him lead. "You're very astute, First Mate Gerrander."

"Oz, please."

"First Mate Oz," I shot back.

His laughter was full and melodic. If I was going to be at sea for months, at least this one was easy on the eyes.

My calves burned from the climb, and Oz's longer legs were an enviable asset. Every one of his steps took two of mine. He was patient and let me set the pace, but even as we reached the main deck and he turned me toward the stern, that sense of wrongness redoubled.

A flicker of movement caught my eye. I tensed, expecting danger, but it was only a crewman coughing into his hand as he hurried by.

"Caelyn smiles on our journey," Oz said. "The captain expects fair weather all the way to Naskatam."

It took a conscious effort to relax my grip on his arm. I couldn't be certain how privy the first mate was to my true destination, so I chose my words carefully. "And once we resupply there? What does Caelyn have in store for the rest of our journey?"

"The Khestian is more forgiving this early in the summer. It should be uneventful."

His answer didn't provide the insight I needed to loosen the knot of foreboding in my stomach, so I simply nodded.

The quarters set aside for me were blessedly not below deck, but right beside the captain's at the stern. Oz held the door for me as I peered inside. A narrow cot, a round table, and a well-worn chair were cast in reddish light streaming in through scarlet drapery.

Scarlet like blood. Like the canopy in the Chancellor's guestroom.

I shuddered.

"Does it displease you, milady?"

I shook off the phantom feeling of Ideghis's touch and cursed myself. "Not at all. It's more than enough, thank you. Might I stay out here a while, though? The carriage ride was rather stuffy."

Oz's gaze strayed to something behind me. His brows furrowed. "Yes, of course."

I frowned, following his gaze to a pair of pale-faced sailors shuffling across the deck behind us.

"Just be mindful of the crew as they work." Oz stepped toward them. "If you'll excuse me."

He didn't wait for an affirmation before hurrying away, flagging down the two sailors and exchanging words I couldn't make out over the wind. As he waved them toward the bow, the oddity of their complexions hit me.

Sailors spent a long time in the sun. Unseasoned crewmen might have such pallid skin, or maybe it was the product of a poor diet of salt pork, ship biscuits, and rum.

The knot in my gut twisted a little more.

Oz watched them go, then started back toward me with an apologetic smile.

"Mr. Gerrander!"

The first mate paused, and a young human with windswept black curls and dark circles under his eyes intercepted him. I secured the door to my cabin and tilted an ear to listen.

"What is it?"

"It's Kinsmet, sir. He's got something on his face."

"He's what?"

"They're sores of some kind. They're not responding to the healer's magic. J-just come and see, sir."

When Oz glanced toward me, I pretended to stare into the network of ropes and sails. I waited until he'd been led away, then drifted to starboard before doubling back to follow them.

Bastian's carriage still sat on the rise. I glanced toward it three times before convincing myself it was best not to look again. We'd be on our way soon, and the temptation to bolt back down the gangplank would fade.

I steered wide of a thick-shouldered sailor scratching at a red pustule on his neck. The wound broke open and yellow fluid gushed over his fingers. Face pinching, I dug for the kerchief tucked inside my skirt.

Before I could offer it to the man, a commotion broke out farther up the bow. More pale sailors rushed by, three with similar red abscesses marring their hands and faces. Another doubled over coughing.

My blood froze as solid as the Ru'Natha in winter.

A slave carrying a sack dropped his burden beside me, spilling grain across the floorboards. His sharply exhaled words gave voice to the fear that had lodged inside me.

"Weeping pox."

A sharp cry followed. The commotion up ahead broke apart, revealing a figure lying on the deck. He rolled over and vomited black bile.

Crewmen swore. One of the deckhands threw himself overboard and splashed into the channel.

"Pox!" a man shouted. "He's got the pox!"

"No," I whispered, stepping back.

Oozing sores covered the fallen man's face.

"Laangor has cursed us!"

Fleshrot had already taken hold of the ones on his neck.

Two more sailors vaulted over the railing. Another man wearing yellow swept down from the forecastle. "Hold! I said hold, you useless scabs! No one leaves the ship!"

Along the boardwalk, black-and-gold-liveried soldiers noticed the commotion. Several of them turned toward the ship, and one reached up to pluck an unlit oil lamp from a nearby post.

Another stab of cold pierced me. Even a single suspected case of the weeping pox would shut this entire port down.

"Raise the plague flag!" Oz's voice. "Do it, now!"

The ship would be towed out to sea and burned. The crew, passengers, and any slaves who had been on board would be quarantined until the city healers could be certain the pox didn't spread. *I* would be detained and my subterfuge discovered. Mascha would suffer for helping me, and I would be enslaved once more.

I glanced toward the railing. It was a long drop to the water, and I had nowhere to go but back to the docks. The paint on my face would wash away and reveal my runes.

Up on the rise, a white flash drew my attention. A second rift opened closer to the docks, and a cloaked figure stepped out. Mascha hesitated. He couldn't rift onto the ship with the wards in place any better than I could rift off.

Rorsch Hekkai stormed the dock, shouting and drawing weapons. They apprehended the slaves loading cargo first, striking them with whips and the flats of blades to herd them back. A jade-robed Aetherian paused to assess the chaos before issuing orders along the boardwalk.

Oz made his way back to me, but Laangor only knew how much he'd already been exposed to the disease. He reached for me. "Kaara, I'm going to need you to—"

I ducked under his arm and kneed him in the groin.

"Agh!" He hit the deck. "Gods!"

"I'm so sorry for that." Backing toward the side of the ship, I sought out Mascha's cloaked form again. If neither of us could rift on or off the ship, I had to get off another way. The wards stabilized the Wall on the vessel itself, but if I could cast one *off* the ship, then maybe I could jump.

I pulled saphyric energy from the beads around my neck. Magic crackled like static through my limbs.

I cast a final calculated look back at Mascha and scowled at the number of trees surrounding him. I aimed for the open ridge instead and threw my will down toward the water. The Wall split wide beside the hull, and the second rift flashed open beside the carriage.

"Wait!" Oz called.

I leaped over the railing and plunged toward the water. Misty cold, not watery cold, enveloped me. Then I struck gravel with a gasp.

The port stretched below me, and the expanse of brush and trees separating the channel from the ridge was a green smear of tropical fronds and vines. Another rift caught my eye, flashing white-violet behind a warehouse down by the ship. Two cloaked figures emerged, their features lost to shadow.

Mascha appeared beside me, blocking my view. He held his hood against the Aetherial wind and hauled me to my feet. "We can't use the carriage. Hang on to me."

Distantly, I understood why—Bastian couldn't be implicated in any way—but the series of rifts Mascha Bent us through, one after another, scrambled my ability to put logic into words. Gravel, grass, buildings, and trees all blurred. My stomach heaved and my shins hurt. Only seconds ago, I'd been on a ship bound for home. I'd been so close to returning to Orowen, to my people, to the war effort. This delay should have devastated me.

So why did I feel relieved?

I clung to Mascha, savoring his scent steeped in iron and leather. His strong, steady hands banished whatever ill feelings I'd grappled with on the docks.

When at last he dumped us out in the shadow of a familiar, private walled garden, he cupped my ears and tilted my head up, assessing me. "Are you alright?"

It took me several heartbeats to realize he expected an answer. I was too busy turning over the conflicting emotions raging through me. I was alright, truly. A little shaken, but it would pass. I was safe. *We* were safe.

"Maralla?"

I threw my arms around him, uncertain I could ever let go again.

CHAPTER FORTY-ONE

MASCHA

FOUR MONTHS LATER

MORNING SUN BROKE OVER the eastern horizon as I stepped out of a rift and into Bastian's secluded garden. A marble fountain burbled to my right, throwing a gentle mist into the air. On my left, scarlet, ochre, and gold flowers set the bushes ablaze and filled the space with a sweet fragrance. Up ahead, soft viol music floated out of the open doors and down the cobbled path. The sound teased a smile from me.

Sorrow crowded in behind it.

After the weeping pox outbreak had quarantined the entire Isle of Durgost for two months, a series of setbacks had delayed Maralla's departure further. The night I'd scheduled her next ship to leave, an accident between three freighters had clogged the Durgostian Channel. The crash forced larger ships to change course for Epillon for over a week while repairs were made. Any smaller ships I'd approached had refused to take on passengers for fear of sickness. Then a spree of stabbings had led to even more guards around the docks.

It had taken a month to secure the next voyage, which was waylaid by a defective bilge pump and a hull riddled with shipworms. The parasites had also infected other ships and damaged Durgost's reputation.

Something could be said for the Deal-Breaker's new security; even I struggled to work around it. On top of his demands that I find and apprehend Kestra Hyanaro and his growing band of rebels, I'd been grasping at straws for Maralla's way out. Fortunately, she and Bastian had taken well to each other, and neither seemed to hold my failures against me.

But I'd finally procured another way out for her: false documents and no questions asked on a ship bound for Brynn. Most crews rarely braved the waters near the port city, but this captain claimed he had personal ties to Uzov Brijjya, the leader of the Iceborn who controlled the area. He assured me he could provide safe passage.

The journey from Brynn to the nearest Alliaansi stronghold was only a month on foot through friendly forests—the closest I could get her to her homeland. I dared to hope the captain was simply a braggart with nothing more nefarious in mind.

As I strode up the moss-laden path, the music stopped abruptly on a single, discordant note. Maralla uttered a string of muffled Syljian curses. As I entered, she began the piece again.

Maralla's section of Bastian's estate was a portion of his own private suite. The few servants the jeweler allowed himself had proven dependable, and I'd compensated them handsomely for their discretion. It was an enormous risk, but there was nothing for it. I'd installed wards to bar sound from traveling outside the garden, and I checked the scrying wards around the perimeter compulsively. I'd strengthened them as delays mounted, and Maralla eventually began to refer to the space as her home.

I peered into the kitchen before chuckling to myself. That space was little used and always tidy. Maralla hated cooking, and she got by on fruits, raw vegetables, and cheeses most often. Bastian's servants provided some meals for her, and I brought her wine and choice cuts of selka, beef, and shellfish whenever I visited.

Her bedroom was much less organized. Without slaves to make the bed or launder her clothing, Maralla let the linens lie about until she ran out of things to wear and then washed everything in the fountain. The bedside table was littered with smudged maps, half-whittled figurines, and piles of abandoned yarn balls that barely passed for knitting.

She was certainly not made for idleness. After many heated arguments, I'd accepted her aid with my vision for Rillion. It was she who'd tracked down Kestra Hyanaro and his circle of rebel commoners. To them, she was known as Enigma, and she carried messages from an anonymous but vastly wealthy donor who wished to see them rise.

I found her seated at a bench in the sitting room. Light from the windows haloed her chiffon-clad figure. She held the viol to her chin, caressing the fingerboard with a dexterity born of hundreds of hours' practice. Every measure of the piece she played rang with perfection—

Until she struck that same discordant note again.

"*Saonis miraar*," Maralla growled.

I leaned against the doorway and folded my arms. "Invoking the gods won't help you here, *neime*."

Maralla shot a playful glare over her shoulder. "Shows how much you know. I happen to have a stellar rapport with Mira."

The goddess of creation had certainly blessed her, but I didn't say it. "I don't doubt it."

She turned to face me. "I didn't hear you come in. I hope you didn't subject yourself to that racket for long."

"What I heard was beautiful. I love it when you play."

Her cheeks darkened. "Flatterer." Setting the instrument aside, she rose and gestured toward the pair of chairs in front of the empty fireplace.

I took my usual seat on the right. At the beginning of her stay at Bastian's, I'd visited often to ensure she had everything she needed. As the weeks wore on, her rooms had become a retreat for me, and I began to appreciate the smaller space for its lack of interruptions.

"Wine?" she asked.

"Please."

Maralla fetched a bottle and sat beside me, one leg curled beneath her. "We're drinking it straight. I'm not in the mood to wash glasses." She uncorked it, took a sip, and passed it to me.

My brows lifted. "I should remind you the last time we drank straight from the bottle, we wound up swimming in the fountain."

She side-eyed me with an impish grin. "As if you'd mind a repeat of that evening."

I tilted my head as if considering. That was the first night we'd fallen asleep in the garden together, after lying on the grass counting stars. I'd woken at sunrise with her head on my shoulder, feeling as if I held the entire world in my arms.

I busied myself with examining the label on the bottle. "No, I suppose I wouldn't."

"See?" She laughed. Maralla tucked a lock of hair behind my ear. "We don't need glasses."

Our eyes met, and I savored the sound of her laughter. Silonas willing, today would be the last day I should ever hear it. The knowledge gripped my chest so tightly that my response stuck in my throat. I took a long pull from the bottle and passed it back to her.

"What is it, Tipori? You look troubled."

I forced a smile. "I have a ride home for you."

"When?"

Her sudden apprehension gave me pause. I could understand her reservation, though; there had been so many disappointments.

"Tomorrow morning." I sucked in a breath. "The ship is bound for Brynn. Captain Lee expects to make port in about four months."

Maralla's jaw worked, but no words came.

Concern nipped along my spine. "I know it's been frustrating for you, being trapped here for so long, but this time it will work."

"Tomorrow morning," she repeated, averting her gaze into her lap.

"*Ciir*. Is that a problem?"

She rose to pace the floor, ignoring my question. "You're certain he's trustworthy, this captain?"

"I doubt it." I turned in my seat to watch her. "But it's the best opportunity I've found in weeks. The captain agreed not to ask any questions."

Maralla continued to pace. "What's his cargo? Does he stop in Eidosinian ports on the way?"

"Spices, he said. And no, I got the sense the Sorcerers' Guild has a price on his head."

"What about the Iceborn? Admiral Brijjya controls the northern seas. He'll have an outpost near Brynn."

"Lee claimed he had a personal tie with Brijjya. He assured me the Iceborn would allow him safe passage."

"A personal tie?" She scoffed. "Unlikely. If anything, he's running weapons for him."

I sat straighter. That explained why the captain was so amenable to my terms. If he was used to smuggling weapons abroad, he would have the means to smuggle people, too.

"If that's the case, I'm sure he'll see you safely across the sea."

She started to pace again. "At least until we make port, and he doubles his profit by selling me to Brijjya."

I remembered the story of how Maralla had arrived in Rillion, chained to the floor of an Iceborn slavers' galley. I abandoned my seat and went to her, pulling her into my arms.

"It's as close as I could ever hope to get you to your people, Maralla. It avoids Eidosinia as you requested, and you'll have your magic. I have no doubt you can keep a ship full of pirates in line." When she didn't look convinced, I cupped her cheeks. "If we keep passing up these opportunities, it could be years before I see you safely out of Durgost. I'll keep my promise no matter how long it takes, but I know you want to go home."

Her eyes misted and she clutched my wrists. "Come with me."

I opened my mouth. Closed it.

So *that* was what this was about.

"*Neime.*" I shook my head. "We have been over this. It wouldn't be safe for you."

She pressed her body flush against mine. "I don't care. Come with me."

A part of me wanted more than anything to give in to that demand. A part of me would gladly leave everything behind to be with her. My love for her was as swift and unstoppable as an ocean current, capable of reshaping the trajectory of my entire life.

But I couldn't abandon my plans. For the last few months, I'd been mapping the Deal-Breaker's network of agents, finding weaknesses in its framework, and building my own web of spies—mostly women—who were loyal to me. With my plans to elevate Catari and Emmi to concubines alongside Scherazeme, partly to share her burden, and partly to accommodate other tastes, I would soon have eyes in every bedroom in Rillion. And once *I* controlled the Rorsch Hekkai in earnest, then real changes could begin.

I let out a slow breath. "I want to be with you. Truly I do. But I still have obligations here."

She put her hands on my chest, one resting over my heart. Maralla bowed her head a moment, her forehead pressed against the hollow of my throat. When she looked up again, there was a new resolve in her eyes. "Then I will stay."

"No." It was an outrageous suggestion. One I wouldn't stand for. "I will not see you languish here on my behalf—"

"I love you."

I blinked. "What?"

"You heard me." She lifted her chin in challenge. "I love you, Mascha, and I'm not going anywhere."

I searched her face. "Maralla..."

"If you plan to overthrow the Deal-Breaker, you're going to need all the help you can get. I'm your only connection to Hyanaro, and I guarantee he won't trust you if you try to step in."

"But your people need you."

She shrugged. "I've been gone nearly two years. They'll have replaced my command by now. I'll still ask you to send saphyrum"—her hand over my heart pressed more firmly. Possessively—"but I'm needed here more."

My sorry attempt at pragmatism dissolved, and a quiet laugh escaped me. "You've been spending too much time with Bastian." The bastard still hadn't let up about my need of a wife.

Mischief sparked in her smile. "He makes good sense."

"How would this even work? What sort of life would that be for you?"

"I spoke to Bastian already. He says I can stay here."

They'd been conspiring against me.

"And it's not like I haven't already been moving about the city, working for Kestra."

I shook my head, disbelieving. "You truly want to stay? With me?"

She nodded. "*Ciir.*"

Joy and love bloomed in my chest with such ferocity that I didn't register my tears until they fell freely down my face. "Why?"

"You've risked everything for me." Maralla reached up to wipe my cheeks. "I would be a fool to walk away from a love like that."

I looked down, fighting to retain control, to tell her how much that meant to me, but I couldn't force anything out around the knot in my throat.

Maralla's fingers sifted into my hair, forcing our eyes to meet. "Kiss me, Tipori."

I didn't have to be told twice. I pulled her to me and pressed my lips firmly against hers. Her perfect curves fit against the contours of my body until there was not a single space between us. I kissed her, and I kept kissing her until I was breathless and trembling.

When at last I broke away, I drew a ragged breath. "I love you."

To say the words aloud was like watching the clouds part after a storm. Like breakers stilling against the shore, a victory stroke on the piccara board, or the final shake on a multi-million gran deal.

She pressed her forehead to mine. "We're in this together now, you and I."

"You and I," I echoed, entwining my fingers with hers. I nodded, savoring just how right that felt, and kissed our joined hands. "Nothing sounds more perfect to me."

This story has been written as a standalone with series potential. If you'd like to see more of Mascha and Maralla in future books, the best way to let me know is to leave a review!

Read on for an Epilogue 'sequel teaser' to see where their story might go next.

Epilogue

Deal-Breaker

Humid air whistled through the balcony balusters and teased a lock of hair from the Deal-Breaker's temple. Surf crashed against the cliffside and drowned the call of seabirds overhead. He crossed one ankle over his knee and sighed, lifting the warm mug to his lips.

A fine morning, made finer by a favorable end to what might have been another unfortunate and costly affair.

We're in this together now, you and I.

The Deal-Breaker smiled and sipped his tea. The scrying runes inside the wards at Clairmont Estates had served him well.

Ship worms and pox, accidents and stabbings. Too much time had been spent manufacturing delays to keep his wayward pet in line. Now, with Mascha's most cherished possession in a box, he only needed to tighten the leash.

The Deal-Breaker before him had been tremendously short-sighted, only using Mascha to breed more pit fighters to make his favored subjects wealthy. He hadn't known that Mascha's true value lay not in his killing prowess, but in his arcane talent. Seer magic was a precious commodity—one that could only pass from parent to child.

And it was this seer magic—specifically the presence of a Clairvoyance rune—that would finally restore the Deal-Breaker's power.

Black mist and the bright flash of a rift drew his attention to the open space near the balcony railing. Svaronei stepped through, jade robes brushing the floor as he bowed.

"Vhedja is in position. The port marshal is prepared to apprehend the weapons smuggler and his crew, Master."

The Deal-Breaker dismissed the news with a wave. "There is no need. Let Captain Lee sail as scheduled."

Svaronei frowned. "You wish for her to escape?"

"Her heart proves a treacherous thing." The Deal-Breaker set his mug aside and adjusted the ruby ring on one finger. "She has decided to stay."

Svaronei's confusion was a tangible ripple in the psionic river of his thoughts. The Deal-Breaker ignored it. His thralls didn't need answers; their purpose was to serve, not to understand.

"He will gain status among the rebels," Svaronei pointed out. "She'll inspire him to fight back."

Another smile tugged at the Deal-Breaker's lips. "Oh." Light glinted red off the gems on his hands. "I know."

NOT ALL THOSE WITH SIGHT WISH TO SEE.

Riisii Evallier's memories are full of dark, dreadful things. Where once she was used for her power—the gift of Foresight—she's since fled Rillion with her family and found a better life.

But she can't outrun her gift. When a servant to the goddess of knowledge requests her aid, Riisii discovers just how pivotal she'll be in the coming war. To save the future, however, she must first overcome her past.

FREE to newsletter subscribers! Claim your short story today!

WWW.THELASTDRAEGION.COM

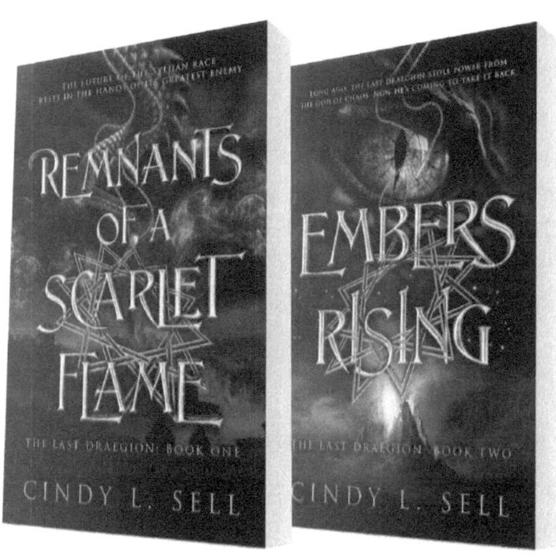

Dive into The Last Draegion Saga!

An on-going epic packed full of jaw-dropping action, political intrigue, and lovable characters (and some you love to hate).

Remnants of a Scarlet Flame: TLDS Book 1

The sorcerers have taken everything from Alar's people. When a leader of the Syljian resistance is captured, Alar must leave his post as a spy in the Sorcerers' Guild to prevent a war his people can't win. But no rescue mission ever goes according to plan, and no prison break is ever easy.

Embers Rising: TLDS Book 2

Sorceress Daeya McVen has escaped north to treat with her enemies, intent upon bartering her newly awakened magic for her father's life. But when she learns that controlling her power requires a sacrifice, it seems her father isn't the only one she stands to lose.

Order from your favorite bookstore today!

Acknowledgements

(And Shenanigans)

Every book is a labor of love, but some are more love than labor. *Tipori* was that book for me. It started off as a bunch of disconnected little snippets, ballooned to a 30,000 word novella, and before I knew it, I was wrangling a 300-hundred-page novel and trying not to start a sequel until *The Last Draegion Saga* was done.

Huge thanks, as always, to everyone who had a hand in this story's creation:

My Greek-Letters Team—Alicia Leatherdale, M.J. Lindsey, K.A. Herdt, Candice Honeycutt, E.R. Donaldson, Hank Ryder, and Derrick Hall—who pushed me to make this story the best it could be.

My E-Team, Emma O'Connell, Ellie Owen, and Erynn Snel, who continue to polish up all my prose and make it sound like I know what I'm doing. I'm truly grateful for all the work you do.

My D&D group, who shoved my ass into the DM's seat, jabbed a finger at the page, and said, "Do the thing." And so I did.

My amazing husband, who deserves a gold medal and chocolate for all the love and support he's given me while I pursue this crazy dream.

My readers. Without y'all, I'd just be chucking words into the Aether.

And a special thanks to Liz, whose roleplay obsession led to my creation of a pretty fucked up culture with way too much story potential.

Pantheon Guide

Saolanni, Greater Goddess of Life

Mira, lesser goddess of creation and birth
Shavaan, lesser goddess of healing
Caelyn, lesser goddess of nature

Ordeolas, Greater God of Order

Silonas, lesser god of fortune and trade
Tiior, lesser goddess of wisdom and knowledge
Delvin, lesser god of law and justice

Baosanni, Greater God of Death

Laangor, lesser god of suffering
Yasuo, Gatekeeper, lesser god of the afterlife
Anordis, lesser god of war and chaos

Pronunciations

Akaaris: (ah-KAHR-iss)
Anelliiq: (an-ill-EEK)
Baghara: (bah-GAR-uh)
Hasanthe: (hass-ON-thay)
Ideghis: (ID-eh-gis)
Johtan Shasnaram: (jo-TAHN shas-nahr-AHM)
Maralla: (mar-AH-luh)
Mascha: (MAHSH-uh)
Nalerta: (nah-LAIR-tuh)
Orowen: (OR-oh-wen)
Raenara: (rie-NAHR-uh)
Rillion: (RILL-ee-on)
Rorsch Hekkai: (ROARSH heck-EYE)
Saarach: (SAHR-ack)
Scherazeme: (share-uh-ZEEM)
Simmion: (SIM-ee-un)
Svaronei: (svahr-oh-NIE)
Tipori: (tip-OR-ee)
Vhedja: (VAYD-ya)

Translations

Rillanese

araschavka (air-uh-SHOV-kuh): a clitoral hood piercing

gheschal (ge-SHAWL): distress

kas hadem (KAHS ha-DEM): shut up

kavvur (kah-VER): discomfort

mascha (MAHSH-uh): death

    Also, 'the mascha,' a move made popular by pit-fighting sensation Mascha of House Ideghis, in which the ribs and back muscles are severed, and the lungs are removed from behind.

meschiir (mesh-EER): sir, Mr.

rascha (RAHSH-uh): (plural, *raschan*) female slave

raschu (RAHSH-oo): (plural, gender-neutral, *raschun*) male slave

sadarah (suh-DAHR-uh): ma'am, Ms.

Syljian

amii (ah-MEE): (plural, *amiien*) friend

ashaan (ash-AHN): (derogatory) half-blood

besaav'ruh (bay-SAHV-roo): be calm

iiren'norvaa (EER-in nor-VAH): good evening (both salutation and farewell)

iithe'ruh caezo (EE-thay-roo KAY-zoh): eat shit

ciir (SEER): yes

crii'ruh (KREE-roo): stop

daatahl (dah-TALL): for her

daatahr (dah-TAR): for him

drest'ruh (DREST-roo): rise

imaane'ruh (im-AH-nay-roo): stay/don't go

kaana'ruh ke'aave tipori (KAH-nuh-roo kay-AH-vay tip-OR-ee): remember to
have mercy

neime (NIGH-may): a term of endearment

oeloraati (oh-lor-AH-tee): a period of intense sexual receptivity in Syljian women
that coincides with fertility, typically occurring for six weeks every three to five
years

ruh (ROO): a suffix added to verbs to express the imperative mood (e.g. give
commands)

saonis miraar (say-ON-is meer-AHR): gods above

vaash'ruh (VOSH-roo): kneel

ABOUT THE AUTHOR

CINDY L. SELL SUPPOSEDLY lives in the Midwestern United States with a home full of furry critters, including her two boys and doting husband, but she really spends most of her time on Dessos battling sorcerers or negotiating trade deals with pirates.

She graduated from Washburn University with a creative writing degree, but didn't bother to do anything with it until COVID when she ran out of excuses. When she's not writing, she enjoys bowling, crochet, and riding her '82 Sportster.

Look for Cindy on Facebook, say hi on Instagram, and visit her website for upcoming events and shenanigans.

Works by Cindy L. Sell

The Last Draegion Saga

Remnants of a Scarlet Flame: September 2024
Embers Rising: August 2025
Tides of Immolation: TBD
Aether and Ash: TBD

Tales from Dessos

Tipori: September 2025

Short Stories

The Trouble With Knowing: August 2024